THE HERO SLAYERS
TEMPT FATE

THE HERO SLAYERS TEMPT FATE

O. S. Marrow

Podium

Cover design by Paulina Bochniak

ISBN: 978-1-0394-8782-6

Published in 2026 by Podium Publishing
www.podiumentertainment.com

Podium

THE HERO SLAYERS TEMPT FATE

CHAPTER ONE

The Boys' Club

The city of Westbara: a glamorous locale, built on the riches of Goldmarch merchants, a joining of the traditional human architecture and the tiled arches of tiefling design from the west. To this day, the very same trade flows through this hub—silks, spices, jewels—and more than there ever was before. Fort West was the epitome of this amalgamation of culture, both in terms of the architecture and the rulers of this large province. Queen—now Empress—Amira so often pointed to this city as evidence of the Goldmarch being made stronger by their acceptance of other peoples, and rightly so; few cities the world over were as beautiful as this one.

It was just a shame I was here to kill someone.

"Hit him again," I told Lore.

The barbarian looked down at their prisoner, tied to a chair in the basement of their own home. A member of the Cult of Ascendency—a group of devout Player-worshippers who believed that if they served the Players enough, they would be taken with them to their home. Of course, me and the team knew that the Ascended World was broken, that the Players were fleeing it—but try telling a cultist that.

Lore punched the man again. "Tell us. Tell us where the Player is."

The cultist said nothing, spitting a globule of blood onto the dusty floor.

Corminar—the only other person in the room—watched on. "Perhaps an arrow might loosen his tongue."

"I told you," I said. "He's weak enough. An arrow could kill him!"

"Well, this certainly isn't working, is it?" Corminar asked. "We have been here for, I am estimating, an hour? At this point, we would be fools not to alter our strategy."

Lore groaned. Again. Then turned to the prisoner. "They've been like this ever since Val and Arzak left. Bickering. If Arzak was here, she'd have put a stop to it by now, but . . . Well, they don't listen to me, do they?"

"I don't know," said the prisoner.

"They don't," Lore insisted, then hit him again.

It was true; Corminar had been getting right on my nerves. I'd tried to hold my tongue at first, because he'd just watched his home fall to invaders. We'd been there to try to stop it, killing a Player in the process, but we'd been too late—the new Golden Empire had made the Dawnwood their latest acquisition. But this excuse only went so far, and I was getting pretty sick of his attitude—something that he said about me, too.

"Reveal the location of the Player now," Corminar growled, drawing the bow gifted to him by Elandor in his dying breath.

"Woah!" I said, jumping between Corminar and the prisoner. "What did I just say?"

"You are not the leader of this team."

"Lore, back me up here," I tried.

I didn't hear anything from the barbarian standing behind me for a moment. "I . . . dunno."

"You're on his side?"

"I'm not on any side!" Lore protested. I heard him turn back to the prisoner and begin mumbling under his breath again. "See what I mean? This is about as bad as it has been, since Arzak and Val left, admittedly, but . . . Oh!"

I whipped my head around to look at Lore, thinking he was in trouble. "What? What's going on?"

"I got an idea!" Lore said. "Can I try my idea?"

"He is not your leader," Corminar reminded him. "You may do as you wish. As long as it is sensible."

Excitedly, Lore turned back to the cultist. "Arzak and Val, they were our friends, see. We didn't know why they'd disappeared at first, but then like a week later, Styk here—he's the disheveled one—"

"Thanks?" I cut in, but Lore ignored me.

"—he decided to tell us. Was a big to-do, asked us to promise not to run away or attack him, and all that. And you know why they left? Because they found out who his mum was." He looked to the cultist. "I think you'll like this part. Styk's mum, she's a Player."

The cultist's eyes widened.

"Yeah, look, see?" Lore said to Corminar and me, pointing at our prisoner. "He likes that!"

The elf and I both sighed, which was about as close as we'd come to agreeing with each other over the past couple of weeks of travel. We'd abandoned our "borrowed" ship at the Great Golden Canal, and we'd headed west, chasing Lore's visions of a Player. His active effect—*Man of Prophesy*—had been gifted to him by the last Player we'd killed, the one who would've led the invasion of the Dawnwood. She was determined that Lore make it to the completion of the Council's plan, foretelling that he was important somehow in ensuring it actually happened. This meant that Lore could now see the path that got him there. We weren't interested in much of it, but the parts that involved killing Players? That, we could get on board with.

And one such vision had brought us to Westbara.

That didn't mean we'd hadn't gotten into some trouble along the way—the Goldmarch was quickly becoming a more violent place—and I'd made plenty of use of my experience gain boost to level up some more. This included upgrading my *Stealth Attack* ability to level 3, which granted me a massive 200 percent increase to damage when I attacked unnoticed, as well as an improved *Cloth Armor* ability on the *Needlework* front.

"Val didn't take kindly to it, we think," Lore continued. "And Arzak went with her; they're good friends. But me and Corminar here, we're pretty open-minded. Corminar especially. We don't mind this kind of thing."

"You . . . have the blood of the Architects running through your veins?" the prisoner asked. It was about the most we'd heard him say in . . . well, ever.

I pulled the Sisyphus Artifact out from under my shirt, where it hung on a chain. "Only way I can use this. Does this mean you're going to tell us where the Player is?"

"I assumed that you meant to hurt them, but if they are family . . . if you mean to aid them . . ."

"No, we—" Lore started, but a pointed cough from Corminar made him slam his mouth shut.

"Sure," I said, very happy to tell any lie if it got me what I wanted. "We just wanna help my . . . cousin."

The cultist narrowed his eyes. "Swear on your mother, the Player."

"I . . . swear?" I said, unable to resist saying the second word like a question, because it couldn't be this easy.

It was that easy. "The Player you are after, he is known in these parts as the Councilman."

"Yes, that sounds like the man we are after," Corminar said. Councilman, Council . . . it was a perfect fit. "Where is he?"

"Right now?" the cultist said. "He should be accepting the key to the city. For services rendered."

Lore grabbed his sword. "Where?"

"Town square," the prisoner replied. "Why? Is he in trouble?"

"He is now," I said, and then I opened a portal to the street outside.

The three of us leaped through the portal and ran, Lore somehow keeping up despite the fact that he had a massive sword to lug around with him. We charged through the narrow, winding streets of this ancient city, and whenever there was enough straight road ahead of us, I opened a portal to close the distance.

My portals attracted the attention of the soldiers in gold. The Goldmarch had changed since it moved from kingdom to empire, its soldiers cracking down on anything they even perceived as a threat to the peace. Anyone who got on their bad side would face down the full, heavily funded, force of the law, and those soldiers who did the cracking down could do whatever they wanted with impunity. We'd discovered in our travels that the best thing to do was keep our heads down.

But there was no time for that now.

We ignored the shouts of the soldiers, charging onward, Corminar and Lore trusting me to use my portals to keep us out of trouble—or to lose ourselves among the winding streets. Finally, I saw the crowd ahead of us, thousands standing in the town square, their attention on the steps that led up to Fort West. With guards still following behind us, I opened a portal for the three of us to step through—spilling us out into the center of the crowd.

"Sorry, sorry," Lore mumbled apologetically as people had to shift to one side to make room for his large frame. A short woman behind him, her view now blocked, coughed pointedly. Lore apologized again, then seemed to try to make himself as short as possible.

Meanwhile, Corminar and I looked up to the steps to Fort West. On it, the duke of Westbara shook the hand of a small, weedy man.

Around us, thousands erupted in applause and cheers, sending their love to the man being honored. Though, looking around, I couldn't help but wonder just how sincere this applause was—with so many Goldmarch soldiers around, did the locals just want to avoid being called traitors to the empire?

Finally, Lore looked up at the man on the steps. "Ah," he said.

"That him?" I asked. "The man with dozens of soldiers at his side, and thousands celebrating him? That's our Player?"

"Yep." Lore nodded. "That's him. That's our Councilman."

"Oh good," I said.

This wasn't going to be easy.

CHAPTER TWO

Another Day on the Job

"Any thoughts?" I asked the two other Slayers who were standing at my side in the midst of this huge crowd.

"I assume a well-placed arrow in this moment is out of the question?" the ranger replied.

I shook my head. "Not unless you can guarantee that you could kill him in one hit." Corminar opened his mouth, inevitably to say that he could, so I quickly continued, "And not unless you can guarantee there aren't wards around to block the hit. I don't want hundreds of soldiers chasing us down; even with my portals, I don't know if I'd be able to get us out of that one."

The ranger sighed. "Then we must scout. Monitor his habits. Discover where and when he is alone."

I nodded. "Agreed. Lore, anything to add?"

The barbarian blinked at us. "Sorry, I got distracted. What we saying?"

"We're gonna follow him."

"Works for me!"

We looked back at the Player, huge grin on his face as he continued to speak enthusiastically to the woman who had handed him the oversized "key to the city." He was saying something about the great and important work he'd done, how he was Westbara's savior, blah blah blah . . . I wasn't really listening.

"He's . . . not moving anytime soon, is he?" Lore asked.

"No," Corminar replied.

"Tavern?" I asked, nodding to one on the edge of the town square.

"Tavern," both the ranger and the barbarian agreed.

We pushed through the crowd toward the tavern, taking care to weave around any soldiers in gold uniform who might recognize us. At the edge of the crowd, I looked around for any more guards, but the only ones in sight were busy kicking a man who was already on the ground. At least . . . they were . . . distracted?

I hurried across the open space to the tavern door, Corminar close behind me, and then we turned to find that Lore had stopped. His eyes were on a shop next door, one that catered toward people organizing fetes and fairs. "Are you coming?" I asked.

"Get me a beer, I'll be there in a pop."

Corminar and I looked to each other and shrugged, then entered the tavern. This close to the city center, the taverns were busy, so when I spotted a free table, I hurried over to grab it. "This round on you?" I asked Corminar.

He looked as though he was about to refuse, but then he shrugged and disappeared to join the mass at the bar.

While I waited, I sat and looked around at the big-city folk in the tavern, those with fancy—and clean!—outfits, freshly trimmed hair, and the occasional ornate weapon. We could have lived like that if we'd wanted to, admittedly—Val seemed to have a never-ending supply of coin—but we had a more important purpose.

My heart dropped as I thought of Val again. I'd known she wouldn't take the news about my Player ancestry well, but I'd thought she of all people would understand that you were more than your blood. I'd thought maybe she'd be in a huff for a few days, or we'd have an argument. I didn't think she would disappear entirely. I almost felt . . . angry that she'd had this reaction? Like I deserved more. I may not have ended up being one of the heroes who saved Sunalor—because, well, nobody saved Sunalor—but we'd still done plenty of good in the world. We'd taken down two evil Players. We were heroes. So why wasn't that more important than where I'd come from?

Lore arrived at the table first, and when he did so, he was wearing a pointy paper hat, tied by a string under his chin.

"What . . . are you wearing?" I asked.

He blinked back at me. "A party hat."

"OK. Why are you wearing a party hat?"

"It's my birthday."

It was my turn to blink with surprise. "Oh. Why didn't you say anything? We'll get a few beers in, celebrate properly."

Lore shrugged. "Didn't wanna make a big deal out of it. And we've got other stuff on our plates, haven't we?"

I nodded in agreement, though I felt a little guilty about it. Maybe I should have bought him a present or something. Could I afford to lose more friends?

When Corminar returned, grasping a triangle of glasses between two hands, we had to have the same conversation again.

"Your hat . . ." he said, placing the beers down. "Is it . . . ?"

"It's a party hat," I replied.

Corminar didn't take his eyes off the hat. "And, may I ask, why—"

"It's his birthday," I said, at the same time that Lore said, "It's my birthday."

The elf paused for a moment. "I see. Perhaps after we deal with this so-called Councilman, I will purchase a cake."

Damn. I should have offered that.

We sipped our beers, one of us occasionally peering outside to see whether the Councilman was finished. The crowd was slowly evaporating, but from what we could tell, the Councilman himself was taking a lot of joy from giving a long, long speech.

"Probably shouldn't have another, should we?" I asked as I drank the last of the beer. "Want to have clear heads when we—"

"He's moving." Lore suddenly noticed.

We rose from the table and hurried out of the tavern, spilling onto the street—one of us still wearing a silly hat.

"Should probably take that off," I told Lore. "Makes you stand out to the guards."

"No, I've thought about this; it's a disguise, see? If they start looking for a guy with a party hat on, I just . . . take it off. Then I'll be invisible to them."

I considered this for a moment, and then shrugged; I couldn't find any flaw in that logic.

We waited for the Councilman to finally finish his speech, in awe of his ability to ignore just how much the crowd was dwindling. Finally, he bowed deeply, long and drawn-out, and the ceremony was finally over. When the Councilman departed, he was flanked by a half dozen rather large soldiers in the golden uniform of the empire, and so we kept our distance; now that there were only three of us, we wouldn't be able to handle so many.

The Councilman traversed the city streets with these soldiers at his side, and I'd expected him to keep to the inner city, where the rich and the powerful lived. But instead, he tore off to the west, toward the . . . well, *slums* might not be the right word, but it wasn't the wrong word, either.

Out here, the number of weapons we saw grew greater, and none of them, now, were ornate. But still, people knew better than to mess with the soldiers of the empire; even if they were to pick a fight and win, they'd then have to deal with the whole of the city watch coming down on them.

That didn't stop people eyeing us up, though, and it took Lore growling at a couple of people—even with the party hat, yes—to warn them off. Eventually, the Councilman turned down a dark alley, and we approached the end of it, peering around the corner, to see what he was up to.

In the alley, facing down the weedy Councilman and his much broader entourage, were three people: a young half-tiefling, half-human woman with a smirk on her face; a large warrior man who would have put us to shame if we didn't have Lore with us; and a very tall woman with a metal contraption on her forearm. It was to the half-tiefling woman that the Councilman spoke, though we couldn't quite make out what he was saying. Not for the first time, I regretted picking *Enhanced Portals* over *Portal Relay* when we'd defeated Niamh, though admittedly the former had come in handy, too.

"What are they saying?" I asked.

"Dunno, can't hear," Lore replied. "Cor?"

"You two talking is not helping matters," the ranger replied. "I believe they are speaking of . . . a deal? Though it is not clear if they are making or resolving said deal."

The Councilman turned away, his guards doing the same, and we yanked our heads back around the corner. I searched around us for a spot to hide, and finally saw another shallow alley over the road. I portaled us over and out of sight just before the Councilman and guards turned the corner.

"What do we think, keep following?" I asked.

Corminar nodded his agreement, and we turned the corner back out onto the street a few seconds after our targets passed. We kept slow, increasing the gap between us and the Councilman so we wouldn't be spotted, and—

A metal dart—for lack of a better word—shot out from the original alley and landed squarely in the center of Lore's party hat, pinning it to the wall of a nearby building. He struggled with the string as he tried to whip it off before it strangled him.

I snapped my head toward the source of the dart, and spotted the tall woman, who had raised the metal contraption on her arm. She was flanked by the two others we'd seen in the alley.

"Why are you spying on us?" the metal-arm woman asked. "The Councilman may not have noticed, but we sure as hell did."

"And why are you wearing that, anyway?" the half tiefling asked, nodding to the party hat nailed into the wall.

"It's his birthday," Corminar and I explained simultaneously.

"Happy birthday. Why're you spending it eavesdropping? Or is this how you boys like to celebrate?" She clicked her fingers, and with that, a familiar purple glow burst into life beneath her feet. The woman fell deftly through it, landing at my side, and then whispered into my ear, "If you're looking for a fight, you've got one."

Before I could react, the woman kicked my leg behind my knee, dropping me to the floor. I spun around with my dagger, but it hit only air—the woman had disappeared through a portal once more.

Another metal dart shot out of the tall woman's device, clipping Lore in the shoulder with enough force that he staggered backward, and Corminar drew his bow on the other stranger, now charging at him.

It looked as though we had a fight on our hands.

CHAPTER THREE

The Trio

All right, three-on-three. We could do this.

It seemed we had already paired off, based on how the enemies had attacked us; Lore was facing down the woman with the metal magicks, while Corminar released his first shot into the Lore lookalike. This left me to face down the other worldbender.

I looked at the street around me, watching people hurry away from the danger and slam doors and window shutters behind them. I found the worldbender in the distance, down the alley, making a show of inspecting her long nails, and I couldn't help but be irritated by this—even though I knew that was the exact reaction she was looking for. I opened a portal beneath my feet and dropped through it, projecting myself across the alley with my dagger swinging.

The other worldbender opened her eyes in surprise—she hadn't expected to be faced with her own magicks—and hesitated, but not long enough that I could make contact with my knife. She opened another portal beneath herself, and I pushed myself through it, using my body to stop it closing.

"Hmm," the worldbender said as I pushed myself through the portal, and then she kicked me in the chest to try to force me back out of it again.

"Yeah, annoying when people do this, isn't it?" I replied.

She replied with another kick, harder this time, and I stumbled back out the portal. After orienting myself once more, I spotted her down the alley, but this time she wasn't making a show of escaping—recognizing now that I did actually pose a threat.

I charged toward her, opening a portal in front of me once more, and I leaped through it. But this time, I opened the portal's partner in the air above her, and I fell down toward her.

The worldbender saw me coming—she must have tried this trick before—and she whipped her hands upward to open a portal. I expected it to open between me and her, but instead she opened it at my side, managing to catch my knife arm. The impact disarmed me, sending the knife clattering to the ground down the alley, and I began to spin through the air.

As I spun, I saw the woman open a portal beneath herself once more, and this time I focused on getting through it before it could close. As I was falling at speed, this was no problem, and I managed to stop myself spinning in the air by holding out my hand and colliding it with the enemy.

I grabbed onto her, not much worrying where my hands went.

The woman gasped. "Oi! Mind yourself!"

I spun us around so that we'd hit the ground enemy-first, but the worldbender saw through my plan. She whipped her hands back and opened a portal on the ground, which we fell through and then came out another one that was launching us directly upward.

Now, I was on the bottom.

As we reached the apex of our launching into the air, I realized the woman would have closed the portal beneath us, so I opened one again.

"Oh, really?" she complained. "Carle? Ama? Any help here? Think we're just gonna go around in circles otherwise."

We fell together through the portals, and now I was on top once more. When no answer came from the woman's colleagues, she grumbled to herself, "Alright, well we'll try this then, won't we?"

Her skin began to ripple, and I thought I was about to see the burning texture of *Ash Husk* come forth, but instead her skin grew . . . cold? "*Frost husk?*" I asked.

"Yeah. Pretty cool, yeah?"

"Yeah, pretty cool. But not as cool as . . ." I activated my *Ash Husk* ability, and my ashen skin began to cause the woman's to sizzle.

The other worldbender yelped, trying to pull herself away, but I held on tight, hoping to distract her long enough that we'd collide with the ground once more. We plummeted fast.

"Raelas!" the woman with the metal magicks cried out, and a large ball of metal suddenly shot toward me. It hit me in the side, spinning me around until I was on the bottom again.

There was just enough time to open a portal, but not enough time to position it well. Raelas and I fell through the portal in the ground, both of us hitting an elbow on the side of the portal and sending us spinning once more.

"I'm starting to see why others find portal magicks annoying," Raelas said.

"Yeah, right?" I agreed.

We flew out of the other portal, flying diagonally across the air and over our allies. Lore was now locked in a tussle with the other large man—Carle, presumably—and Corminar was using his agility to avoid the metal mage's attacks while loosing the odd arrow. Switching enemies had probably been a good idea.

"Need help?" I called out as the other worldbender and I soared over them.

"Yes!" both Corminar and Lore complained.

I opened a portal beneath both of the other two enemies, dropping them onto their heads and giving my friends an advantage, before closing them again and opening another portal to catch myself. This portal I paired with one horizontal to the ground, and Raelas and I came tumbling to a stop on the dusty street.

"You can do two sets?" the other worldbender exclaimed.

"Yep."

"Any chance we can call the portal magicks a wash, and like, not use them? Might make this quicker."

I shrugged. "Sure."

"Really?"

With the flick of my wrist, I opened a portal below her. "No."

Raelas fell tumbling through, and I opened another portal beneath her which I paired with one directly above. One thing I'd realized since my portal magicks upgrade was that having two pairs made it easy to trap someone in an unending loop. While Raelas fell, over and over and over, I turned my attention to the others. Corminar seemed to be the one having the most trouble.

I opened a portal beneath my discarded dagger, dropped it into my hands, and then leaped into the air. Using my magicks, in the blink of an eye I was above the metal mage—who hadn't yet realized I was no longer occupied. I fell, knife pointing down, and I was just about to land the tip of my dagger in her flesh when Corminar made the mistake of glancing at me.

Ama realized I was there in an instant, and she ripped some of the liquid metal from her sleeve and cast it above her—making a solid sheet between me and her. My dagger bounced off the sheet, the impact knocking it from my hand, and my wrist cried out in pain.

"Think I broke something!" I shouted.

"Not your dagger, I hope?" Corminar asked.

"No, my wrist."

"Good."

At that moment, the other burly man swept Lore's leg, knocking him to the ground. I whipped my good hand over to them, opening a portal to save Lore before Carle could bring his sword down into him, and Lore tumbled out at my side.

"Concentrate on the mage!" I shouted. "We gotta thin their ranks!"

At that moment, I saw a flash of movement out of the corner of my eye—one which was followed up by a punch to the nose. "Broke something else!" I shouted, stumbling backward.

Raelas stood before me, having broken out of my infinite fall trap. I cursed myself; of course she'd have had no problem with that, she had portal magicks to use.

Lore put himself between me and the other worldbender, and tried to punch her right back, but she used her portal magicks to be out of reach in a flash. "This lot are ruining my birthday," he grumbled.

"That's your fault for taking jobs on your birthday, then, isn't it, big boy?" Raelas shouted.

All three of us hesitated. "What do you mean, 'taking jobs'?" I asked.

Now it was Raelas's turn to hesitate. "I mean . . . you took the bounty on us, right? The Councilman sent you to tie up loose ends?"

All efforts at attacks were starting to fade.

I blinked at the half-tiefling woman. "What? We didn't take any bounty."

"Then why were you here?"

"Spying on him!"

Raelas's eyes narrowed. "Not on us?"

"My dear, we do not know who in all the hells of creation you are," Corminar replied.

The worldbender glanced at him and then back to me, apparently thinking I was going to be easier to deal with. And maybe I was, these days. "We're . . . well, we don't have any official name, but people call us the Trio."

"It sounds like you're just called the Trio, then," I replied.

"No, people just call us that," the worldbender insisted. "So, you've heard of us?"

"No."

Raelas looked to Ama, then shrugged. "Who are you lot, then?"

"The Slayers. Maybe you've—"

"No," Raelas immediately cut me off. "Though perhaps I should have, one of you being so handsome and all . . ."

Both Corminar and Lore beamed.

"Stop smiling!" I snapped at them. "They tried to kill us!"

"Oh, right," Lore mumbled.

I turned back to Raelas. "One thing I don't understand. You were making a deal with him, weren't you? The Councilman? Why would he want to kill you?"

Raelas smiled. "Because that big job he did? The one that saved Westbara, and got him the key to the city? He didn't do it.

"We did."

CHAPTER FOUR

More Important Things to Worry About

None of us three Slayers said anything for a moment. Lore, in the end, was the one who opened his mouth first. "What job?"

Raelas slouched. "You lot aren't from round here, are you?"

"Tundras," I replied.

"The Dawnwood," Corminar said.

"I am. I'm from here," Lore finished. We all turned to look at him, and he looked back at us, confused. "Grew up round here, didn't I? Well, further west. Northwest, really. In the Beached Armada proper. A little town called Coldharbor. But these sorts of parts, at least. And I thought that would count." He looked at Raelas. "Does that count?"

"I . . ." Raelas started, then didn't seem to find an end to that sentence.

"If you are not here in order to kill us," Carle said, in an accent far posher than I had expected, given his whole . . . vibe, "then why are you here? Surely you do not mean to kill a Player?"

"No, course not," I replied, instinctively. Admitting such a thing in any parts—particularly here, under the empire—was a recipe for dying fast. "Who'd wanna do that? Even saying that would put the whole city on our case, and we—"

"Cos we do," Raelas interrupted. "We wanna kill him."

I trailed off. "Oh, right. In that case, yeah. Yeah, we do, too."

"Nice. Not often you meet people who want to kill the offspring of the Architects, is it? Some like-minded souls and all that."

"Really?" Lore asked. "This isn't some kind of trap? You'd really kill a Player?"

Raelas shrugged. "We kill all sorts; we don't discriminate. You wanna team up?"

This wasn't quite the heroic response it could have been. She could have said they slayed evil no matter who it was, but the way she phrased it seemed to imply that the "evil" bit was optional. Still, with Arzak and Val still missing, we could use all the help we could get.

"Do you know where he lives?" I asked.

The half tiefling smiled. "I'm going to take that as a 'yes.'"

I'd suggested going to a tavern and talking through the plan over a pint or two, but this idea had been met with raised eyebrows. Ama had said, "We would want a clear head if we are going after a Player," in a tone like you'd use to talk to a child. So instead, we were sitting in a place that served only food—you couldn't even buy beer if you wanted!—that had a slightly obscured view of the manor where the Councilman took residence.

"We're all clear on the plan, then?" Raelas asked. After the nods and murmurs of agreement, she reached toward the large breadcrumbs she'd used to mark our positions on the table in front of us. She reached across me, almost uncomfortably close, and swept the crumbs onto the floor. Raelas lingered there to glance at me, surely noticing how rigidly I was sitting in my chair. "You OK there, handsome?"

"I still think we should portal him elsewhere," I said, stumbling on my words, flustered. "We don't know how many guards he has inside there with him. Wouldn't it be better to fight on our terms?" I didn't really buy this logic that was coming out of my mouth, but it was better than acknowledging the other worldbender's question.

"We don't know how many guards are inside, correct," Ama said. "But we also do know how many are outside."

"Thousands," Lore said, nodding knowingly.

I opened my mouth to defend this point of view further, but snapped it shut again when I realized I'd only be digging myself deeper. Anything else I might have said instead was completely lost when Raelas winked at me.

Lore caught my eye from across the table, and then glanced at Raelas. "Why do you wanna kill him, anyway?"

This question drew Raelas's attention away from me and to the barbarian instead. I smiled my thanks to Lore, though I admittedly wasn't completely sure this was why he'd done it.

"We completed work for him, and he didn't pay. That's what you three stumbled onto. Thinks he can get the key to Westbara and then bring his new guards with him to tell us he's not paying. Only reason we took the damned job was because it paid well."

"And if we were to let this slide, then of course that might give future employers ideas about not paying us either . . ." Carle added.

We'd heard a similar thing from the Red Thorn. Of course, we had been the ones who hadn't paid up, back then. "Yeah, I know a few elves who'd agree with you." I gestured to Corminar. "He still has one of their bows, actually. Gave it to him after the Battle of Sunalor."

Ama raised her eyebrows. "You were there?"

"There?" I repeated. "Corminar here was leading the—"

The elf shook his head abruptly, and I changed course. Fair enough, really; I probably wouldn't want people talking about my failures, either.

"We were there, yeah."

"You've been all around, huh?" Raelas asked, her eyes trained squarely on me. As she held my gaze, she fiddled with her long hair, adjusting it around her short, curling horns.

I did not know what to do with such unabashed attention.

Lore coughed. "Yeah, we were there. Us three, Arzak, Val . . ."

I had to assume that this comment was for my benefit, even though I hadn't done anything; it was Raelas who was being so forthcoming here.

"And where is this Val?" the fellow worldbender asked.

"She—"

"Oh, good heavens, look at the time," Corminar said, looking up at the sun hanging low in the sky. "Perhaps we should be killing a Player now?"

I smiled to Corminar, thanking him for the interruption, and the six of us rose from our seats.

Raelas threw down a large handful of coins onto the table to pay for our food. "It's on me," she said, her eyes fixed on me to let me know that this act was entirely for my benefit.

We strolled along the road, taking care not to glance at the manor in which the Player was staying all that much, and slowed to a halt at the junction.

"Alright," Raelas said. "Remember the plan: Styk, you create a distraction. I'll portal the rest of us inside. Then you'll join us, yeah?"

"I'll join you," I confirmed.

"Don't be long, now," the other worldbender said with eyes that seemed to challenge me.

"I—"

"I knew it!" a voice suddenly shouted.

Our six faces whipped up to face the source of the cry—a window in the manor house overlooking the cobbled street.

"I knew you would not be able to let it go!" The Councilman beamed, his tone sounding almost excitable as he looked down on the Trio from up above. "Archnemesis . . . es at last!"

"Nemeses," Carle corrected him.

"Archnemeses at last. They always told me you could not rise so high without drawing the envious eyes of the locals, and here we are, about to do battle because—"

"We ain't envious!" Raelas shouted up to him. It was nice for her attention to be fixed on someone else for a moment.

"Well, what are you, then?"

"Unpaid," Ama answered.

"Yes, well, one and the same, are they not? You are envious of the money that I have not handed over for services that you claim you rendered."

"We did render them!"

"As I say, 'claim.'"

"Are we gonna stand around here bickering all day, or are we gonna fight?" I interrupted.

The Councilman looked down at me. "And who is this? A member of your 'Trio'?"

"You do know what 'trio' means, don't you?" Ama asked.

Lore raised a hand. "Are we still doing the plan, or . . . ?"

"They're here to kill you, same as us," Raelas informed the Councilman.

"Well don't say so that loudly!" I hissed at her. This was all going off the rails fast. I wasn't sure I'd ever seen a plan go so wrong so quickly, in fact.

The worldbender shrugged. "Why not?" She looked around; most of the nearby people were hurrying off since the use of the word *kill*, but a few guards were suddenly very, very interested in this conversation. "Oh, right, yeah. You don't mind a few guards, though, do you?"

"I mean, we're about to fight a Player, aren't we? Kinda think we need all the advantages we can get."

"He's right, you know," the Councilman said, glancing at me. "We should begin. Oh, it's been so long since I was in a decent fight." He flicked his wrist, and blue-white flames engulfed his hand. When they died away, a ghostly blue axe was in his hand.

The Trio had already told me that the Councilman had decent *Conjuration* and warrior skills, but it was weird to see a man as small and weedy as this one holding an axe. It almost felt like he should have been a pure magicks user.

"Guards?" the Councilman called out to the approaching soldiers in golden uniform. "Arrest these six for the crime of treason. And kill them if you must."

Treason—that's what it was, these days, to seek to kill a Player. The Players were the agents of Amira, Empress of the Golden Empire, and so trying to kill one of them was like hurting the empire itself. It was no wonder, then, that the soldiers jumped to follow his command.

I looked around at those in golden uniform, encroaching on us in a broad circle, about seven of them so far, but more surely on the way. "Yeah, maybe we should take this inside." I reached one hand to the road beneath our feet, and the other up to the room the Councilman was peering out from, and was about to activate a portal, when—

Screams erupted from the near distance.

All of our faces snapped to the source of the noise, friend and foe alike. Along the road from here we could just about see the western gate—and people running, dragging their children, away from some evil that we could not see.

"What?" the Councilman asked, voice suddenly panicking. "What is it?"

Only Corminar, using his improved elven vision, could give an answer. "Malae," he said. "Malae are attacking the city."

A chill ran down my spine, and the soldiers turned away from us. Suddenly, the accusation of treason didn't seem so important.

CHAPTER FIVE

Monster Hunting

"How many? How many malae?" I demanded of Corminar. From the looks of it—that is, people running screaming—there were a lot of them.

"At least four," he said. "Perhaps more."

The thing about malae was that four was a lot. Even one had the potential to destroy a city this size, its touch likely to corrupt, its very presence pulling forth everyone's greatest fears.

Corminar's eye twitched.

"Bees?" I asked, thinking back to the last time we'd encountered a mala together.

"Just buzzing," he replied. "For now."

"Lore?" I asked.

He shook his head, saying nothing, but his face was pale.

"No visions, either?"

Again, he shook his head. "Nothing that I saw. No malae."

"OK," I said, and raised my voice to include not just the Slayers, but the Trio, too. There was a speech that needed to be given whenever you faced down the malae; something I knew from prior experience. Corminar had been there the last time we'd faced down the malae, back when we'd been trying to fulfil his debt to the Red Thorn, but Lore had only heard us talk about the malae, back when we'd discovered the witchfinders had used them to power their experiments. And the others? As far as I knew, they had no real working knowledge of the monsters. "There are three things you need to know before fighting a mala," I shouted. "One: don't let it touch you. If it touches you—"

"Then we'll have to kill you," Lore said, his eyes trained fiercely on the gate where the malae were roaming. "Two: you're gonna feel some fear. Fear about things you didn't even know you were scared of. You gotta ignore it; it ain't real."

"Lore, how do you—" I began to ask.

"And last: it's like depth-raiders—the stronger you are, the stronger *they* are."

I hesitated as I looked at Lore, there being a fire in his eyes that I wasn't sure I'd seen before. Was it possible he'd encountered the malae in the past, too? Was it possible that he had also lost someone to them?

"You're talking like we're going to fight them," Raelas said. "We've faced them before; it . . . ain't easy."

Carle nodded. "I would much rather we leave town. There is a city guard to deal with this."

I shook my head. "No. No, there's some things that go beyond all else. It doesn't matter right now that the guards want us dead; if we don't do something— if we don't help—then many innocent people will die."

" . . . And it might earn us some favor with the guards?" Ama added.

It was this addition, not my reasoning, that seemed to convince the rest of the Trio.

"Alright," Raelas said. "Malae. Never fought malae before. Could be fun."

"It won't be." Lore's eyes remained on the western gate.

As we were about to move, a voice rang out from above. "*Excuse me!*" The Councilman. "Are we, or are we not, about to have our epic showdown?"

I glanced to Corminar and Lore. "Is it just me, or is this Player not anywhere near as intimidating as the others?"

"Others?" Raelas asked, eyebrows raised, whipping around to look at me. "Impressive . . ."

"There are malae attacking the city," Corminar called up to the Player. "Do you not think this comes before your petty squabbles?" How far he'd come since I met him, when he was trading in these creatures. Watching his home city fall to the enemy had matured him, though I hadn't told him that; he would have thought he was mature already.

"I *think* you should finish what you started," the Councilman replied.

In response, the six of us turned away.

"Fire?" I asked. "Anyone have fire?" I looked to the three new allies, who all shook their heads or shrugged.

"I have a single explosive potion," Corminar said. "Though only one; we would need to use it well."

I nodded, then looked to Raelas. "OK. I have some ideas on that, but I'll need your help." The other worldbender nodded. "The rest of you: draw the malae's attention away from the others, but don't let them get too close. And *definitely* don't let them touch you. Understand?"

Lore nodded knowingly, while the others expressed their agreement.

"Alright," I said, "let's go."

Raelas opened a portal that flicked the six of us closer to the action, all while the Councilman was prattling on about the supposed destined fight in the background.

We stepped through, and out into chaos. Screams erupted around me as people ran, clutching their heads, shouting about things that weren't there—and only existed in their minds, conjured by the malae. And there, on the center of the road, were two of the monsters. They approached slowly.

Shlop. Shlop. Shlop.

"You said four!" I shouted to Corminar, and was answered by a new wave of screams erupting from a nearby traveler's inn, followed by people storming out. "Ah. Found 'em."

I turned back to the other two malae, taking stock of the situation, and adjusting my plan accordingly. "You reckon that inn has insurance?"

"I don't know, but I *love* where this is going," Raelas said. "What you thinking, handsome?"

I ignored her; even if I wanted to acknowledge that descriptor, there wasn't time. "Lore, Ama, Corminar . . . get those two's attention," I said, pointing to the two malae that were still outside. "Bring them into the tavern. Corminar, chuck me the explosive potion."

The elf approached and placed it gently in my hand. "It is fragile. Do not 'chuck' it until you intend to use it."

"You got a plan?" Lore asked.

"Yes."

"I don't always like your plans."

"I know, buddy." I turned, gesturing for Raelas and Carle to follow me. I hoped I could wrangle these two into doing what I wanted, and I could trust Corminar and Lore to deal with the other malae sensibly. We ran into the tavern, slipping around people still stumbling out, and as soon as I entered, I staggered to a halt.

There, standing directly in front of me, was Val.

She stared back at me with dead, graying eyes, and her skin began to rot and flake away. The image was so intense that I couldn't tear my eyes away, the horror of what was before me snaking its way into my heart.

Someone grabbed me by the arm, and I was finally able to look away, to see Raelas staring up at me. "You OK?" she asked, and this time there was none of the flirty drawl I was becoming used to; she recognized the seriousness of the situation.

"It's Val," I croaked, looking back at her. "She . . ." But there was nothing there now. It was a vision. It was my greatest fear made real.

I almost felt guilty. Last time I had encountered the malae, it was another woman I'd seen—or heard, rather. A woman I'd long since lost, that parts of me were beginning to move on from. But wasn't it time? Wasn't it time I moved on with my life, and made something with someone else? Someone who had disappeared in the night, admittedly.

"Styk," Raelas said, shaking my arm. "Come on!"

We plunged into the center of the tavern's main chamber—a large, two-story room with a railed balcony around the next floor up. Light poured in through large panes of glass in the roof, illuminating the tavern floor and the woodwork below. As well as two malae.

"What now?" Carle asked, choking back the same sensation I felt growing within me—fear.

"Keep them busy. Get everyone else out."

The two of them nodded, and while Carle went one way, Raelas and I went for the other creature. It grew closer to a young tiefling couple, who cowered in the corner, too overwhelmed by feelings of fear to flee—something that was very understandable, all things considered.

While Raelas tried to open a portal beneath the mala, I knew better. The monster stretched instinctively around the purple portal as it burst into life, stopping itself from falling through, and continuing on its slow advance toward the tiefling couple.

But I'd opened a portal, too, and I'd opened it beneath the cowering couple. They tumbled out at my side, and I picked them up with one arm each. "Run!" I shouted. "Now!"

The shock of the fall had been enough to bring them back to their senses, and they did as I instructed without hesitation. As they left, they ran past new figures entering the building.

The guards who had once been about to kill us arrived at our sides, and they jumped into attacking the creatures without any question of sorting us out first—malae really were the great unifiers.

"Keep them occupied!" I shouted to the soldiers. "I can deal with them, but we need the other two in here first!"

Nobody complained, so I took that as agreement, that they were on board with my plan. But though the soldiers might have deferred to my plan, they clearly weren't experts in fighting malae. They got in close, swords slashing toward the dark, tiny enemies, thinking that killing them was as easy as chopping them in two. But when swords met void-like flesh, the malae parted around them, unharmed. And then they were close enough for the malae to strike.

One of the monsters hopped onto a soldier's leg, wrapping itself around it. The soldier began to panic, and his colleague tried to slice it free—but it was already too late for the man, whether they knew it or not.

I opened a portal beneath man and mala, and together they plunged through it, out into the middle of the courtyard. At least, when the enemies were attached to a person, it was easier to move them around with portals—they were too busy feasting to prevent themselves from falling through.

The soldier gasped as the mala drove its tendrils into its flesh, feeding on his mind, his sapience, his very soul.

"Carle!" I shouted to the gentleman warrior who was dealing with the other mala not far from where I'd just thrown the dying soldier. "He's corrupted!"

The man stared blankly back at me.

"You need to kill him, before he turns!"

If the warrior had any questions, he was sensible enough to keep them to himself. The man flicked the other mala back with the tip of his long sword and then turned to the dying man—and the mala feasting upon him.

"No!" one of the soldiers shouted, flinging a hand forward as he charged toward his colleague, apparently still looking to save him.

I flicked a hand up, meaning to open a portal in front of the charging soldier to stop him—but another portal appeared there before I could. I turned to Raelas, and we nodded to one another simultaneously.

Carle brought his sword down onto the soldier's neck, separating it in—unfortunately—not one blow but three. But it was still quick enough to kill him before he could be corrupted, like I'd seen happen before.

Val's voice echoed through my mind. "Maybe me next. How do you know _I_ haven't been corrupted, if there's all these malae running about?"

I shook my head, ignoring her.

"What do you see?" Raelas shouted across the interior courtyard.

"Nothing I want to talk about," I cried back. "You?"

"Poverty."

I was about to question this, but the second mala was approaching Carle once more, and he was going to need help if he was to keep out of their range. I leaped into the air, blinked through a portal in a now very well-practiced maneuver, and arrived at his side. As the mala _shlopped_ closer, I threateningly flailed a _Knifestorm_ attack forth—but of course these weren't the sort of creatures to be intimidated.

Instead, I opened another portal, this time to my pocket world, and I dumped out dozens of _Needlework_ supplies onto the mala. It was a costly attack—cloth wasn't cheap—but anything was worth it if it meant killing these monsters. Besides, this cloth would burn.

The tavern doors burst open, and Corminar, Lore and Ama charged inside, followed quickly by the other two malae. They'd done it—the plan was coming together. All that was left was . . .

I hurried to Carle's side, then opened a portal below us that would get us out of the center of the courtyard. I just needed to get these two recently arrived monsters into the same spot, and then my plan could really begin. But how could I get them through the portals?

I cast my eyes around the well-lit tavern interior until I found my answer: another casualty from before we arrived. I opened a portal below them and tossed the body next to the two new malae, who immediately hopped onto it to feed. As soon as they were settled—and distracted—I opened some more portals to throw the body and malae next to the others.

Now, they were all in one place. Now, I could throw that potion.

I pulled Corminar's explosive potion from my pocket, and I tossed it into the center of the tavern. Flames burst forth as glass shattered, lighting the wooden interior and my *Needlework* supplies alike.

The malae squealed as they faced fire, their greatest weakness, but only two of them died.

---

2 x Level ? Corruption defeated!

Worldbending: +2,200XP
Worldbending increased to level 52!
Base Points Gained: +2 INT, +2 Free Points (INT/WIS/CHA)

As for the others? I'd hurt them, yes, but what I'd mostly done was enrage them. And now, they were headed right for me.

CHAPTER SIX

Like a House on Fire

"Oh, now the tavern's on fire," Lore said. "Cool, cool." His eyes were wide, flicking toward something in the corner of the room that wasn't there; the malae's fear magicks had gotten to him like they had me.

The two monsters *shloped* toward me, slow and steady, never ceasing. They'd escaped the fire—the only thing that could potentially kill them. But the fire was spreading fast, and the fight wasn't over yet. "Raelas!" I shouted. "You got *Portal Slice?*"

"Got what?"

"I'll take that as a 'no.'" Styk raised a hand to the wooden beams above. "Gonna need your portals—watch what I do!"

Corminar fired an arrow at the approaching malae to slow them down, but he was too busy being distracted by visions of *Witchcraft*-imbued demon bees to aim well.

I opened a portal that dumped some of my burning *Needlework* supplies onto the wooden beams above. The fire took a moment to spread, but the beams caught before the cloth could fall back to the floor once more.

Good. Now we have more to play with.

I *Portal Sliced* through a small section of the beams, dropping a flaming block of wood to the ground. I tried opening a portal during its fall that would land it on the enemies, but I wasn't fast enough—the wooden block landed at their side.

"I think I see where you're heading with this," Raelas said, appearing close at my side. "Again."

The others—soldiers and nonsoldiers alike—formed a wall in front of us, doing their best to slow the malae movements with makeshift shields. Their efforts were minimal, however, because they all knew that they couldn't risk letting the creatures touch them.

I *sliced* through the wooden beams once more, and Raelas whipped her hands around to catch the flaming debris with a portal. The flaming chunks appeared out the other half of the pair and smashed into one of the malae, the void-like flesh extinguishing the flames. It squealed with pain, its flesh rippling and burning, but it wasn't enough to kill it. Not yet, at least.

"Again!" Raelas shouted.

I dropped another section of recently lit beam down, and Raelas again moved to catch it. Even as the wood fell, I could tell that her aim wasn't quite so good this time, but her portals gave me enough time to move to correct it. I opened another portal in front of Raelas's and redirected it back toward the same creature. It hit square and true, and if I wasn't mistaken, the mala was looking a little smaller, as though some of it had burned away.

"Feels like we're a pretty good match, huh?" Raelas said.

Corminar glanced over at me. "You have a type."

"I don't think now's the time," I snapped back at him, and then dropped another chunk of flaming wood for Raelas to throw at the enemy. She opened a portal, and—

"You *dare* turn your back on me?" a voice boomed behind us.

Both Raelas and I hesitated, then turned to see the Councilman standing in the tavern's doorway, furious. "There was . . ." I started.

"Do you not know who I am? I am a Player! I am the spawn of the great Architects themselves! And you think you can challenge me then turn away?"

"We're kinda in the middle of something, darling?" Raelas said.

"Yeah, can't you see the . . ." I gestured to the two remaining malae. We turned back to attack them once more.

"I don't *care* that you—"

"After," I told him.

The Councilman spluttered with fury behind me, and I let him do so—but not without someone to keep an eye on him. "Lore?" I asked, gesturing to the Player.

The barbarian nodded, and then circled around us to stand between us and the Councilman.

We continued, smashing a couple more pieces of flaming wood to the same mala until it hissed away into nothing. Raelas was right about one thing; we did work well together.

Level ? Corruption defeated!

Worldbending: +1,200XP

And then, there was just one left.

As the flames spread, one of the supporting wooden pillars began to crack, and part of the balcony on the floor above began to buckle. I flicked my eyes down to Ama, who was standing under it, and opened a portal beneath her for her to fall through just before the flaming balcony above could crush her.

She spilled out at my side and brushed her legs as she stood. "You could've warned me."

"Usually, people just say thank you." I moved my hands back to dump more flaming beams onto the enemy, and was about to do so when Lore yelped.

I whipped around to see Lore tangling with the Councilman's ghostly axe, the aura flickering into his flesh and singeing it. Lore shouldn't have had any problem with this skirmish, but his eyes were darting—the mala had its teeth in him, inflicting fear in someone it deemed powerful. From the looks of the Player, he wasn't having quite as much trouble with fear—but was that due to weakness or the strength to ignore his fears?

As I glanced over, the Councilman parried Lore's Bane Sword away and pushed past him, apparently fixating instead on me—presumably for having infuriated him.

"Corminar!" I called out, and the elf tore away from the shield wall while I kept my attention on attacking the last of the malae.

He spun around in a graceful maneuver as he drew an arrow into his bow, and then shot it at the charging Councilman. Except, at the last moment, something buzzed in his vision, putting him off at the last second. The resulting arrow shot over the sprinting Player's shoulder. Corminar hurried to fire another arrow, and this one hit the Councilman in the shoulder.

This was enough, apparently, for the Player to retrain his focus on the elf, rather than me.

"Nobody attacks a Player and lives to tell the tale!" the Councilman shouted. I had plenty of evidence to the contrary, however. The Player charged through the spreading flames, and swung his axe through the air at Corminar.

The elf leaped back, retreating deeper into the tavern, to avoid the hit and managed to loose another arrow into the Councilman's chest at the same time. As I knew full well, the malae's visions of fear came and went—he could fight undistracted for now, at least.

I sliced another major chunk of beam free, and as it hit the ground where Raelas dumped it, it made the building shake. More of the flaming balcony dropped to the floor, right where Corminar had been moments earlier—the rest of us were separated from his fight with the Player.

"Oi, handsome!" Raelas nudged me, drawing my attention back to the mala. "More fire, please."

I was about to let loose more of the wood, when I heard Corminar cry out with pain. I looked back over to my friend, through the flames, and saw the Councilman standing, axe raised, over the fallen elf.

"I may be in need of assistance!" the ranger shouted.

I threw my hands forward to open a portal, but only a purple glow fizzled forth.

"Damn *mana* reserves," I mumbled. My newer *Enhanced Portals* ability only required mana to open the portals, rather than sustain them, but there was still a hefty mana cost to conjuring them at all—and I hadn't been keeping an eye on it. I might not have had enough mana for any more portals, but I did still have enough for another *Worldbending* ability. My skin rippled and changed as I used almost the last of my mana to activate my *Ash Husk* ability. With this new fire resistance, I charged through the flames, but even with this ability, the heat was enough to hurt.

I gasped as I emerged from the other side, but I didn't slow down, instead throwing myself into a tackle that pushed the Councilman to the ground. The Player should have had enough time to kill the elf, and yet my friend was still breathing. Still, that didn't change what I had to do.

I drew my knife and swung it around toward the enemy's neck.

But in that same moment, his ghostly axe changed form, morphing into a long, sharp, chain-like object. It moved seemingly of its own accord, and wrapped itself around my wrist before I could land the attack.

The enemy's weapon wrenched me sideways, to the ground, and the Councilman stood over me, silhouetted by the raging inferno.

"And now," he said, his voice croaking, "I must . . ." The Councilman swung his axe, and his ghostly chain darted at me.

But then, he hesitated.

The chain came to a stop just before my neck.

And he . . . gulped.

"What's . . . going on?" I asked.

The Councilman shook his head.

"Have you never killed someone before?"

"Your friend seems awfully chipper about the prospect of dying," Carle shouted over the raging battle.

"Yeah, usually dying's not a big deal for him!" Lore shouted back. And he was right—this one wouldn't take either, considering my Sisyphus Artifact currently had a charge in it.

"I'm . . . gonna stand up now?" I said, and couldn't help but frame this sentence as a question. I slowly retreated from the points of the enemy's ghostly weapon, and clambered back to my feet. "You've really never killed someone before, have you?"

"I'm *trying!*" the Councilman insisted. "It's just . . . it's just . . ."

He didn't get to finish that sentence, because at that moment, Corminar reappeared and dumped a heavy barstool onto his head, knocking him unconscious.

The elf and I made eye contact.

"Probably the easiest Player yet, right?"

"Indeed."

We turned our attention back to the last remaining mala, and I saw Raelas trying to throw flaming items of furniture onto it. There was no need for *Portal Slicing* anymore, considering half the tavern was now alight.

"Little help?" she shouted across the room to me.

But she couldn't see that the battle was already won. The building was disintegrating, more and more flaming debris collapsing inward. Soon enough, the mala would be surrounded—all we needed to do was let it happen.

"Time to go!" I shouted.

"But the—"

"It'll be dead in a minute anyway. And if we hang around here, we will be, too." I turned around, grabbed the unconscious Player by the scruff of his tunic, and opened a portal to dump us outside—and out of trouble.

It was time to find out what this pathetic excuse for a Player had to do with Tana's grand plan.

CHAPTER SEVEN

Council Work

I learned something new that evening.

If you need to carry a body—or a body-shaped object—through a crowded city without drawing trouble, just put a cloth over it. Anyone with an ounce of sense would know it was a body that the burly Lore was carrying over his shoulder, but the fabric gave them an excuse not to check. This applied to the locals, at least—they didn't want any trouble—but the guards were another matter.

We'd had to keep to the winding alleyways of Westbara that Raelas knew so well, and staged an elaborate distraction at the gate, to keep out of sight of the guards.

From there, it was simple, and one decently sized bribe later, we were standing in the basement of a traveler's inn with the Councilman tied to a pillar. We were really starting to get the hang of this "kidnapping and interrogation" thing.

It took Corminar slapping the Player lightly on the face in order to wake him up. When he awoke, he did so with a start, glancing worriedly at the six of us glaring down at him.

"At last," Lore said. "Was beginning to think Corminar hits harder than we thought."

"I—" the Player started, but I interrupted him.

"We got a few questions."

The Councilman snarled. "I don't answer questions coming from—"

"Interrupt me again, and Lore here will punch you in the mouth."

Lore punched him in the mouth.

Both the prisoner and I blinked at the barbarian. "I said if he interrupted me again."

Lore scratched the back of his head sheepishly. "Oh, right. Sorry."

"I thought you said you were good at this," Ama called out from the back of the room.

I held up a hand to beg her for her patience, then turned back to the Player. "You work for the Council"—the prisoner looked around shiftily—"so tell us: what's their plan?"

"I . . ." The Councilman trailed off.

"OK, new rule: interrupt me *or* fail to answer me, and Lore will punch you in the mouth."

Lore moved again to hit the prisoner, and I held out a hand to stop him.

"Last chance," I said. "What's the Council's plan?"

"I . . . I think it's . . ."

"OK, hit him."

Lore connected his fist with the man's face, and this time blood splattered out of his mouth.

"What's their plan?" I demanded. Still, the Player didn't look like he was going to respond. "We know they're after us. We know they've put a bounty on us; Niamh saw to that. We know Tana is organizing . . . *something.* We just don't know how it all comes together."

"It is time for you to fill in our gaps in knowledge," Corminar added. "Now. Else we kill you."

"I . . ." the Player spluttered through bloody teeth.

"Tell us," Lore said.

"Now," I added.

"I . . . I . . ." The Councilman's eyes flicked around the room, damp and pitiful. He didn't find a friendly face. "I don't . . . know?"

"How can you not know?" I cried back, exasperated. I kept my volume down so as to not to let any patrons upstairs in the tavern know what was going on down here. "You're the Councilman! You are, therefore, a member of the Council, aren't you?"

Silence swept over the basement.

"Oh, gods," Corminar breathed.

I shook my head in disbelief. "You're not a member of the Council at all, are you?"

The Player's voice cracked as he replied. "They . . . rejected my application."

"And so you calling yourself 'The Councilman' is . . . ?"

"Have you ever heard the phrase 'dress for the job you want'?" the Player replied. "This is like that."

"No, it isn't."

None of this was adding up. First of all, this man's insane logic—I couldn't figure out how he'd come to justify calling himself the Councilman when he wasn't a member of any council I knew of. But secondly, also . . . Lore's visions had led us to him. And if they'd led us to him, then us having met him was a vital stage on our journey toward Tana's grand plan. Yet it was hard to believe that this pitiful soul had—or would have had—anything to do with it.

"When are you gonna ask him about our payment?" Raelas asked, piping up from the back of the room.

". . . Never? I don't care about that."

The Councilman—though maybe we shouldn't still call him that, all things considered—snarled. "Payment? Payment for what?"

"We did the job!"

"Well *clearly* you did not!" the Player shouted back at her. "Considering what just happened."

I raised an eyebrow. "What . . . does he mean, exactly?" I asked Raelas. "Just what was the job you did for him?"

"Err . . ." the half tiefling replied, noncommittally.

But the Player answered for her. "Killing malae!" he shouted. "Westbara's been having a bit of a mala problem lately—you saw it. *You* were supposed to eliminate the threat."

"We thought we had," Ama replied. "We eliminated the one we found."

"One?" the Player repeated. "*One?* I sent you to kill dozens!"

"Guess they'll have to take back that key to the city, huh? Considering you didn't save Westbara, like you said."

"*You* didn't save—"

"Alright, enough!" I shouted, risking a loud voice and potentially alerting those above us to the commotion. There was something in this; I could feel it. And, judging by the look I shared with both Lore and Corminar, they saw it, too. We wondered why the so-called Councilman was important in getting us to Tana's great plan? Well, maybe this was the answer.

A few weeks ago, now, we'd stumbled across an abandoned witchfinder village. In that village, we'd seen some strange contraptions, and the witchfinders themselves had seemed to be trapped in a tear between worlds. We'd fixed the tear, potentially trapping them forever—they were witch hunters, so who cares?—and then we'd found the experiment's notes.

It had been a mala that had powered those devices. The same creature we now stumbled across.

What with Lore's visions having led us this far, I couldn't just discount this as a coincidence.

"Tell me about the malae," I snapped—both at the prisoner and at the Trio.

Both Raelas and the Councilman spoke at once, and I couldn't understand what either of them were saying.

"Not both at once!" I cried over them.

"Then perhaps don't ask them all at once," Ama suggested.

"Yeah, thank you." This mismatched group were proving even more dysfunctional than the mismatched group I was used to. I missed Val already, but right then I *really* missed her. "Raelas, you first."

"Been a few sightings of those malae in the area. Mostly around the fringes, picking off travelers and stuff, yeah? And the duke and his cronies here don't care about that. But then they started coming *inside* the city, and people started panicking."

"Yeah, so they should," Lore said.

Raelas raised her eyebrows; she didn't disagree. "Anyway, they put out a bounty on the malae, this idiot"—she waved to the Councilman—"responded, and . . . what's the word?"

"Subcontracted," Corminar said.

"Yeah, subcontracted it to us, and the rest is history."

I tried to resist the urge to put my head in my hands. I failed. "Gods alive . . ."

"Rather the mess you have put yourselves into," Corminar added, echoing my thoughts.

"Yeah, idiot," Raelas agreed, not realizing that the elf was including the Trio in that *you.*

I turned away from the prisoner, trying to figure out what to do next. It seemed sensible to follow this line of investigation—if the malae were entering the city, then they were breeding out there. And who was to say that wasn't being managed by a member of the Council, seeking to power their machines?

"You," I said, prodding my finger into the Player's chest.

He widened his eyes in surprise.

"These malae, what do you know about them? You had to have a plan beyond getting the key to the city, right? You want to be in the Council, and I'm guessing you thought this would get you there. So, what is it? Are you clearing up their messes?"

From the way the lanky Player's lip twitched on his hanging mouth as he struggled to find the words, I realized I was onto something.

"Don't make me make him hit you," I said.

Lore cracked his knuckles for dramatic effect; we'd practiced that particular bit of theatre.

The Player looked hesitantly at the barbarian's hands before glancing back up at me. If I wasn't mistaken, he was shaking slightly. Was he really this new to actually being hurt? "Alright, alright," he said. "I tell you, you let me go, though."

"As a rule," Corminar said, "we do not allow Players their freedom."

"Why not?"

"Because you kill people," Lore answered.

The Player pushed against his bindings, and I got the sense he was trying to raise his hands to protest his innocence. "I don't! I've never killed anyone."

"This guy just gets more and more pathetic by the minute, huh?" Raelas mumbled.

"We don't believe you," Lore said.

"Err . . ." I muttered, and everyone looked at me. "I really don't think he has. He had the chance to kill Corminar, and he had the chance to kill me, and he just . . . didn't. I think he might be . . ." I looked into the Player's eyes. "I think he might be *afraid* to kill."

The man's eyes widened in fear—not from the fear that we had him tied up and might've been about to kill him, but instead due to his greatest fear made a reality. We'd found him out. The secret was out. "I . . . I . . ." he stuttered.

I pounced on the opening. "Tell us *everything* about the malae, and we'll leave you alive. Otherwise . . ."

"Styk . . ." Corminar said, grabbing my arm.

I looked around at him. "What harm could it do? He won't kill anyone. And it feels like a bit of a pisstake to kill someone like him, even if he is a Player."

The elf frowned, but said nothing else on the matter.

"Tell us," I ordered the Councilman. "Now."

The man held my gaze for a moment, running the calculations, before finally realizing that giving us what we wanted was his best chance of getting out of here.

"Alright," he said. "The malae. I suppose I can tell you—but if you do run into any other Players, you didn't hear it from me."

"We make no promises," Corminar said.

"Ignore him," I said. "The malae."

The Councilman drew in a deep breath. "I came to Westbara because I heard that a member of the Council was here. Yusef, his name was. The leader of the Cult of Ascendancy—do you know it?"

I nodded; we'd had dealings with these Player-worshippers before. In fact, the reason I'd even gotten access to the *Worldbending* skill tree had been through a defeat of one of these cultists.

"I wanted to impress him. I wanted to show him that I could be a valuable asset to the team. So he tested me. He asked me to . . . to . . ."

"Kill someone," Carle guessed from the rear of the room.

The Player gulped, then nodded.

"So you failed the test," I said, "your application rejected. What's this got to do with the malae?"

"Because he's the source. I saw it, when I was there with him, out in the Beached Armada. He is in the trade of collecting them for the Council for schemes unknown. Those that have been seen around the peripheries of Westbara . . . they are those that escaped."

I made eye contact with Corminar. "So, if we wanted to find this Player . . . ?"

"Then you would follow the malae," the prisoner finished.

Corminar nodded.

"Good," I said. "We're done here." I gestured up the wooden steps to the tavern proper, and the Trio were the first to climb.

"Guess we're not getting that payment, then . . ." Raelas grumbled, just loud enough for me to hear.

Lore, Corminar, and I walked away next, leaving the Player to call after us.

"Wait!" he cried. "Wait! You said you'd let me go!"

From the top of the staircase, I crouched down and made sure to look the Player in the eyes. "No, I said we'd leave you alive. I didn't say anything about letting you go." With that, I slammed the door shut, leaving the Councilman in the dark, and tipped the bard upstairs to play as loud as he could until the tavern closed for the night, drowning out the Player's shouting.

Then, we set our sights on the next step: mala hunting.

CHAPTER EIGHT

Quench the Thirst

We'd left the city of Westbara the morning after abandoning the pitiful Player in the tavern basement, and I was surprised to find that the Trio came with us. When I'd asked them about it, Carle and Ama had glanced at one another, while Raelas had shrugged, telling us that tracking down these malae was—and I quote—the "right thing to do." It wasn't what I was coming to expect of this small gang of mercenaries, but I wasn't exactly going to argue this point with them.

And so, from Westbara, we traveled further west still, which was the furthest both Corminar and I had ever been from our respective homes and made me feel strangely anxious. Lore, on the other hand, was loving it—there was nothing quite like a return home, he said.

"If you keep on this road," he continued, blabbering on even though nobody had responded to him in the past five minutes or so, "you get to the Naval Temple. They took lots of the old ships from when the Beached Armada invaded, and they turned them into holy sites. You can go there, you can see a bit of history, you can pray to the creators—that's what they called the Architects—and you can drink. You know anywhere else in the world where you can drink at church? I don't. It's very low alcohol, admittedly, what with all the heat, but it's still nice."

I nodded politely.

"And at certain times of year, the sun lines up with the hull of the ship, and the shadows make patterns that ripple across the dunes. It's great. We should go."

"May I remind you that we are here for a specific purpose?" Corminar said.

"Well, yeah, but maybe we can go after."

As we continued on the western merchants' road, the greenery started to become more like . . . yellowery, and then the plants became fewer and further between. Lush green fields gave way to a brown excuse for grass, and before much longer there was more sand than grass. It was strange—I knew the temperature out here wasn't much higher than in certain parts of the Goldmarch, but it definitely *felt* it. It wasn't long before my water tankard was empty, and I—and the others, from the looks of it—needed a place to rest awhile.

There was no shortage of taverns on the merchants' road, capitalizing on this thirst. Some of them were proper buildings, formed of clay, while others were large, glorified tents. The next one we came across was a clay building, though I would have been fine with either at this point. There were no windows, only holes in the thick, beige walls, but the furniture inside was strangely ornate— wood carved with patterns that must have come in with the ancient tiefling invaders.

I sat on a plush stool next to this ornate wooden bar, bought a round of beer with coins swiped from a wealthy diplomat's house in Westbara—it was amazing that it had taken me this long to realize that portals were an ideal skill for the purposes of burglary—and handed them out. Carle and Ama thanked me and took theirs to the edge of the building, where they stared out at the sand dunes while still just about shielded from the midday sun. Lore and Corminar inspected their beers before, finally, thanking me, and I couldn't blame them—the beer was flatter than I had expected.

And this left only the half tiefling gazing at me along the bar. Realizing I could avoid her attention no longer—I'd only managed it so far because Lore was strangely protective of Val, even though she'd abandoned us—I slid the beer to the other worldbender.

"Nah, I don't drink," Raelas said, pushing the glass back toward me. "Bad habit."

"Could've told me before I ordered. You don't drink cos it's unhealthy?"

"Cos if you get in a fight when you're drunk, you ain't sure to win it."

I pulled a face, then looked down at the surface of my beer, considering this a moment. On balance, I decided it was worth the risk. The beer might have been flat, but it tasted good, if unlike any beer I'd had before—there was a floral aroma to it.

Raelas watched me as I drank. "Nice to have another worldbender around. Not often you get to meet them, is it?"

I shrugged. "The elves have plenty of them," I replied. "Or . . . had? I don't know how many of them escaped." I glanced over at the others, and I saw Lore sheepishly approach Carle and Ama, his eyes on the other big guy.

"What were you doing there? I heard it fell to Amira, but . . ."

"Trying to stop that from happening."

Raelas smiled. "Just the three of you?"

"Well, we had two others. And a whole bunch of criminal elves, but . . . yeah. We killed their general, but it wasn't enough. We were too slow. I don't think Corminar has forgiven himself for it."

The bar grew quiet, the only sounds being a blanket flapping in the breeze and Lore talking Carle's ear off about sheep. I took another sip of one of the two beers in front of me, and I tried to put our failure out of my mind. I didn't manage it.

"Must've gotten some decent abilities out of all that, though?" Raelas asked, and I couldn't help but think she was trying to lighten the mood.

"*Enhanced Portals*," I replied. "You got that yet?"

Raelas shook her head, pulling a face. "Never even got the option. Though, I don't think I specced into portals as much as you did. Manipulating material, however . . ." She reached out to the half-empty glass of beer, wrapping her hand around it, and soon the glass began to . . . melt?

"Isn't that hot?"

"Don't always need heat to melt things," Raelas replied. "I saw you went for *Ash Husk*, though. Probably a smart move; there's so many—"

"—fire mages about," I finished for her.

The woman smiled. "Yeah, that's it exactly. Makes my *Frost Husk* not so good. Bad decision."

I opened my mouth to speak, but hesitated. The question I wanted to ask—had to ask, really—had the potential of pushing her away. And it was nice to have a little attention since Val fled, all things considered.

"What is it?" she asked.

"Why are you with us? Really?"

Raelas shrugged. "Maybe I just wanna keep looking at your handsome face?"

"You know I'm traveling with Lore and Corminar, right?" I replied. "Usually they—"

The worldbender waved me down. "They're a bit pretty for my taste."

"Be serious."

"I am! They're too pretty. I tend to like—"

I shook my head. "No, not about that. About why you're with us."

Again, the half tiefling shrugged. "Killing malae? There's gotta be a decent reward for that, hasn't there?"

This was all the answer I ever got, though in part that was because I was distracted. Across the inn's floor, I heard someone use a word that was on my mind. Malae.

I stood from the barstool and must have rushed over a little too fast, because the two old men blinked and recoiled slightly. "You mentioned malae? Where?"

One old man looked to the other before replying, "A half day north, they said. On the merchants' road."

"How many?" I asked. "How many malae?"

"They didn't say," he croaked. "All they said was too many."

Once our flasks were full of water, our bellies full of food, and the sun was hanging lower in the sky, we set out once more across the Armadan Desert. As we got further west, it turned out we'd barely hit the worst of it. Soon there was not a tree in sight, and absolutely no water sources to speak of.

Raelas—who was now walking by my side, Lore having given up on getting between us—told me that the only water sources out here had small villages built around them, and that we wouldn't find water until we found civilization. So it was worth rationing the water. It was at this point that I regretted filling one of my two flasks with that delicious lowish-alcohol beer, but I kept the fact that I'd done that to myself.

I was assured that there would be another village coming up soon, where we could barter for some water. It would be expensive, but it sounded like I had more than enough stolen funds to cover it. So I drank water while I could, knowing I'd have to ration it later.

My flask was empty—again! I had little self-control—when we finally climbed a dune and saw the village stretched before us. I was on the verge of storming down toward it when Corminar suddenly whipped out his hand to block my path.

His elven eyes had spotted something.

"What does your intense friend see?" Ama asked.

"You know, he wasn't always this—" I started, then realized the Battle of Sunalor probably wasn't useful context right now. "Never mind."

"What you see, Cor?" Lore asked.

"Nothing."

I narrowed my eyes. "In that case . . ." After I moved to take a step forward, Corminar blocked my path once more.

"Nothing," he repeated. "There is not a soul in the village."

My heart dropped. "Malae?"

"I see no corruption. If malae are to blame, they have since departed, or they are hidden inside one of these structures."

I nodded. This time, when I took a step forward, he didn't stop me. "We move slow," I said. "Keep an eye out for movement. If you see any, announce it immediately. We can't afford any malae getting the jump on us."

We crept into the abandoned village, each of us focusing in different directions, not a single part of the settlement avoiding notice. But as we pushed between the buildings, we saw and heard nothing but the squawk of a bird circling above.

"Vultures," Ama grumbled, pursing her lips.

"Then there has been death here," Carle added.

We continued through the town, toward the largest of the buildings, where Raelas whispered that the water would be. As I stepped inside, I called out, "Hello? Anyone home? We've come to purchase some water." When nobody replied, I added, "We can pay well!"

But still, there was nobody in sight.

"I don't like this," Raelas said.

"Yeah," Lore agreed, and it was about the first time those two had agreed on anything.

The vulture—multiple vultures, in fact—cried out overhead once more. Feeling suddenly very mortal, I set my eyes on a trough of water at the far end of the building, and filled up both my flasks, tipping the beer onto the floor. Ama watched me, eyebrow raised.

"What you waiting for? Fill up," I told them, swigging from the flask while we still had more water available.

"What if the water was the problem?" Ama asked.

I stopped drinking midsip, and everyone watched me.

". . . Feel anything?" Raelas asked.

"Like what?"

"Poison."

I paused again. ". . . No?"

Everyone nodded and went about filling up their flasks. I stepped outside while they did so, keeping to the shadow of the building, and stared up at the vultures circling above. They were bigger than any vultures I'd ever seen, though I'd admit that my experience was limited.

The others joined me at the door. "Where to next?" Raelas asked.

I shrugged. "Don't see any malae here; can't be where those men were talking about. I say we move on. Keep going. Sooner or later, we—"

"Err, guys?" Lore said, which was the exact thing he usually said before delivering horrific news. I looked around at him to see him peering up at the sky, hand over his face to block out the harsh light. "I don't think those are vultures."

"Yes they—" Ama began, at the same moment that Corminar looked up and paled.

"Get to cover!" he roared.

And then the "vultures" dived to attack.

CHAPTER NINE

Winged Beasts

We fled back into the village's main building—a communal marketplace, of sorts—and each dived behind the cover of a nearby item of furniture. The architectural style meant that the building was open to the elements on two of its sides—and from the looks of it, these were closed up only by thick sheets of fabric which were currently rolled up at the top. This design choice meant that the "vultures" had no problem swooping into the building after their would-be prey: us.

Keeping behind the cover and out of sight, I didn't get a proper chance to look at them, so I shouted across the building to Corminar. "What are they?"

"Vultures!" he shouted back.

"What? I thought Lore just said—" But I didn't get a chance to finish that sentence because at that moment, one of the birds soared into the building, shrieking. I got more of a look at it as it swooped overhead. It was a vulture, sure, but there was more at play here. Its body was black, its skin beginning to rot, and a strange ooze was dripping from its wings.

I'd seen this before. And so had Lore.

"They've been touched!" the barbarian shouted across the room. "They've been touched by malae!"

"At least we know we're on the right track . . ." Ama grumbled at my side as she hid behind the same unit.

The bird fluttered to the ground at the far edge of the building, then tilted its head as it looked around. Its dark eyes landed on Raelas.

"Corminar! Fire!" I shouted as I looked around desperately for anything to use as a weapon. A market stall at Lore's side caught my eye—a stall that had once sold lanterns, many of them upturned. And some of them were oil lanterns.

"Lore—" My shout was drowned out by the second of the corrupted vultures swooping into the building, again shrieking as it did so. The first turned slowly around to face Raelas, who scrambled backward into the wall.

As the vulture charged at her, its wings raised and its beak low, I whipped a portal over its head and dropped the unit Ama and I were hiding behind onto its long neck.

Raelas nodded her thanks and ran for the exit, only to find the third and final vulture circling above, ready to pick out whoever left. She opened a portal beneath herself as it swooped down for her, and disappeared from sight.

Meanwhile, Ama and I were now exposed, so I opened another portal to drop us at the side of Corminar—whom I had a very important question to ask. "How many?"

"Three vultures," he replied.

"No. How many fire potions. You knew we were after malae, so I assume you did make some fire potions?"

". . . One."

"*One?*" I repeated, aghast.

"My supplies are lacking."

I shook my head, sighing. Corminar clearly wanted to say something about this reaction, but he didn't, correctly recognizing that there were more important things going on right now. "Give it," I said, holding out my upturned hand.

Corminar glared, but handed over the small vial, burning red and hot. "Use it well," he said. "I assume you have a plan?"

I did, but I wasn't going to waste time explaining myself. I turned to Ama. "You, Carle, and Corminar keep them busy, OK? And don't let them touch you!"

I didn't give the woman time to argue, and I disappeared down through a new portal that spilled me out at Lore's side.

"You're really getting the hang of portals," he said. He stood with his Bane Sword raised, his eyes on the closest of the corrupted vultures. Lore was experienced enough with malae corruption to know not to charge it like he normally would; here, patience was a virtue. And so was fire.

"Thanks." I reached onto the market stand and began shaking the oil lanterns, listening for the sound of liquid sloshing around. Finally, I found not one but two with oil already filled. "Lob this at the wall," I said.

Lore did so without a second thought, and he did so with enough power to smash the admittedly flimsy glass in the center of the lantern. The oil within began to seep out onto the floor.

"Feed the flames!" I cried to him, then lobbed Corminar's single fire potion onto the oil, where it, too, smashed. The flames took immediately, setting the clay wall and floor ablaze. But it would die out soon without flammables thrown onto it. "Now!" I shouted, reiterating the urgency.

I ripped open the top of the other lantern as Lore charged over to a chair and threw the cushions onto the new fire. Ahead of me, I saw a corrupted bird fixing its gaze on Carle and beginning to move toward him. I had to act fast.

Taking my dagger from its sheath, I dipped it into the oil and then dropped it, clattering to the hard stone floor. I looked from enemy to Carle to Corminar to flames, and I came up with a quick strategy—one that made having *Enhanced Portals* absolutely critical.

I leaped through the air, and as I did so, I opened two pairs of portals. One, I opened under my knife, dropping it into the flames, and the other I opened in front of me. This one spilled me back out next to Ama and Corminar, and I pushed the oil lantern in the latter's direction.

"Hello again," Ama said.

"Dip your arrows," I told Corminar, and then whipped myself around to close one portal and open another, dropping the now flaming, oil-dipped dagger back into the air in front of me. I activated *Ash Husk* as it fell, knowing it was going to be hot and wanting to reduce any resulting damage, and I snatched it from the air.

As Corminar pulled his arrows back out, I held my flaming blade next to them, and they caught alight. But this oil wouldn't last long.

"Carle!" I shouted, pointing to the large muscular gentleman as he swung an axe to try to ward off the advancing creature of darkness.

Corminar shot a flaming arrow into the vulture's side, and its flesh fizzled and warped at the flame's touch. The monster immediately became more interested in Corminar than Carle, and it turned to charge at the ranger.

But Corminar was quick, and he used the bow Elandor had left to him to loose arrow after arrow after arrow, each one burning away more of the monster's form. By the time it reached him, it was already disintegrating on the ground.

I didn't hang around to watch, mostly because another of the creatures was in that moment swooping down toward me. I ran away from Ama and Corminar just enough to prevent them from being touched by the monster's corrupted wing, and then I opened a portal to drop me out of the enemy's path.

I stumbled back to my feet at the side of the building, just in time to see a circle of glowing purple magicks fizzling into life near the center of the ceiling. Raelas was still alive then, and using her *Worldbending* abilities to her advantage. With a squawk, a vulture emerged from the portal and flew fast into the interior wall, hitting it hard.

"Having fun out there?" I shouted to Raelas.

"Yes!"

It was all well and good, but now there were two enemies inside this small space once more. The other vulture looked around to see where I'd gone, and its head stopped tilting when it spotted me. It hopped up into the air and swooped at me once more, but this time I was ready for it.

I raised my hands in front of me, forcing myself to wait until the last possible moment before I activated the portals. I lobbed my flaming knife with one hand to distract the enemy—barely catching it; I really missed my *Throwing Knives* ability right about now—but it was still enough. The creature squawked its alarm, and in that same second, I opened a portal between us. It disappeared through it and emerged from its partner. Landing right into the fire.

Lore—who had still been feeding the flames—looked around in alarm, because the monster had almost touched him.

I bit my lip. "Sorry!" I shouted.

Ignoring the notifications that were piling up, I turned my attention to the third and last of the enemies. The bird had its eyes fixed on me.

"Corminar?" I asked.

"Alas, my fires are extinguished."

"Alright," I cried back, and then focused my attention on repeating my last strategy. The flames on my dagger, too, had gone out, so I couldn't rely on a flaming throwing knife to distract it. I'd need to time this perfectly.

The bird swooped toward me.

I raised my hands.

This one was the largest of the three, with the greatest wingspan. Just one wrong move, and one of those corrupted feathers could touch me. My life would be over.

It grew closer, and my eyes remained on those wings.

I opened the portals before I really knew I'd done so, and the vulture swooped to one side. The enemy caught the edge of the portal with one of its wings, sending it spinning through the air toward me. I had to dive to one side just to avoid its touch, and I found myself back out in the afternoon sun. As the vulture batted its wings to get back to its feet, I turned around to face it once more.

The enemy monster knew my strategy, but as they say, there's more than one way to slice up a rockrat.

Again, I'd need two sets of portals for this to work. At least. I could only hope that Raelas understood what I was doing. I let the vulture swoop at me once more, and then I opened another portal—this time beneath my feet, knowing that there was no certainty the void monster would go through it. I stumbled out against the outside wall of the building, and I shouted out to get its attention once more.

"Over here, you big idiot!"

Maybe Val was right, and I really did need to work on my insults.

Still, it did the job—I don't think the vulture spoke the common tongue anyway—and the monster turned back toward me. From on top of the sand dune where I'd disappeared, it swooped at me once more.

This time, I really did wait until the last moment.

I crouched as it approached, flinging one arm in front of my face to protect it—even though corruption was corruption, no matter where it touched—and I opened a portal beneath me to fall through. As I plummeted, the vulture collided with the wall—hard.

I spun out onto the side of a sand dune, and I didn't waste the half second it would have taken to stand up. I opened one pair of portals, then another—both positioned against the side of the dune to send tons of sand pouring onto the spot where the vulture had dropped to the ground.

Another portal, doing the same, announced Raelas's presence, and her understanding of my strategy.

At first, the mala-touched bird tried to fight it, beating its large wings to pull itself away from the ground. But the amount of sand coming was just too great. It couldn't fight it.

It could only be buried.

---

3 x Level ? Corrupted Vultures defeated!

Worldbending: +4,200XP
Worldbending increased to level 53!
Base Points Gained: +2 INT, +2 Free Points (INT/WIS/CHA)
Knifework: +1,450XP
Knifework increased to level 40!
Base Points Gained: +1 DEX, +1 STR, +2 Free Points (VIT/DEX/STR)
Ability Selection Unlocked
Select an ability from the list below:
. . .

I breathed a sigh of relief. It was over. For now, at least; I knew there was only more malae in our future, if we were going to find the Player responsible for trading in them. That was a problem for later, though. Right now, I had an ability to select.

CHAPTER TEN

Corruption Spreads

All six of us were silent as we regrouped in the small village's main building, each of us rattled by the stress of the fight before. When a monster could kill you simply by touching you, then you couldn't let your guard down even for a moment. Not that I much wanted to let my guard down and get stabbed with a sword or whatever, either.

We stood around the remains of the corrupted bird that Corminar had shot down with his flaming arrows. The one that I had thrown into the flames was now completely disintegrated, while the third was buried beneath a mound of sand taller than the building itself. This one, then, remained the most visible, and acted as a reminder of the danger we'd just faced.

"They survived it," Lore said, echoing the thought that was going through my mind in that same moment. "They survived the corruption."

"I'm gonna take it that's not normal?" the other worldbender asked.

I shook my head. "No. Only the strongest people usually survive. And even then . . . it's only the body that survives. Not the mind. Not the soul."

Lore nodded thoughtfully.

"I suppose this does not bode well for the future?" Corminar asked, though the question was rhetorical. "If there is a mala infestation out in these western lands, and those corrupted survive long enough to spread this disease further . . ."

"Then it's only a matter of time before the Beached Armada falls," Ama muttered, her eyes remaining on the creature, drifting toward the remains of its head.

At this, Lore looked up at Corminar. "I won't watch my home fall," he said.

The elf nodded a single nod; he understood this sentiment very, very well after the events of the past few months.

"Carle, look at this," Ama said, pointing down at what remained of the creature's beak.

The warrior crouched, and for a moment I thought he was going to touch it.

"Careful," I said.

Carle nodded up at me, confirming his understanding, and then removed a pair of small half-moon spectacles from his pocket and placed them gently atop his nose. To look at him now, I wondered how I ever thought Lore and him were similar—they were just muscular and had trained up in "hitting things" skills; that's where the similarities ended.

"The beak?" he asked Ama.

The metal mage nodded. "The scars indicate to me a higher density of corruption. Could this mean this was where the mala latched on?"

Carle paused for a moment before replying. "No."

"No?"

"No, I hypothesize that mala didn't latch on at all. I think these vultures might have been *eating* them—or trying to." He looked up at me. "Could this be how lowly beasts survived the corruption?"

I shrugged. "I'm no doctor."

Carle looked next at Lore, who held out his hands, palms up, to express that he also had no bloody idea.

"We can know only one thing for sure," Corminar said. "If we are to stop this corruption, we must act fast. I will not see another land fall to evil."

I nodded. "Gather your stuff. Fill your flasks. It's time to move."

We traversed west, using the last of my *Needlework* supplies to create makeshift hats that held off the worst of the sun's rays. We were heading for the next water well, as both Lore and Raelas agreed that there was our best bet—the vultures would usually have a water source to return to after feasting, and this was the nearest one. If they'd come from anywhere, it was there. And besides, even if this turned out to have been a faulty guess, we'd still be able to replenish the water in our rapidly diminishing flasks.

While we walked, we kept talking to a minimum due to the heat—with the exception of Lore who still seemed used to this discomfort from growing up around here. Even Raelas seemed to not be after my attention, which was fine by me, as it gave me a moment to circle back around on the ability selection I'd received from our fight with the corrupted birds.

Ability Selection Unlocked
Select an ability from the list below:

> **Option 1: Dual Wield (Knifework)**—*Passive*. You can now use a dagger in each hand with equal ability. Ability level is copied from dominant hand to nondominant hand.

Two knives! It was hard to go too far wrong with that, I thought. Double the damage, surely? But then I thought it through. For a start, I only had *one* dagger at the moment, except that part was at least easily rectified at the next weaponsmith. There was a larger problem, however. If I had a dagger in each hand, it was going to be harder to use my portals.

I *could* open portals without gesturing, but they tended to not end up quite where I wanted them. And precision was key with portals—opening them a foot to the left of where I really needed them could be make-or-break.

I kept this option in the running but moved on to the next of the three options.

> **Option 2: Execution III (Knifework)**—*Upgrade to Execution II.* Attack a target while undetected for +300 percent damage.

It may have been a little less exciting than the first option, but I'd learned my lesson on upgrades—depth of ability, assuming you picked well, was usually better than breadth. I could almost hear Val nattering in my ear, telling me to upgrade this ability cos I used it so often.

And she—or my imagined version of her—was right. An extra half damage again, up from 200 percent to 300 percent, was a substantial increase, particularly when combined with my bonus to damage from my *Stealth* passives. I really had to give this one proper consideration.

But there was still one more option.

> **Option 3: Mana-Fueled II (Knifework)**—*Upgrade to Mana-Fueled. Passive.* Optionally, use mana in place of stamina to activate *Knifework* abilities. When mana is used, cost is reduced by 20 percent.

This was another upgrade, and pretty inconveniently it was another upgrade to an ability I used regularly. I'd not invested too many of my free points in Dexterity, and so my stamina reserves were pretty pitiful. This didn't matter, because I *had* put loads of points into Intelligence, and therefore had plenty of mana. At least, usually I did. I had run out when fighting that particularly long battle in Sunalor, and then against Niamh. If I could reduce my stamina costs by 20 percent, then maybe that went a long way . . .

In the end, after much consideration, I decided that there was a clear winner this time around, and I made my selection.

> **Ability Upgraded**: Execution III
> **Execution III (Knifework)**: Attack a target while undetected for +300 percent damage.

Yes, I decided once I was locked into my choice, *this is the right decision.*

We continued onward, following the stony merchants' road across the dunes, the sun beating down on us. I swigged from my flask, finding it draining quicker than I would have liked, and based on the filthy look Corminar gave his own flask, he was running into the same issue.

In the distance, I saw the mountains that I knew stood tall in the center of the Beached Armada, their peaks white with snow even in this hot environment. I'd have done anything to be lying in some snow right about then. Not even snow; I'd take sleet. Or a shallow puddle, even.

"Just ahead!" Raelas, at the front of the pack, shouted—it was as though the Architects had heard my prayer.

The oasis stretched in front of us, palm trees and lush green grass spreading irregularly around it, birds—none of them corrupted—sitting at the side of the pool, lapping up the refreshing water.

I would have run to join them, to charge into the water, if I hadn't thought it was properly inappropriate to contaminate a water source with my sweat and dirt. But there was another reason I didn't, too; three dozen people huddled around it, far too many of them nursing fresh wounds. And these weren't the usual sort of wounds, either—not slashes from swords or burn marks from fireballs—these were whole limbs, cut clean through. Almost as if they'd *intended* to cut them off.

So we approached slowly, and I wasn't the only one of us who made sure their weapon was easily accessible.

"Hold!" one of them shouted. They were an older tiefling man, skin leathery from the sun, his eyes red not just in the iris where we might have expected it.

I came to a stop, and so did the rest of my party behind me. "We don't want any trouble," I said. "We want water, and . . ." I gestured to some of their injured. "And to help where we can."

"Speak for your—" Ama started, but was cut off by Raelas coughing pointedly.

"What's happened here?" I asked, in part to bring the man's attention off Ama and back to me.

The man stared back at me with red, empty eyes. "Malae," he said.

CHAPTER ELEVEN

A Chasm, A Void

I had a great many burning questions, but the priority right then was to help those in need. Lore, Corminar, and I followed the older tiefling man to a man about his age lying on the floor, cradling an elbow point that was bleeding profusely and carried no hand.

Corminar pulled out a healing potion and poured just the smallest amount down the man's throat.

I blinked at him. "Will that be enough?"

"I have only two in my possession."

"Can you make more?" Lore asked.

Corminar hesitated. "Scout the oasis," he said. "The primary ingredient I need to create more are soothing succulents."

"What'll they look like?" I asked.

"They will have thick leaves," the elf replied as he inspected the man's wound. The worst of the bleeding seemed to have stopped. "Sturdy. The relevant plants in this continent are said to have a blue trim."

I nodded, and Lore and I hurried over to the oasis. I considered opening a portal to close the gap, but it would save only a handful of seconds, and I didn't want to startle anyone. The last thing these people needed was to think that they were under attack.

At the water's edge, Lore and I parted, each traversing around one side. There were few plants here that fit Corminar's specifications, only a handful, and one that I could see with the telltale blue trim that the elf had told us to watch out for. I sliced it from the ground with my dagger, revealing an almost fleshy, gel-like interior, and hurried back to Corminar's side.

The elf nodded, and handed Lore and I a healing vial each. "Ration them," he said. "Even with this, I will still only be able to brew so much."

I nodded, and as I turned back to the rest of the injured, I noticed the Trio watching on, out of the corner of my eye. Ama was muttering something to Raelas, but at this distance, I couldn't hear what. I considered shouting out, demanding their help, but instead turned my attention to the next of the injured—a younger tiefling who'd lost a leg.

"Here," I said, tipping a little of the potion into her mouth. I could see the wound heal some—enough, at least, to keep her alive for now. "Who did this?" I asked, nodding to the wound.

She stared blankly back at me, and in that moment I understood. She'd done it to herself. It had been the only way to stop the corruption spreading, and to survive. Except . . . those vultures had survived it somehow—in a way, at least.

"You'll get to a healer. They'll be able to . . ." I stopped myself from saying more; at this point, it was best not to promise anything.

Lore and I continued around the injured as Corminar finished brewing more, and he flashed a nod for us to give more to each injured person. Before long, we'd stopped the worst of the bleeding, and no more would die this day. As Lore and I returned to Corminar's side, the elf was speaking with the older tiefling who'd first met us.

"Thank you," he said. "The Architects bless you, thank you."

"Yes, yes, that is quite alright," Corminar replied.

The tiefling flung himself forward and wrapped his arms around the elf, hugging him tight. "You saved my husband! You saved all of them!"

"I only use my alchemical gifts to . . ." Corminar began to reply, blushing helplessly in the tiefling's arms.

"Sent by the gods themselves!" the older man continued.

When it all became too much, Corminar wrenched himself free of the tiefling's arms, and the tiefling instead shifting his attention to Lore. The barbarian met the older man's hug with as keen a hug of his own. When it came to be my turn, I *portaled* myself to the other side of Corminar to avoid it.

"We need to find where these creatures are coming from," I said, hoping to trade on the goodwill we'd brought with Corminar's potions and move on from the whole hugging thing.

The man narrowed his eyes. "Why?"

"We seek to put a cork in the metaphorical bottle. We seek to kill them all," Corminar replied, and this answer put the tiefling at ease.

"I don't know where they all came from originally, but I can tell you where lots of them are now."

"The ones that hurt you? Tried to corrupt you?" I asked.

The tiefling shook his head. "No, our battle took place in our home, a few hours to the southeast. Corrupted vultures swooped down from on high, to—"

"We know," Corminar cut in. "We fought them."

The tiefling raised his eyebrows. "And you escaped without injury?"

"No," I said. "We didn't escape; we killed them."

The older man took a very literal step backward, though I felt that it was out of a sense of theatrics rather than genuine surprise. "Then perhaps you stand a chance after all! Perhaps we may rid these holy lands of the blight. Perhaps we might live our lives once more."

"You . . . mentioned malae?" Lore cut in. "Other malae? Where?"

"I . . ." the tiefling said, and his so recently bright expression faded to one of darkness. "I think it is best I show you. Would you and your . . ."—he looked over to the Trio, still watching on—"friends like to join us?"

"Traveling companions," Corminar corrected him. "Not friends. Though yes, they should be provided with the same information as ourselves."

The tiefling nodded, then begged our patience while he returned to his partner and picked up an old, rusting metal flask. He pointed north, toward the hills. "This way," he said.

"Is it far?" I asked, considering filling up my own water flask.

"Not as far as we would like," came the reply.

The tiefling turned out to be correct—it took only ten minutes or so before we grew near; something I sensed only because the man grew hesitant to proceed. We'd climbed across increasingly steep sand dunes, and across outcrops of bright orange rock that seemed to be slowly pushing forth from the ground. And then, in front of us, we saw a canyon cut into the rock below.

The tiefling whipped out his hand in front of Corminar to halt us. "We should not step closer," he said. "We might disturb them."

"We must see for ourselves," the elf replied, and though still glum, the tiefling removed his arm from Corminar's path.

The six of us approached the canyon edge slowly, and fear reared its ugly head in my gut. From the pace of the others, I suspected they were feeling much the same.

Our guide had said the canyon had formed in eons past, the river that had carved it long since dried up—or diverted by tiefling settlements. Now, it was dry, and a reminder of what this land might have been if it was properly tended to.

As we approached, we realized just how deep the canyon went, the opposite cliff face growing larger and larger with every step we took closer. And then, when we finally reached the cliff edge, we saw that the canyon floor was covered in darkness.

Lore staggered backward, paling.

My heart dropped.

I realized then what I was seeing. Not darkness, not shadow, but a layer of malae crowded on the canyon floor. Not one. Not even dozens. Hundreds.

Behind me, Lore roared, clutching his hands to his head. He was the only other one among us who had truly seen what the malae were capable of. What a *single* mala was capable of. Let alone hundreds. This many could destroy entire continents. Maybe even entire *worlds*.

"We'll find a way, Lore," I told him. "We'll find a way to kill them."

"No," he breathed, still clutching his head.

"We will. We'll rain fire down on them from the heavens above if we have to. We'll—"

"It's not that," he croaked. "You haven't got it, have you? There's hundreds in there."

"Yes, I saw. We—"

"That doesn't just *happen*, Styk! They don't just reproduce like that. Don't you see? The Councilman was wrong! These people ain't just trading in malae. They're . . . they're . . ." Lore stumbled over the words, seemingly unable to bring himself to say them.

But I could. I'd made the leap in logic, now. I'd realized what he had a minute earlier, when he'd stared down into the chasm and seen the void incarnate staring back at him.

"They're not trading them," I finished for the barbarian. "They're breeding them."

Lore gulped, then nodded.

The Councilman

The barkeep finally freed Simm the next morning. Not only had he suffered the indignity of being tied up, but he'd also been drinking heavily the previous day, and a full bladder had eventually become wet trousers. The woman sniffed her nose as she untied him.

"Councilman," she said with a smirk.

Simm considered snapping something back at her, but nothing came; there was really nothing he could say that would make this look good. Instead, he stood, flexed his limbs, and hurried out of the tavern.

He kept his head low as he walked through the streets of Westbara on that busy morning, hoping nobody would recognize him. The stink on his trousers drew some attention, but at least none of the locals seemed to realize he was the Player who had saved Westbara from the mala threat.

Except, of course, he hadn't. Not only had he outsourced the problem—his weapon was for training only; he rarely used it on beasts, at least not powerful ones—but also, they had failed to deliver. He cursed to himself—this was the last time he hired mercenaries with no brand recognition. And to brand themselves "The Trio" simply because there were three of them? That was pretty uninspired. That should have been the first clue.

It was as though the gods from home were turning a blind eye to his troubles today, for when he arrived back at his manor, he found that the door was ajar. Someone had broken in.

Simm summoned his bound alter blade and gripped it tightly, ready to defend himself. Not that he'd kill, of course; killing someone in retribution for a simple burglary was hardly just.

He stepped inside and closed the door gently behind him. As his eyes adjusted to the lower level of light, he saw a figure walking down one of the two grand staircases at either side of the atrium, and he raised his blade. "You there! What are you . . ."

Simm trailed off when he recognized the face—one of the Duke of Westbara's aides. And the man was carrying his ceremonial key.

"In lieu of yesterday's events—the mala incursion on the western gate—the duke sees fit to strip you of your reward."

"But I—"

The aide looked down at the oversized key. "I argued he should let you keep it, for what it's worth. It's not as though it unlocks anything, and despite yesterday's rather long ceremony, the people will forget you the next time a hero comes along anyway. But he insisted. He said these things matter, that we should rescind your award as a point of principle. And so . . . here I am." The aide continued down the staircase toward the front door that Simm still stood in front of.

Another indignity.

It was all too much, after the day Simm had had. Bloodied, beaten, urinated on—admittedly that last bit was his own doing—and now this.

"You don't look well, friend," the aide said as he approached, nose twitching as he picked up the smell of urine. "Did someone get the best of you?"

Too much. Before Simm knew he was doing it, he reached out to snatch back the key to the city. "It's mine! I won't let you take it!"

But the aide held on tight, trying to pull it out of the Councilman's hands. "It doesn't open anything!"

"It's mine!" Simm repeated, and he tried to yank it once more, but the aide got the better of him—the key slipped from his hands. And so Simm drew his alter blade, concentrating on keeping it in axe form—his preferred weapon— though such raised emotions played havoc with this sort of magick.

"Really?" the aide asked, both smirking and raising an eyebrow for good measure. "You really think I'll believe you'll attack me?" He moved to push past Simm, but the Councilman didn't budge. "Simm, please. Move."

"That's 'Councilman' to you," Simm growled.

The aide's smirk grew greater. "You know, my employer has dealing with Players all around the continent. Some of them are those in Amira's pocket. The Council themselves. And do you know what they said, when I asked about you?"

Simm's nostrils flared. "What?"

"They said . . . 'Who?'"

The Councilman's anger got the better of him, a wave of red rising within. And with this anger, his weapon changed. He couldn't control it—or, if he could, he didn't want to. At least, not in that moment.

The axe became a chain, and the chain shot straight forward, lashing out, Simm's anger made weapon.

And it shot forward directly through the man's heart.

The aide blinked down at his chest, at the huge gaping wound from which blood was already starting to pour. ". . . Oh," he said as he dropped first to his knees, and then to the ground.

The Councilman rushed to the aide, horror at what he'd just done making vomit rise up his throat. He choked it back.

"No, no . . ." Simm gasped, pushing his hands onto the wound to try to stem the bleeding. "No, I didn't mean to . . ." He already knew this effort would be in vain if he didn't cry out; without the serious attention of a healer, fast, this man was not going to live. "Guards!" he shouted, but stopped himself midword.

Simm looked down at the man dying in front of him. If he shouted, if he got the soldiers' attention, there was the smallest chance that the aide might live. But there was a *certainty* that he would be locked up, potentially for the rest of his life in this world. This world would no longer be available to him, and what with the corruption that was sweeping across so many of the others . . .

Simm stood, releasing the wound, letting the blood flow.

The aide tried to cry out, but whatever they'd wanted to say was lost beneath the blood pouring from their mouth.

"I'm sorry," the Councilman said. "I'm . . . I'm . . . I'm sorry. I didn't mean to. But I . . . I can't go to jail. I can't. I'm sorry."

He forced himself to watch the man die.

Today, after so many years, he'd done the one thing he told himself he'd never do. He killed a living soul. One of the locals of this world. An innocent.

Simm stumbled backward, panic rising and a terrible sense of change washing over his body. He looked around erratically, trying to force himself to ignore his emotions, to be practical. The emotions were there, and they were just like he'd always expected: horror, terror, and above all . . . guilt. Guilt that he'd done something unforgivable.

But at the same time . . . it wasn't so bad. It felt terrible, sure, but it wasn't insurmountable. He could breathe. He could settle his heart rate. He could . . . cope.

Did, then, a whole new world open to him? Could he kill after all? And if he relented to such a base instinct, could he rise to even greater heights? Would the Council finally grant him entry?

A memory of the previous night flashed before his mind. The worldbender: *We know they're after us. We know they've put a bounty on us; Niamh saw to that.*

Simm stared down at his hands and sleeves, both dyed red with the aide's blood. There was one way he could prove himself to the Council—he could deliver this bounty. He could take down the meddlers.

He could kill again.

CHAPTER TWELVE

The Road to Home

There was little we could do about this many malae.

One, two, maybe even up to a dozen we could handle, given some fire. But this many? We'd die before we really made a dent in their number. We had no choice but to leave the malae where they were, but that didn't mean we were happy about it—or were about to leave them unguarded.

"You and your people," I said to the old tiefling who'd shown us to the canyon. "Do you think you can watch over this place? Stop any travelers from stumbling upon the malae?"

The old man looked back at me with his vibrant red eyes, fear in them.

"You don't have to get close. And I don't think the malae are going anywhere; they're fenced in well. We just don't want—"

The tiefling shook his head. "It's not that. It's . . . sooner or later, the traders will return. Black market merchants. They are powerful people—individually, but even more so as a whole. I can't stand in their way; I won't do that to my family."

I glanced to Lore, who nodded; he knew these parts, and if he agreed with what the man was saying, then that was good enough for me. "OK. Stay out of the traders' way, but everyone else . . ."

"I will keep them away."

"Thank you," I said.

This was a far from perfect plan; without anyone guarding the malae, then someone would come along for them eventually. They'd trade them away, and the corruption would spread. But equally, we couldn't stay here. Maybe we would kill off a few black marketeers, but more would keep coming. We wouldn't address the root problem.

We had to go elsewhere; we had to find the Player behind this trading, and we had to find the person responsible for breeding the malae—presumably to meet Yusef's demand.

There was a question about just *where* we would go next, as we had no idea where these malae had really come from. But this was swiftly answered when Corminar spotted an old rusting knife buried in the sand by the canyon. Treating it as a clue, he handed it around for us each to look at, but only Lore—who knew these parts well—was able to provide additional context.

"This mark here," he said, pointing to a spot on the blade, near the base. "It's a touchmark—the mark of a specific blacksmith. And this one, I know."

"You know touchmarks by heart?" Ama asked, eyebrow raised.

"Just this one," the barbarian said. "It's famous. Famous all around the northern Armada. It belongs to a blacksmith in Coldharbor, where I'm from. I'd know that symbol anywhere—even the guards used to carry his weapons, and I saw no shortage of their swords as a kid."

I made a note to ask Lore about his supposedly criminal background later; for now, we had a job to do. I clapped the barbarian around the shoulder. "Sounds like you're going home, then."

Lore smiled.

Two days later, the sprawling city of Coldharbor stretched before us. Though it was still very much a desert city, greenery had returned over the past few hours of walking. Palm trees stood over the sides of the road, obviously tended to and placed strategically to make the entrance to the town more appealing—though also a sign that there was plentiful enough water for this to be possible.

And of course there was, what with Coldharbor being a coastal city. The bay known as the Coldwater stretched as far as the eye could see behind the city, obscured only by a tall stone palace ornately designed despite its humble building material. It was the same body of water I'd seen from the Tundras a few times over the years, though here the sea was a vibrant blue green, and looked warm enough that its name didn't really fit.

The city itself shared some of the traits I'd come to expect of cities—it had the familiar tall walls of a central old town, with the city having grown far beyond them in the years since its founding. The buildings were a pale yellow white, matching the local rock, though there were patches of bright color as large fabrics created shade on the many rooftops. Tall spires—ancient monuments to the Architects—shot forth from the city skyline here and there, stripes of dazzling gold reflecting the high, bright sun.

Lore sighed when Coldharbor had first come into view, a smile on his face.

"It's been a long time," he said, though halfway through that sentence the joyful tones seemed to waver, just for a moment.

We proceeded down the palm tree–shaded road into the sprawling outer city, and the noise seemed to hit us like a wave. This was a city full of life, and unapologetically so—people shouted across the rooftops, people cried out about the wares they were selling, and there was the general racket of people . . . enjoying themselves? It was very different to what we'd seen in the Goldmarch over the past few weeks, what with the soldiers of the new Golden Empire cracking down on pretty much anything that brought people joy in the name of keeping them in line.

"Don't suppose you remember where the blacksmith—" I started to ask Lore, only to turn to my side to find him gone. "Lore?"

Carle caught my eye and nodded toward a nearby market stall—one that served steaming buns of some variety I'd never seen before. Currently handing over some coin, with three buns cradled in his left arm, was Lore.

I sighed and approached, and was at his side at the same moment that he finished the interaction and turned around.

". . . What?" he asked, presumably in response to the unimpressed glare I was giving him. He picked up one of the buns from his arm. "You want one?"

"Where's the blacksmith?" I asked.

"Oh. Right. Yeah." Lore took a moment to look around, getting his bearings. "You know, it's been a while since I was here, but . . . I think it's . . . this way?"

And so that way we went. I should have known, looking back, that Lore's memory of the place was a little iffy, considering he phrased that last bit as a question rather than a statement. By the time he *actually* led us to the blacksmith, it was almost an hour later, and I couldn't help but think we weren't more than ten minutes away from where we'd started.

The blacksmith itself was a big operation.

They seemed to have a whole building to themselves—and it wasn't some tiny shop, either; it was four stories tall and each floor was about the size of a tavern. Most of the ground floor was dedicated to customer service—blacksmiths, still covered in soot from the forges, took client orders down and passed the notes back to the dozens of other workers behind them. The rest of the ground floor was dedicated to the forging itself, it seemed—though I could see leather being passed up for pommels and I could hear the sound of grindstones being used for sharpening blades.

And there was a queue. A big queue. I wasn't sure, looking back, I'd ever seen a queue that size before—and I hoped never to again. We left the Trio in the shade across the road, and Corminar, Lore, and I joined the queue at the back, the big man peering over the heads and counting how many were still ahead of us. It wasn't massively thrilling to hear that number be so large.

But it moved quickly, at least; they had this operation running as efficiently as possible, and it was maybe twenty minutes before we reached the front—and a tiefling blacksmith with her hair tied up in a headscarf.

"Your order?" she shouted over the noise, skipping the pleasantries.

"Information, actually," I said, placing the rusty dagger down on the desk in front of her. "We wanted to know who you made this for."

"This line's for orders only," she said without looking up.

"Is there an information queue, then?" I asked.

"No." With a sigh, she looked up and took a look at the discarded blade. "You haven't looked after this much, have you?"

"It's not mine. Like I said, we're just looking for who you made it for. You have records?"

"Yep," she said, tapping her skull. "Up in here. Doesn't mean I'm telling you, though."

"We just want to return it," I lied.

"You ever heard of blacksmith-client confidentiality?" she asked.

"No," I replied, and this time I was telling the complete truth.

"Well, like I say: can't tell you."

I sighed, then turned to my two friends, huddling us in close together. "I think we need a bribe," I whispered to them, both of whom nodded. We turned back to the smith and both Corminar and Lore slid something across the table to her—a pile of coins and a steamed bun, respectively.

The smith looked from the coins, to the bun, and to Lore. I was just about to interrupt and apologize for my friend when she smiled at him, picked up the bun, and began to eat it—completely ignoring the coins.

Corminar and I shared a look, then shrugged.

"One of Yusef's lot," she said through mouthfuls of pastry. "Can't remember who precisely, but one of his team. That's all I can tell you."

Lore smiled, winked at the smith, and then turned away—to be faced with Corminar's and my suspicious faces.

"A bun?" I asked. "And that worked?"

"People like food round here."

"Is that where you get it from?"

I shook my head, then led Lore and Corminar back to the Trio.

"You get what you need?" Raelas asked.

I nodded. "We're on the right track—the blade was made for one of Yusef's team. That's evidence enough for me; he isn't just trading the malae, he's involved in their breeding, too."

The Trio was silent for a moment, before one of them asked the obvious question.

"So, what is next?" Carle asked.

"Now, we go find him."

CHAPTER THIRTEEN

Those Lost

We found some beds for the night at an inn, one that Corminar described as a "boutique inn." The stone walls were bare and flush, decorated only occasionally by ornate water fountains which the owner insisted we could all drink from whenever we wanted. There was talk of a palm wine–tasting downstairs this evening, but with all the hot sun I'd suffered over the past couple of days, even I wasn't that interested.

So instead I retreated to my—single!—room, and I continued to work on my cloth armor. I was working on some simple cloth-based bracers, which were supposedly the simplest thing to make. And if they were simple, then hopefully that meant I could make them to a higher quality. Besides, some cloth bracers were a whole lot better than the armor I had currently, which was . . . nothing.

I thought of Val as I worked on the last part. Where was she right now? Was she away in some far-off land continuing the work? Or had she had enough of Players, staying away from them—or *us*, as she might have thought—for the time being?

I finished the last stitch and took in my latest creation.

Needlework: +3,150XP

Needlework increased to level 17!
Needlework increased to level 18!
Base Points Gained: +2 DEX, +2 CHA, +2 Free Points (DEX/CHA)

> *Level up!*
> *You increased to level 19!*

With my *Legacy of Sisyphus* active effect upgraded by the life force of Niamh, I was progressing fast. Obviously, my overall level was more of a vanity metric than anything else, but it made me feel a bit more comfortable in myself that I was comparable in level to those I passed on the street. And it had taken so little time, in the grand scheme of things. Who knew that fifteen times the experience points and a lifestyle with action could be so conducive to leveling up.

Conducive, I thought, *big word. Maybe I've been spending too much time around Corminar.*

I pulled the bracers onto my arms. They fit fairly nicely, which was good considering I'd made them with myself in mind. They could have been better, admittedly, but they were worth it for the option of knocking away any glancing strikes. Satisfied, I took them off again—it was the early hours of the morning by this point, and I didn't intend to get into a fight right about now.

Placing the bracers to one side, I got into bed. For an inn that cost so much per night, the beds really weren't as comfortable as they should have been. I tossed and turned for a while, until I heard movement in the hallway. With sleep not taking me, I crept across the room to see which of our party was heading out at this time. I inched the door open just in time to see Lore disappearing down the staircase.

Maybe it was not being able to sleep, or maybe it was some innate nosiness, but I instinctively decided to follow him. I hurried back inside my room and yanked my trousers back on before hurrying down the stairs. I spilled out onto the moonlit street and saw the silhouette of the big man heading west, toward the outskirts of town.

I could have called out to him at that point, but some instinct within told me to keep quiet. If Lore was heading out at this time, he probably didn't want anyone to know about it. Maybe I should have given him some privacy, but he'd been acting increasingly antsy over the course of the evening, and this surely had something to do with it. I kept my distance as I followed him, and hovered a hand over the dagger I'd thought to bring with me; if *I* ever returned home, then I'd definitely have a fight or two on my hands.

But nobody came to ambush Lore, and nobody even spoke to him, the streets being as deserted as they were. And eventually the barbarian arrived at his destination: a small cemetery on the outskirts of the city. I hesitated on the boundary.

"You coming, Styk?" Lore called out without looking back.

I paused for a moment, but the jig was up. "How'd you know it was me?"

"Battlesense abilities aren't just good in a fight," he said.

I approached the man's side. "You mind?"

Lore shook his head and led us into the cemetery. He took a route that said he knew exactly where he was going, through the winding graves, his eyes fixed on a small one at the far side. There, he removed one of the steamed buns from his pocket, knelt down, and placed it atop the gravestone.

PLYAS ERELOS
DAUGHTER, SISTER, HERO

I waited to ask the question, giving Lore the moment of peace that he'd wanted, that I'd intruded on. "Who is she?" I finally asked.

"My sister."

"Plyas? That's a tiefling name, isn't it?"

The barbarian nodded. "Foster sister. I was adopted."

"Oh, I didn't—"

"My parents, they were merchants. Came through here. Weren't doing well. Couldn't afford to feed me. Left me on the doorstep of the Erelos family."

I found a lump in my throat. "You never said."

Lore shrugged. "I was young, I don't remember them. Didn't even know my own name, so they let me name myself."

Well, that's the mystery of the cool name answered, at least.

"What happened to her?" I asked, then immediately added, "If you don't mind talking about it."

I knew the answer before Lore spoke it. "A mala," he said. "Back when they were rare. We were playing in the dunes—saw it coming, but were too young to know what it was. Plyas . . . she was always the braver of us . . . she touched it."

The rest of the story hung in the air, Lore not wanting—or needing—to spell it out.

"I left about a year after that. I was angry. I fought a lot. Fell into a *Barbarian* class and barely looked back. It was only when I checked in on the folks a few years later that I'd learned one of the malae had slipped through a mercenary's attack on them."

"A Player, I'm guessing?"

Lore nodded. "I didn't blame him, not at first. These things happen. But when I spoke to him, when I mentioned it . . . he didn't care. He didn't care that a kid had been killed by his carelessness. And I'd thought he'd be a hero. No, the only hero around here was her." He nodded down to Plyas's grave.

"I lost someone to malae, too," I said.

"I thought you might've, yeah."

"Losing her . . . it hurt. Made it hard to open up to someone again, after that."

Lore turned to me. "Until Val?"

I gulped. "Until Val."

"She'll come back," the big man said. But I wasn't quite so sure.

I woke up late the next day, finding the bed surprisingly comfortable after all. The sun was high in the sky, pouring in through the wooden shutters. I staggered downstairs to get some food from the kitchen and found only Corminar and Lore sitting in the hall—the latter still yawning and looking very sleepy.

"The Trio?" I asked, grabbing a seat on the bench next to Lore.

The elf shook his head. "Absent."

"They've left?"

"Belongings remain in their rooms. I broke in."

"I'm a bad influence on you," I told him.

As I ate a hearty breakfast, we spoke about our plan for the day—namely, hunting down the Player behind the mala breeding: Yusef. We had absolutely no leads. We didn't even know if he was still in the city, just that he'd been through here at some point. So, the first step was asking around to find out. Surely, if a Player was still in Coldharbor, someone would know about it.

We stepped out into the near midday sun, and I immediately insisted we stop for a lot of drinks. This was something Lore in particular was keen on, though I suspected that was just because he wanted to pay a visit to some old haunts from his youth. We walked wherever our legs carried us, having no real destination, which sent us west once more. Though instead of veering off toward the cemetery, we stuck to the main road, heading toward the Mountain Gate.

Lore had fallen into the role of casually asking people about any Players coming through town, or occasionally about Yusef specifically. Though it was quite a direct question, the barbarian seemed to phrase it in ways that resonated with the locals—he understood their ways and culture so well, having grown up here. All knew of Yusef, their eyes lighting up at his very mention, but none knew his current whereabouts—suggesting that he was not in Coldharbor.

We were just about to find another spot to get a drink when the hairs on the back of my neck stood on end. There was some silent, indiscernible change to the bustling main road, one which caused all three of us to stop, searching for its cause. And we found it staggering in through the gate.

It wasn't a mala, this time, but a man.

A man who cradled his arm—an arm touched by dark corruption.

I ran to help him, pushing through an amassing crowd of locals. "Don't touch him!" I shouted. "Don't touch him!"

But the locals all looked at me like I was crazy. "Well *of course* we don't touch him," one of them said, "he's been attacked by a mala." The same woman turned to the corrupted man. "Stay with us, OK? We know what to do: we need to get you to the scientist. She specializes in this kind of thing."

I flashed a questioning look to Lore. "You know about this scientist?"

The barbarian shook his head. "Nope, never heard of her."

"Then maybe we go pay them a visit."

CHAPTER FOURTEEN

The Scientific Method

We followed the two locals as they carefully steered the corrupted man the way of the scientist, using thick reams of cloth to hold him upright while preventing the risk of getting corrupted themselves. I—and Lore and Corminar, from the looks of them—felt surplus to requirements, but this was our only lead on someone who might know a bit more about the malae, so we stuck with them, trailing some way behind.

The locals led the corrupted man around the outskirts of the city, to a neighborhood that looked dingier than the rest, with people well armed and watching newcomers carefully. That is to say, my kind of place. But Lore seemed to be right at home here, his eyes lighting up at the sight of old, dirty inns and shops and stalls. He even cried out a greeting to an old cloth merchant who waved back, confused, not recognizing the young boy who'd left in the burly barbarian who had returned.

We finally came across a building cleaner than the rest, with fresh paintwork and glowing, newfangled *Light*-magick bulbs across the top of the front. It was in here that the two women hurried the corrupted man, and then as soon as he was across the threshold, they scurried away—presumably not wanting to be on the hook for any medical costs. But someone inside moved to support the man—a tiefling woman covered from head to toe in a transparent, protective material, ready for such a situation.

When she looked up at the three of us, her eyes fixed on Lore and widened. "Lore?" she asked, voice lilting with joy.

"*Alenna?*" the barbarian replied, equally excited.

The scientist almost dropped her patient as she moved to hug Lore, arms wide, then realized the man needed support. "We'll hug later," she said, then began pulling the man deeper into her clinic. "He a friend?"

"No," Lore replied, "we just stumbled across him." Then he came to an abrupt stop and took in the clinic properly. And fair enough, really; this was unlike anything I'd ever seen before.

One wall of the shop was lined from floor to ceiling in shelves filled with glass specimen jars. Almost all contained an alchemical ingredient or a monster part or glowing magicks, and only some of them I *recognized*, let alone understood what they did. Alenna had a waist-high stone plinth in the center of the room, upon which she urged the corrupted man. In the corner of the room, hot enough that I could feel it from here, was a stone oven with a raging fire inside—and I got the impression that was where any corrupted body parts went, because it took fire to kill corruption.

"Will I keep the arm?" the man asked the scientist, glancing at the three of us nervously, as though he had no idea why we were there.

"We're gonna do our best!" Alenna shouted, then pushed the man's shoulder back down onto the stone plinth. "Lie still?"

"Is that a question?"

"Lie still." Alenna turned to her wall of medical supplies and tapped a finger against her chin. "What do we need? What do we need," she murmured, then suddenly seemed to have a moment of revelation, and pulled a jar full of green-glowing worms from the shelf. She turned back to the corrupted arm and tossed the worms onto where the mala had touched him.

I leaned over to Corminar. "Do you have any idea what she's doing?"

"None whatsoever."

Alenna put her face close to the corruption, watching the glow-worms closely. As the man began to move, she leaped backward. "Still! Lie *still!*"

The injured man stopped shifting. ". . . OK."

"OK," Alenna said, turning away. "The glow-worms aren't working. I've had some luck with them before, but I think they might only like elf flesh."

Corminar shifted nervously.

"Tiefling flesh? Not so much."

"What's that mean for me?" the patient asked.

Alenna turned back to him, an axe in hand. "It means you're gonna lose the arm." Before the patient could react, she flung a hand forward and released blue magicks that emerged as a glowing rope, binding him in place. "Sorry," she told the corrupted man, "but it's for your own good."

Then, as if practiced in the motion, she brought the axe down on the affected limb, above the spread of corruption. Alenna clearly had more strength than she looked like she had, because she took the arm off in only one strike. As the man screamed, the scientist immediately held cloth to the wound. "Lore, would you mind . . ." She nodded to the cloth, and the barbarian took it, holding it in place.

Meanwhile, Alenna took the corrupted arm and tossed it into the oversized oven. She sighed when it was done. "Phew," she said. "Hard work, this."

"Lenna . . ." Lore said nervously.

The scientist jumped. "Oh! Right." She took the cloth from Lore and began feeding low levels of yellow-white *Healing* magicks into the wound. The patient, meanwhile, had passed out.

It was some time before Alenna had stabilized the once-corrupted man, and she had us wait upstairs in her living quarters, telling us to make ourselves at home. Lore clearly took the scientist at her word, because he was immediately looking in her cupboards for snacks and something to drink—both of which he found.

As we sat nibbling on biscuits and sipping some sort of hot, spiced drink I hadn't had before, the scientist finally arrived upstairs.

"How about that hug now, big guy?" she said, arms stretched wide.

Lore practically sprinted to his old friend, grabbing her in his arms and returning the hug so enthusiastically that he lifted her from the ground. When he finally put her down, the two of them traded stories of what they'd been up to in the years since they saw each other, while Corminar and I sat uncomfortably, feeling like we were intruding.

From the sounds of it, Lore had seen Alenna only once since he'd left home, but before that they'd been close friends. Alenna knew Plyas, too, because she referenced her before Lore did—drawing a confused expression from the ranger in the process.

The tiefling, for her part, had applied herself in the magicks before realizing that maybe there was another route to helping people—using the natural ingredients of the world in a way similar to alchemy, but without the magicks element, just using their innate properties. She'd had some success, as evidenced by the clinic, but the growing mala scourge had brought with it a new challenge.

"It's what I've been trying to do here," Alenna said. "Come up with a way to make people survive the corruption through a combination of magicks and science. I'd had some success with those worms eating up the corruption enough that the host survives—the worms don't—but they don't always take. And then the host gives in a few days or weeks later. It's progress, but it's not enough. So then we have to resort to more traditional methods."

"Cutting it off," I said.

The scientist nodded. "Yeah."

"It looks as though people understand you are making progress," Corminar said, nodding to the room—as finely decorated up here as the clinic itself had been, if not cozier.

The scientist blinked as though caught off guard. "Oh?"

"I noticed there was no charge for the patient, yet it would require significant funding to have a place such as this. Donations, I would assume? Perhaps from a handful of wealthy benefactors?"

Alenna hesitated before smiling. "Right on the money. You have smart friends, Lore." She hit the man playfully on the upper arm, and Lore didn't seem to notice.

"That's why we're here, actually," I said, wanting to bring up the topic that had put us on Alenna's doorstep. "We're looking for leads on the malae. As far as we can tell, someone is breeding them, and we think that person might be—"

Lore coughed pointedly; though this woman was a friend, clearly she was still as fooled by Players as most of the world. If I spoke negatively of them in her presence, she would be less likely to help us.

"We think that person might be in the city," I finished, switching up from what I'd originally intended to say. "Have you heard anything? Do you know anything that would help us?"

The scientist licked her lips thoughtfully before replying, training her eyes on me in a way I didn't quite like—what was going on in that brain? "What do you intend to do with the malae once you find them?"

"We are here to exterminate them all," Corminar said, sparing no drama.

Alenna nodded. "Good. There's getting to be too many of them—not that one isn't too many. But, fair warning: many adventurers and mercenaries have tried to wipe them out, and many of them have ended up back in my clinic. Or never shown up at all." She turned to Lore. "You'll be careful out there, won't you?"

The barbarian nodded, a kind smile on his face.

"Good." Alenna stood from her seat and hurried across the room. Halfway down the stairs, she called out, "I'll be right back; got something that might help you." When she returned, she carried a stone in her hand—one with glowing green energy hovering around it. "I borrowed some magicks to make this."

"*Witchcraft?*" I asked, noting the color of the spell.

Alenna shrugged. "We do what we must. This spell, here, it looks for *Witchcraft* magicks. A particular *kind* of *Witchcraft*, in fact—those associated with the malae."

Lore held out his hand to take the stone, eyes fixed upon it. "Are you saying what I think you're saying?"

The scientist nodded. "It tracks malae. And you can have it, but I ask one thing in return."

"What's that?"

"If you do find any malae, give them to me to study. The only way I can save people is if I know what I'm working with."

Lore met the woman's eyes and nodded, that kind smile still on his face. "We can do that," he said.

CHAPTER FIFTEEN

The Coldharbor Sprawl

Lore gave the mala-locator stone to Corminar to monitor as we roamed the city, suggesting that he trusted Corminar to use it better than he trusted himself. But as we weaved through the narrow streets of Coldharbor, I began to think it was for another reason: so he could concentrate on looking around the city he'd grown up in.

He took us into the odd shop here and there, for food, for drink, sometimes just to have a look around—mostly it was for food—and enthusiastically explained who had owned each business, how long they had been there, and a handful of supposedly amusing anecdotes from his childhood. After a while, it felt like he'd forgotten why we were here in the first place.

So I reminded him. "Lore, you know we're hunting malae, not . . . shopping?"

The big man's smile faltered. ". . . Yes?"

From the way he'd said it, I could tell this was a lie; he wasn't exactly the best liar in the world.

"Just one more stop," Lore said.

"We really—" Corminar started, but the barbarian interrupted him.

"You'll like this one. I promise."

And so, reluctantly—and with no shortage of sighs on the elf's part—we followed Corminar toward the center of town. Here, in the heart of the city, the buildings stood tall and were crammed close together, every square foot of real estate built upon over the course of the years. Lore led us between these tall buildings—I was grateful for the shade from the midafternoon sun—then came to a stop. He closed his eyes and drew in a deep breath.

While he . . . did whatever he was doing, I looked at the sprawling market in front of us. It was wedged between the tall buildings, stalls, and stores crammed into every nook and cranny, continuing in the distance through arches and tunnels under buildings. The stalls here sold vibrant cloths, aromatic spices, and no shortage of the curved blades that the tieflings of the Beached Armada so preferred. It was a feast for the senses, and I understood why Lore had brought us here.

"The Coldharbor market!" Lore proclaimed, almost shouting—but there was enough of a din from the throngs of customers that few seemed to even notice. "Isn't it great?"

"I'm assuming they sell snacks here," I replied.

"Ahem," Corminar coughed pointedly, clearly keen to be getting on. I, however, could see the appeal of this place, and what harm was there really in letting Lore relive a few childhood memories?

"Lots!" Lore replied. "Buncakes and spit-veg and roca and—"

"Ahem," Corminar repeated.

I turned to him. "Yes, we'll be getting—" And then I saw that he was looking down at the magical device that Alenna, the scientist, had given us. "Ah."

"What's . . ." Lore started, and then he caught up with what was going on—there was a mala nearby. "Oh. How close?"

Corminar looked up, straight ahead of him, following the indication on the locator stone. He stared at a woman who froze abruptly to the spot, fabric disguising her face and clutching something in her hand that was covered by a bright magenta cloth. She was hiding the creature in plain sight. "Oh, not far," he said.

We burst into a sprint toward the woman, and she at the same moment turned to flee into the dense market. The three of us immediately hit the wall that was the milling crowd, none of them in any rush to get out of our way and much more interested in browsing wares at their own pace. It was Lore who had the least trouble with the crowd, which was surprising considering that he was by far the largest of us—but I supposed if you saw him barreling toward you, you'd get out of his way in a hurry, too.

I glimpsed our target fleeing into the distance, weaving among the market stalls, able to move faster than us even with a large, disguised crate in one hand—she was from the city, and seemed to know innately how it moved.

"She's getting away!" I shouted to the other two, and then caught myself. "Wait, what am I doing?"

I first reached forward to open a portal in front of our target, but I couldn't aim properly through such a dense, ever-shifting crowd. So instead, I aimed roughly above her and opened a portal for me to fall through to catch up to her. As I leaped through the portal on my side, I saw Corminar leaping through to join me. He'd really gotten his head around all this portal stuff at last.

We fell out the other side and tumbled down into the crowd—me landing on top of a young couple who were holding tails, and Corminar onto the roof of a market stall. If he had been Lore, he would have crushed it and put someone out of business, but instead he bounced off the top and fell nimbly to his feet.

The two of us—and Lore, not so far behind—continued to charge after the woman, winding through the stalls and around a sharp corner. We stumbled to a halt when we didn't initially see her, but then Corminar threw his hand forward, gesturing to some reams of cloth swaying in the wind—where the target had just run through.

I opened more portals to close the gap some, bringing us to the cloth merchants, and we burst through the same wall of fabric that our target presumably had. I saw nobody on the other side, but Corminar's sharper elven senses had him running to the right, down a narrow alley that stretched away from the marketplace and into thick shadow.

I charged after him, hearing Lore approaching—and apologizing to people he pushed through—at my rear. The alley grew narrow as it steered off to the left, not wide enough for two people to pass through side by side, and maybe even not wide enough for Lore to get through without sucking in his stomach.

The alley turned again, sharply, putting Corminar out of sight, and I charged down it. It suddenly opened up into a courtyard, and I collided with Corminar's back as the elf had stumbled to a halt. I was about to insult him for stopping so abruptly when I looked around to see the reason *why*.

Here, there wasn't just one person with cloth covering her lower face. There was a dozen. Our target had fled for the support of her allies—and now, we were greatly outnumbered.

"Err . . . hi?" I said, waving timidly. "Nice to meet you all."

Lore charged into the courtyard and collided with both me and Corminar, sending us falling forward to the dirt. "Sorry," he mumbled as the elf and I jumped quickly back to our feet, anticipating the fight that was to come.

"I think we've taken a wrong turn somewhere," I said, edging backward, my ranger friend following suit. "We'll just be—"

One of the disguised enemies, an archer looming over us on a balcony at our left, loosed two shots in quick succession. One landing just where I'd been about to place my foot, and the other landing just where Corminar had been about to step.

"Impressive . . ." the elf murmured. He appreciated good archery when he saw it.

Back down on our level, one of the enemies stepped forward, out of the shadows of one of the buildings.

"Ooh, very good," Lore said. "Very dramatic."

The man who'd just stepped into the light glared at the barbarian like he was being sarcastic, but I knew him well enough to realize he'd been sincere. Still, it probably wasn't worth calling that out right about now. "Why do you harass my employees?" he asked, staring at Lore with bright red eyes.

"I promise you, he's not harassed anyone in his life," I replied. "Besides, I think we should be the ones asking the questions here. Questions like . . . why are you carrying malae around? And who are you selling them to?"

A few of the enemies drew their blades at the mention of the malae, but the man in charge waved them down. For now.

I kept one hand behind my back, ready to portal us out of here if the inevitable battle turned out to be one-sided—and not one-sided in our favor.

"I don't think that's any of your concern," the mysterious stranger replied. "That's our business. Not yours."

"It's everyone's business when those malae you're trading are out there killing people. That canyon, to the southwest—is that your doing, too?"

The man's eyes gave no answer, but he did at least hesitate. Was this canyon news to him? And did that mean it was unrelated to this particular piece of enterprise? Maybe he just headed up the trade in Coldharbor, rather than the Armada as a whole. This man would surely have a boss, wouldn't he?

"You must know," Corminar said, "we cannot leave here until we exterminate your stock."

I lowered my portal-ready hand; Corminar was right. We'd need to give this our all, not have one foot out the door. Those dead from corruption deserved that.

"And *you* must know," the stranger replied, "we cannot let *you* leave."

I sighed, raised my blade, and readied myself to fight.

CHAPTER SIXTEEN

A Bazaar Battle

As Lore and I drew our blades—one bigger than the other—the enemies attacked. I skirted my eyes over them, counting exactly how many, and came up with nine. That would mean taking down three each—fairly long odds unless we figured out a good plan fast.

The archer on the balcony above loosed a shot and it skimmed my ear, drawing blood. It was about as close as it could get without doing real damage. Seven more of them—their leader not included—stepped menacingly toward us . . . and still I had no plan.

"Regroup?" I asked my friends.

"Regroup," Lore agreed verbally, and Corminar did so with a nod.

We turned and ran, weaving down the winding narrow alleyway, Lore allowing Corminar and me to go first as he could bear more damage.

"Wish the others were here right now!" I cried.

"Val and Arzak?" Lore replied.

". . . Yes!" I lied. Had I so quickly replaced them with the Trio in my mind?

Lore grunted behind me as he swung his blade to fend off the enemies. They'd grown close already, and we needed to put some distance back between us if we were going to come up with a plan. One idea flashed through my mind—take the battle back to the markets, and hope to lose the enemies in the crowd. But then I got suspicions that these enemies wouldn't mind a little collateral damage—or, at least, they'd mind it less than we did.

I pushed my hands forward instinctively to open a portal ahead of us, but the alley was narrow and winding enough that I couldn't open a portal far enough ahead for it to do any good.

"Rooftops?" Corminar shouted, and I figured out where he was going with that—he wanted me to portal us up there.

"Can't see them, and they're too high! Out of range!"

Instead, we continued to flee down the alleyway, stumbling back out into the marketplace. I looked around quickly for a plan, and spotted a number of balconies hanging over the bazaar. I opened a portal next to myself and Corminar and paired it with one on the closest balcony. "Through! Through!" I shouted, and Corminar did so with only a second's hesitation.

But a second was too long.

Though the ranger had made it onto the balconies—and was in this moment readying an arrow to fire at one of our pursuers—the enemies had grown too close. Now that the alley had broadened out into a street, the mala traders had been able to get around Lore. Most of them very sensibly realized that he wasn't the easiest pickings, and so they were now charging at another member of the team—me.

One of them swung their blade at me before I could disappear through the portal, and I dived backward to avoid the attack. I aimed my movement poorly, not getting through the open portal but instead clipping my shoulder on it, sending me spiraling toward the ground. I didn't have a second to spare on another attempt, so I burst back up into a sprint, vacating the spot where a sword was arching down just in time.

And, just like that, I found myself among the crowds once more. I was about to open another portal to get me out of trouble, but the masses had grown so dense that I couldn't even see a spot to open one to enter. I pushed through the shoppers, five or six of the enemies charging after me. I wanted to call out to Corminar for help, but I knew that as soon as I did, the enemies would know he was there, and would find cover.

But there was another way.

I spun around just long enough to fling my hands in the direction of my pursuers, glimpsed through the crowds, and instead of opening a portal—which would have been ineffective in such a crowd—I used another of my abilities that hadn't proved all that versatile so far. I activated *Silence*.

A giant, faintly purple bubble appeared around the enemies and shoppers alike, and immediately all of them blinked at the sudden change in sensation—all sound having been eradicated for them. Some of them even stumbled to a halt. But the confusion would be temporary.

"Corminar!" I shouted, not taking my eyes off the enemies so they couldn't see who I was yelling to. "Get them!"

He immediately fired an arrow that caught one of the traders in the shoulder, sending them to the ground, clutching their wound. It wasn't a fatal one, but it was enough to eliminate them from the fight—at least until they saw a healer.

I felt the uncomfortable sensation of an unread notification popping up, but I ignored it for now—there were still at least five others to deal with.

I continued pushing through the crowd, stretching my head above them to look for a way out. The masses were good for slowing my attackers down, but they also slowed me down—and rendered my portals useless. I needed a little space. To my left, I spotted another cloth merchant—one I'd need to return to later, to restock my *Needlework* supplies—with their wares hung on solid ropes that stretched across an off-shooting road. I swerved toward their store.

Shouting behind me announced Lore's return to the fray, and I glimpsed him managing to take out another of the mala traders before they could notice him coming—their attention fixed on me. But then the four remaining turned on him, and even Lore wasn't strong enough to hold off that many.

"Lore!" I shouted. "Over here!"

Corminar's arrows had been few and far between, and it was only at this point that I realized why. He was as limited as I was by the crowds—with these dense masses moving in unpredictable patterns, he couldn't always get a shot with no risk of hitting an innocent. I saw him leap across the narrow-ish street, from balcony to balcony, trying to find a better angle.

Lore stumbled out of the thick crowd near me, and we charged on down the quieter street. As we passed under the first line of colorful cloths, one of the enemies caught up, striking a blade toward me. Instinctively, I raised my hands to protect myself—which would have been a foolish move if I hadn't been wearing my new bracers. They stopped the worst of the attack, the blade only just catching my skin, but they were ruined in the process. Already.

Lore roared and tackled my attacker to the ground, which would have been a kind gesture if it didn't leave me with three others to deal with.

I backed up down the street, passing through the pieces of fabric and glancing up, a thought suddenly occurring to me. "Lore!" I shouted. "Be ready!"

The barbarian headbutted the trader he was dealing with, sending them to the ground, clutching their nose, then he looked at me. In the same moment, I reached a hand up and used *Portal Slice* on one end of the ropes from which the fabric was hanging.

And at the same moment, the three traders charged at me.

"Now!" I shouted as one end of the rope fell to the ground at Lore's feet.

The barbarian thought just quickly enough to grab the rope from the ground and yank it taut—just as the three attackers ran into it. Two of them fell from the impact, and Lore whipped the rope again to topple the other one.

From there, it was easy.

"Come out! Now!" I bellowed to the leader of the traders as we reentered the courtyard, his employees bound by the rope I'd taken from the cloth merchant.

I'd paid him for his troubles and promised to return to buy more of his wares, and at that point he'd been happy enough with the deal to even help us tie up the prisoners. All the mala traders who'd still been conscious had snarled and spat at us as we did so—all of them except one, the archer, who had been strangely quiet.

The leader of the mala traders sneered at us as we approached, though I got the impression that the sneer was as much for his employees as it was for us. What did it say about how he ran his business that his team had managed to get captured even though they'd greatly outnumbered us?

"Now, my good fellow," Corminar said, "you are going to tell us everything you know about the Armadan mala trade, and then you are going to show us to your stock. Do you understand?"

The man didn't reply.

"I asked you: do you understand?"

Still, nothing.

"I don't think he understands," Lore said.

Instead of speaking, the enemy finally answered by striking his arms down at his side—with particular dramatic flair, I've got to admit—and forming within his hands the blue-white glow of *Conjuration* magicks.

Corminar raised his bow to strike, landing an arrow firmly in the man's chest. As a droplet of blood dripped down the side of his mouth, the dust underneath each of his hands began to fly into the air, twisting and turning and taking shape. The shapes of men.

"Sand spirits!" Lore shouted.

I moved to charge them with him, dagger in hand, readying to activate *Knifestorm* to deal damage fast, but the barbarian whipped out his arm to block me.

"Swords are useless," he said. "They'll shift around them."

From his confident tone, I could tell he'd encountered these before. He knew what he was talking about.

"Do you have, then, any suggestions?" Corminar shouted above the blustery wind that kept the sand spirits' shapes.

"I . . ."

The spirits charged toward me and Lore, and I instinctively opened a portal to block them. Only I didn't open a typical portal. I opened an entrance to a pocket world—one that they blasted right into.

When I snapped the portal shut again, the winds died.

"You dare—" the injured merchant leader began, but was cut off by Corminar firing another arrow at him—this one doing the job.

". . . Huh," Lore said to me. "I wouldn't have thought of that."

Corminar nodded approvingly. "Best be careful when you next access your pocket world. Though perhaps the magicks will have faded by then."

I breathed a sigh of relief; fighting in this heat was not much fun, and only then did I allow the notifications to come in.

---

6 x Merchants of the Dark Markets defeated!

Worldbending: +5,350XP
Worldbending increased to level 54!
Worldbending increased to level 55!
Base Points Gained: +4 INT, +4 Free Points (INT/WIS/CHA)
Ability Selection Unlocked
Select an ability from the list below:

. . .

The ability choice would have to wait for now, at least until we'd decided what to do with these traders. Already, Corminar had begun by taking it upon himself to pull the cloth from their chins, revealing each of the traders' faces. He moved down the line, revealing mostly tieflings, but the odd human in there, too. There was even an elf, sporting on his wrist the red rose symbol of the Red Thorn—a member of the organization of elves still technically exiled from the Dawnwood, even if it was now under imperial control.

And then Corminar reached the end of the line, standing in front of the archer.

"I must say," the elf said. "You are a fine shot. A shame that you take—" But Corminar stumbled over his sentence when he pulled the cloth from the human's face—revealing his identity as someone we knew well.

". . . Lambkin?" Lore asked.

Captain Lambkin. Or, *ex*-captain Lambkin, at least. The last time we'd seen him, he'd helped us take down Jacob, the pyroknight and the first Player I'd killed. Then, he'd gone off to oversee Tokas, to make sure she didn't get into any trouble after we'd learned she'd made a deal with the very same Player. From the looks of it, we'd picked the wrong man for the job—because this . . . This was trouble and a half.

"Call the guards, then get me out of here," Lambkin said. "I will explain everything."

CHAPTER SEVENTEEN

Old Friends

As the guards descended on the courtyard, we hurried Lambkin out of sight. The mala traders needed locking up, and so, too, did Lambkin, probably—but we had some questions to ask him first.

Lore held our captive by the wrists bound behind his back as we weaved through the crowds of the marketplace. You might have thought that so many people being around would mean that someone would surely spot that Lambkin was a prisoner, and perhaps even question what was going on. But the truth was that the crowds were so dense, so tightly pressed together, that nobody could even see the ropes around the man's wrists.

As we walked in silence away from the courtyard, through browsers and guards charging to the scene of the crime, I perused my ability selection choices. Having regretted not picking it first time around, I skimmed the list first, looking for another shot at *Portal Relay* or an improved version of it, but found nothing—not yet anyway.

Ability Selection Unlocked
Select an ability from the list below:

Option 1: Warped Shield II (Worldbending)—*Upgrade to Warped Shield. Passive.* If an enemy strikes you with a melee weapon, *Warped Shield* automatically activates to open a portal that deflects this attack. You must not have any portals currently active. Uses mana on activation.

I already had *Warped Shield*, of course, though I tended not to get into situations where I had to use it. The original ability was nowhere near as useful as I'd thought it would be, considering it had only applied to nonenchanted weapons. The whole world seemed to be carrying enchanted weapons these days, and even if the enchantment was minor, it meant that my ability wouldn't kick in.

I mentally earmarked this option as I knocked into a broad, scarred man's shoulder. I glared up at him, thought better of getting into another fight, and hurried through the crowd after Lore.

Option 2: Saved Portal II (Worldbending)—*Upgrade to Saved Portal.* Select a location to "save" for future portals. Until your save point is moved, you may always open a portal here, even if it is beyond your current *Local Portal* range. Mana is used only upon opening the portal.

This was the problem with getting a skill to a decent level—every ability choice you had to select from was very compelling.

I'd passed over the original *Saved Portal* for another ability before. I don't remember what that other choice had been, but I *did* remember feeling bad about not picking this one. There were so many applications to it, not least of which was around making a "base" for the team to operate from. But nowadays, with Val and Arzak gone, that didn't seem so important. Still, it meant that we'd always be able to quickly retreat from a fight if we got in over our heads—and the Architects knew that we did that very often—so it was still a very compelling option.

But, as the crowds started to thin ahead of us as we approached the end of the bazaar, I looked at my third and final ability choice.

Hidden condition met! Alternative ability choice unlocked.
Option 3: Disintegrate Seams (Worldbending) [Requires: *Needlework* level 15]—Use your magicks to tear away at the seams of light or medium armor, immediately weakening the armor.

I almost laughed when I envisioned using this ability. I face down a huge, towering enemy—the large guy I'd just bumped into a minute ago sprung to mind—and I have no hope of piercing his armor with my dagger. So I activate this, then the string that holds the man's armor together falls apart . . . and so, too, does the armor itself, dropping to the ground. Maybe it even reveals some embarrassing underclothes.

It really *was* tempting, simply for that reason. But my mind won over my heart, and I picked the option that I'd told myself I would select next time it came up.

Ability Upgraded: Saved Portals II

Saved Portals II (Worldbending): Select a location to "save" for future portals. Until your save point is moved, you may always open a portal here, even if it is beyond your current *Local Portal* range. Mana is used only upon opening the portal.

My instinct whenever I got a new ability was to try it out straightaway and see what I was dealing with. In this case, though, there was no location around me that was useful to keep saved, so I had to hold back. Maybe we'd find somewhere soon. Maybe we would even go track down a safehouse for this precise reason.

Finally, we left the din of the marketplace behind us, and Lore hurried Lambkin into the cover of a small, dark alleyway.

"You could unbind my hands now, good sir," Lambkin said.

Lore didn't do any such thing. "Nah, first you tell us why you're involved with mala traders."

Lambkin looked to me next, holding his hands out behind his back. But I shook my head; I was in no mood to disagree with Lore here. The ex-captain, seeing he wasn't getting anywhere, hung his head down and sighed. "I am not involved with mala traders."

"You were in their camp!" Lore protested. "You fought alongside them!"

"You're literally wearing the same headscarf as them," I added.

"Yet you will notice I damaged none of you?" Lambkin said. "And as Corminar Cladenor here says"—he nodded to the ranger—"I am a fine shot. I would have hit you if I'd wanted to, as the second highest leveled archer in the Tundras."

"We are not in the Tundras," Corminar growled.

"Be that as it may—"

"I think . . . we're getting a little off topic," I interjected, not wanting this to devolve into another pissing contest between the two rangers. "Why were you there, Lambkin? You should be in Aptleed, keeping an eye on Tokas, and you not being there would worry me, let alone . . ." I gestured back the way we'd came.

"I am no mala trader," Lambkin said. "I was *infiltrating* the traders. Months of work, it was, to get me this far—and all that had now gone down the drain."

"Down the drain?" I asked. "The guards will arrest them, and—"

"You think that is the extent of the operation?" Lambkin asked, echoing my earlier doubts. "No, Styk. They are just one unit. One local unit. Who knows how many more are out there, and who knows who they report to? My intention was to work my way to the top, to understand—"

"It's a Player," Lore said. "It's a Player in charge. His name is Yusef."

Lambkin held the barbarian's gaze, then nodded. "Then it's as she suspected," he said, and then immediately paled.

"... What was that?"

"Nothing."

"You said something about 'as she suspected.' Who is 'she,' Lambkin? Tell me it's not her. Tell me you didn't."

"I . . ." Lambkin started.

"You were supposed to watch her! Not *team up with her!*"

The bound man gave shrugging his best attempt. "We thought you were all dead!"

"Why?"

Lambkin blinked at me. "There was a Player-led invasion of the Tundras. And where were you? We figured that the Player-slaying had fallen to us, considering that you were nowhere to be seen. Though, I must admit that the Player in question fell through our fingers and died over the course of her next invasion, as far as I could—"

Corminar coughed pointedly.

"... You were in the Dawnwood," Lambkin realized aloud.

"We were."

"Ah. And you . . ."

"Eliminated the Player, yes," Corminar finished for him.

"You might have written to me."

It was my turn to blink now. "We were a bit busy!"

"Before then!" Lambkin said next. "I moved halfway across the continent on behalf of my new friends to watch over a tiefling gone awry, and I *expected* they might check in on us every now and then."

"Well, I figured you'd be making a new life with Sae. That's what you said, didn't you? Thought you'd put all this behind you."

Lambkin mumbled something under his breath.

"What's that?"

"She didn't come, alright?" the ex-captain repeated. "When I got back to Umlok, she was gone. Her father, the baron, he'd taken advantage of my absence to marry her off to some cousin of a duke. Never saw her again. And so the only friend I've had is . . ."

"Tokas," Lore finished.

The bound man nodded, and finally I reached forward with my knife to slice the ropes from his wrists.

"Alright," I said. "We'll let you go free on one condition: take us to Tokas."

"And if she doesn't repeat everything you just told us," Lore said, "we're gonna have some *words*, you and me." The barbarian towered over the ranger as he delivered this implied threat.

Lambkin nodded, and then began to lead us through the winding streets of Coldharbor to see a woman who we'd thought we'd never see again.

To see a woman who'd betrayed us.

CHAPTER EIGHTEEN

Rehabilitation

Even Lore was quiet as we followed Lambkin through the streets of Coldharbor toward where Tokas, the woman who had betrayed us, was staying. I couldn't quite work out how the tiefling—not exactly the most charming woman I'd ever met—had convinced Lambkin to work with her, but maybe the latter had gotten tired of the quiet life, particularly if Sae wasn't living it with him.

I cast my mind back to the moment of realization, when we'd fled Jacob the pyroknight after our first, doomed attempt to kill him. We'd been cowering in a cave when it had all come together, and I'd reached out to take Tokas's obscurem from her. When I'd shattered it, I'd seen her true face—that of the pyroknight healer who had been there during the devastation of Plainside. She'd been involved in a deed so evil that there was surely no forgiveness.

Lambkin finally came to a halt in front of an unassuming door near the edge of town, the faded blue-green paint peeling from the woodwork, dust lining the windows. He gestured for us to enter, but . . . none of us did.

"You can go in," he said. "This has been our base of operations for the past few weeks. It's safe."

"It's not that," Lore said. "It's . . ."

He didn't need to say it; I was right there with him. And from the expression on Corminar's face, the elf agreed, too: we were not in a rush to see Tokas again. But we all knew we had to, that we had to make sure Lambkin had been telling the truth, and that we had to find out what she knew. We each drew in one last, deep breath before following the Tundran archer into the house.

As we stepped inside into a narrow hallway, the floor consisting of a mosaic of tiles so common in this area, our shoes against the ceramic announced our arrival. And at the end of the hallway, turning around from a stove placed in front of a large window, we saw the silhouette of a tiefling. A familiar tiefling.

"Hi, Tokas," Lore said.

There was a moment of silence that could have been anything from a second to a full minute before the tiefling replied. "Hi, Lore."

Two children with worryingly loud footsteps—steps that seemed to make the very ground shake—rushed out into the hallway to see who had arrived. Tokas's kids, Punnas and Lopas, emerged smiling, blissfully unaware of their mother's past crimes. As they should be; they were too young, still, to hear such things.

"Woah!" Lore said enthusiastically, putting it on a bit as he crouched down to meet them at their eye level. "Haven't you two grown! You gotta be, what, ten feet tall by now?"

"Nooo!" Punnas replied, chuckling. "Not *ten feet*!"

"Well, you two look it to me," the barbarian said, then glanced up at Corminar and Tokas. "Why don't we go play in the other room, let the grown-ups talk?"

"But *you're* a grown-up!" the other child protested.

"You don't have to become grown up if you don't wanna," Lore said. "That's the secret they don't tell you." He continued nattering on about something or other as he led the two children up the staircase and out of earshot. I met the barbarian's knowing gaze for just a second and nodded my thanks. Not for the first time, I took a moment to note that the big man was smarter than he looked—something I often forgot.

"So," Tokas finally said, holding Corminar's gaze. "They told you I was here, did they?"

Both the elf and I narrowed our eyes, but it was Lambkin who answered first, shaking his head. "We ran afoul of each other. Chance, nothing more. They weren't searching for you."

If I wasn't mistaken, this answer caused a little sadness to emerge behind the tiefling's eyes; she wanted us to have been looking for her. She wanted us to want her. It was a feeling I could empathize with—I'd spent a lot of time alone in the past.

"You brought them with you? The kids?" I asked, trying my best to move Tokas's thoughts along. For all her past transgressions, it was hard to see her as sad as she was.

Tokas shrugged, then looked to the ex-captain. "Lambkin has explained to me that I was overrelying on my father's kindness and offers for childcare. Besides, it is important they see and understand my work, for once they learn what I did . . ." The tiefling's voice cracked, just for a moment. "They won't think me all bad. They will understand that there is good and bad in everyone, their mother included. Though I suppose all children learn that at some point."

Corminar and I nodded glumly, while Lambkin didn't react. Clearly his childhood had been healthier than that of everyone else in the room.

"And just what, may I ask, is it that you are here for?" Corminar asked. When Lambkin moved like he was about to speak, the elf whipped a hand up to demand his silence; we had to make sure that their stories aligned.

"Lambkin told you about the mala trade?"

"We knew already," I replied. "We just didn't expect to find him a part of it. So you came here to take it down?"

Tokas shook her head. "Not initially. We're here to take down Players."

Corminar gulped.

"You're continuing the work?" I asked. "You're back slaying again?"

"I never stopped. Lambkin and I, we've already taken down one together—a man named Sandar, if you really have to know—and when we heard about Yusef from merchants traveling across the Coldwater, we knew he was our next target."

I nodded. "The same man we're here for. Do you know his location? Or his weaknesses, how we can kill him?"

The tiefling shook her head. "No, you're not understanding me. We're not here to kill anyone. We're here to take them down. *Expose* them." Tokas turned to look out the dusty window and at the street beyond, clearly preferring it to forcing herself to meet our gazes. "You remember the Tundran invasion?"

"Kinda hard to forget," I replied.

Tokas nodded. "The dukes, the barons, the leaders . . . they only allowed Amira's forces to help them because Amira had a Player speaking for them. And we know what most people think of Players—that they're heroes, that they can do no wrong, and so on. But really, they're just people, like the rest of us. Some of us . . . make mistakes. And some of us are evil. That's true of them, too."

"You're here to demonstrate that," Corminar said. "How?"

"That's about as far as we got. We suspected that Yusef was involved in the mala trade, and so we began to infiltrate. If we could get undeniable proof from the inside that he was involved . . . we could spread it. We could show people that Players aren't to be lauded. That some are manipulative, evil, and able to force you to do terrible things."

This was the third time, by my count, that Tokas had referenced her crime of teaming up with the pyroknight. It was as though she wanted to talk about it. But it was up to Corminar, not me, to decide if he was ready to.

He wasn't. "I am on board with such a plan," he said. "Styk?"

I nodded. "Works for me. As you say, if people knew what Players were really like, the Tundras would never have been invaded. And the Dawnwood . . ." I trailed off; we could all fill in the blanks here, and it didn't help Corminar to keep spelling it out. I looked to the elf for guidance here, as it seemed like if we wanted the same thing as Tokas, then it would make sense to work with her.

And yet . . . after what I saw the pyroknight do in Plainside, back when this all began, and with her at his side . . . Well, I didn't know if I could deal with her traveling with us.

But Corminar seemed to be on the same page. "Good. Then we will share information in our efforts. We will continue our investigations, and if we learn of anything significant, we will share this with you." He nodded to the tiefling. "Tokas," he said, like he was breaking off this interaction, then turned and did the same to the other ranger. "Lambkin."

I nodded a timid goodbye, too, and we shifted toward the door just for a second before the tiefling spoke again.

"If you do see them," she said, voice now definitely shaking, her eyes fixed on the floor, "will you tell her I'm sorry?"

"Who?" I asked.

Only then did Tokas glance up at us, any sadness behind those eyes replaced by confusion. "Arzak. You're here with them, aren't you? In the Armada?"

My heart dropped.

"Arzak and Val are in the Beached Armada?" Corminar asked, with a much more level tone of voice than I would have managed.

"You didn't know."

"No," I said, surprised to find my voice coming out as little more than a breath.

Tokas furrowed her brow. "Then it seems I am not the only one to have hurt them."

I opened my mouth to speak, but Corminar grabbed my arm and turned me away; this was a can of siltworms he didn't want to open.

"If we learn any more of the Player, we will tell you," the elf said to Tokas and Lambkin. "You will have our cooperation."

Corminar left out the end of that sentence, which was, to my mind, ". . . and nothing more."

As we left the building, I was sure I heard a voice whisper behind us.

"I'm sorry."

CHAPTER NINETEEN

Special Delivery

"There's kinda a lot going on."

When Corminar, Lore, and I had returned to the inn after our long day, we'd found the Trio tucking into a hearty meal—one that we joined them for without any hesitation. While they were fairly vague about their day in Coldharbor— telling us they'd just been "looking into a few things"—we'd given them the basics as to our own day.

We told them we hadn't found the Player responsible for the malae, but people around here knew of him. We told them we'd met a scientist, who'd turned out to have been an old friend of Lore's, and was looking into a cure for the mala-inflicted corruption. We mentioned taking down the local gang involved in the mala trade, leaving them for the guards. And we even mentioned running into a couple of other people we used to know, Lambkin and Tokas, but we left out the part about the latter's terrible betrayal; that would only have resulted in a lot of questions.

I'd thought until this point that it had been a productive day, but really we were no closer to finding Yusef, the Player seemingly responsible for the mala trade in the continent as a whole. Still, we'd done some small good, at least, in helping that mala-touched man to Alenna and by sorting out some black market traders. We'd earned our stew tonight.

Corminar and Lore left soon after dinner, neither of them having spoken much, really, since we'd left Tokas behind. Both of them were still chewing the matter over, and I supposed they had more history with Tokas than I had, excluding the part where she'd been there in Plainside the first time I'd died. This left me with Raelas, Carle, and Ama, though I'd just popped over to the bar to order a pint when I turned around to find that only the tiefling was left. Something told me she'd had a lot to do with the sudden disappearance of her friends.

I sat back at the table, opposite her, keenly aware of those bright red eyes upon me as I concentrated my attention on the beer instead. "You know I'm . . ." I started, realizing I was going to have to put to words why I was wary of Raelas's advances. "You know I'm kinda with someone, right?"

Raelas didn't look away for a second. "Yeah. Val, right? But where is she, cos I've been traveling with you for a week now and I haven't seen her." She brushed a lock of her hair behind a small, curly horn.

"We've been going through something."

"Wanna talk about it?"

I shook my head. "Not really."

Raelas smiled. "That's OK." From her tone, it seemed she meant it. Not that I was comparing her and Val or anything, but it was nice to be talking to someone who wasn't combative all the time. "You know, we found someone touched by malae today, too," she said, kindly changing the subject. "Came in through a gate."

"You get them to Alenna?"

The tiefling shook her head. "They were too far gone."

"Might not have been if we had a cure," I replied. I thought back to the malae we'd found in the traders' courtyard. We'd left them there, alive but firmly caged, as evidence of what the merchants were involved in, showing why we'd left them tied up. The guards would put two and two together and sentence the traders sufficiently for their crimes, as everybody in these parts knew what a mala was capable of. But maybe we should have taken one of the monsters with us, delivered it to Alenna to study, and make good on our deal.

Lore wouldn't have been on board with the idea. He'd already lost Plyas to the malae, and taking a living one to his only remaining childhood friend was a recipe for digging up past trauma. He didn't have to know about it, though.

"You wanna get out of here?" I asked Raelas.

The tiefling's eyes lit up. "What did you have in mind?" She didn't need to spell it out for me to know what she was implying.

"Not that," I said. "Instead . . . I was thinking we'd go steal something."

Raelas wasn't quite as excited by the prospect of theft as Val would have been, but she was still a willing participant. Though I got the impression that she was doing this only because I had asked, and—as she had suggested many times— because she thought this was a bit like a date.

The last time she mentioned this being like a date was while we were pressed up against each other in a tiny broom closet.

"What kind of dates do you usually go on?" I hissed back at her, and Raelas didn't quite get to reply because we heard the voices of guards approaching.

We'd followed Alenna's mala-locator stone to find where the city guards had taken the living evidence of the traders' crimes, and it had taken us to a smaller outpost not too far from the bazaar. What with three pairs of portals between us, as well as us both having leveled up the *Stealth* skill somewhat, it wasn't too hard for us to get inside. What *was* hard was getting to the right room, which just so happened to be the basement. We'd portaled our way inside, almost run afoul of guards *immediately*, and then darted for the nearest doorway, hoping for somewhere to hide.

And that brings us up to date, to the pair of us wedged into a broom closet, me pretending I couldn't smell Raelas's floral perfume and feel her fingertips resting gently on my forearm.

The guards seemed to come to a stop just outside the door, and—fearing that they were about to find need of a broom—I pointed my hand toward the ground. As Raelas repositioned herself closer still, I cast the spell, sending us falling through one portal and out into the darkness of the basement.

Stealth: +2,250XP

Stealth increased to level 23!
Stealth increased to level 24!
Base Points Gained: +2 DEX, +2 WIS, +4 Free Points (DEX/WIS)

"I can't . . ." I started, but Raelas had anticipated the complaint, and with a flick of her wrist she summoned a purple mote of light.

"One of those ability choices I made while you were busy speccing into portals," she said. We looked around the dimly lit basement at hundreds of crates of evidence, and I sighed. "Any ideas where they are?"

"If the guards were smart, they already killed them," I said, removing the locator stone from my pocket. "But then if they had . . . this wouldn't be working."

"You've got to let me borrow that at some point," Raelas said.

"To do some mala hunting?"

"Something like that."

I followed the glowing arrow on the stone as it pointed me across the room, toward a stack of familiar-looking crates by the door. The guards had just dumped them here, then. They should've known better.

But it was handy for me.

I picked up one of the crates and shook it slightly. Only when I heard a familiar squeaking noise from inside did I know that there actually was a monster inside.

"You got it?" Raelas asked.

I nodded, then passed her the crate to hold. "Careful."

"You worried about me?" the tiefling said with a smile.

I ignored her—clearly Raelas wasn't going to be put off, no matter what I said—and returned to the remaining crates of mala. I activated my *Ash Husk* ability, but just on one finger, and I used my smoldering fingertip to singe a message into the side of one of the wooden crates.

"*Burn me immediately*," Raelas read aloud.

"Think they'll get the message?"

"Dunno how they could miss it."

I knocked on Alenna's door a third time, on this occasion far louder than the ones before.

"Alright, alright," I heard a voice cry out from inside. "I'm coming. I'm coming. But this better be a real emergency. You better have corruption on your damn—" Alenna stopped talking when she swung her door open and saw me standing there with Raelas at my side, crate in hand.

"Fast-track delivery," I said. "Thought you wouldn't want to wait."

"You thought right, yeah," Alenna said. "Come in, come in." She practically yanked Raelas inside, her eyes on the crate in the woman's hands.

After I nodded, Raelas let the scientist take the crate from her hands.

"Oh, goodie! Been a while since I got my hands on a live one." Alenna looked up at me. "You've done good. This is gonna help a lot of people. But, can I ask . . ."

"Lore's fine," I replied, getting where she was going with the question. "I just didn't think he'd like me putting you in danger. Especially after what happened with . . ."

I trailed off, but Alenna said her name. "Plyas."

Raelas raised an eyebrow at this, but didn't ask. Good on her. Other people I knew—me included—would have asked without a moment's hesitation.

"You reckon you'll be able to find a cure with this?" I asked.

Alenna shrugged. "Could do . . . but that's the thing with science; you don't know how close you are to a breakthrough until you've actually . . . broken through. So I can't promise anything, but . . . yeah, it'll help."

"Alright," I said, turning away to leave the scientist to her work. "Glad to have helped. If there's anything else we can do . . ."

Raelas grabbed me by the arm as I was halfway out the door. "You forgot to ask for payment," she whispered.

"No, I—" I started, but Alenna called out behind me, cutting me off.

"You know," she said. "There is *one* more thing you could do to help . . ."

CHAPTER TWENTY

The Return of the Estat Order

"You went back to Alenna without me?" Lore asked.

We—the six of us; three Slayers, three Trio members—were sitting in the tavern once more, having some breakfast, and Lore and Carle were eating more than the rest of us combined. If I wasn't mistaken, there was a little friendly rivalry going on around who could eat more. Maybe they had some things in common after all.

I shrugged. "We couldn't sleep."

"We?"

Raelas waved to signal that she was the other half of "we," and Lore frowned to show that he wasn't a fan of that at all.

"A date?" the barbarian asked.

"Yes," Raelas said, at the same time that I said, "No."

Carle and Ama looked to one another, vaguely amused expressions on their faces. I got the impression then that I wasn't the first person Raelas had pursued aggressively in this way.

"Look," I said, "the point is: there's something else we can do to help her. She needs information. Experimenting on those touched by the malae is all well and good, but there's other related research out there that's already been done. She just needs to read it."

Lore's eyes lingered on Raelas for a moment. "OK, so where do we get this research for her, then?"

I mumbled the answer under my breath.

"What's that?" Ama asked.

I sighed. "From a library of the Estat Order."

". . . Ah," Lore replied; he'd been there the last time we'd had to deal with this lot.

"They are the librarians with the excessive late returns policy, yes?" Corminar asked. "Those with whom you two have tussled before?"

"They're the ones who kill you for late returns, yeah," I replied. "I . . . don't think we ever got to the bottom of why they do that, did we?"

Lore shrugged. "Maybe they're just a bit weird."

"'Just a bit weird' is putting sugar in your stew. Killing people for forgetting to return books is just a *little* bit passed that, don't you think?"

Carle raised an eyebrow. "A peculiar returns policy indeed. And they still get patronage?"

"I wonder if this policy isn't intended to discourage such a thing," the ranger replied.

Ama leaned forward, cutting through the rest of the conversation and steering us back to the most important aspect of the matter at hand. "And this job . . . it pays?"

"Yes, Raelas was quick to establish that."

The tiefling nodded enthusiastically.

"Is that all that matters to you?" Lore asked, with more irritation in the typically gentle man's voice than I was used to. "Saving people isn't its own reward?"

Ama smiled. "No reason we can't have two rewards!"

It was supposed to be a quick day trip. We'd leave Coldharbor in the morning, straight after our surprisingly tasty breakfast, and we'd head southwest to Fallenstone. We'd visit the ruins of the ancient city—in which a small town was beginning to form around the water well—and we'd track down the library. We'd go in, request the book in question, pray that this particular library was staffed by more reasonable people, and we'd head back in time for dinner.

That was the plan, anyway, but I had doubts about one part in particular: that these particular members of the Estat Order would be more reasonable than the last. They didn't have a good track record.

You'll be unsurprised to learn that it was Raelas who walked at my side as we traveled.

"You really won't tell me a little about your past?" she asked.

"What's there to tell? I stabbed some people, got stabbed a few times, and drank a lot of beer."

Raelas raised her eyebrows as we climbed up the latest sand dune along the traveler's road. "We both know there's more to you than that. You've killed Players, tried to stop an invasion—"

"*Failed* to stop an invasion," I corrected her, then glanced around to make sure Corminar wasn't in earshot; he wouldn't like the reminder.

"—and you've done all this without going past level nineteen. And don't think I haven't noticed that strange relic hanging around your neck."

I whipped my hand away from the Sisyphus Artifact, then tried to act casual about it. I could maybe trust the Trio with some details about our Player-killing, but I wasn't in any hurry to reveal the truth about the artifact—or the Player blood required to use it. It was time to change the subject. "Well, I don't exactly hear you volunteering anything about your own past."

"You haven't asked!"

"Consider this me asking."

Raelas smiled. "So, you're interested after all?"

I sighed; this woman could make something out of anything.

"So, Carle, Ama, and I, we've known each other forever. As far back as I can remember, at least. We grew up together on the streets of Oalem—no parents, no money, no prospects. Called ourselves the Trio since we were small. Had to steal food, find shelter where we could . . ." Raelas glanced over at me. "And I'm guessing that's all pretty familiar to you, too?"

I shrugged.

"See? Lots in common. Don't suppose this *Val* had to go through what we—"

At a glare from me, Raelas stopped midsentence.

"OK, OK. Sorry. Just thought it had to be said, is all. Anyway, one day some rich merchant comes to town. An elf, from the Dawnwood. She's visiting the local lords, and they all throw some huge feast in the palace gardens. We're not allowed in—nobody is—but we can see enough to know that there's too much food. It's going to go to waste. We're hungry—starving, maybe—and that food isn't going to get eaten. So, when the feast is winding down, we sneak in, and we try to reduce food waste.

"It's the merchant who caught us. She alerted the guards, and they catch me. I tell them we were just hungry, that we just thought nobody would mind. But they keep going on about how it's theft, like it's against the law so it must be morally wrong, too. No . . . what's the word?"

"Nuance?" I suggested.

"Not the word I was looking for, but it works. Nuance. Yeah. So they arrest me, and they want me to pay a fine to let me go. Carle and Ama don't have the money, obviously, and eventually the jailhouse gets too full and they let me go anyway. When I found the others, do you know what we swore?"

"That you'd try to feed the poor?" I asked. "Make sure nobody ever goes hungry again?"

Raelas laughed. "No. We swore that we would get filthy, filthy rich. At any cost. We swore *we'd* never go hungry again."

When we finally arrived in Fallenstone, the midday sun high in the sky above us and making me desperate not for beer, but for water, Lore grabbed me and Corminar by the arm. Though Ama watched with pursed lips and an unabashed raised eyebrow, none of the Trio tried to eavesdrop on whatever was going on here. From the familiar look on Lore's face, I had some idea.

"Another vision?" I asked.

He nodded glumly. "I was speaking with the Player we're after. Yusef. I was asking him about . . . about prophecy. About these visions. Like he was an expert."

"A vision about visions? Very cool."

But Lore didn't seem to find this funny. "What if . . . what if we shouldn't be here? These visions, they're supposed to get us to where Niamh wanted us, right? For that Council's plan to get done?"

"Are you saying we *shouldn't* kill a Player involved in a transcontinental mala trade?" I asked.

At this, he hesitated. ". . . No. Course not. I just . . . I dunno. Feels like we're . . ."

"Damned if we do, and damned if we don't, as you humans say," Corminar finished for him.

Lore nodded, sadness in his eyes.

I clasped the big guy around the shoulder. "Alright," I said. "I hear you. We'll think on it, yeah? Maybe there's a way to kill Yusef without helping the Council. And if there is, we'll find it."

Again, the barbarian nodded, but didn't seem reassured by this. Whatever he was seeing due to his own active effect, it felt very real to him. More real than I could imagine.

We returned to the others and fixed our attention on the library—which, as it turned out, hadn't been all that hard to find in a town of maybe fifty buildings.

"Alright," I said. "We know the plan. Corminar, Lore, Ama, and Carle, you're going in the front entrance. You'll ask for the book and hopefully the librarians will hand it over. And if they don't . . ."

"We're sneaking in the back anyway while they're distracted," Raelas said.

Raelas and I hurried around to the rear of the building while the rest of the team approached the front door. I picked a spot that *felt* like it would have nobody inside to spot us entering, but of course that was guesswork as I could see nothing. At least with my *Tamed Portals* passive, the portals wouldn't glow brightly; if we were quick enough, Raelas and I might be able to sneak inside even if there *were* people about.

"Ready?" I asked.

Raelas stepped in close. "Ready."

I opened a portal below our feet, and the other worldbender and I fell through. The moment we were out through the other end of the portal, inside the library, I cut off the spell and crouched toward the floor. Nobody immediately started crying out, which was a pretty good sign as far as breaking and entering went, and the only talking I could hear was on the other side of the building. Keeping still, I could hear that it was Corminar asking politely for the book in question.

Even better, I *had* picked a spot where there was nobody around. And there was nobody around because Raelas and I were surrounded by tall bookcases, full of—no points for guessing—books.

"Any idea how we find the one we want?" Raelas asked, echoing my own internal monologue.

I cast my eyes over the spines. "Looks like it's alphabetical by title."

"Must have taken them a while."

"Yeah, maybe we need to introduce these librarians to a hobby."

We moved down the aisle toward where the book in question should have logically been, and had to come to a sudden stop when an older tiefling man in a long robe glided by. I hadn't heard his footsteps at all—they were really serious about being quiet in libraries, huh?—but fortunately he seemed too absorbed in the book he held to notice us. Raelas and I remained deathly still as he passed through the junction ahead of us, not daring to move.

He drifted away, and I breathed a controlled sigh of relief.

"Alright, good," I said, turning to Raelas. "Now, let's—"

But the other worldbender had idly drifted her fingertips along the spines of the books. And neither of us had known that the shelves would be protected.

A layer of blue light rippled where Raelas had touched the books, and for half a second I thought we'd gotten away with it.

But then the siren blared.

Stealth: +1,650XP

Stealth increased to level 25!
Base Points Gained: +1 DEX, +1 WIS, +2 Free Points (DEX/WIS)
Ability Selection Unlocked
Select an ability from the list below:
. . .

The notifications were a sure sign that we'd now been spotted, and though I was excited to finally have another *Stealth* ability selection, it was going to have to wait.

Shouting erupted at the other side of the library, and the old librarian whipped around to face the source of the noise—us. He lowered his book to the safety of a nearby bookshelf.

Once again, we had to do battle with the Estat Order.

CHAPTER TWENTY-ONE

The Book Thieves

"Hi," I said to the librarian who'd spotted us, and in that same moment shouts erupted from the other side of the building. Corminar, Lore, Carle, and Ama had understood exactly what had happened and had thrown themselves into the fight I'd hoped to avoid—though I couldn't see them because rows of tall, heavy bookcases stood in the way.

The old librarian swung his hands up and together, and a blast of crackling blue energy shot toward us. Raelas shifted in front of me, catching the worst of the blast to the chest and sending her soaring backward into a bookcase. The unit wobbled but didn't tumble, and Raelas fell, winded, to the floor.

As the librarian moved to blast again, I dived to the left, behind the cover of the bookshelves that I knew the staff here wouldn't risk damaging.

. . . And the spell passed right through it without harming the books.

Lightning magicks caught me in the arm, burning the skin and making my muscles tense enough that I dropped the dagger I'd just drawn. I groaned as I spun to the floor, and I whipped a hand out just in time to stop myself from colliding with the wood nose-first. Using a quick portal, I collected my dagger from where it had fallen on the floor and tossed it through another portal above me before snatching it from the air. Quickly rearming myself was a useful case for portals that I'd only recently come to properly appreciate.

Having experience with these librarians of the Estat Order already, I knew how to fight them. Reaching up, I yanked a handful of heavy hardback tomes from the nearest shelf, and I tossed them toward the floor. After peering back around the corner at the charging librarian, I waited for him to attack again before countering with an attack of my own. As the librarian pushed his hands together, I opened a portal beneath the books on the floor and dumped them just in front of the enemy. The heavy books collided with the librarian's head and distracted him enough from the attack, just as a handful of metal spikes shot down the gap between the bookcases.

From another glance, I realized these were part of one of Ama's spells, and hadn't been aimed this way. She'd been fighting a librarian of her own, but had missed. It was a wonder she hadn't hit me in the process.

With the nearest librarian still staggering from my whole "dumping books on top of him" attack, I pressed the advantage. I charged toward him, dagger arching through the air.

But the librarian recovered as I approached, flinging another lightning attack at me. I veered to one side, avoiding the worst of the attack, but a groan behind me announced that I'd moved aside just to let Raelas get hit by it again.

"Oops! Sorry!" I called out.

Raelas responded with another groan.

Suddenly, Carle and Ama cried out, and I glimpsed them soaring backward through the next aisle between the bookshelves, apparently having been caught by another librarian's spell.

"Going alright over there?" I shouted to them.

"*Yes*," they groaned in unison.

As I shot forth once more, the librarian responded with another spell, and I regretted that I didn't have a *Throwing Knife* ability, which would have been perfect in this scenario. Instead, I settled for opening a portal beneath me and falling through it to avoid this latest attack, emerging from the portal's partner above the enemy. As I fell, I activated *Knifestorm*, spinning toward the ground and lashing out with my blades as I did so.

The old man cast a ward, but not before I'd slashed up his left shoulder some. As I bounced off the ward, the librarian nursed his fresh wounds, and I thought I glimpsed fear in his eyes.

"Artur!" the librarian shouted, presumably to one of his colleagues. "Activate the—" But neither the other staff member nor I heard the rest of this instruction, because I'd thought quickly enough to activate a spell of *Silence* around him.

I charged into this sphere of silence roaring, which of course was abruptly cut off as I entered the area of the spell's influence, and I arched my blade through the air toward the enemy.

The librarian responded by pushing his two hands forward, fingers splayed, and he summoned a magical ball between us. As this glowing blue sphere expanded, we were both blasted backward, outside the *Silence* area.

I ran immediately back into and through it, pushing my knife forward into a *Stab*, with all my weight behind it. I was just about to pierce flesh with knife-point when—

"Stop!" the librarian said holding his hands up in the air. "Stop! Stop."

I paused midstab, not quite sure what to do with this. I wasn't used to being asked to stop midfight. "What?" The others—friend and foe alike—also seemed to stop fighting, as evidenced by a break in the shouting, grunting, and fizzling noise of spellwork.

"Everything alright?" Lore called out from somewhere across the library.

Still with his hands in the air, the librarian continued, "It's clear you're stronger than me. Please, this doesn't need to end in blood."

"Stronger? I'm level nineteen." Though I'd said this, I was admittedly pretty pleased that someone considered me strong; it had been a while since that had happened.

"Do you think us librarians are really so blind?" the old man croaked. "We read, perhaps more than anyone else in the western continents. We know our history. We know that there are things more important than levels, than strong versus weak, than citizens versus Architects. We see what is happening out there, both far abroad and on our doorsteps. If there is a reason you need a book—a *good* reason, one that helps people—then we can bend the rules. We can make an exception."

I lowered my blade slowly, allowing my hand to fall to my side. Across the library, I saw another of the staff lowering their weapon, too.

"Well?" the librarian prompted me. "Is it? Is it for a good reason?"

"It's to help people."

"Tell me," the man said. "Which book?"

"*Elgar's Meditations on the Cosmic Barrier*," I replied, and then got ahead of the next question by adding, "No, I don't know what it's about, either."

The old librarian held my gaze for a moment, then retreated backward down between the bookshelves. Last time I was in one of these libraries, the fight had ended with me pushing over these bookshelves in a domino-like effect; if this man really was going to help me, then I'd make sure that didn't happen again. The librarian reached behind him and took a book from the shelf without looking, familiar enough with the layout of this dense library to have known exactly where the book in question would be.

He held it in his hands and made no attempt to approach. "Promise me."

"Huh?"

"You say you want to do good with this book. There's no way you can provide any evidence that this is true. So, I'll have to ask for the next best thing: a promise. Promise me that you will use the knowledge I give freely for good, not evil."

"It's for good," I said. "I promise. It's for a scientist. Someone who is trying to find a cure for the mala corruption. She thinks . . . she thinks that book holds the key. That's all."

Still, the librarian didn't approach, but Lore and Corminar shuffled over from across the library, nobody making any attempt to attack them.

"Do you know why we are forced to kill those who do not return these books?" the old man asked. "We take no joy in it. It seems almost absurd a policy, doesn't it?"

"Yep," Lore murmured.

"We kill because we have to. The books in here—many of them, at least—they contain knowledge which defies the laws of the System. Knowledge that, with prolonged exposure, can turn the strongest of us mad." He tapped the cover of the leatherbound book in his hands. "This one I catalogued, and so I know a little of its contents. It refers to the creation of wards—wards powerful enough to withstand practically anything. But they take their power from the soul. Elgar, who wrote the book? They disappeared after publishing, never to be seen again, though they left behind a house with messages scrawled on the walls. Messages scrawled in blood. You say you want to cure mala corruption, but I can't understand how this knowledge gets you there. So, I ask again: do you promise?"

The librarian held out the book in front of himself as he repeated this question, and I placed my hand on the book as I held his gaze.

"I promise," I said.

CHAPTER TWENTY-TWO

Flock

We left the library, spilling back out into the town of Fallenstone, and I couldn't help but be happy that we'd parted ways with the Estat Order on better terms this time. We'd damaged far fewer books, hadn't smashed in a window to escape, and in general there wasn't going to be as much of a cleanup job. That didn't stop the members of the Trio grumbling about it, however, each of whom thought libraries really shouldn't operate like that.

The six of us sat down on the side of the road, enjoying the shade of an old palm tree as we took a quick breather. I'll admit that I was the one who suggested doing so, and I'd suggested it purely because I had a *Stealth* ability to select.

Ability Selection Unlocked
Select an ability from the list below:

Option 1: Danger-Sense III (Stealth)—*Passive.* Your senses grow keener; you notice all but the most elaborate traps and ambushes.

I'd been offered a *Danger-Sense* ability twice before, since having to start my progression from scratch. And both times, I'd opted for something else instead. This wasn't to say I didn't think these abilities were valuable—back in my thievery days, I'd relied on this ability for almost every job—but were they as valuable as other options? Very possibly not, especially now that "item relocation" wasn't my day-to-day employment. I kept an open mind on this ability choice anyway, before shifting to the next one.

> **Option 2: Gentle Step (Stealth)**—*Passive.* Your footsteps are dampened on even the hardest of surfaces. Reduce noise of movement by 80 percent.

My initial reaction was that this option was a bit more useful. I had both *Stealth Attack* and *Execution* which massively improved my damage when I was unnoticed, and if I could disguise my presence further with an ability like this, that would make those other abilities even more viable.

I already had *Silence*, a *Worldbending* ability which completely eradicated sound within a bubble that I summoned, however there were few things in life more alarming than a spell bubble suddenly forming around you. This meant that the *Silence* ability was useful when I was trying to avoid combat, but less so when I was trying to sneak up on someone.

Taking *Gentle Step* would fix that, so it was top of my list so far, but there was still one ability choice left . . .

> **Option 3: Rogue's Instinct (Stealth)**—*Passive.* You have a 50 percent greater chance of noticing others who are using *Stealth* abilities.

This, my third and final option, was almost the inverse of *Gentle Step*. Instead of making it harder for others to notice me, it would make it easier for me to notice others. And that was tempting! With my health points being fairly limited as I hadn't invested much in Vitality, I was weak to a sudden, high-damage attack like an assassin might hit me with. I had *Warped Shield* which occasionally helped with that kind of thing, but it was far from enough.

And yet . . .

What was more likely? A scenario where I was sneaking up on someone else, or a scenario where someone else was sneaking up on me? Considering I was usually surrounded by at least two other members of the team, there was a clear answer.

> **Ability Unlocked**: Gentle Step

> **Gentle Step (Stealth)**: *Passive.* Your footsteps are dampened on even the hardest of surfaces. Reduce noise of movement by 80 percent.

As soon as it was done, I slapped my thighs and stood up. "Well?" I asked the others. "Ready to move?"

Corminar groaned. Yes, *groaned*. How far he'd fallen that he would make noises like that. "It is a long journey," he said. "And the sun is still high in the sky. Might we not rest for a moment longer?"

"It would be, but—" I started.

"I could go for a snack," Raelas volunteered, raising her hands. "Fighting is hungry work."

Lore nodded his agreement, as he always did when someone suggested eating.

"It's not a—" I tried again to explain myself, trying to reveal the trick I had up my sleeve to surprise them all with.

"Do you think they would serve grilled vegetable skewers?" Carle asked Lore. "I have a craving."

"He's on a low-fat diet," Ama explained.

"I'm trying to tell you that . . ." I tried for the third and final time, but this time I trailed off on my own, without anyone interrupting me. The reason? I'd glimpsed movement on the road at the edge of town—hundreds of people walking into Fallenstone, all wearing the same pale orange robes, and all the robes sporting the same emblem: a golden sun with a line through it.

The Cult of Ascendancy.

I took an unconscious step backward; never before had I seen so many in one place. These were dangerous people, people who believed in serving the Players above all else, who believed that if the world worshipped them enough, the Players might bring us with them to Olympus, the Ascended World, the land of the gods. This, of course, was the exact opposite of the Slayers' own cause, which wasn't so much about worshipping Players as it was about killing them.

"Guys . . ." I said, and everyone followed my line of sight. Both Corminar and Lore—knowing what this meant—stood, just in case we had a fight on our hands. Not that we'd be able to fight off hundreds.

We watched this group stroll into town, none of them slowing even for a moment.

I reached out and touched one of the cultists gently on the arm to get their attention; I couldn't help myself, I had to know.

"What is this?" I asked the stranger. "Where are you going?"

The cultist blinked down at my hand, and then looked me in the eyes. From his expression, I could tell he thought this was a ridiculous question. "It is Yusef," he said. "The Seer. He heads to Coldharbor; we pilgrimage to have our destinies read."

The man moved away, and I let my hand fall.

"What did he just say?" Lore asked. "Destinies read? Do you think he . . ."

"Has the powers of *Divination*," Corminar finished for him.

"You think that's why you've seen yourself asking him about your visions?" I asked Lore, forgetting about the presence of the Trio for a moment.

"His what?" Ama asked, but the three of us ignored her.

"Forget Lore's visions," Corminar said. "If this Yusef has the gift of foresight, then there are broader complications."

I nodded. "Maybe he sees us coming. And then what hope do we have of killing him?"

THE HERO SLAYERS TEMPT FATE

"Wait, you want us to kill someone who can *see the future*?" Raelas asked, standing and arriving at my side. "We didn't sign up for this. No reward is worth dying for."

"Depends on the reward," I replied, unconsciously touching the Sisyphus Artifact that hung from my neck. I'd died for that, and I'd do it again, given the choice; it had gotten me out of plenty of trouble already, and even better: it still had a charge in it. I could die again.

"No," Ama said, standing as well. "No, we're out. We'll help you stop the mala trade, sure, for the right money, but we won't go up against a diviner."

Corminar shook his head. "There is no stopping the trade without killing him. He is a Player, a Council member, a man with near unlimited resources at his disposal. If he remains alive, then anything of the trade we undo, he will build back. We must kill him."

"He's right," I said, finally tearing my eyes away from Yusef's pilgrims and facing down the Trio. "We have to kill him. If you want to run, fine. Run. But we will succeed. This is what we do: we find Players, we find ways of killing them, and you know what we do next?"

"We actually kill them," Lore said.

I pointed to him to signify that this was the correct answer. "They said Yusef is heading to Coldharbor. He's not there yet. We have a head start—we can return, and we can prepare a trap."

"While I do agree with this course of action," Corminar said, "I must stress that we are the best part of a days' journey from Coldharbor; he may beat us there."

And then, I smiled. "You know, back when we were fighting the mala traders, I got a new *Worldbending* skill. A really, really handy one. One called *Saved Portals*, which allows me to specify a certain location where I can always open a portal, from any distance."

I flicked my wrist, and a portal appeared in front of us.

"Before we left, I made sure to do so."

With that, I stepped through the portal and emerged half a world away. One by one, the team followed me, appearing at my side on the grand staircase that led up to Coldharbor's house of government, that overlooked the city's central square. Hundreds of people looked on, curious, as we appeared among the crowds, but none were so interested that they gave us more than a second look.

"Now," I said, "shall we get to work?"

Arzak

"Mm," Arzak grunted. "Orange not my color."

She and Val had donned the robes of the Cult of Ascendancy in an effort to hide in plain sight. Of course, Yusef's pilgrims had thus far shown them only acceptance, welcoming the orc and the human into their midst without so much as batting an eyelid, and making any attempts at stealth largely unnecessary. But this was now; would that change once Yusef was dead?

For the witch's part, she pulled off the orange robes as well as she did everything else—something that Val reminded Arzak of far too often. It was frustrating to dress for the orcish build and her pallid green skin tone, at least while observing human and tiefling fashion senses.

Arzak looked down and pulled on the waist of her robes, pulling it taut. The orange hue nearly perfectly matched the smooth sides of the surrounding sand dunes, as though this particular dye was chosen in an attempt to blend in. This wasn't the real explanation, of course; it couldn't be, not when the pilgrims otherwise made every attempt to be seen and attract others to their cause. No, instead Arzak suspected there was a spiritual meaning behind this chosen color. In the eyes of the Players, those of this world were as meaningful and as consequential as grains of sand—this color was an effort at humbling the self.

The warrior tried to communicate this theory to Val, but as ever this was too complex a concept for the clumsy common tongue. Instead, she settled on saying only, "Hate it."

"Well, it's an assassination attempt, not a fashion show, Arzak," Val replied, her eyes on the masses of pilgrims huddled in the shade of the cliff.

"You think we close?"

The witch cast her eyes again over the crowds, and Arzak could tell that Val had just now seen what she'd seen. The looser body language, the smiles, the twinkling in the eyes—there was excitement here. Anticipation. A sense that they were close to the supposed prophet.

"Not long now," Val said. "We ready?"

Arzak nodded. Would the other pilgrims stare on at them now and notice that they stood away from the rest of the group? Would they see that there was something different about the orc and the human? Would they recognize that they were not true believers?

And even if they did see all that, could they ever imagine what the orc and the human would do next? Only one person involved had the gift of foresight, and that was the Player himself. Arzak could only hope that she and Val would seem inconsequential enough that Yusef didn't read their futures . . . and foresee his own death.

Yusef possessed a humble godliness.

Unlike the other Players that Arzak had encountered over the years, this man did not surround himself with gold and fine threads and all the other trappings of extreme wealth. Instead, he dressed as a humble man, even Arzak's new robes seeming finer than those he wore. At least, that was as far as Arzak could tell at this distance.

They were two days' journey south of Zelas, among the foothills of the Ullite mountain range, their steep, orange spears seeming to pierce the heavens in the backdrop of Yusef's makeshift stage. The Player proselytized to a silent audience—never before had Arzak seen so many so enchanted by the words of one man that they wouldn't speak—and he spoke of the Ascended World. The supposed prophet knew his audience.

"It is a world where each soul has the freedom to achieve a better life. It is a world where the hardest of workers are rewarded with riches beyond their wildest dreams. A world of social mobility, of opportunity, of accessible heaven."

"If it's so good, why did they leave?" Val murmured, echoing Arzak's own doubts. Already, Yusef had proven himself not to be trusted; his words conflicted with Niamh's own testimony—that their home world was destroyed—and she had been a woman with no reason to lie. This man, however, wielded hope as a weapon; if those who followed him worked hard, and did his bidding, then maybe they, too, would be rewarded. This was a far more dangerous weapon than any sword, or any spell.

"Now we know he a liar," Arzak summarized.

The sermon went on for hours, this Yusef enjoying the sound of his own voice a touch more than was healthy. When finally the Player ceased his talked of the Ascended World, he made the offer that the pilgrims had spoken of. He offered to read their futures.

This was the moment that Arzak and Val had been waiting for. They didn't want their futures read, of course. Even if they *hadn't* been intending to kill the Player, Arzak didn't imagine anything good could come of that foresight. When they had put the other Slayers behind them, Lore had been struggling with this very issue, and it hadn't seemed to be doing him any favors.

Instead, the pair skirted around the crowd, using their robes to blend in with the other pilgrims, those who weren't here to kill the man being worshipped. They slipped through the crowd slowly, taking their time, making sure only to push forward where there were gaps, rather than risking attracting any unwanted attention. The reading would last hours, so the pilgrims said, and so they had time. They needed to be patient.

As one by one the pilgrims were shown their destinies, Arzak and Val slipped through to the front of the crowd. The enemy was a hundred yards away, then fifty, then twenty, and then . . . almost within their grasp.

Arzak turned to Val, who nodded. It was time.

The orc placed a hand on the knife hidden underneath her robe, one commissioned exclusively for this purpose. It was a dagger in the orc's eyes, but large enough for the smaller races that it was considered a *One-Handed* weapon—and therefore Arzak could put all her lifetime of progression behind it. It had, too, a specialist enchantment, one created by an old friend of Val's called Steve—a peculiar man, though the orc kept that view to herself. This enchantment would replicate something Arzak had seen of Styk's progression; it would deal significantly higher damage if the user went unnoticed.

Which is what led them to this moment. To Arzak and Val slipping forth from the crowd, their eyes on the Player's back, to a glorified knife sliding forth from its sheath and arcing through the air, to an expectation that they would put down this Player before they could do even more damage to the world Arzak called home.

Yusef spun where he stood, bringing forth no weapon nor the blue glow of sorcery. Instead, he attacked with the only power he seemed to possess: *Divination*. A ball of yellow magicks shot forth from his hand, catching Arzak in the chest. For a moment, she expected to be sent flying backward, but instead the spell washed over her like a warm shower.

"I will—" Arzak started, and then the vision began.

Familiar black eyes stared back at Arzak, that color unusual even for a tiefling.

Tokas looked up at her, those dark eyes communicating . . . what? Sadness? Regret? Anger? Arzak could only see it as some combination of the three.

The tiefling was close, almost touching her. "It had to be this way," she said.

Only then did Arzak blink and look down at the knife, pierced through her thick flesh, her rib cage, her heart.

Tokas twisted. "It . . . had to."

What more could Arzak expect of her oldest friend, these days, than betrayal?

Arzak collapsed to the ground, the horror of what she'd been forced to foresee washing over her. Tokas's first betrayal had been bad enough, making the orc loathe to trust anyone again—a cynicism that had led to her finding out the truth about Styk and the Sisyphus Artifact, even before Val.

But even that first betrayal could not come close to this.

Tokas, her oldest friend, would be the one to end her life. Tokas—the woman she'd treated like a sister. Tokas—the woman who Arzak had pulled back from the brink of oblivion.

As the orc lay paralyzed on the ground, she felt her heart break. She couldn't bring herself to react to the crowd of orange descending on Val, restraining her with hands and spells. Even when one of the pilgrims brought forth a knife, Arzak could only manage numb acceptance.

It was the Player, not her, who would end up saving Val's life.

"No," Yusef said, staring down at Arzak but speaking to his flock. "There is no need for violence. Given time, all will see the light."

CHAPTER TWENTY-THREE

Visions & Strength

While Corminar led the Trio to Tokas and Lambkin in preparation for the Player's imminent arrival, Lore and I took our borrowed—and *cursed*—library book to Alenna. This meant that they could get the introductions out the way without us, and I was almost sad to miss that; I kind of wanted to see how Corminar would manage introducing Tokas.

I imagined him introducing Tokas to the Trio as follows: *This is Tokas. She was blackmailed by a Player over the death of her children to stand idly by while he slaughtered dozens of people, and blackmailed all her friends in the process. We will now be working with her.*

For the record, I couldn't imagine introducing Lambkin was going to be much easier: *This is Lambkin. He is a disillusioned ex-guard who thought that a level 2 person was responsible for the devastation of Plainside, rather than believe a Player could be involved. Yes, we know he's an idiot.*

And finally, there was the Trio: *These three are the Trio. We still don't really know what they're about just yet, to be honest, just that they have a dumb name for their team.*

For a moment, I considered parting ways with Lore to catch up with them, but a glance at him stopped me in my tracks. From the expression on his face, I could see he was seeing another vision of the future, and from the grimacing I could tell that it was another bloody one.

"Anything fun?" I asked.

"You were thinking about going to join the others, weren't you?" Lore replied.

"How could you tell?"

"These visions, I don't think any of them are certain to happen. In fact, I think I only see them when people are about to make important decisions."

I raised an eyebrow. "And leaving you to hang out with an old friend is an important decision?"

"Apparently. You leaving me now causes Arzak to die."

I stopped in my tracks. "Arzak? Was Val there?"

Lore shrugged. "I dunno. It's the first I've seen of them."

I tried pressing him further on the matter, but he wouldn't budge. Whatever he'd seen was—again—bloody enough that he didn't want to dwell on it.

When the scientist opened the door to find her old friend there, she wrapped her arms around him in a big hug, and Lore didn't seem to mind that her hands were covered in blood.

"Another one?" I asked.

Alenna hesitated for a moment, then realized I was referring to her bloody hands. "Ah. Yeah. More every day. No luck sorting out the mala problem, then, I'm guessing?"

Lore shrugged. "A bit of luck, but we ain't there yet. Disassembled the local trading group, or one of them, but . . ."

"But there's a lot more out there," Alenna finished for him.

"Yeah."

The scientist turned to me. "You got it? The book?" She paused for a moment before adding, "Or anything else?" I knew exactly what she was referring to; she was asking if we had any more mala bodies for her to dissect, but she didn't want to spell it out in front of Lore.

I waved the book in the air in answer, and Alenna hurried us in. I noticed Lore tried to keep his eyes off the body on the stone plinth in the center of the room. For my part, however, I couldn't help but stare. Alenna had made incisions all around the dead woman's body but primarily around the neck and shoulders. Whatever she'd been trying to do, clearly it hadn't worked.

We followed Alenna upstairs and away from the metallic scent of spilled blood. In her living quarters, she began brewing a batch of the local, earthy drink, and I took a seat at the table, placing the book down in front of me.

"So this'll help, will it?" I asked, nodding to the book.

"Can't promise anything, but yeah, I think it will."

"Lenn . . ." Lore started.

"Yeah?"

"The guy in the library said that this book was about soul-powered wards."

The tiefling nodded. "Yep, that's the one."

"I . . ." Lore said, again hesitantly.

I hurried this conversation along. "He's asking how that's gonna help."

Alenna sighed. "It's about using the malae's own . . ." She trailed off, apparently rethinking her explanation. "You know much about the history of the Beached Armada? I'm talking back in invasion times."

"History isn't my strongest subject," I replied.

Lore turned to me. "What *is* your strongest subject?"

"Sociology."

The barbarian's face didn't move; he didn't know quite what to make of that.

Alenna got us back on track. "OK, right, so. The tiefling locals weren't always here, right? They came from well out west, from islands that there isn't even a name for in the common tongue. They were a naval empire, and they spread and they spread and they spread until . . ."

"They ran out of sea?" I suggested.

The scientist pointed at me. "Exactly. When they got to these continents, they found landmasses that stretched for an eternity north and south, and they couldn't go around them. So what we nowadays call the Beached Armada is . . . a beached armada. A navy forced into fighting a land war. A war we shouldn't have won.

"But there's this old tiefling concept about using your enemy's strength against them, and that's the only reason that the tiefling empire actually . . . *won*. These locals, back then, they were stronger. They were used to fighting on land, and they knew the area, which is, you know, pretty important when you're fighting in a desert."

"Ooh!" Lore said excitedly, understanding where this was going. "Water! Water sources."

"Water sources, yeah. The locals knew where they were, and the tieflings didn't. That was their enemy's greatest strength. So the empire sent out scouts all across the continents. They climbed the Ullites, found the source of the streams and the rivers, and they . . . poisoned them all with their magicks. Really, we as a people should carry a lot more guilt with us than we do, but other people don't know their history like I do. History is fun, though? When it's not about poisoning people, at least."

"Yeah, probably worth specifying that last bit," I said.

"The point is, that's how the old empire won. That was how they always won. Now, I'm not saying that what they were doing was *good*, by any means. But you'd be a fool to think it wasn't *effective*. They won far more often than they lost, and it all came back to that one central idea: use your enemy's strength against them. *That*, in a nutshell, is what I want to do with the mala problem. With the corruption. I want to use the malae's power against them. This is the only way we can win. And we must, *must*, win."

Her eyes drifted to Lore, and I could see the pain within them that spoke of their shared loss—of Plyas, lost to the malae. That was Alenna's driving force here; she'd already lost too much to these monsters.

". . . Does that answer your question?"

Lore and I glanced at one another. "Not really," we both said at once.

Again, the tiefling smiled. "It will. In time. Trust me."

Lore looked as satisfied by this answer as I was. That is, not at all satisfied. "Just . . . be careful, will you, Lenn? The librarian said the guy who wrote the book went mad. Said the book's cursed. Once you've gotten the info you need, you'll put it down, yeah? You'll let us take it back to the Estat Order?"

Alenna approached the barbarian's side and squeezed his shoulder. "After all this time, it still surprises me that you're a big softy."

"Promise you'll be careful," Lore said, not letting the point drop.

The scientist smiled. "I'll be careful. I promise."

Lore breathed a sigh of relief. "Good. Now . . ." He gestured to the empty cup in front of him. "Where's the loo?"

While Lore stepped away, I took the opportunity to ask Alenna about the mala that Raelas and I had secretly delivered to her. "Did it help? What we . . ." I left the rest unsaid, just on the off chance Lore could still hear.

Alenna smiled. "Every step is a step forward."

From that, all I could take was that she was moving in the right direction with her research; hopefully the delivered book would help more. All this science stuff was beyond me, but I trusted her—Lore was a good judge of character after all, and if Alenna said she was getting there, then I believed her.

But with the number of mala attacks growing, even with the work we'd been doing . . . I just hoped she wouldn't be too late.

CHAPTER TWENTY-FOUR

Setting the Trap

When Lore and I arrived at the house where Tokas and Lambkin were staying, we found that the introductions were well and truly complete. Lambkin, Corminar, and Raelas stood bent over a map of the city, Tokas and Carle were reading books on the *Divination* skill tree, and Ama was . . .

"Where's Ama?" Lore asked.

"In the other room, with the kids," Raelas replied.

". . . Traumatizing them?" I asked.

The tiefling blinked at me. "Playing with them. She likes children."

"I didn't think that woman liked *anything*."

Lore and I shuffled over to the table, and the sketched map of the city thereon. "What we thinking?"

"Unlike in Sunalor, we do not have the forces to make use of the city walls," Corminar said, apparently having put his "Lieutenant Cladenor" hat back on for the first time since the fall of his homeland. He was thinking like a leader, at least. "The defensive nature of this city—though nothing like that of the Dawnwood capital—is useless to us without a great number of allies. Instead, we search for an area to which we might lure the Player. One where we might spring a trap."

I nodded. "Alright. Where are you thinking?"

"We don't know," Lambkin answered.

"Less alright."

"We are open to suggestions, Styk."

I studied the map further. There was the main square, outside Coldharbor's house of government, with the high staircase overlooking the rest of the plaza, and where I had my *Saved Portal* ability set to. But would high ground help us here? Otherwise, there were the markets—we could potentially use the chaos of the hubbub to our advantage, but then . . . maybe Yusef was used to that environment? And then there were the rooftops, a potential arena away from the locals and collateral damage. Here, maybe Raelas and I could use our portals to the team's advantage, shifting us around from rooftop to rooftop and keeping ourselves out of harm's way.

I couldn't answer, and the reason was simple: we just didn't know enough about our enemy. We didn't know how strong he was, we didn't know what abilities he had. All we really knew was that he could foretell the future in some way, though even that we didn't know the limitations of.

"I don't know, either," I finally admitted. "With what little we know about Yusef, how can we know what plan would work best? If I had to choose now, then maybe the rooftops? Raelas and I could use portals to move us all around, while we limit the movement of the enemy. But for all we know, the Player can jump thirty feet in the air."

"I'm game if you are," Raelas said.

Corminar nodded. "We will pencil in the rooftops of the southwestern district until such a time as we have a better plan."

"Perhaps we need to take a step back, here?" Lambkin asked.

Lore took a step back from the table. "I don't see how this helps."

"Not . . . not literally. I mean, maybe we're approaching this the wrong way. Styk is right; what do we really know about this Yusef? We know he is strong, that he has earned the loyalty of the Cult of Ascendancy, that he has some affinity for *Divination*, but how might we overcome such power, regardless of location?"

Lore's eyes lit up. "We turn his strength against him."

Raelas looked up at him with recognition in her eyes; she, too, knew her Armadan history.

I nodded. "Yes. But how? The Cult of Ascendancy has so many people by now that surely we can't hope to get close to him. We'd need to either separate him, or . . ." I trailed off as an idea came to me.

"You got something, handsome?" *someone*—no points for guessing—asked.

"Yusef's strength is in the number of cultists. But the weakness is that he can't possibly know them all. What if we found some of their robes? We blended in? We could get close to the enemy without him even knowing we were there." It was my thieving past coming in handy again; surely nobody else on the team would have thought of this. Well, Val might have done, but she wasn't here.

"You're saying we assassinate him?" Raelas asked.

"But he's a Player," Tokas piped up from across the room. "He will be too strong. How can we deliver so much damage so quickly?"

"We'd need to strike all at once, yeah," I said. "Our strongest attacks. Maybe some new weapons, and poisons. I don't know all your classes, so I leave that up to you to figure out your strongest attacks. But for me—"

"Oh," Lambkin said.

"Oh?" the elven ranger asked.

"Yes, *oh*. I just thought of something."

We waited for a moment for him to continue, before I prompted, "Are you gonna tell us, or . . . ?"

"The mala trader group. The one that Tokas and I were infiltrating? They were armed to the teeth. I don't know who was providing such powerful weaponry, but—"

"The Player," Corminar and I said at once, before the elf continued, "He would want those trading in the malae to be able to protect themselves. He would know the value in protecting his trading organization."

Lambkin nodded. "The point is: they had weapons. Weapons that we can use. Weapons we might turn against the Player, in the spirit of turning his strength into weakness."

"We should head back to the markets," Tokas said. "We should retrieve the weapons before—"

But Lambkin shook his head. "The guards will have already seized the cache. They will be selling the weapons for some 'under the table' coin. A guard salary isn't sufficient; trust me, I'd know."

"So we gotta steal the weapons from the guards?" Lore asked. "If Val was here, she'd love that. Loves a heist."

"Alright," I said, returning us to the task at hand. As we'd been discussing, Ama had returned from the other room and was standing in the doorway. "Disguises and weapons. What else? We need more than this if we're definitely gonna win this one. We've gotta have enough of an advantage that we can kill the Player even if he *can* see us coming with his magicks."

Tokas threw her book to the sofa and joined us at the table. "You've got to remember, Lambkin and I weren't here just to kill him. We were here to expose him, to turn others against him and his kind. This should still play a part in our strategy; the more allies we have . . ."

"The better chance we have," I finished for her. A couple of weeks ago I *really* wouldn't have expected to be planning a slaying at Tokas's side, but here we were. The enemy of your enemy really was your ally after all. Once this was over, though . . . Well, it was hard to put my memories of the devastation of Plainside behind me. If Tokas was after redemption, then that was going to be a long, long journey.

I nodded. "OK, good. We have a plan. Let's—"

Lambkin raised his hand, and at that moment I realized all eyes were on me. Somehow, I had fallen into the role of the team's leader; everyone else looked to me for confirmation. ". . . Yeah? You don't need to raise your hand, you know. You can just speak."

"I didn't want to interrupt."

"Lambkin, pretty much all we do on this team is interrupt each other."

"It's a bit rude, though."

I shrugged. "No argument there. You got something else?"

"It's what Toke just said," he replied. Toke? Were they on a nickname basis now? I hadn't realized they'd grown so close. "About having more allies." He looked over to Raelas and Carle, who were standing to my right. "I hope you don't mind me saying, but you three are mercenaries, right?"

"Why would we mind you saying that?" Raelas asked, not realizing that Lambkin was honorable enough to think *mercenary* was a dirty word.

"You're here for the money," Lambkin said. "Whatever Styk and the team are offering you."

We *really* needed to figure out where the payment we'd promised to the Trio was going to come from.

"And that's fine. We can use all the allies we can get. But why not reach out for more? Over the past two months, Tokas and I have seen no end of mercenaries traveling through Coldharbor. We should use them in this fight."

"Ooh, time for some networking," Raelas said excitedly. "It is nice to meet others in the business."

"And who's gonna pay them?" I asked. "Because I don't have any money." I hesitated, feeling Ama's eyes on me. ". . . Besides what we're gonna pay the Trio, obviously."

"I have been siphoning money from the traders since I joined. I thought stealing from them would be the honorable thing to do, though I have not spent a penny of it. Who could justify spending money earned from mala trading?"

Lore nodded thoughtfully.

"I will pay for aid out of this pot. Mercenaries, yes, but enchanters, too. Anyone who might give us an advantage."

"You're right," I said, realizing this was a departure from how the Slayers usually worked. "We shouldn't just keep this to ourselves. Everything we can get, we should use. Lambkin, you lead us to the guardhouse. We'll steal the weapons from there. Afterward, you begin recruitment while the rest of us steal Ascendancy robes and begin to sow dissent among the cultists. Everyone on board with that?"

There was a murmur of agreement before people began to grab their jackets and weapons. Only Lore stood still, raising his hand, having picked up Lambkin's bad habit.

"Yeah?" I asked.

"What if the Player gets here before we're done?"

"We better hope he doesn't. And we better hurry."

CHAPTER TWENTY-FIVE

Cash for Cache

Lambkin led us across the city of Coldharbor to the guardhouse nearest where the mala traders had been set up. The plan was simple: he would sweet-talk the guards, acting as though we were interested in buying the recently acquired weapons cache, and by doing so he'd learn its location. As soon as we knew where it was, the rest of the team would portal in and steal it.

It was a pretty straightforward plan, but that was what the situation deserved; Lambkin said the guardhouse wasn't going to be equipped with traps or anything, so this plan would do just fine. After all, them having acquired the cache to sell under the table wasn't *strictly* by the book. Or, you know, not at all by the book.

When we arrived outside the guardhouse, Lambkin and Raelas approached the woman in uniform out front, and the rest of us stayed back, in the cover of shadows. We watched in silence as Lambkin and Raelas charmed the guard, Corminar shifting uncomfortably from side to side, apparently still thinking *he* should have been the one to go over. We awaited the moment that Raelas would make her excuses and come over to us to tell us where the cache was, but . . .

That didn't happen.

Instead, the pair of them turned away from the guardhouse looking dejected, and I felt dread hanging heavy in my gut. "What is it?"

"They've sold them already," Lambkin said.

"All of them?"

"All of them."

"Yeah," Raelas added. "Lammy wasn't kidding about there being a lot of mercenaries coming through here; apparently some bought up all the weapons within about an hour. Sounds like the guards underpriced them, though, so maybe that's got something to do with it."

"They wouldn't have experience with high-strength weaponry. Their swords, their bows, they are all simple and unenchanted. I should have realized. I should have suggested we come sooner." The man looked genuinely disappointed in himself.

There was another option, though. "You know where they went? These mercenaries?"

Lambkin hesitated, then turned away and approached the guard once more. Another minute later, after some coin had changed hands, the ex-captain returned with more of a smile on his face. "They're staying in a camp outside the western gate, she said. If we hurry, we might catch them."

And so it was that the seven of us—yes, *seven*, I counted; everyone but Tokas was here, who had been unable to find someone to watch the kids so last minute—traversed the city and poured out the western gate. Carle was the one who spotted the mercenary camp first, being one of us who knew what to look for. I wasn't sure what made him so confident that one particular camp was the mercenary camp, but he seemed sure. I put it down to there being some signs that someone was a mercenary that was imperceptible to me but very obvious to someone in the industry.

We took shelter behind a sand dune not too far from the camp, and Corminar and I crawled slowly to the top of it, to peek over.

"Seventeen," he said.

"What?"

"There are seventeen of them. There are only seven of us. That means there are ten more of them than there are of us."

"I can do simple math, Cor."

"You have said the opposite in the past."

"No, I—" I stopped myself. "Forget it. You see the weapons?"

The elf's eyes were naturally keener than mine, so of course he'd seen them already. "The tent to the northwest," he said. "It is the only one guarded; the others must be sleeping quarters. May I ask if you have any thoughts on how we retrieve the weapons?"

"Could portal them?"

"You can't portal *everything*, Styk."

"I can bloody well try."

Corminar sighed. "And when this plan fails, they will be alerted to our presence. You do not know that the crates would fit through your portal. You do not know if the tent is warded against magicks. There are too many unknowns for 'portal it' to be plan B, let alone plan A."

"You're no fun sometimes."

"It is more important to be right than to be fun."

I almost replied with *Sunalor changed you, Corminar*, before realizing that was probably a bit much. I kept it to myself, instead opting for, "OK, what's your plan, then?"

There was no reply.

"You don't have one, do you?"

"I am considering."

"Considering what?"

"Considering our options."

"And what are they?" I asked.

"Perhaps if you give me a moment, I will determine the answer to that very question."

I turned my attention back to the camp in front of us. This was a large group of mercenaries, far more than I'd been expecting. What was the need for so many? Ousting rogue leaders? Clearing infested dungeons? I could see why they'd need to buy so many new weapons, at least.

A large handful of the mercenaries were building a fire in the middle of the camp, preparing for the sun to set. Their body language was casual, unworried; they didn't think anyone would plan to attack them, that anyone who did would be foolish to do so. Maybe we *were* foolish, but I really, really wanted that weapons cache.

"A distraction," Corminar said.

"That's what you've come up with? A distraction? That's like textbook stuff."

"I didn't know you read textbooks."

I ignored him. "Any thoughts on what that distraction could be?"

"Someone could insult them and then run away."

I hesitated, not sure if he was joking.

"I am not joking," he clarified, anticipating my reaction. "Unless you have a better idea, I think drawing as many of the enemies away would be our best approach."

With a sigh, I nodded. I really didn't have any better ideas this time—which is pretty shocking, really, considering I was supposed to be good at this kind of thing. "Alright. Who should . . ." I started, and then we both said at once, "Raelas."

We shuffled away from the peak of the dune and then hurried, crouching, to the rest of the team's side.

"Alright, we have a plan," I said. "Raelas, you're going to insult them. Be really creative. *Really* creative. We want as many of them chasing after you as possible."

"Wait, how many are they? How many are gonna be chasing me?" the tiefling replied.

"Seventeen, if possible," the elven ranger answered.

"*Seventeen?*" Raelas replied, eyebrows raised. "I don't think I can outrun seventeen different—"

"Portals," I whispered to her.

"Oh yeah."

"Happy?"

"Kiss on the cheek for luck?" Raelas replied.

"No."

"Fine." The tiefling drew a deep breath, then scurried off around the encampment to the other side, so that she'd be drawing the attention away from us. Corminar and I returned to our places, poking our heads over the top of the dune, and waited for Raelas to do the honors.

When the tiefling finally stepped out into the open, she cupped her hands around her mouth and shouted the most horrific, appalling things I have ever heard in my life. They were so creatively nasty—creative because she completely avoided any discriminatory language—that I don't think I can even repeat them here. Suffice to say, I was taken aback by it and Corminar's mouth hung open in surprise.

And the insults were good enough to draw away a good handful of the mercenaries, leaving only nine for us to deal with. In an ideal world, she would have drawn them all away, but these soldiers for hire were sensible enough not to leave their camp completely unprotected; eight going after one woman would surely be enough, from their perspectives.

"Eight," Corminar said.

"Yes, I can count."

We watched as Raelas turned and ran, and we waited until the departing mercenaries were far enough away that they wouldn't hear any fighting back at their camp. At that point, the elf and I rose to our feet, and the rest of the gang charged up the dune behind us.

The team knew the order—incapacitate, don't kill. These mercenaries hadn't done anything wrong, as far as we knew. Even stealing from them was a bit unkind, really, but I'd justified that because it was to take down a Player—and their mala-breeding operation.

As we charged into the fight, I hoped everyone had taken this instruction to heart . . .

CHAPTER TWENTY-SIX

The Trouble with Mercenaries

I made a beeline straight for the weapons cache while the others occupied the mercenaries.

Sadly, though, our enemies weren't quite on board with this plan. One of them—a tall woman who I'd expected from her solid build to be a barbarian—pushed herself into my way, and activated a warding spell. I bounced off the shimmering blue bubble into the air, though not high enough that I had time to open a portal before crashing into the sand.

I tumbled head over heels once before whipping a leg out to steady myself, and then I charged toward the woman who'd attacked me as the rest of the gang dealt with enemies of their own.

The woman raised her hands to prepare another ward, but I knew what was coming, this time. As I closed the gap on the mage, I opened a portal in front of me and leaped through it, appearing behind the enemy before she knew I was there. Once there, I took a page from Lore's book, bringing the butt of my knife down into the back of the woman's head—to render her unconscious, not kill her. With both my *Stealth Attack* and *Execution* abilities, I did enough to drop the woman to the sand in only one hit.

Level 19 Lightwarder defeated!

Worldbending: +1,050XP
Knifework: +1,300XP
Stealth: +750XP

But there were still others to deal with.

I whipped my head around, searching for who to attack next. Lambkin, who was most effective at range, was rapidly being encroached upon by a man wielding two swords. Before long, he would be in trouble.

I opened a portal beneath my feet and dropped through it without looking, appearing in the air above the dual-wielding enemy. As I fell, I activated the very same abilities that would boost my damage, and slammed the butt of the knife into the man's head. Again, they fell in one hit—though in part that was because this enemy already had some tactically placed arrows in him, each of them coated in poisons of drowsiness.

Level 22 Blade of Urcat defeated!

Worldbending: +1,900XP *Worldbending increased to level 56!* **Base Points Gained**: +2 INT, +2 Free Points (INT/WIS/CHA)

Knifework: +1,450XP *Knifework increased to level 41!* **Base Points Gained**: +1 DEX, +1 STR, +2 Free Points (VIT/DEX/STR)

Stealth: +700XP

"Just like that?" Lambkin asked.

"Just like that."

"You're stronger than your level suggests."

I cast my eyes around the battleground as I replied to him. "That's what an efficient build will do. How many level nineteen people do you know with a level fifty-five skill?" Spotting two enemies approaching Ama, I left Lambkin without hearing his reply, once again falling through a portal to arrive behind one of the enemies.

I once again arced my blade through the air to knock the enemy out, but even with my *Gentle Step* passive, they noticed me joining the fray. The enemy twisted to block my attack with their forearm, and though I still caught them with my attack, it was only a glancing blow. They were about to launch some spell at me with their other hand when Ama attacked.

The mage lifted her hand, pulling forth thousands of grains of iron from the sand around us. These grains came together in an arrowhead-like shape, melting into one solid object, and then with the flick of Ama's hand, launched at the enemy with enough power to—

"Ama, no!" I had just enough time to shout, realizing what she intended to do, before this metal object shot toward the enemy, slicing through the side of their neck. Blood sprayed over me, covering my face and torso, and the enemy fell to the ground, clutching their neck.

Level 20 Firespouter defeated!

Worldbending: +900XP
Knifework: +950XP

While the next nearest mercenary blinked on at their colleague in terror, I shouted to Ama, "This isn't what we decided!"

The metal mage shrugged. "An accident. It happens."

"That was *not* a bloody—" I started, but we'd have to finish up this argument later because the other enemy had recovered and was charging Ama.

The metal mage stretched both hands toward where her crafted object had shot into the sand, trying to wrench it back out. Before she could succeed, I made a split-second decision. I portaled myself to her side, activating the same damage-boosting abilities as before, and I brought the butt of my blade down into the back of her head. It didn't fell her in one, but fortunately she was so caught aback by this that she didn't immediately react, and I had the chance to do it again. The mercenary hit her with a frost attack to the side of the head, unsteadying her, and when my blade once more bashed into her skull, she became unconscious.

Level 28 Metal Mage of The Trio defeated!

Worldbending: +650X
Knifework: +950XP

The mercenary was on me before I had a moment to regather myself, so I opened a portal beneath me that I fell through . . . but the enemy did, too. We tumbled out onto a dune not so far away, and I was first to steady myself once more. I pounced the enemy, knowing that there was no chance of breaking line of sight, and so instead of relying on the *Stealth* abilities, I tried something else. I held my dagger with the blade facing me, and I activated *Knifestorm*. As I spun, blade in hand, I hit the enemy again and again and again in the side of his temple. Somewhere in that—I'll admit I don't know when—I knocked them out.

Level 23 Frostcaster defeated!

Worldbending: +250XP
Knifework: +1,950XP

I staggered back up to my feet, and saw someone charging at me. I was ready to attack them, about to open another portal at my feet, when I realized that the person charging was . . . Carle.

"Styk, what are you *doing*?" Lore shouted as he finished off the mercenary he'd been battling with.

"She killed one of them!" I cried. "That wasn't what we agreed!"

"Ah," Lore said.

"And so you—" Carle started.

"I just knocked her out! She'll be fine! We'll get one of Corminar's healing potions in her, and she'll be right as—"

Nobody had interrupted me, but I'd seen something over the big man's shoulder. The mercenaries who had chased Raelas away were returning. Fast.

Carle followed my eyeline, and his eyes narrowed. "We will have to talk about this later," he told me, before turning to do battle once more.

We were again outnumbered, having not quite dealt with all eight of the mercenaries who remained. With all seven of the others coming back—I hoped this didn't mean something had happened to Raelas—we were outnumbered more than we'd been initially, even.

But we didn't need to take them all down; that wasn't why we were here.

"Occupy them!" I shouted to the team at large while I opened yet another portal to fall through, this time stepping out next to the storage tent. I kept low as I crept inside, managing to avoid being spotted by the mercenaries returning to find their camp under attack, and I looked around.

Lambkin hadn't been kidding.

Inside was crate upon crate upon crate, and from what I could tell, more of them were filled with swords, axes, armor . . . even a couple of spell books which were good for one-off spell uses. They were all very neatly packaged in crates too big to fit through a portal, so it was a shame that I now had to tip everything onto the ground.

Bracers and chest plates and swords and shields all went crashing onto the ground—or, at least, they would have crashed if I hadn't cast a spell of *Silence* to hide what was going on. Only when I was done did I poke my head outside the tent.

The rest of the team were all grouped together, still standing—well, except for Ama, who was currently draped over Carle's shoulder—but losing seemed to be a case of "when" rather than "if." So it was probably a good thing that I was ready to go.

I reached my arm out of the tent, pointing it behind the team and then again far in the distance. I opened a portal at each location, the one far away a little higher above the ground than I'd intended, but it was hard to aim perfectly at that distance. "Run!" I shouted, and the team did as instructed without hesitation. I didn't quite know how I felt about that; from their point of view, they were leaving me alone in a camp with ten enemies, but I suppose they knew that I could quickly get away with portals myself.

When the last of my friends and acquaintances were through the portal, I closed it and prepared another one under the pile of weapons and armor at my feet. This time, I used a *Saved Portal*, and I fell back into Coldharbor's central plaza among a pile of stolen goods.

Step one was complete.

CHAPTER TWENTY-SEVEN

Finding Faith

From what I could tell, as I stood among the busy central plaza outside Coldharbor's house of government surrounded by a stack of weapons and armor, the Player had not yet arrived. People were still going about their day-to-day business as though nothing had changed, and I saw only one or two orange robes of the Ascendancy Cult among the crowds. It was because everything was still normal that there was a guard on the steps of the plaza very curious about my stack of items.

"Trouble here, sir?" he said. The tiefling's eyes weren't on me but on the pile of weapons and armor around my feet.

"Nope. No trouble!"

This didn't seem to satisfy the guard. "You sure?"

"I just . . . dropped all my weapons."

"Your bag of holding go wrong?" he asked.

"Err . . . sure."

"That's a lot of weapons for one person."

This guy really wasn't giving up anytime soon. "I like to be prepared for all eventualities."

"Oh yeah? Well, piece of advice: you drop hundreds of coins' worth of weapons around here, expect to be robbed. I'd get moving, if I were you."

"I'll get right on that." With no way of holding all the items, I opened a portal to my pocket world and started tossing objects inside. The guard stood there watching me, so I gave him a big thumbs-up to signal that everything was fine. He soon lost interest.

I quickly got to the point where my pocket world couldn't hold any more items, and I still had a lot of stuff around me that was starting to draw unnecessary attention. I was just choosing between some Shoes of Minor Waterwalking—I didn't know how this could be "minor," surely you walked on water, or you didn't—and a spell book that detailed how to put out fires with a breath when a familiar face arrived.

"I thought I'd find you here," Raelas said.

I looked over her shoulder to see if the rest of the Trio was with her, but she was alone. "How'd you . . ."

The tiefling shrugged. "When the mercenaries gave up chasing me, I knew they'd go back to camp. So you'd need to get out of there fast, with the goods if possible. And you did say this was where you'd saved your portal location to for now. You get anything good?" She picked up a short sword from the ground.

"There's something I should probably tell you," I said.

Raelas's smile faltered just for a second. "What?"

"I had to knock Ama out."

"You *what*?"

"She was killing the mercenaries. You know, the one thing I explicitly said we shouldn't do; they hadn't done anything wrong."

Raelas considered me for a moment, then sighed. "Fine. Alright. If you had to do it, then I guess I believe you. You have trustworthy eyes."

Just this once, to keep her on my side, I didn't rebuff her attentions. "Don't suppose you can give me a hand with what's left?"

Ama, now conscious once more, stormed at me as I entered Tokas and Lambkin's rented house—which seemed to have become our center of operations.

"Woah, woah, woah," I said, putting my hands up.

A clothes iron flew from a bookcase as Ama flicked her wrist, soaring toward my head. Raelas stepped in front of me, and the lump of metal came to an abrupt halt, though I got the impression that it was going to regardless of whether or not the tiefling was in the way; Ama wasn't interested in killing me, only intimidating me.

"Ama, stop," Raelas said, flinging the armful of weapons down onto the floor. I followed suit.

But the metal mage didn't stop glowering, and the clothes iron didn't fall from the air. "He knocked me out!"

"Sounds like you gave him no choice."

At this, the mage's expression faltered. "This again? You promised men weren't going to get between us anymore."

"This isn't that," the other worldbender insisted. "It doesn't matter that he's handsome; you were in the wrong."

"Last I checked, we were mercenaries. Killing other mercenaries is sometimes part of the job."

"Last I checked, mercenaries follow the orders of those paying us. And *you* weren't following orders!"

With a grimace, Ama threw the clothes iron into the wall. The plaster buckled beneath the force.

"I guess we're not getting our deposit back," Lambkin grumbled, staring glumly at the damage.

"They're the ones paying us," Raelas pressed on. "So they're the ones we take orders from. Understand?"

Ama looked to Carle for backup, but after a moment of hesitation, the big guy shook his head. "Fine," the metal mage said with a scoff. From the glare she was still giving me, I had a sneaking suspicion it *wasn't* fine, but we had other things to deal with right now.

Corminar approached the pile of weapons and armor on the floor and nudged it with the tip of his boot. "Is this all? I thought—"

I opened a portal to my pocket world above the pile, and the other eighty percent of the weaponry poured out with a crash. The noise summoned Punnas and Lopas, and the two half tieflings watched from the doorway, their heads poking around the frame.

". . . Ah," Corminar said.

"Ah is right," I replied. "There's a lot to sort through. I figured some of us could stay behind and do that while the rest of us steal these disguises?"

Ama and Carle volunteered immediately, and I couldn't help but assume that it was to get away from me. I wasn't going to argue that point, though, as they definitely needed some time to cool off. Lambkin and Tokas, too, said they'd stay behind and help.

"I will earmark any useless items to sell, too," the ex-captain said. "I know someone who will buy them; any extra coin can go toward hiring more mercenaries."

I nodded. "Good. Raelas, Corminar, Lore, you're coming with me. Should be enough to sneak into the local sect, steal some robes, and start sowing dissent among the cultists."

"Him?" Ama asked. I followed her line of sight to Lore.

"What's wrong with that?" I asked. Probably Ama was just in the mood to pick a fight over anything I said. "He knows the city; he's probably the best one of us to help convince people that the Player isn't the man they think he is."

"He's not just good for hitting things, then?"

Lore seemed taken aback, and fair enough, really; there was no reason he should be taking stray shots from this brewing resentment. "No?" he replied, then pulled a rock out of his pocket. "I got this rock charm, too, see?"

From the glint of mischief in his eye, I could see he was messing with her, so I played along. "Oh yeah? What's it do?"

"It's a . . . banishing rock."

"Nice. Where'd you get it?"

Lore nodded. "I picked it up earlier. Thought it looked pretty."

"Are you two going to stand around talking rubbish or are we going to get to work before the Player arrives?" Ama asked.

"Could do a bit more rubbish?" Lore suggested.

I almost played along with him to mess with Ama some more, but she was right; time was precious. Instead, I gathered Lore, Corminar, and Raelas, and we traversed the city to the nearest temple of Ascendancy.

It was a pretty humble affair, all things considered. I'd really expected a temple to the "great" Players and Architects to be something elaborate and colorful, perhaps with stained glass and tall spires. Instead, it was just . . . a hall. The building was formed on plain sandstone, and the interior—as we soon discovered—was bare. We stepped into a lobby where a woman smiled up at us from behind a desk, and at her rear I could see two open double doors through which there was the temple's main chamber.

"Church of Ascendancy," the woman behind the desk said. "How may we be of service?" Of course, the cultists never called it the *cult* of Ascendancy; that'd be a bit too on the nose.

I peered behind her. Only two other cultists were in the building at that particular moment; we could take them. "Ready, team?" I asked.

Corminar drew his bow. "Ready."

The cultist's hands shot immediately into the air. "There's no need for violence! We'll give you whatever you want!"

"Oh. Really?" I asked.

"What is it you're after?" the woman asked, voice shaky. "Coin?"

"We want . . . your robes?" Lore replied.

The cultist slowly lowered her hands. "You mean you want to . . . sign up?"

"Wait, is that an option?" I asked. "You just let anyone join?"

"Of course! What would make you think otherwise?"

I took a minute to work out my answer. "I don't know? I don't have any experience with organized religion."

"Well, allow me to assure you: there is no need for violence. Were you going to fight me for the robes?" the cultist asked.

"I . . . err . . ." I stuttered, trying to think of the correct answer here. We'd really started on the wrong foot.

"I admire your conviction. It is an honor to welcome such passionate new initiates to the fold," the woman said, sliding a box of orange fabric across her desk. She then pointed to a doorway coming off the lobby. "You can get changed in there."

With a polite smile, I took the case of robes off the cultist and nodded for the rest of the team to follow me into the room—which, as it turned out, was a storage room. Only when the door was closed behind me, did I tell the team.

"Remember: we need to get spares for the rest of them. Lore, get a spare for Carle. I'll cover Lambkin. Corminar, you do Tokas and Ama."

"Do you mean to say I have a feminine build?" the ranger asked.

"Yes."

"Good."

We ruffled through the crate of Ascendancy Cult robes until we found a size that would fit us, then pulled them on over our other clothes.

"OK," I said. "So next thing we do; get out there into the temple and start convincing people that the Player isn't someone to worship. Be subtle, though; saying it outright isn't gonna convince anyone. But the more people we have disillusioned, the fewer allies he'll have at his side when it comes time to kill him." I turned to Raelas. "Can you do subtle?"

"When I have to," the other worldbender replied with a smile. "Why? Would that work on you?"

Someone coughed in the doorway, and we all immediately froze before turning to see who had walked in on us. A young man in an orange robe—one of the cultists—blinked back at us.

". . . How long were you standing there?" I asked him.

"Long enough to hear you say you wanted to kill a—"

Lore launched his so-called "rock charm" at the cultist, hitting him in the head and knocking him, unconscious, to the floor. "See? Banished."

"Bet you wish Ama was here for that punch line, huh?"

"Yep," the barbarian replied, then shrugged. "Can't have everything, though."

I nodded. "Right. Ready to say some insulting things about a Player?"

"Always," Corminar said.

CHAPTER TWENTY-EIGHT

Friends of the Cult

We hurried the unconscious cultist into a crate tucked into the very corner of the storage room, then sauntered as casually as we could out of the room, wearing our new pale orange robes. I led the team toward the church's main atrium, where more of the cultists were gathering, when the woman at the front desk cleared her throat.

"And where do you think you're going?" the receptionist asked, hands on hips.

My heart dropped. Had she noticed her colleague enter the room and never leave? "We . . . err . . ."

"You haven't had your induction presentation yet!"

"Oh!" I replied. "That's OK. We were just gonna go talk to our fellow cul—"

Corminar coughed pointedly.

"—worshippers," I corrected myself.

The receptionist smiled. "There will be plenty of time for that after the presentation. There's free T-shirts at the end!"

"Ooh!" said the barbarian.

"Lore."

"Is this a vision?" Corminar asked. "Do you see our attendance here to be important?"

"No, it's just . . . free stuff."

Corminar, Raelas, and I stared Lore down.

"OK, no free stuff, then."

I turned back to the receptionist. "I think we're good. We know the gist of it;

Players are great, am I right? We'll just be . . ." I gestured to the ten or so cultists in the main hall.

The receptionist hissed through her teeth. "Oh, I'm afraid access to the main hall requires the induction. Church rules. I'm sorry."

"And there's no bending them just for us?" I asked, trying on my winning smile. "We're kinda in a hurry."

"I would if I could, but the rules came straight from the top."

"From . . . ?"

"Yusef himself."

I cast my eyes back to the main hall. In normal circumstances, we could fight our way in, but we were here to change minds, and that would hardly have been starting off on the right foot. I sighed. "Well, if a *Player* said so . . ."

The woman's eyes lit up, and we followed her into another small room adjoined to the hallway. In this room was a number of very uncomfortable-looking fold-out chairs facing a blackboard. I grimaced; if there was one thing I hated more than a group of Players doing untold damage to this world to further their own goals, it was the sound of chalk on slate.

"Welcome! Welcome!" the woman said, clapping her hands together. "Please, take a seat. My name is Wuila, and I am the deputy administrator of the western Coldharbor Church of Ascendancy."

"Quite the job title," Corminar muttered under his breath.

Wuila's eyes flicked over to him to suggest she'd heard, but she didn't comment. "It is lovely to have so many new faces joining us today. Perhaps we could all go around the room, and both introduce ourselves and say one interesting fact about ourselves?"

Nobody said anything, all of us staring back at her.

"OK, I'll start! As I said, my name is Wuila, and I won bronze in the Coldharbor junior gymnastics championships when I was fifteen. And now . . ."

Still, nobody said anything.

"I'll pick someone, shall I?" Wuila looked around the room, casting her eyes over all of us, before landing on Corminar.

The elf shook his head.

Wuila looked to me instead. "Could you . . ."

I sighed. "My name is Styk, and I have died twice."

The cultist narrowed her eyes. "Um . . ."

I nudged my elven friend.

"My name is Corminar, and I watched my homeland fall to foreign invaders while it was under my command. Raelas?"

The tiefling smiled a saccharine smile. "My name is Raelas, and I think this guy is superhot."

I kept my eyes fixed on the cultist, not meeting the other tiefling's gaze.

"OK, but that's not really about *you*, is it?" Wuila pointed out.

Raelas nodded. "Fair point. Here's one: as a child, I was once so close to starving that after I fell unconscious, I woke up in a morgue." She turned to Lore. "Big fella?"

"My name is Lore, and I like sheep!" Lore's smile was less saccharine, more sincere. "Also, I have an active effect that forces me to see possible futures whether I like it or not, including occasionally the deaths of my closest friends!"

"Huh," Raelas said, this being the first she'd heard about all that.

Wuila stood at the end of the room in stunned silence, and we looked back at her. After a moment, she clapped her hands together. "OK! Maybe I will skip the introductions section in the future." She turned and began scrawling on the blackboard with the chalk, and all four of us cringed at the noise.

Lore raised his hand. "When do we get the free stuff? You said it includes T-shirts?"

"At the end," Wuila muttered, finishing up her scrawling on the board. The message she'd written read *CHURCH OF ASCENDANCY*, with a tick next to it, followed by *CULT* with a big cross next to it. "The first thing you must know about the church is that it is *not* a cult. Malicious agents around the western continents have sown the seeds of this idea, and alas, it has taken hold. So, again: not a cult, just a group of lovely people worshipping Players so that we might ascend to heaven. But as you're here, you know all this."

"Sure," Lore said encouragingly.

"Our church began as a small number of loyal followers of Yusef, the Player gifted with knowledge of the future."

"Like me!" the barbarian added.

"I'd keep that to yourself," Wuila suggested. "Trust me." She turned back to the room at large. "Yusef will in time lead us all to the land of the Architects. However, until this day comes, we must obey his every instruction, and live as he wishes us to live. In normal induction meetings, I would now reiterate Yusef's orders: to obey all Players, to eliminate those who would oppose them, and so on. However, I received glad tidings this very morning—Yusef is coming to Coldharbor!"

The cultist went silent for a moment, as though expecting applause. Raelas and I figured this out first and began cheering and clapping as much as we could manage without looking like we were taking the piss. Lore and Corminar joined in.

"Yeah!" Wuila said, also now clapping and cheering, not realizing that we were only doing so to fit in. "That's it, yeah! Very exciting times! Yusef will be here in the next few days, according to my reports, and so you'll soon be able to hear from the man himself—probably on the steps of the central plaza, as that's where he usually speaks. You might even find people are hanging about there already, as space will be at a premium!"

When Wuila trailed off, I raised a hand. "Are we done?"

Raelas nodded. "Yeah, we'd love to go meet our fellow cul—"

Again, Corminar coughed pointedly.

"We'd love to go meet our *new friends*."

"We're done! I'll go get the T-shirts."

As Wuila disappeared from the room, Raelas and I rose from our seats, then hesitated when it looked like Lore and Corminar weren't following.

"Aren't you coming?" I asked.

Lore stared back at me, confused. "Didn't you hear? She's getting the T-shirts."

I tried Corminar instead. "I expected this of him, but you?"

The elf shrugged. "Perhaps they will be fashionable."

I shook my head, exasperated, then led Raelas out of the room and into the main hall. Even more cultists had gathered there, apparently having been drawn in by the news of Yusef's arrival in the near future. I glanced over them, figuring out who would be the best person to start with, then realized that I was probably going to have to sow the seeds of doubt in all of them anyway. While Raelas went right, I went left, toward a group of young tieflings in the same pale orange robes as me.

"How's it going, fellow worshippers?" I asked, butting in on their conversation. They all blinked back at me. "My name's Styk. Just joined. Players are pretty great, right?"

". . . Yeah, they're pretty great," one of them replied.

"Well, most of them, at least," I carried on. "Don't suppose you heard about what happened in the Dawnwood?"

The tieflings looked to one another, and their eyes changed from distrustful to interested. "No?"

"You didn't? Huh. I suppose we're a long way from there."

"What happened? Was a Player hurt?"

Well, yes, but that's not the point I want to linger on, particularly because I was the one who hurt her. "A Player went rogue! Led an attack on the elven homelands. Slaughtered thousands. Tens of thousands, maybe. I didn't know a Player could do that."

"A Player—" one of the tieflings started, but I didn't let this narrative get thrown off course.

"I imagine Yusef will sort it out, though, won't he? He wouldn't let that happen."

One of the tieflings, with a furrowed brow—in fact, they all had a furrowed brow, not being able to comprehend this—leaned in. "Yusef would not stain his hands with the blood of—"

"Spawn?" a voice called across the room.

I ignored it at first. "So you're saying he would let that go unchecked? That's not very benevolent of him."

"Spawn!" a voice shouted louder, marked with the tangs of the orcish accent.

Only at this time did I look over, and I saw an orc in orange robes having just entered the room. I didn't recognize her at first, but she certainly recognized me—because I was the "spawn" she was talking about.

And then my heart dropped. I remembered. A long way back, just after we'd taken down the pyroknight, I'd traveled north with Arzak to get more information on the Sisyphus Artifact. Up there, I'd sought out an artifact expert named Lillya, who'd told me that only those with Player blood in them could use the device.

And it was this orc who stood before me.

"Spawn of Architects!" she shouted, arms raised at her sides as though meaning to embrace me.

"No! No no no . . ." I started.

"It is him! He with Player blood inside!" Lillya was pointing at me by this point, and the whole room was looking.

"You guys already have a Player to worship!" I protested.

"Yes. But there is thing better than Player."

I knew I was going to regret this, but I asked anyway. "What?"

"*Two* Players!"

Mouths began to open, adoring eyes falling upon me. This wasn't good. I needed to be invisible if I was going to have any chance of killing Yusef. Being known to all his cultists was hardly invisible.

"I . . . err . . ."

And then I turned and ran.

CHAPTER TWENTY-NINE

God-Chasers

I burst through the temple's doors out onto the busy streets of Coldharbor. I didn't stop to check how many were following me, but I heard at least two pairs of footsteps.

"Styk!" Raelas cried. "Wait!"

I didn't wait. The best thing for me right now was to get out of this situation as fast as possible. The less time I gave the cultists to see my face, the less chance there would be of them remembering me when the time came. But I knew in my heart of hearts that much of the damage was done; word would spread quickly that there was already someone with Player blood here in town.

"Styk!" another voice cried. Lore's. "There's nobody following!"

I came to an abrupt halt and looked around. He was right; there was only the pair of them there, Corminar apparently still inside. Was I really that arrogant that I thought the cultists would chase me just because of what Lillya said? I was only the spawn of a Player after all. Surely that was different.

". . . Oh," I said.

Then a dozen cultists burst forth from the temple. Lillya scanned the street and then, seeing me—in my not-very-camouflaged orange robe—pointed. "He there!"

"Oh," I said again.

"OK," Lore said. "My bad."

The three of us turned and ran.

"What's going on?" Raelas shouted as we weaved through the crowds. "Are they trying to kill you?"

"No, worse!" I cried back.

"What's worse than that?!"

"They're trying to *worship* me!"

As a gap appeared in the crowds before me, I opened a portal for the three of us to hop through, which brought us stumbling out a good way down the street—but not out of sight of my pursuers.

"Is that . . . bad?" Raelas asked.

"It is when your whole plan depends on being invisible!"

"Fair point."

I collided with someone as they stepped out of a shop, spilling the pile of fruit they'd been clutching in their arms. "Sorry!" I shouted back, then opened another portal. I risked a glance back at the cultists as I did so, and noticed one of them gaining on me—a small tiefling woman who seemed able to move faster than anyone I'd seen before. The crowds were no obstacle, either, as whenever she found her path blocked, she winked out of sight and then reappeared at their other side—magicks not entirely dissimilar to my portals.

I leaped through my portal, followed by Raelas and then Lore, and then the big guy suddenly cried out, clutching his head.

Another vision.

"Lore, come on!" I said, trying to yank him forward. "Now's not the time."

"I can't control it!"

Raelas appeared at my side, trying to tear me away. "Styk . . ."

"I see . . . I see . . ." Lore snapped his head up at me, and I saw his eyes glowing yellow. "If we go after Yusef, Alenna will die."

I stared back at him for a moment, before catching sight of the fast tiefling behind him. "We'll talk about this later—we gotta go!"

"They're not after him!" Raelas said. "They're after *you*; leave him behind."

I didn't like the phrasing of "leave him behind"—especially not when he was seeing his friend die—but she had a point. I let go of Lore's arm, then turned and ran, pushing through the crowds. Raelas and I knocked an old couple to the ground by accident, and I hissed in embarrassment. I took some solace in the fact that everyone around would look at our robes and think the Cult of Ascendancy was responsible; they deserved that and far, far worse.

"So it's true?" Raelas asked between breaths. "You actually have Player blood in you?"

"Well don't go announcing it to everyone!"

"No, it's just . . . you didn't tell me!"

I darted around a corner, hoping that we'd done so without our pursuers noticing. But we weren't that lucky. "And why would I have?"

"Well, I thought—"

"Don't pretend you're telling *me* stuff! Or are we really saying you, Carle, and Ama are here just for what we're paying you?"

Raelas remained suspiciously quiet on this point.

The alley ahead of us grew narrower and narrower, and at its very end, I saw a flash of orange. The same shade of orange as my robes.

"There!" a familiar voice shouted again, and I realized turning had been a bad idea; Lillya and a few of the other cultists had circled around to cut me off. Presumably they knew these winding streets far better than I did. I stumbled to a halt, then turned to run back the way we'd come, only to see the tiefling cultists appearing from that side.

"What do we do? Fight?" Raelas asked.

"That's about the only thing that'll get me even *more* well-known," I replied, then backed against one of the two walls, placing my hands against it.

Raelas saw what I was doing, and then charged at and collided with me just as I opened the portal. We fell through it together, straight into the building's living space. I stumbled backward over a low table, and saw a young tiefling child staring back at me, nibbling on a piece of vegetable.

"Cult?" he asked.

"Eat your vegetables and don't tell your parents I was here," I replied, before opening another portal that would take me, Raelas, and the low table out onto the street on the other side of the building.

"You'd make a good dad," Raelas said.

"Don't get any ideas." I stumbled back to my feet and cast my gaze around. Both ends of this street were clear of cultists—at least of any who were chasing me, though there seemed to be more around than usual—and so I picked a direction at random.

Raelas and I charged down the alleyway toward the next junction . . . just as the tiefling appeared around the corner to the right. Instead of stopping and going the other way, I instinctively pushed my hands forward and opened a portal in front of us. Raelas and I sprinted through, appearing some way down the street, but I had no doubt that the cultists were still on our tail.

"I can't shake them!" I shouted. "They're a stubborn bunch of—"

"Wait, what about your saved portals?" Raelas asked.

". . . Oh yeah." I threw my hands forward once more and opened yet another portal, which Raelas and I leaped through, to spill out onto the steps of the busy central plaza.

---

8 x Cultists of Ascendancy escaped!

Worldbending: +2,650XP
Worldbending increased to level 57!
Base Points Gained: +2 INT, +2 Free Points (INT/WIS/CHA)

Once the portal was closed behind me—and once I'd checked that none of those following us had squeezed through—I dusted myself down and breathed a sigh of relief. "It's kinda weird that they pretend they're not in a cult when the notifications literally say that they are," I mumbled, causing Raelas to shrug.

"Couldn't you have thought of this earlier?" the tiefling asked. "My stamina reserves are . . ." She trailed off.

"Well, that's the thing about having so many abilities; you forget you have some of them."

"Err," Raelas started.

"What? Really? You don't? Cos I'm not practiced enough in—"

The tiefling tugged me gently on the shoulder. "Styk?"

"Yeah?" I asked, looking up at her.

Raelas's eyes were fixed on something in the center of the plaza, so I followed her line of sight.

I'd known the plaza was busy. What I *hadn't* realized was that it was far more busy than normal. And those extra people? So many of them were wearing the same pale orange robes as us. They stood not disorganized, but in an almost uniform formation, in circles around something in the center of the plaza.

No, I realized. Not *something*. Someone.

Standing atop a makeshift stage was a face I'd never seen before, but recognized instantly. I saw on their face the confidence of a god; I heard in their booming voice the unabashed sense of power. Before me, I saw a Player.

While we'd been preparing for the battle ahead, Yusef had already arrived.

CHAPTER THIRTY

Armed to the Teeth

"He's here."

I grabbed Raelas by the arm, my grasp firm but not tight. "Get back to the temple," I told her. "Fetch Corminar and Lore, bring them to the house. I'll get the others ready. Understand?"

The tiefling nodded. No smiles, no batting of her eyelashes, just a nod.

"Good." I turned away and began sprinting through the sea of orange robes, resisting the urge to portal my way through. That would surely get me noticed, and even if it didn't, it could plant a seed in the back of the Player's mind—one that might have him expecting a portal. My feet hit the hard cobbled streets as I slid between flocking pilgrims and unimpressed locals, working my way across the city and back toward the house that Tokas and Lambkin had rented for the duration of their work here.

As I approached the front door, I spotted Lambkin coming from the other direction. He raised a hand to get my attention, but before he could say anything, I shouted, "Inside. Now." A serious expression crossed his face in a flash.

When I bombed through the door, four faces looked up at me. Tokas, Ama, Carle, and Punnas—Lopas nowhere in sight—stood and crouched around piles of the equipment commandeered from the mercenaries.

"What—" Ama started, but Tokas caught on quick.

"He's here," the tiefling said.

"Yes."

"And the others?"

"On the way. They'll be here soon." I looked around at the piles of equipment.

From what I could tell of the piles, they'd organized them into weapons, armor, artifacts, and . . . a mix. Possibly those items not useful to anyone in this makeshift team, to be sold to pay for hired help. But there wasn't time for that now. Yusef was here for a reason, and the longer we waited to strike, the more chances we'd have of finding out what that reason was. I *really* didn't want to find out. "What do we got?"

Tokas stood from her crouched position, stretching her back as she did so. "Weapons were the easiest. We're looking for damage-boosting equipment, and that usually happens on the weapon side rather than the armor. But that doesn't mean the armor was a complete bust." The tiefling strolled across the room to the pile of weapons, and pulled a thin dagger from the pile. She brought it up toward me fast.

I flinched.

Tokas's face paled, and as she gulped, an awkward silence swept over the room. After a second, she flipped the blade around, facing the handle toward me for me to take. Neither of us made eye contact with one another; we didn't want to talk about the reasons I'd flinched—that I could never really trust her—but at the same time that meant we couldn't resolve it.

I kept my eyes on the blade as I took it from Tokas's hands, and I saw sigils on the dagger glow gently, the glow taking on the purple hue of *Worldbending* to my touch.

Item Equipped: Sorcerer's Friend

Sorcerer's Friend: +100 percent to damage when user has magicks active.

"We figured this was ideal for you," Tokas said, looking at nobody in particular. "I know it says 'sorcerer,' but the description says it works for all magicks. *Worldbending*, we figured, would be included."

I held up my other arm and activated my *Ash Husk* ability. As my skin rippled and re-formed into fire magick–repelling ash, the sigils on the blade glowed purple once more. "Looks like you were right," I said.

And wasn't this handy? If I went unnoticed by my target, then I could use my *Stealth Attack* ability for an additional 200 percent damage, and the *Execution Knifework* ability for another 300 percent. Now that I had this weapon equipped, too, that was seven times the usual rate of damage—assuming it added its bonus rather than multiplying, which was how these things usually worked.

I forced myself to look up at Tokas. "Thanks," I said.

The tiefling met my eye for just a second. She nodded, before turning away once more. This time, she went to the armor pile, and pulled a pair of bracers. She handed the equipment over to me slowly.

I began pulling the armor on.

> **Item Equipped**: Whirlwind Bracers
> **Whirlwind Bracers (Rare)**: *Knifework* attacks require 30 percent less stamina.
> *Warning: you do not meet level requirements to wield this item effectively!*
> *Requirement: Knifework—Level 50*

I wrenched the straps tight as the warning message flashed before me, and the bracers themselves seemed to start humming with energy. "Ah," I said. "I don't meet the—"

One bracer shot off my right arm, shooting across the room into the wall, creating another dent in it. Then, just as the front door opened, the other bracer shot off me, repelled by the missing level requirements.

Lore stepped inside just in time to get hit in the head by the flying bracer. "Ow?" he said, looking at the bracer and then around the room with a very confused expression on his face.

"Sorry," I said through clenched teeth. "My bad."

"Don't have the level requirement?" Raelas asked as she stepped inside behind Corminar. "We can do something about that."

"You can—" Lambkin started to ask.

"You got any belts there?" Raelas asked Carle. "Without any level requirements."

The barbarian immediately whipped his hand up, four leather belts therein; he'd been on the same page.

Raelas retrieved the bracer that had hit Lore from the floor, and grabbed the belts with her other hand. "Alright," she said, handing me the bracer. "Put this on, and hold it in place."

I hesitated.

"Don't you trust me?" she asked.

"No."

Raelas looked up at me, apparently genuinely upset by this answer.

"Alright, fine," I said, then wrenched the bracer on once more, pulling the straps tight. Already I could feel the energy building up within it, about to spring off me once more.

But the tiefling moved in with the belts, and using two of them, she wrapped the bracer tight, fixing it to my arm. When Raelas was done, she stepped back hesitantly.

Though the bracer wanted to spring off—I could feel it pulling away from my arm—the belts held it in place. ". . . Huh."

"And this . . . *works*?" Corminar asked.

"I'd say about seven times in ten," the tiefling replied.

This answer didn't fill me with confidence, but I allowed Raelas to do the same with the other bracer.

"OK," she said. "Now, don't fidget."

I slowly began to move my arms around, making sure I could use my full range of motion without dislodging the armor. I couldn't live my life like this, but I could bear with it for the time it took to assassinate a Player.

Tokas, Ama, and Carle distributed the rest of the useful items to the team. Lore and Carle took new armor that gave them good resistance to melee attacks. Ama had already taken her equipment, namely a quiver full of arrows made entirely from metal. Corminar rejected the bow he was offered, apparently happy with the bow Elandor had left him, so this bow was given to Lambkin instead, who was much happier about it. Instead, the elf took bracers—why were there suddenly so many bracers in the world?—which improved the potency of his alchemical creations. And finally, Raelas was given an obscurem, to hide any glows from her magicks and help her retain the element of surprise.

"Hey!" I protested. "I want one of those! Why give that to her and not me?"

"Your portals are fainter," Ama said.

I shrugged. "So I got *Tamed Portals*, and what? I—"

Lore placed his hand gently on my shoulder. He didn't need to say anything to communicate that he thought this wasn't a battle worth fighting. And so my quest for an obscurem would continue.

"What about you, Tokas?" Raelas asked the tiefling. "What are you taking?"

Tokas went oddly still. "Me? Oh, I . . . I don't need anything."

"Why not? You're coming with us, aren't you?"

The tiefling's eyes darted to Corminar, lingering for half a second. "No. No, I have to stay with the kids. Besides, I wouldn't want to . . . to get in the way." She glanced at Corminar again.

"You won't get in the way," Lore said. "And the kids will be—"

"She's right," Corminar interrupted him. "It's best she stays here. It's best she . . . watches the children."

The room went quiet. Everyone here knew something had just happened, but the Trio didn't know quite what that was. Still, the atmosphere was awkward enough that nobody—not even Ama—worked up the courage to ask.

Lambkin stood from a chair, slapping his knees. "Right, then," he said. "If that's everything . . . I suppose it's time to kill a Player?"

Once again, the occupants and visitors of this house looked to me. I nodded.

"Remember," I told them. "We hit him hard and fast."

CHAPTER THIRTY-ONE

A Death Foretold

A sea of orange stretched before us.

The crowd that had been dwindling before was now a thousand strong, two thousand strong, worshippers having flocked from all around the lands to be here. Yusef stood on a stage near the steps that led up to Coldharbor's governing building, facing the plaza at large. It was a shame he wasn't *on* the steps; a little further back and he would have been just where my *Saved Portal* location was. *Oh well, you can't have everything.*

The Player was preaching already, but at this distance—us on a balcony at the other side of the square—I couldn't make out a word he was saying. Part of me wished I'd taken that *Worldbending* ability that let sound travel through my portals, as it'd have been nice to know what we were dealing with.

At my side stood Raelas, Lore, and Corminar, as well as the homeowner who we'd bribed for access. The old woman must have assumed we were fellow devotees based on our pale orange robes, and couldn't have known she was about to be an accessory to an assassination.

"What's that he say?" the homeowner asked.

"Not sure," Carle mumbled back to her. "Can't hear him."

The old woman shrugged. "No refunds." She shuffled off back into her apartment proper.

"Think we can aim our portals well enough from here?" Raelas asked. That was the plan; she would make a portal to drop her and Carle over the Player's head, while I'd do the same for myself and Lore. We'd considered dropping the others in, too, but figured that the process would be too slow. Much better was it that Corminar, Lambkin, and Ama entered the crowd hours earlier, and schmoozed, bribed, and intimidated their way to the front. They'd be ready to strike at a moment's notice, the signal being the purple glow of Raelas's portal. They were out there among the thousands right this second.

"It's not that I'm worried about," I replied. "It's getting back out again."

"Agreed," Carle murmured, drawing in a deep breath. "Perhaps we should rethink our fee, Rae. I'm not sure we accounted for this much peril."

"Now's not the time," the tiefling replied. "Besides, we've got . . ." She trailed off for a moment. "We've got good reason for being here."

Carle didn't react.

"How much longer should we give 'em?" Lore asked. "Should be in there by now, shouldn't—"

A scream cut him off, and the four of us wrenched our upper bodies over the edge of the balcony. The cry had come from the streets down below us, just off to our left.

My heart skipped a beat, and for good reason; the last couple of times we'd heard screaming in the city streets, it had announced the presence of malae. And from what Tokas had said, there'd been more sightings in the last day, handled by the guards—but not without loss of life. This time was no different.

There amidst shouting, fleeing locals was a small black blob—the most powerful monster anyone could possibly expect to see in their lives, except maybe for elderbeests or depth-raiders.

I cast my eyes back to the distant Player, the man we were here to kill. Many of his crowd, mostly those toward the rear, were becoming aware of the creature's presence, and panic was rippling through them like a wave. I had a choice now: begin the assassination attempt amidst the chaos, or . . . do what's right, and try to stop it before innocent lives were lost.

I sighed before I opened a portal just off the edge of the balcony. "Guess we've got some work to do first," I said to the other three as I leaped over the low wall and fell through my purple magicks. I dropped nimbly to the dusty cobbled street a good distance away from the mala and straightened up once more as the others fell one by one to my side.

"Let's be quick," I told the others. "Raelas, you're with me. Portals. Lore, Carle, find something to catch it in." They nodded, and I took a step closer to the mala.

It was funny. In my first life, I wouldn't have *dreamed* of willingly approaching one of these monsters like this. And back then, I'd been a higher level than I was now. I felt stronger, this time around, my build being more efficient, having more synergy, being tall rather than wide. To look at me, I was only level 19, but I was confident I could beat someone as high as level 28 or so in a fair one-on-one fight. A mala was more powerful than a level 28 person, admittedly, but I wasn't alone; I had friends at my side.

I opened a portal beneath the creature, dropping it into the sky high above, where it began to fall. I knew from experience, though, that these monsters adapted quickly; I wouldn't get many more portals before it started stretching to avoid falling through them.

"Got one!" Lore shouted. I glanced to my left to see him raising an open crate, a bunch of oranges falling out of it onto the ground. He winced, then apologized to a nearby stall owner, who seemed more interested in fleeing the mala than any damage to his produce. Lore threw the open crate to the ground, open end pointing upward.

"Good!" I shouted, then opened another portal beneath the enemy to throw it into the empty crate.

Immediately, the monster had adapted, stretching out in midair to grow too wide to fit through the portal, wrapping its black tendrils around the side of the ring. I opened another pair of portals to one side, and began throwing things at the creature.

Raelas, seeing where I was going with this, followed suit, and soon there were two portals raining heavy market furniture down on the creature. The creature squealed as the larger objects hit it, but didn't budge.

"Rae!" Carle shouted, and I glanced over to him to see him lifting an anvil off the ground. Yes, a literal anvil; even Lore's eyes bulged.

The tiefling nodded, then opened a portal in front of him. Carle heaved the anvil until it was placed perfectly above the mala, then dropped it.

I closed the portal immediately, the monster only partway through, because I didn't want the anvil slipping through, too, and potentially demolishing the wooden crate.

Lore slammed the lid of the crate shut immediately, using a hammer and nails to reinforce the opening, and the anvil cracked the cobblestones as it smashed to the ground.

Level ? Corruption defeated!

Worldbending: +1,700XP

I breathed a sigh of relief. It was done. We had a much more dangerous battle ahead of us, but we'd managed this without anyone getting hurt and without draining our reserves too much, so I was gonna chalk this up as a victory.

Carle approached the crate, wrapping his hands around it. "I will leave to dispose of the creature," he said.

"You'll what?" I replied. "No, the guards can deal with that. We need you for Yusef."

"I—" the warrior man began to protest, but was interrupted by Lore shouting out for guards' help. A couple of them finally turned the corner, eyes on Lore.

Not a great response time, I thought, but perhaps they'd been there the whole time and were just afraid to face down a mala. If that's what Carle was going through—fear of the inevitable fight—then I couldn't blame him.

Once satisfied the guards knew how to dispose of the mala, we turned our attention back to that sea of orange robes.

We reached the same balcony using portals, figuring that we'd already drawn attention to the magicks when we'd used them to fight the mala. From there, we looked on at Yusef's thousand or more followers, who had settled back into the same position as before, now that the mala incursion was dealt with. Visibly, those at the rear were more on edge now, but hopefully that hadn't set in closer to Yusef—we needed them as relaxed, and as slow to react, as possible.

"I guess there's no time delaying any longer," I said, and with one last sigh, I pulled my dagger from the sheath, and raised one hand to the air above Yusef's stage. At my side, Raelas did the same. "Everyone ready?" I asked.

Lore and Carle adjusted their grips on their weapons. They knew they were going through first, to take the brunt of any retaliation, but Raelas and I would be through soon after.

"Then let's . . . do it."

I activated my portal. Though mine was *Tamed*, and therefore didn't glow brightly in the air, Raelas didn't have that passive ability, so hers did. Lore and Carle leaped through the two portals, and Raelas and I didn't have time to watch them fall from the other side before tumbling through ourselves. I activated all my relevant abilities—*Stab*, *Execution*, and my *Stealth Attack* passive that was already working in my favor—and I slammed toward the ground, and Yusef. It was a move that reminded me of my final attack on the pyroknight, all that time ago.

But at that distance, I'd aimed poorly, and Yusef was just out of reach. So instead I landed, pushed myself into a sprint, and charged at him. Lore, Carle, and Raelas did the same, having emerged from the portals while the others pushed forth from the crowd.

It was, of course, too easy.

A hand snapped out to grab my wrist, knocking the belt holding the bracers to it. The armor slipped from its binding, flying through the air and slamming into the shoulder of one of the nearby cultists. Around me, the others met the same response, those cultists closest to Yusef reaching out and moving to block their attacks. Lambkin's nocked bow fired an arrow high into the sky, while a familiar orc leaped to grab Ama's metal arrows from the air. Lillya.

"Hello again, spawn," the orc worshipper said.

I wrenched against the hands holding me back, desperately trying to free myself, and a glance at the others showed me that they'd suffered the same fate.

We'd been fools to think that striking fast would be enough, that blending in and avoiding his notice would mean he wouldn't see our future; this was a man with a far higher *Divination* skill than we could have possibly expected. He'd known we were coming.

"Here at last," Yusef said, dark brown eyes sweeping over the team. Behind him and around us, people in orange robes roared and shouted and tried to burst forth to attack us, but a hand held up by the Player instructed them to stand back.

Yusef strolled over first to Corminar, then to Lore, and then finally to me. My heart dropped when I realized what it meant that he'd picked out the three of us.

"The Slayers," he said. "We meet at last."

CHAPTER THIRTY-TWO

The Greater Good

Corminar spat at the Player's feet, and cultists roared at him, desperate to deliver justice but unable to disobey their leader's orders.

For his part, Yusef only smiled back at the elf, sadness in his eyes. He raised his hand and waved some of his most loyal followers in. "Keep them restrained and move them to my new home." He turned back to us, hands clasped behind his back, and he sighed. "I have orders to eliminate you on sight, you know. Orders straight from the Council—kill those who have been killing our members. But I do not yield violence as a weapon; instead, I convert with rhetoric and with knowledge of all that is to come. We will speak, and, in time, you will see the light."

"See the light?" I asked, snarling, pulling in vain against the hands that gripped me tight. "And what if we don't?"

"Then, like the rest of your team, I will have to imprison you until you do."

My heart dropped. We'd known Val and Arzak were in the area. We'd known that they were after him. But we didn't know that they'd already been caught. Probably those two would have had a better plan of attack than sneaking out of the crowd to assassinate the Player, and even they had been caught at his hand. Would they be there, where Yusef wanted to take us? Would I have to face Val again? Somehow, that part was more terrifying than anything else.

The Player turned to his most trusted and gestured again. "Go."

With that, each of us was dragged back by our arms and shoulders, out of the crowds, our feet left to drag along the cobbled streets until the sea of orange was far behind us. Enough cultists remained with us that fighting back was futile; we were outnumbered five to one. If we were going to escape, we'd need to choose the right moment.

The locals actively looked away when they noticed what was happening; they knew better than to involve themselves in the business of the cult, especially when it now seemed to be taking prisoners. It was a survival mechanism, and one that I definitely could *not* blame them for.

We took an abrupt turn off the main street and soon entered a small, cramped apartment—one that Yusef seemed to have made his own. For all that it was humble in size, in decoration, and in furnishing, it also . . . didn't seem to be his. The little decoration that did still exist included a sketch of a happy tiefling family, hanging on the wall. Where were they now? Had they given their home up willingly, or had the cult taken it from them by force?

Those in orange, finally dumped us on chairs surrounding a large dining table—one large enough for the large family that had been evicted under mysterious circumstances—before binding our hands behind our back. Though perhaps they were making the mistake of using regular, not magically reinforced, rope.

We were positioned, bound, to face a single chair on the other side of the table—one which Yusef took, notably without any rope bindings. He scratched his long, wild beard as he considered us with those dark eyes. He looked to Carle, Ama, and Raelas before flicking to Lambkin. "You, I have intelligence on, but . . ." he looked back to Ama. "You are . . . ?"

"Mercenaries," I replied for them.

"Ah! To replace those you lost in your team's schism? Very good."

Lillya, who was apparently part of the cult's inner circle, appeared from the kitchen to place a jug and empty cups of iced tea in the center of the table.

"Thank you, Lillya," Yusef said, and the orc took a step back to wait on him from the corner of the room. The Player began to pour out a cup of tea for Corminar, then paused. "Ah. The bindings, yes."

"You foresaw that problem, did you?" I growled at him.

Again, Yusef's reaction was only to smile. He considered us again, silently, carefully.

It was Lore who spoke next, that silent resentment boiling up until it was silent no more. "You're breeding malae," he said. It wasn't a question, only a statement, but it came attached to flaring nostrils and a deep, out-of-character scowl.

The Player nodded. "I am."

Lore hesitated.

"Were you expecting me to deny it?"

"I was expecting some shame at least."

Yusef drank from the cup he'd begun pouring for Corminar, taking his time before replying. "Is it shameful? Out of context, perhaps. But in context, given that we need such abundant *Witchcraft* magicks to complete Tana's plan . . . perhaps not."

"We saw the canyon," Corminar said, holding the man's gaze.

"Ah. A shame. I had instructed no guard presence as I did not want to draw attention to it, but alas that gambit seems not to have paid off."

"You will kill hundreds," the elf continued. "Thousands. More."

Again, the Player took a sip of his tea before replying, and pulled one foot up over the other knee to rest it there. "Agreed. But it is for the greater good. Our tests in the eastern Goldmarch showed us that the malae were the only way. And for our needs . . . we will need them in great number."

"Don't suppose you're about to tell us what your needs are?" Lambkin tried. It was a good attempt—don't ask, don't get, and all that—but the Player was hardly going to—

"Of course!" Yusef replied. "Like I say, my weapon is the truth, and the future. How could I convert you without bringing you into my confidence?"

Lore opened his mouth to reply, and I silenced him with a glare.

"It was Tana's plan, originally, but she could not do it alone. She recruited Players from this world—those whose presence was faded in most other worlds—and formed the Council. You see, the Council is not some dark, mysterious organization; we are only a group of friends working toward some common goal."

"Niamh didn't seem to think so," I said, interrupting only because I thought this provocation might encourage Yusef to reveal more than he already had.

The Player nodded. "Perhaps. Our goal is . . . important. It's only natural that emotions run high. You see, if we rebuild the land of the Architects, we will have a home once more."

Lillya, among others in orange, visibly raised their eyebrows at this revelation; this was news to them, that the Architects' world needed rebuilding.

"And to rebuild this world—or create a rough approximation of it—we will need the power that the malae afford. *That* is why we risk the lives of those here, because it will save millions more. Because it will give us a home once more. That is it, our grand plan: to go home."

Silence swept over us for a moment. Lore shattered it.

"The towers," he said. "I saw them." Lore had told us what he'd seen in his visions: three great towers, standing around the city of Auricia, each taller than the grand palace itself, each crackling with the green energy of *Witchcraft* magicks. And him, there, looking up at them, the depth-raider at his side.

I furrowed my brow. "You saw them? You mean in the witchfinder village? Our scouts confirmed that it was your team that fixed the experiment gone awry."

"No," Lore said, and my heart dropped. He was doing it; the one thing we'd told him not to do. He was revealing Niamh's final gift. "I saw it in my visions. I was there. Niamh made sure that I saw that I was there. That I *needed* to be there."

The Player before us didn't move, didn't adjust his posture or sip on his tea.

Instead, he sat there stunned for a moment; this, he really hadn't seen coming. "You . . . are blessed with the gift of prophecy?"

Lore nodded. "Niamh cursed me."

Yusef narrowed his eyes, then his posture softened. "Niamh always was jealous of my gifts; it's no wonder she developed *Divination* within herself. But to give it to you . . . that *is* curious. She wanted you there so badly? She saw that you were so important to our success?"

"See for yourself," Lore said. "You have prophecy, too."

"Tell me," Yusef said, rising from his chair and moving around the table to slouch against it in front of Lore. "What, precisely, did you foresee?"

"The three towers. Activating. I saw that I needed to be there for it to work, though I don't understand why. And if I don't get there . . ." Lore trailed off and glanced to me.

"Yes? If you don't get there, then our plan is unsuccessful?" Yusef prompted him.

"Sure. You're unsuccessful. But also . . . Styk and Val die."

I gulped. "What? You didn't tell—"

"I just want them all to live. I've lost too many friends over the years already," Lore replied.

The Player stared back at him, those eyes considering once more. "Interesting." He raised his hand and gestured for his followers to approach. "Free them," he said.

"Free them?" Lillya repeated, hesitating.

"Do you disobey?"

"No. I only think . . ."

"Do not think. Do."

Lillya and the rest of the cultists approached, knives drawn, slicing the bindings between our hands. Lillya, who'd approached me, found that mine were already cut; I'd used my *Portal Slice* ability already, freeing myself to move when the opportunity presented itself.

"You . . ." I started.

"You may go," Yusef interrupted us.

". . . Just like that?" Raelas asked. "Good villain you are."

The Player winced. "Not a villain," he said. "Just a man who wants to go home. And it seems that your freedom is necessary, if our plan is to be a success. Even I would not mess with matters of prophecy. But make no mistake, if you come for me again, I will execute your friends and I will set a thousand worshippers upon you. You would not live to see sunrise." Yusef shifted his gaze to Lore. "You excluded. You . . . We will speak again soon."

We rose from our seats, and I would be lying if I said I wasn't a bit stunned. In this strange, revelatory, confused daze, I stumbled out onto the streets of Coldharbor under the midday sun. The seven of us soon began to hurry away, taking our freedom before the Player could change his mind.

Some distance away, I turned back to the others.

"We've been arrogant," I said. "*I've* been arrogant. We shouldn't have under-estimated Yusef's powers of *Divination*. He was always going to see us coming. If we're going to kill him, we're going to need to get creative. More creative than ever before. We're going to need to do something that even someone with the gift of prophecy won't see coming. And we're going to need to free Val and Arzak first."

I heard a round of agreement from everyone but Lore. Instead, the barbarian stared blankly back at me, his face glum, and his eyes glowing yellow.

Lillya

"We will speak again soon."

Lillya watched the would-be assassins leave, aghast that the descendant of the Architects was simply allowing them to go. She knew his core tenet was to convert, not harm, but to see it put into action against such a dangerous group of individuals shook her to her core. Of course, there was one among them who had Player blood running through his veins, which only complicated Lillya's feelings further.

"Oh, Divine Player," one of her fellow worshippers said, practically throwing himself at Yusef's feet, "with great humility, may I ask, is this wise? We must assume such fanatics will not give up so easily. Is there something you see in their future that gives you context we do not have?"

Yusef's eyes remained on the doorway. "Give it time," he said. "I foresaw their arrival, and just the same, I foresee their conversion. And what did I say about that form of address? I am Yusef. That is my name. That is what you will call me."

"Of course . . . Yusef," the man in orange said, bowing even further, his eyes fixed to the floor at the Player's feet so as to not look upon him. So many of these westerners believed that they were not worthy. Up in the Northern Reaches, members of the church did not share this belief. Lillya met Yusef's eye when she spoke to him, and though he had instructed them all to do so, the orc couldn't help but think he was taken aback when it actually happened.

"You like me to arrange the big man come back?" Lillya asked. "You say you speak again to him soon. Is instruction or prophecy?"

"In good time," Yusef said, as he so often did, though the orc noted that this was no answer one way or the other. The prophet could be so terribly vague in his replies, though Lillya suspected that he did not wish to cast too big a stone into the rivers of fate with his revelations. "I will have some alone time now," he continued, "to divine. Please ensure those we displaced are fed."

All of those in orange hesitated, lingering for a moment. All of them wished to ask about something Yusef had said just minutes earlier—about the realm of the Architects needing rebuilding. Not once, in all those parables and allegorical stories, had Yusef mentioned this. And yet these Slayers entered, and the truth—if that's what it was—came out. Why had he not told his closest aides that his world, and their intended destination, was in disrepair?

But it was too bold a question to emerge from anyone's lips, so everyone soon did as the Player commanded. Except . . . Lillya lingered on the threshold.

"Is there something else?" Yusef asked.

The orc gulped, steeling herself, before turning around and closing the door gently behind her. "You say something earlier."

"About the Ascended Realm?" Yusef asked.

"No. Yes, this too, but also . . ." Lillya hesitated once more; she hadn't dreamed of being so bold as to ask about the world of the Architects, but there was another, perhaps less dangerous, question on her lips. "You say earlier you foresee Slayers coming."

"I did."

"But . . . I *tell* you they coming."

Yusef drew in a deep breath before turning to her. "Sometimes, the art of *Divination* can be . . . fickle. Elusive. We must plug any gaps as they emerge. You understand?"

"So you . . ."

"I don't lie, I augment." Yusef said, apparently having foreseen Lillya's question. Or was she simply that predictable? Before the orc could open her mouth once more, the Player continued, "That'll be all, Lillya." From his stern tone, there was no room for argument here.

And so Lillya left Yusef alone to work his magicks. She knew well enough by now—from previous weeks spent in the Player's employ—that moments such as these were few and far between. She should take the opportunity to get some rest.

Lillya's current lodgings were in a small room at the top of the house, shared with another follower of the Player who she'd liked well enough, but with whom she had little in common. The younger tiefling woman was in the room as Lillya arrived, apparently having come to the same conclusion.

"Weird one, huh?" she asked, her tone suggesting this was idle conversation rather than the start of a meaningful discussion. But Lillya did not do this "small talk" that the other races were so fond of.

"He say the Ascended World need repair?" Lillya asked. "You know of this?"

The tiefling hesitated, trained well enough to think before she spoke on such potentially dangerous matters. "I wouldn't repeat what you heard in that room outside it. Few know about this. If you were to say it in front of the wrong person . . . well, they might just accuse you of heresy."

"But how can be heresy when said by Yusef?" Lillya retorted. "Refuting what he say is the heresy, not repeating it."

"I know that, and you know that, Lillya, but the others? They wouldn't understand. And if word about the Ascended Realm got out . . . that might just lose Yusef followers. We can't have that. At least, not until the Council gets their way—after that, it won't matter. We'll have our realm once more, and Yusef says we'll all ascend with him."

But Lillya had doubts. Doubts that she knew she had to keep to herself. If Yusef had this . . . casual relationship with the truth, then what else had he not been entirely honest about? He had kept this pivotal news hidden, and he had used Lillya's gathered intelligence to "augment" his prophecies. Just what else was out there?

Lillya shook her head—causing a raised eyebrow from her roommate in response—and tried to quell these doubts within herself. If she did not trust Yusef, then why was she here? What was her purpose? And if she could not trust him, then would she ever enter the Ascended World? And then, too, if she never entered this paradise, then was this it? Was her time on this world all she really had?

Again, she shook her head. She had to trust Yusef. She had to.

But if she didn't, wasn't there another Player in town? Or, at least, the next best thing? The young human man known as Styk, the man who'd slipped through her fingers back in Rose Home, he was half Player.

What wise words might he have, in Yusef's place?

CHAPTER THIRTY-THREE

On the Orange Sea

Yusef hadn't been kidding about how many followers he had. We'd seen only some of them before on the road to Coldharbor, when I'd made the mistake of thinking *that* was a lot of followers. And then, when Yusef had threatened us with retribution by setting "a thousand worshippers" upon us, I'd thought he'd meant that was the whole of his flock. But, judging by the sight before us, that would only have been some small part of it.

Beyond the calls of Coldharbor was a sea of tents, stretching if not as far as the eye could see, at least some great distance. Amidst these tents, almost everyone wore those familiar orange robes—the robes that the team were still wearing, too, seeing no good reason to lose our disguises. There were merchants among them, and armorers, and mages, and bards, people from all walks of life, united by Yusef and his words of hope.

It had been two days since Yusef had revealed that he was holding Val and Arzak prisoner, and we'd spent the time trying to track them down. Lambkin's bribed eyes and ears in the city had proven most valuable, and we'd learned quite early on that Arzak and Val were among the camp somewhere. But this camp was large enough that we'd needed more specifics . . .

Slowly, we'd unpicked the inner workings of this large mass of followers. They worked their trades as they traveled, selling their goods on the road at prices that undercut the locals, with any profit going toward supporting their church. It had taken us a moment to understand how they could afford to go so low on prices, but we'd stumbled across an interaction between the cult and a local mining guild, and . . . Well, to cut a long story short, the answer was intimidation. If people didn't sell to them cheap, then *who knows what might happen*? It was funny how these people thought that just because they were with a Player, they could do whatever they wanted—that the rules didn't apply to them. It infuriated me, but there wasn't much we could do. Except kill their leader, of course.

But this couldn't happen until we'd freed Val and Arzak, as we couldn't have their lives hanging in the balance.

All this led to this moment, where we walked through the camp in our orange robes, doing our best to look as though we belonged. We strode with purpose, our brows furrowed, doing our best to emulate the true followers so we would blend in. Our destination was toward the outer perimeter of the camp, away from the prying eyes of the city and the Coldharbor patrols, but also away from the merchant roads into town. Out here, hidden in plain sight, the cultists could do what they wanted.

I checked the map our informant had sketched for us, before handing it back over to Lambkin. He seemed to have a far better sense of direction with this kind of thing, and I suspected it was something to do with his *Ranger* build. He took one look at the sketch, cast his head around, then nodded; he agreed we were heading in the right direction. I locked my eyes upon a large tent some way off, and figured that was our destination—any prisoners they had would need space to move around, at least if they were being treated right. For all Yusef's fault, I thought he was probably above mistreating his prisoners. Or at least he *considered* himself above it, which played to our favor.

"Got it," I said, then the others at my side—Lambkin, Corminar, Lore, and the Trio, prepared themselves. We didn't know what we'd find in the tent, if we'd need to swing into action or if we could simply walk our old friends out of there. So we had to be prepared for every eventuality.

As I approached the tent flap entrance, a woman happened to emerge from it at the same moment. She took a step back when she looked up and saw me and the others staring back at her. ". . . Can I help you?" she asked.

"The Divine Prophet sent us," I said, adopting the cult's usual deference for the Player, even though it made me feel a bit sick.

"The Divine Prophet sent you . . . here?" the tiefling woman in orange replied. "I didn't know he took such interest in our work?"

I could see elation behind the woman's eyes; for all that she was skeptical of it, she really wanted to believe that Yusef took an interest in her personally. He held that much power over her.

"Of course he does!" Corminar said. "Our Divine Lord takes great interest in all of his most loyal." Though he wore a big smile, there was nausea behind his eyes to match mine.

"He sent us for . . ." I gestured to the tent behind her.

"For the packages?" she asked.

"The . . ." Corminar frowned.

"You know, the packages?" the cultist replied. "The ones we collected a few days back?"

"Ah yes," I said, catching on. I gave the woman a knowing wink. "The 'packages.' We're here for the *packages*."

The worshipper stared blankly back at me, and then stood aside, granting us access to the large tent.

Inside, Corminar and I saw not prisoners, but stacks of crates, filled with fresh fruit and ironed robes. I turned back to the tiefling woman. "Where are they?" I asked.

"The packages?" The worshipper gestured to the crates in front of us.

I nodded. "Ah. I think there's been some—"

"Err, Styk?" Lore said, poking his head between the sheets of fabric and looking around. "Wrong tent."

I smiled an apology to the tiefling woman, and then Corminar followed me back out into the sun. Across the makeshift alleyway, Raelas held a flap of fabric open, revealing an array of desks inside this neighboring tent. People in orange were bent over the desks, studying books and making notes, and I wouldn't have thought anything of it if they hadn't been guarded.

I poked my head in the tent, caught the eye of a guard, and then pulled back into the sun once more.

"You see 'em?" Lore asked. "Val and Arzak?"

"It was crowded, but I'm pretty sure I caught a glimpse of an orc woman in there, yeah. Considering they were . . ."

"Much taller?"

"Yep."

"And Val?" the big guy asked, and I could see a certain level of expectation on his face.

"I didn't see her."

"But she might have been in there?"

I shrugged. "I dunno. Maybe?"

"Is this the manifestation of your awkward feelings surrounding Val, or do you sincerely, in fact, not know?" Corminar asked.

"I sincerely don't know."

"Would you like to have another look inside?"

"What, and tip off the guards? What do you think they'll reckon about me poking my head in and out over and over?"

Lore raised his hand to have a go at answering. "Maybe that you really like the game 'peekaboo'?"

"I honestly don't think that's any better than them thinking we're doing a prison break." I turned instead to the Trio, who stood there with painfully neutral expressions as this conversation unfolded.

Ama raised her hand, copying Lore. "So, are we doing this, or . . . ?"

"It pays extra, I assume?" Carle added. Really, we should have had that discussion before we'd gotten this far, but maybe that was part of this bartering strategy.

"Sure," I told him, mostly to keep us focused. I had no idea where the reward money for killing the Player was going to come from anyway, so what was the harm in making it a larger amount? That was a problem for another day. "Shall we?"

Without waiting for an answer, I flipped open the tent flap, and strode in confidently, my eyes on the people at the desk, ignoring the guards as though I wasn't worried by their presence. I clasped my hands behind my back, as I thought that made me look more like I knew what I was doing. It must have worked, because although the guards stirred at our presence, they didn't immediately jump to attack.

I found the orc woman in the rows of desks once more, and made my way toward her. In this low light, I couldn't quite tell if it was indeed Arzak, but there was an easy way to find out. I made my way through the rows of desks, the rest of the team remaining at the side of the large tent. As I walked, I cast my eyes down at what these people were working on.

A man at my left was copying out one of Yusef's speeches onto new parchment. The next prisoner along adjusted a large bracelet on her wrist before stretching her fingers and going back to copying out another speech. Was that all that was going on in here? Were they just put to work copying out Yusef's words? Or was there more to it? Were they expected to internalize the words they were copying? Were they expected to be converted?

As I passed the next desk, a hand shot out to grab my wrist. Instinctively, I reached toward my dagger, but then I saw who'd reached out for me. A familiar face looked up from her desk, quill in her ink-stained hand.

". . . Styk?" Val asked.

CHAPTER THIRTY-FOUR

Saving the Saved

"Styk?" Val asked again, after I hadn't replied.

At seeing her, I'd frozen. A huge mess of emotion had come rushing back as I'd met those deep brown eyes. Complicated feelings—ones of love, and ones of betrayal, not to mention everything else in between. I'd recoiled my hand, pulling myself from Val's grasp, and her eyes had widened.

But this was hardly the full extent of our problems in this moment. When Val had called me by name, the guards had started putting two and two together. One of the prisoners knew me—and probably the rest of the visiting group—by name. We either had once been friends . . . or still were. They'd not worried about our presence here because we wore their uniform, but now narrowed eyes suggested they realized the robes were just robes, that they were no guarantees that we were allies.

As the first soldier pulled her sword free, Lore pounced, pushing her into the edge of the tent, tearing the fabric as they fell through. Everyone else leaped into action, the tent devolving into chaos that I couldn't keep track of. While the others fought off the guards, I focused on why we were here: freeing Val and Arzak. If we didn't get out of here soon, then more cultists would surely descend on us.

I grabbed Val by the wrist just as Arzak rose from her desk some ten yards away, jamming her quill into one cultist's neck.

"Styk . . ." Val said, but thinking she wanted to discuss things beyond the immediate moment, I didn't reply. It was time for action, not introspection.

I threw my other hand forward and opened one end of my *Saved Portal* in the center of the tent. It crackled into life, revealing the steps overlooking

Coldharbor's central plaza. A woman stumbled backward on the other side, having been just about to collide with it.

"Through," I told Val. "Now."

"The bracelets!" the witch said, waving her hand in front of me.

"Yes, very nice."

"They're not a bloody fashion accessory, Styk. They're trapping us here. Remember the prison in Tarenthe? It's Council work."

It took me a moment, but then it came back to me. Once upon a time—it felt like eons ago, now—we'd had to save a friend of Corminar's called Aiwin from a Goldmarch prison. This hadn't just been any prison break, though, and we hadn't just had guards to contend with. All prisoners had a belt that they couldn't remove. If they strayed too far from a gem-based artifact, this belt would close around them and continue closing until they were cut in half. From the looks of it, Val and Arzak's bracelets were of a similar style.

"Alright," I said, and nodded. I looked around at the chaotic fighting just in time to see Lambkin fire an arrow at a guard that the guard rebounded with a spell. I did *not* look in time to react to it heading toward me. "Ow?" I said as I pulled the arrow from my shoulder.

Val approached to heal it, and I allowed her to without making eye contact. Raelas glanced at me from across the skirmish.

"Where's the artifact?" I shouted over the din.

"Next tent over!" the witch cried back. "But, Styk, it's surrounded by a metal box, you won't be able to—"

I didn't wait for the end of that sentence; I had a plan. I opened another portal and leaped through it, landing at the edge of the tent and crashing into two new guards who'd just stormed in, knocking them to the ground. But it hadn't been them I was after. I swung around, activated my *Knifestorm* ability, and tore to shreds a cultist who had been attacking some of my hired help.

Level 18 Protector of the Divine Servants defeated!

Worldbending: +900XP
Knifework: +1,350XP
Knifework increased to level 42!
Base Points Gained: +1 DEX, +1 STR, +2 Free Points (VIT/DEX/STR)
Stealth: +650XP
Stealth increased to level 26!
Base Points Gained: +1 DEX, +1 WIS, +2 Free Points (DEX/WIS)

Level up!
You increased to level 20!

There wasn't time to celebrate my leveling up. "Ama," I said. "With me." The woman nodded, and I opened another portal that took us back out into the sun and the makeshift alleyways between the rows of tents. Dozens of cultists, weapons raised, were storming toward us. "Better act fast."

Ama nodded again, slightly more aggressively this time.

I wasted no time in launching myself at the next tent along, again using my *Knifestorm* ability but this time to slash the tent fabric, rather than flesh, into shreds. The cries of battle grew louder behind me as my friends held off the enemies. Glancing back, I realized I should have told someone to get the other prisoners ready to flee—it would hardly be heroic to leave them behind. My instinct was to open a portal, but without the ability to transmit sound through it, I'd need to stick my head through and shout for someone, and I simply didn't have the seconds to spare, what with so many enemies storming toward us.

"The metal box!" I shouted to Ama. "Break it!"

For all Ama's faults—including killing people when I'd *explicitly told her not to*—she always jumped at the opportunity for destruction. She gritted her teeth together and roared with effort as she wrenched the metal box apart with her magicks, this protective box apparently reinforced by enemy magicks.

Soldiers burst in behind us, and I opened a portal to drop through the ground at my feet, reappearing behind them. I had just enough time to slay two of them, my damage boosted by having broken their line of sight, before the other three turned to me.

---

2 x Divination Students defeated!

Worldbending: +1,950XP
Worldbending increased to level 58!
Base Points Gained: +2 INT, +2 Free Points (INT/WIS/CHA)

Clearly their *Divination* studies hadn't gone that well. Faced down by the other three cultists, I hesitated, unsure in that split second how to act next.

But Ama answered that question for me. "Out of the way!"

I glanced at her and saw her hands raised at her sides, the fragments of the metal box floating in the air around her. I had enough time to get out of the way, as instructed, because I opened a portal beneath me. The other three . . . they *didn't* have enough time.

Scraps of metal tore into them, and before long, we were the only ones left in the tent. For now.

I ran for the gem, arching my Sorcerer's Friend blade through the air in a *Stab*, and . . . my blade ricocheted from the gem. We needed something stronger.

So instead, I grabbed the gem from the remains of the crate and portaled Ama and I back into the action.

There were . . . *far more* enemies in this tent now. But at least their prisoners had now risen from the desks, and even though most of them weren't fighting back, they were doing a very good job of getting in the way, which was just as good.

"Lore!" I shouted across the tent to the big guy, then threw the gem through the air without waiting for a response.

One of the guards, apparently recognizing the gem for what it was, leaped through the air and snatched it.

". . . Oh." I shook my head, pressing after the guard with Ama at my side. As I passed Lambkin and Raelas, I shouted to them, "Get everyone ready to go!"

"The other prisoners?" Raelas asked.

"*Everyone!*" I reiterated.

Ama and I were on the enemy with the gem only seconds later, and I went to my new crutch ability, *Knifestorm*, to attack. The enemy brought up an armored arm to block it, and in doing so knocked loose one of the belts holding my remaining bracer in place—the other one had been lost somewhere in the chaos. The bracer leaped free of my arm, and this time shot upward, hitting me in the nose.

I staggered backward and blubbed to Ama through a bloody nose. "Get it!"

Ama raised her hands, and a second later ripped free all the pegs holding the top of the tent in place. These metal stakes all turned to face the enemy with the gem. Before Ama fired them, she said, "After this, I'm out of mana."

"Don't miss, then," I suggested.

To her credit, she didn't. The metal stakes almost all struck firm, but the enemy was armored enough not to be completely felled by this attack. I pressed the advantage, leaping forward and tearing the gem from their hand, before running with it to Lore this time.

As I appeared at his side, I stabbed a cultist in the side, which gave Lore an opening to finish the job.

Level 16 Office Manager's Assistant defeated!

Worldbending: +650XP
Knifework: +850XP

I threw the gem down on the ground. "Both at once!" I shouted, and we moved immediately, because there wasn't a moment to waste in this chaos. Lore brought his great Bane Sword down on the gem, and I timed my *Stab*—coupled with *Closed Reach* to attack from inside the gem—to hit at the same time. The gem splintered into a dozen pieces, and all around me, I saw bracelets falling to the sand.

"Alright!" I shouted to the prisoners. "Through the portal! Now!"

Nobody seemed to be moving.

"I'm on *your* side, idiots!" I shouted, and this—of all things—was what stirred them into action.

Carle and Raelas began physically pushing the prisoners through, and they spilled out onto the plaza in the center of Coldharbor. Val was one of them, pushed through rather enthusiastically by Raelas, and soon there was only the team—and Arzak—left. Carle, Arzak, and Lore took positions around the portal whilst the last of us filtered through, doing so without any discussion as they knew they'd last the longest against the onslaught. But I wasn't going to force them to find out how long that was.

As Corminar and Lambkin stepped through, I grabbed Raelas's arm and pushed her through in a manner not dissimilar to how she'd pushed Val, then called out to the three of us left behind, "Now!"

They all turned at once and leaped through the portal in quick succession—Carle, then Arzak, and then Lore. As Lore was halfway through, I let the portal close, and it shut the moment the tip of his last shoe was through.

Back in Coldharbor, and out of trouble—for now—we collapsed to the ground, breathing heavily. A crowd had formed around us, perplexed by the portal opened in the center of the plaza and the fighting on the other side of it, and no small proportion of them were members of the Cult of Ascendancy.

"Traitors," I explained to them, through a bloodied nose and wheezy breath, and this seemed to satisfy them.

Gathering myself, I staggered back to my feet and turned to meet the eyes of the team.

Well, not quite the whole team. Still, I couldn't meet Val's gaze.

CHAPTER THIRTY-FIVE

Friction

We walked across the city of Coldharbor back toward the house Tokas and Lambkin were renting with few words shared. I could feel how tense everyone was, including the typically carefree Lore, with Val and Arzak eyeing our new—hired—acquaintances with suspicion, Raelas returning the favor to Val, and Corminar keeping a close eye on both me and Val. When we finally arrived outside the house, it was almost a relief, but as I was about to reach out to touch the door, Corminar turned to the rest of the group.

"Before we enter, there is something else you should know," he said, eyes on Val and Arzak.

". . . What?" the witch asked.

"We did not stumble across only Lambkin out there."

"What you mean, Cor?" Arzak asked, glancing nervously at the door. "What you mean?"

"I . . ."

But before Corminar could answer, Arzak pushed him aside and swung the front door open. Through the hallway, she could see into the kitchen area, and the tiefling standing there, bowl in hand, child at her side.

Tokas froze, meeting Arzak's gaze.

"Oh no," Val breathed.

From how tense Val had suddenly become, I'd thought Arzak was going to get violent, that this was going to end in tears. Punnas and Lopas's tears, mostly. But instead, the orc turned around and slammed the door behind her.

"Keep her away from me," she growled at Corminar, then strode away from the building, showing no signs of stopping.

"Arzak!" Lore cried after her, but it made no difference.

"I'll check on her," Lambkin said, gesturing toward the door. "She won't . . . have taken that well."

"It was a cruel surprise," Corminar said. "For us to spring Tokas's presence on her, after all that she did."

"She's not the same woman," the other ranger replied. "The one who betrayed you, she's gone. Tokas has grieved. She has done good. She has tried to make amends. She doesn't deserve—"

"Let's not get into what she deserves," I cut in, before Corminar could. "See to her. We'll be in the tavern."

Lambkin nodded then turned away, and I hurried after Arzak.

"You should said earlier," the orc growled as I appeared at her side, Val hurrying after me.

"We didn't know how to break the news. We couldn't think of a good way."

Arzak turned, scowling, and for the first time I felt the receiving end of her terror. "There *no* good way! She was best friend. She betray me. Us." The orc shook her head. "And greater betrayal still to come." This last bit was under her breath, as though she couldn't quite bear to speak it.

"What do you—" I started, but Val stepped in, putting her hand on the orc's arm.

"Let's get a drink," she said, and led us toward the tavern, having heard my interaction with Lambkin. "We've . . . got a lot to talk about."

I forced myself to meet her eyes, but found that Val was still looking at anyone but me—which included the three members of the Trio. Raelas, Carle, and Ama were following at a distance, their scrunched-up body language betraying that they felt they were intruding on this pretty awkward interaction.

"A drink," I said. "Good idea."

"So . . ." Lore said, with less of his usual cheeriness, "anyone wanna go first?"

The eight of us were sitting around a large table in the center of the tavern, the raucous laughter of drunk locals erupting sporadically around us. A drunk woman staggered backward into Ama, who responded with a swift elbow to the leg.

"Sorry we didn't warn you about Tokas," I said, though the apology was a little forced; we had a job to do, and I didn't like apologizing for taking all the help we could get.

"You should be," Val snapped, then immediately caught herself, blushing.

"You said she's going to betray us again?" I prodded.

"Not us. Me," Arzak replied. "She kill me. I saw it."

Lore leaned forward, resting his elbows on the table. "Did Yusef show you this?"

The orc nodded.

"He showed me things, too."

All faces snapped to Lore.

"He *what*?" Raelas and I asked him at the same time.

Val looked to the tiefling, then back to me, eyebrow raised.

"What he show you?" Arzak asked.

"How to save you all."

We all grew quiet. Really, this was a great way to dampen the spirits of a conversation; I took note for next time I wanted someone to stop speaking to me.

"We save everyone by killing the Player," I said. "That's why we're all here. That's why *Tokas* is here, because we need every advantage we can get. We've never fought anyone this strong before—the pyroknight, Niamh, they were strong in their own rights, sure, but they couldn't *see us coming*."

"And how do you suppose we get around that?" Ama asked.

"Who these three?" Arzak asked.

"Hired help."

"And friends," Raelas added. This resulted in her getting a dirty look from Val—one that the tiefling met with a feigned, polite smile on her face.

"He always going see us coming," the orc continued, ignoring the three new faces. This wasn't like her; she was usually polite. Clearly her brief encounter with Tokas had thrown her for a loop. Though maybe this was fair enough if Tokas really was prophesied to kill her. "We cannot kill him."

"Nobody is unkillable." Except me, sometimes, but I left that bit out. "All we gotta do is bake some redundancy into the plan. OK, he might see the first strike coming, but the second? Third? Fourth? Fifth? Si—"

"And so on," Corminar cut in.

"He will see," Arzak said.

"What do *you* suggest, then?" Raelas asked. "Cos Styk has got us this far, and—"

"Undo his work," Val said, glaring at the tiefling woman now, making absolutely no attempt to hide it. If Raelas was bothered by this, she didn't show it. Right now, I was regretting sitting next to the tiefling woman.

"You know about his work?" Arzak asked.

"The mala trading," Corminar replied. "We conducted sufficient investigation to acquire this knowledge, yes."

"*That*, we can do something about," Val said.

"We already did! We took down his operations in the city. Got them all arrested. Job done. So now, we—"

"All of them?" The witch seemed to suddenly have the confidence to meet my eyes, but I suspected it was powered by Raelas-inflicted wrath. "Because that's not what we heard."

"Well sorry if you didn't get the most up-to-date information, considering you were *prisoners*."

"This has nothing to do with us being prisoners, it has to do with—"

"Alright," Lore said, standing up and slamming his hands down on the table. "You two need to sort this thing out." Neither Val nor I needed to look at him to know he was talking about us.

"Maybe later," Val said as Raelas scooted her chair ever so slightly closer to me. Lore glared at her.

"There still mala trading in city. Shipment went east yesterday," Arzak said. "If we stop this, he not get his way. *Council* not get their way. Almost as good as killing him."

"Almost," Corminar echoed.

"We'll take almost," Val said.

I forced myself to keep meeting her gaze. "No, we won't."

"I'm with Styk," Raelas said.

"*We know*," said Val and Lore in unison.

Carle raised a hand. "Should we be here?"

"If we aren't going to kill him, we'll take our payment now," Ama added.

"Can we talk about that later?" Corminar asked.

Val began swigging from her beer, and my instinct was to do the same, but I resisted. Lore thumped his head down against the top of the table, while Raelas put her hand on my arm reassuring me, causing me to snap my hand back—but not before Val saw. Ama was still looking at me expectantly, while Corminar slumped his shoulders and sighed.

This reunion wasn't going like *anyone* wanted it to.

At that moment—and I almost thanked the Architects themselves for their timing here—the tavern's door slammed open, revealing Lambkin and a young half-tiefling boy. They looked around, and upon spotting us, the ranger pointed the boy in our direction.

As they approached, Corminar looked up at him and said under his breath, "Oh, thank Hades." He put his hand to his mouth when he realized what he'd just said; never before had he been happy to see Lambkin, his rival in *Archery*.

"Drink, Lammy?" Lore asked.

"Apparently, beer is the only positive thing to come out of this meeting," Carle added.

Lambkin looked around at us all nervously, though I couldn't tell if that had to do with the furious expressions on some of our faces, Tokas's wellbeing, or the reason that the boy was here with him.

"Who's this? Your son?" Val asked.

Lambkin looked down at the young boy.

"Could it be? *Father*?" the kid asked, blinking big eyes up at him.

The ranger hesitated. "No, I—"

"Just kidding. I'm a courier. Got a message for a Mister Lore?"

Lore raised his hand.

"See, I told you he was here," Lambkin grumbled.

"What's the message?" I asked, cutting through whatever bickering was going on between the ranger and the young lad.

"Alenna needs ya. Says there's a problem. A mala problem."

"See?" Val murmured.

I sighed, sinking down in my chair. This was not going to be fun.

CHAPTER THIRTY-SIX

Corruption Evolves

The re-formation of the Slayers hadn't gone very well.

I think anyone among us would have admitted that, what with the usual bickering having evolved into arguing, and with our open emotional wounds showing no signs of healing. It was maybe no wonder, then, that the message from the young courier—that Alenna needed our help—caused the group to split once more.

Lore, Corminar, and I, as well as the Trio, left the tavern to go see what Alenna had found, while Arzak and Val stayed behind, the latter showing no sign of slowing down on the drinking. At least we'd agreed that we would remain in touch, sharing information, and that we'd need to work together in some capacity if we were going to defeat Yusef. It was only after I left the tavern that I realized I'd included Lambkin and Tokas in that "together," which maybe Arzak needed spelling out. It surprised me, too, that my subconscious had included Tokas in our group after our earlier betrayal, but maybe that spoke to how anxious I was about taking down this Player—that we really did need all the help we could get.

There was a lingering pain in my chest as we put the tavern behind us. At some point, Val and I would need to talk. Properly. I'd need to find out why she left. Not that I didn't know the answer—I knew it was because of my ancestry—but I needed to hear her say it. And I needed to hear that she couldn't get past it. Only then, maybe, would I be able to move on. With that thought, *move on*, chaos erupted in my chest; no part of me wanted that, but maybe it was what I needed.

Alenna was waiting in her doorway as we approached, her face pale. If before she shared her old friend's penchant for cheeriness in the face of horror, she didn't anymore. And Lore, for that matter, wasn't his usual jolly self, either, ever since that interaction with Yusef. It really felt that everything had started going wrong during that fight with Niamh—since then, nothing came naturally, and everything seemed to lead to disaster and melancholy.

Or maybe I was just in a bad mood.

"Everything OK?" Alenna asked as Lore passed her, entering her place of business.

"It will be. Eventually."

Judging by her expression, this answer didn't satisfy the scientist, but there were apparently other priorities right now. We settled around the two chairs in the downstairs surgery, Ama and Corminar taking those seats while the rest of us stood around them. Carle was about to prop himself up on the medical plinth before Lore gently stopped him by pointing to a piece of flesh that hadn't been cleaned up.

"What is it?" Raelas asked. "Take it it's not a surprise birthday party for Ama?"

"It is your birthday?" Corminar asked.

"Next week."

"Happy birthday for then. Lore has a party hat you may wish to borrow."

Alenna remained still, staring on glumly. A cough from Lore refocused us on why we were here.

"There's a man on the loose," the scientist said. "He's been . . . touched by the malae. It's corrupted him."

I glanced to Corminar, who met my gaze across the room. We were on the same page: this was reminiscent of the vultures we'd come across. "Let me guess," I said. "He's not all there?"

"He's not there at all. He might look like a man, but he's a monster. He needs to be . . . put down."

Corminar rose from his seat, drawing in a deep breath. "A simple enough problem," he said, which was probably not the correct description of any mala-related issue. "Do you have a location?"

Alenna nodded glumly. "To the west, that's all I know. You'll see the chaos. But . . . I don't think you're taking this seriously enough. This corruption has the brain of a man. It is smarter than any mala you have dealt with before, and that's not to say they're dumb usually. This 'man,' it's . . . hiding. Striking from the shadows. It's . . . *adapting*."

We followed breadcrumbs of destruction.

At first, the screaming had been a pretty good indicator of where to pick up the trail. A woman, attacked by the walking corruption, lay dead on the street, guards holding their friend back while they—sensibly, if horrifically—began to burn the body. Further north, a wooden building extension had been smashed through, the strength required for such a feat being beyond what the local population were capable of. We next found ourselves back in the narrow, winding markets in the center of the city, where there was no shortage of witnesses who'd seen the "man of shadows," who pointed us deeper into the market still.

It was at that point that I realized where we were headed—back to that small courtyard where that mala-trading operation had been based. I turned to Corminar with a furrowed brow, who nodded to confirm that he was on the same page.

"Why there?" I asked.

"Could the answer be as simple as 'coincidence'?"

I shook my head. "I think we'd be idiots to put it down to that."

"Agreed. But then . . . what else might be the reason?"

We entered the courtyard in single file, this formation necessary due to the narrowness of the alley entry, but we did so with our weapons raised, ready to strike. Lore, at the front of the pack, waved the flaming torch he'd picked up at the market on the way, making sure to keep it between himself and the enemy.

But the enemy wasn't there. Not in sight, at least.

Keeping our footsteps quiet, we crept toward the building that had once been the headquarters of this mala-trading operation. Lore pushed the door open gently, causing it to creak on its hinges. We paused, waiting for the noise to alert the monster to our presence, but nothing jumped out at us. Nothing ambushed us.

So we entered, our breaths shallow, our weapons raised, and our eyes peeled for any signs of movement.

"I don't like this . . ." Ama whispered, getting a nod from Raelas in response.

I spotted something in the corner of one of the rooms. It was an otherwise bare room, no furnishings, not so much as paper or paint on the walls, with only one exit. The only distinguishing feature in here was a large burn mark on the floor. It was where the guards had dealt with the traders' stock.

Corminar crouched down at my side, sweeping his fingertips through the ash. "Perhaps it seeks its brothers," the elf said, voice hushed.

"Or to mourn them."

"Slayers?" Carle called out from another room, a bit louder than I would have liked considering the creature could still be around here somewhere.

Instead of shouting back, Corminar and I went to the source of the cry, to find Carle leafing through correspondence atop a nearby desk.

"How much did you investigate this operation?" Carle asked.

"Well, there wasn't exactly any time, considering we had to get Lambkin out of—"

"Did your friend know these traders were here before the Player?"

I hesitated, then half snatched the letter from his hands. Corminar read it over my shoulder, and I could tell that he was a faster reader considering he groaned a few seconds before I did.

"What?" Lore asked in whispered tones. "What is it?"

"It's from Yusef," I said, handing him the letter. "He didn't create this operation. He *bought* it."

"So that means—"

"It was here already," I finished.

"If, seemingly, on a smaller scale," Corminar added.

Lore, face pale, handed the letter back to me, and I folded it neatly before pushing it into a pocket. It was evidence, and evidence that might come in handy later, if Tokas and Lambkin were to complete their mission of exposing rather than killing the Player.

"Alright," Raelas said. "So, before the Player knew about these traders . . . who was buying? Supply and demand, isn't it? This business wouldn't exist unless someone needed the malae. But who? For what?"

"That, my dear, is the question," the elf—and the only person I'd ever met who had the phrase *my dear* in their vocabulary—replied.

"We'll ask Lambkin about it later," I said. "Maybe there's more to the story."

"Would he keep information back?" Corminar asked. "I do not believe so; he is not that kind of man." How far the elf had come in his views of the rival ranger; once upon a time, he wouldn't *dream* of defending Lambkin, and yet here we were.

I shrugged. "Well unless you have any better—"

Something scuffed the ground in the next room, and all six of us froze. Our heads snapped toward the source of the noise. Now, if this was a story I was telling you in a tavern, or maybe a bard's tale, this situation would normally be followed up by us discovering that the source of the noise was something inane. Maybe a stray dog. Or a rat.

In this case, I'm afraid to say, there was no wry twist at the end of the story. A figure shuffled into the doorway—one that, in the low light, we might have been forgiven for thinking was a man. But we knew better. The awkward gait, the spluttering noises, and the lack of the "what are you doing in here?" question gave it away.

As all six of us took a step backward, adjusting our grips on our weapons, the figure stepped forth, into a stream of light pouring in through the open front door. The once-man's skin had turned gray. His jaw hung open, slack. His eyes, while still the usual tiefling pink-red hue, had no life behind them. And, perhaps most worryingly of all, a strange black ooze seeped from the man's eyes and pores—an ooze that matched the once-vultures we'd seen on the road to Coldharbor.

Lore handed the flaming torch to Carle, before grabbing a nearby wooden chair and smashing it against the ground. As he tore a piece of wood free and held it against the torch, the corrupted man snarled.

And then it lunged.

CHAPTER THIRTY-SEVEN

Spoken like a True Monster

All of us took a semiunconscious step back, our base instincts driving us to put as much space between us and the corrupted man as possible. But it wouldn't be enough. If this corruption played by the same rules as all the mala-created corruption we'd faced down in the past, then we absolutely could not let him—it?—touch us.

"Out!" I shouted.

Lore, Ama, and Carle, who were closest to the door, bombed outside. At the same moment, I opened a portal. Corminar, having been around me long enough, knew that it was coming, and jumped through immediately. But Raelas took another half second to realize, so I grabbed her by the arm and yanked her through, allowing the portal to close behind me just as the monster reached out for us.

The portal snapped shut, and—

No, I realized, it hadn't. The creature's fingertips were already across the portal's threshold, and it pushed itself into the faint purple magicks. Fingertips became hand, which became arm, which became snarling body. Alenna hadn't been kidding; this monster had brains. It really was a level up on the malae we'd battled before, not that they were unintelligent by any means.

The creature snarled as it pushed itself through the portal, stumbling to the ground in the courtyard, and it hissed something that I almost thought was a word. *Missed? Must?*

"Plan, Styk?" Raelas asked.

"Same as always: kill it with fire." I looked to Lore, and on this signal he charged to the front of the group, Carle following close at his side, both of them wielding flaming torches.

The monster recoiled at the sight of fire, snarling, but it wasn't warded off. Not that we wanted to ward it off; if it ran, then it could hurt more people before we could put it down.

"Ama," I shouted, glancing to the metal mage then nodding to the one alley-way leading out of the courtyard, "take the exit. Make sure it doesn't escape."

The woman nodded, and did immediately as commanded. Whatever Raelas had said to her about following orders had worked.

Lore and Carle pressed forward with their torches, pushing the creature back into the corner of the courtyard, keeping it hemmed in. But I wasn't under any illusions that it would be this easy; already I could see those black eyes darting around, searching for a way to fight back.

Corminar hurried to the side of the two large men, then raised a clothbound arrowhead to Lore's torch, setting it alight. In a flash, he nocked the now-flaming arrow and shot it at the monster's chest. As fire met corruption, its flesh sizzled like food in a frying pan, and the creature squealed with pain.

When the sizzling faded, it snapped its dark eyes to Corminar, and it growled.

"Cor, I think it's—" Lore started.

The corrupted man then launched into the air, soaring above both Lore and Carle—no easy feat—and landing behind them, at Corminar's side. The elf froze for just a moment, but fortunately I was quicker to react. I whipped a hand forward and opened a portal behind Corminar, the haste making my aim sloppy, putting its edge just under his feet. The elf teetered on the edge for a moment, but when the mala-corrupted man moved to attack, he took a step backward and found no ground beneath him.

As the monster leaped toward where Corminar had been only moments earlier, I realized that it was going to keep flying through the air into Carle. My breath catching, I opened my other pair of portals—thanking my past self for picking the *Enhanced Portals* ability back at level 50, allowing me to open two pairs at once. This second set I placed between Carle and the enemy, expecting the creature to fly through it.

But it reacted quickly upon seeing the portal, flinging its limbs wide and catching the edge of the magick to avoid falling through.

At that moment, two metal projectiles—courtesy of Ama—shot toward the monster, burying themselves in its flesh. Each impact visibly knocked the monster backward, but they weren't enough to push it through the portal and out the other side, which I'd positioned high in the sky above us.

Corminar, meanwhile, had skirted around the edge of the battleground, once again lighting an arrow from Lore's torch. If it had worked before, it would work again, but I had a feeling that killing this creature was going to take more fire than any one arrow could deliver.

As this flaming arrow met its target, the creature shrieked. Once again, among the noise, I could swear I could hear a word. A word in the common tongue. Was the man's brain not entirely corrupted?

Carle charged, roaring, bringing his flaming torch in an arc through the air and down toward the beast.

In that moment, I made a—possibly *bad*—split-second decision. "Stop!" I shouted.

The warrior hesitated, stopping his attack in midswing, then looked to me, confused. For the record, everyone else in the courtyard was also giving me that same expression—one that silently asked, "Have you gone *mad*?"

"I think it's . . ." I started, meeting the creature's black eyes. "I think there's still a man in there."

"A man who's killed multiple people," Ama shouted back.

"A man who'll kill anyone he touches," Carle added.

When did they become such experts in malae? I ignored the pair of them, keeping my eyes on the creature, whose demeanor had changed. It no longer snarled, it no longer looked like it was about to attack. Had we just been dealing with a cornered animal? One with no real malicious intent? A creature just looking to survive?

"Lore," I cried to him, keeping my eyes on the possible enemy. "Do you have any visions? Do you see what happens if we don't kill it?"

"*Don't* kill it?" Raelas repeated.

I ignored her, too. "Do you see anything, Lore?"

"Nothing." The reply was glum.

"Never come when you want them to, huh?"

To this, Lore had no reply. Was that a disagreement? If so, what had he seen already that he'd wanted to? What possible fates had he avoided?

"Can you hear me?" I asked the creature.

It didn't reply, but stared back at me with bleak eyes.

"Can you understand me? Is there still a man in there?" I pressed the question.

This time, it made some kind of noise, again a noise that—if generous—you might describe as being a word in the common tongue.

"It does not understand you, Styk," Corminar said. "It is a monster. Nothing—"

"*Stand*," the creature hissed, and my heart dropped.

"*That* was definitely a word," Raelas said.

"We're all already standing," Lore added, a tad perplexed.

"*Under . . . stand*," the corrupted man said, this time managing the full word.

I continued holding the creature's gaze. This posed a pretty bad problem. Carle and Ama had been right—this "man" had killed people already, and would again, if left alive. Anyone it touched, even unintentionally, would succumb to the corruption. And yet . . . it was an innocent. A victim. A cornered animal.

"I don't know what to do here," I said.

"Kill it," Corminar snapped.

"It didn't do anything wrong! Not intentionally, at least."

"You do not know that. Alenna said this creature was far more intelligent than any mala we have faced before; perhaps this is a ploy?"

The corrupted man held my gaze, too, and in those dark eyes, I could swear I saw sadness.

I gulped. My heart began beating so hard that I could hear it reverberating around my head. I took a steady step forward toward the corrupted man.

"Styk?" Raelas asked, and I could hear the genuine concern in her tone.

I took another step forward.

The creature didn't recoil.

"I dunno if this is such a good idea . . ." Lore said, also worried.

"A vision tell you that?" I asked.

"No, just common sense."

I ignored the big guy and kept moving, holding one hand out in front of me to reach toward the monster, gesturing that I was coming in peace, the other hand pointing at the ground.

"Don't let it touch you!" Ama shouted.

"Yes, I know the drill."

"Then why—"

I shook my head firmly, and continued to look into the eyes of the corrupted tiefling. "I'm not going to hurt you, OK?"

The creature said nothing, but cast its eyes over at Carle and Lore's torches.

"Put the torches away," I told them.

"Do no such thing," Corminar said.

The two larger men settled instead for holding the still-flaming torches behind their backs.

I took another step toward the creature. "We're going to help you. We're going to get you to someone who can help. We're going to get you to the scientist."

And then, the monster snarled once more.

It bared its grime-covered teeth at me.

And it lunged.

CHAPTER THIRTY-EIGHT

Created

With my right hand still pointing to the ground, I activated a portal, and I slipped through just in time to avoid the creature's swiping hand. As I stumbled out at Raelas's side, I breathed a sigh of relief.

At least, until the tiefling stared up at my head with wide, terrified eyes.

"What?" I asked. "What's wrong?"

Without replying, Raelas suddenly leaped for my sheath, yanking the knife free. I thought for a moment that she was about to stab me with it, but instead she whipped it fast over the top of my head. Locks of my long hair fell to the ground at my side, and looking down upon them I saw the corruption just starting to take hold.

Raelas had just saved my life.

"Thanks," I offered her.

"Is that all I'm getting? Not even a kiss?"

"Now's not the time."

"A kiss later, then. Got it."

Ignoring her, I turned my attention to the corrupted locks of hair, and portaled them to Lore's side. He knew exactly what to do, bending over with his torch to burn the hair from existence.

The creature still had its eyes trained squarely on me—something had focused it away from the flames and instead on the one guy who'd tried to save it. Him? It? I still wasn't sure.

"I was *trying* to help you," I told the creature.

It responded by charging across the courtyard toward me, arms flailing wildly. I opened a portal behind me with plenty of time to spare for Raelas and I to step through.

"There is no reasoning with this creature," Corminar said as he loosed another flaming arrow. "We must eliminate it."

The corrupted man shrieked again as the fire hit its grimy flesh, but still this wasn't enough to distract it from me. As it charged again, I shifted to the left to keep Raelas well out of harm's way and I stepped through another portal.

"It *really* doesn't like you," Raelas said.

Ama followed that up with something under her breath, and I was pretty sure I could work out what it was. But now wasn't the time to get into an argument.

"Remember Westbara?" I shouted to Raelas, who was now at the other side of the courtyard from me.

The tiefling nodded. "We bring the house down on it."

I opened a portal at Lore's side, and he stepped through to the other end— into the building that the traders had been using as their headquarters. The *clay* building. You know, a material that famously didn't burn.

"Err, Lore?"

The big guy poked his head back out of the door. "Yeah?"

"Is there enough wood in there?"

". . . Not much!"

The monster charged at me again, and once more I shifted out of the way using a portal. This was good—the longer I could keep it occupied with its anger toward me, the longer we could figure out how to kill it.

"Any bright ideas?" Raelas asked. "Anywhere we can get something to burn, and fast?"

As everyone looked around, I kept my eyes on the charging monster, making absolutely sure I didn't let it get close—either to me or to anyone else. As I opened the latest portal, something occurred to me. I'd seen plenty of wood lately, and it was just on the other side of my *Saved Portal*. But those in orange robes were *not* going to like it.

"I'm about to open a portal!" I shouted to the team. "There's plenty of wood just a *Portal Slice* away, but we're going to need to move fast. Raelas, can you be ready with the portals? And Carle, Corminar, you'll throw the wood in."

"Yeah," Raelas said. "Of course, but where are you—"

I opened the *Saved Portal* in the middle of the courtyard, revealing the stairs overlooking Coldharbor's central plaza—and the Player's wooden stage thereon.

"Ah," the tiefling said. "Got it."

I shoved my head through the portal and activated *Portal Slice* after *Portal Slice*, cutting through the foundations of the nonenchanted wood. Lillya, who was onstage among a number of other cultists, looked on with wide eyes as the floor beneath them began to shake, and then, quickly, collapsed.

As Carle, Corminar, and Raelas leaped through the portal, I retreated, leading the enemy away from our source of wood. The monster began to charge once more, and then, midcharge, slowed to a halt. It turned gradually toward the *Saved Portal*, where plank after plank after plank of wood was soaring out after being catapulted through by Raelas's portals.

"Oh no you don't!" I shouted, waving my hands to get its attention. "Over here! It's me you want."

But still the corrupted tiefling was turning, apparently working out what we meant to do next.

"What was it I said before? Something made you *really* hate me. Was it saying I'd help you? Was it saying—"

The creature charged, grimy arms flailing once more, but this time it headed for the portal. "Cor, Rae, I—" I started, but realized any warning would be too late. Instead, I snapped the *Saved Portal* closed for a moment, stranding the others in the courtyard, but causing the monster to charge through that spot without interfering.

As I opened the portal once more, next to me, a piece of wood soared out and knocked me in the side. "Ouch?" I said.

Any more complaints I had were quickly silenced by Corminar, Raelas, and Carle leaping through the portal, a hundred cultists in orange robes charging after them.

"They weren't happy," Carle explained.

"No, I bet."

Ama moved away from the exit to the courtyard, but I held out a hand to stop her.

"No! Stay there. We have to keep him here at all costs."

The metal mage nodded her agreement.

"The rest of you, well . . ." I opened a portal beneath the pile of wood, throwing it inside the building.

"I'm still in here!" Lore shouted to remind me, popping out the building amidst a rush of debris.

"Sorry!"

The barbarian lit the pile of wood, and the flames lit fast. Now, all there was to do, was—

Raelas opened a portal, the flaming interior of the trader headquarters visible on the other side. "Push it through!" she roared.

—well, that.

The monster croaked something I chose not to understand, before Corminar loosed a flaming arrow and Carle threw a nearby rock into its chest. The corrupted man stumbled backward, but it wasn't enough. Ama, pressing the attack, yanked four metal-headed arrows from Corminar's quiver with her magicks, and threw them all at once into the creature. It stumbled back, into the portal, the flames licking at its back, and it grabbed at the edges of the portal.

It howled.

And then it ran.

Ama's eyes widened as the creature charged her—or not her, really, but the single exit to the courtyard.

I opened a portal in front of the monster, but it was smart enough to avoid it, twisting to one side to move around it. I opened another portal, and again the creature anticipated it, this time sliding across the ground underneath the very faint purple magicks.

But there was another option.

"I can't believe I'm doing this *again*," I grumbled as I activated my *Pocket World* ability. Dozens of scraps of cloth rained down upon the creature, knocking it to the ground at Ama's feet. It dragged itself forward, both toward Ama and the exit, but Corminar was ready.

"Lore!" he shouted across the courtyard.

The barbarian was ready. He raised his torch into the air, eyes glowing yellow once more. And Corminar shot. The clothbound arrow passed through the flames, lighting instantly—an ability afforded by Corminar's potions—and landed squarely in the pile of cloth.

My *Needlework* supplies, and the enemy, went up in flames.

The corrupted tiefling staggered, trying to stand even when sapped by fire—the mala's only weakness. Corminar and I arrived at its side just in time for the ranger to release another flaming arrow into it, knocking it to the ground once more.

"*Kill . . . creator . . .*" it said.

Level ? Corruption defeated!

Worldbending: +5,200XP
Worldbending increased to level 59!
Base Points Gained: +2 INT, +2 Free Points (INT/WIS/CHA)

Corminar and I stood at the corrupted man's side, and the ranger loosed another shot, even though we had the notification to confirm that we'd defeated it. It was better to be safe than sorry with this kind of danger after all.

As Ama scooted backward, away from the dead creature, I put my hands on my sides and sighed. "You know, at some point, I'm actually going to do some *Needlework* with these supplies," I said as I watched the cloth burn.

"I shall believe it when I see it," Corminar replied. "How much did this cost you?"

"I don't wanna talk about it."

"I . . . Err . . ." Ama started as Lore, Raelas, and Carle appeared at our sides.

"Yes, you'll be paid for this," I said. "I'll add it to the bill."

"That's great, but—"

"We can talk amounts later. Any idea what that meant, about killing the—"

Ama said nothing, but she raised her foot. The skin around her ankle was . . . paling. It was gray. The corruption had taken hold. And, unlike my locks of hair, there was no simply cutting it off.

"Ah," I said.

CHAPTER THIRTY-NINE

Emergency Surgery

"Go," Corminar said to me, face paling, the fire spreading throughout the building behind us. "*Go.*"

"But the—" I started, gesturing to the flames.

"We'll handle it," Lore said. "Go."

I nodded. We were on the same page; there was only one chance to stop the corruption before it claimed Ama's life. "Raelas," I told the tiefling. "We're portaling. Get ready." Without waiting for a reaction, I opened a portal beneath Ama, dropping her into the sky high above.

And then we ran. We sprinted through the streets of Coldharbor, opening portals beneath the tumbling Ama, magicking her back into the sky once more. Raelas opened portals at our sides so that we could traverse the city quickly, while I focused my own portals on the woman touched by the mala. I considered using my *Saved Portal* once more, but this was a situation where it wasn't helpful; its location at Coldharbor's central plaza was about as far from Alenna's surgery as we were. And, of course, it was surrounded by hundreds or thousands of cultists. For all their idiocy in worshipping Players, they didn't deserve to be put at risk of being corrupted. Few—if any—deserved that.

And so, on we went, Ama's screaming having long since faded, but thankfully this was due to her getting used to falling rather than the corruption having spread too far already. From what I glimpsed as she tumbled toward the lower of the latest pair of portals, the corruption was still located only on her leg. Hopefully, we still had time. Hopefully.

It wasn't long until we reached Alenna's practice, and I opened the final portal facing upward, not dropping Ama from a height, but instead using the momentum to send her up into the air. At the peak of her flight, I whipped open another portal below her, so she only had to fall a couple of feet before she was on the ground.

Raelas was already knocking on the door of the surgery, pounding it with all her might.

"*What?*" a familiar voice cried when the door swung open, and Raelas replied to Alenna simply by pointing at Ama, on the ground outside.

The scientist's face paled. "What happened? Was it . . ."

I knew what the rest of the question would be. Was it the corrupted man that she'd sent us after? Well, I wasn't going to lie to her. "You can make it up to us by fixing her. Stop it spreading."

"She—" Alenna started.

"Do whatever you need to," Raelas interrupted. "Anything. As long as she lives."

Alenna nodded glumly. "Wait there. Don't touch her."

For a few moments, I had to stretch out my arms to warn away the crowd that was forming. The crowd was only interested in our portal magicks, but as soon as they saw Ama, they backed up. Fast.

Alenna stepped forth from the building again, this time wearing a thick apron and a face mask, and she chucked both me and Raelas an apron each. "Alright," she said. "Bring her in."

Alenna insisted on doing her surgery behind a curtain, though it seemed this wasn't so much about protecting her secrets as it was about protecting us from the trauma of watching. When the other three—Lore, Corminar, and Carle—arrived, they entered the room in silence that matched our own, and the five of us waited without speaking for Alenna to reappear.

At one point, I glanced over in Lore's direction, and I saw his eyes glowing yellow once more. The visions were coming harder and faster than ever before. Not that you'd know without looking at him—he'd gone from talking about every single one to not mentioning them at all. Was this because their contents had changed? We knew he'd foreseen some of our deaths, and had worked secretly to avoid them, but what else was he *not* telling us? Was he seeing things even worse than that?

There was a knock on the door as we waited, and when nobody else moved, I dragged myself up from my perch to swing it open, expecting to have to tell people that the scientist was busy. But standing there, in the street, were two familiar faces—Val and Arzak.

"Hey," Val said.

"Lambkin say you here. We want talk."

I stepped aside to reveal the rest of the team sitting, heads in hands or faces pale, waiting for Alenna to be done. The other two members of the Slayers looked past me and one of them, at least, read the room.

"We talk outside, maybe," Arzak said.

"No, it can wait, Arz," Val said, glancing pointedly to the crowd of glum adventurers further into the building. "It can wait."

The orc nodded. "Where you stay? Not with Tokas? We not stay with Tokas."

"No, not us, either," I replied, semiexasperatedly. "You don't think we've forgiven her, do you? After all she did? It's a means to an end—gotta take all the help we can get."

Arzak opened her mouth, but I wasn't in the mood for this to spiral into an argument.

"We're in the Crooked Well, toward the western side of town. You want me to show you the—" I started to ask.

"We can find it," the witch replied. "We'll . . . see you there?"

I nodded, then turned away, back toward the rest of the team. Only when I was sure Val was far enough away that she wouldn't look back, I glanced back over at her, a heavy weight in my stomach.

The best part of another hour passed before Alenna finally appeared once more, pulling back the curtain to reveal Ama. The metal mage was pulling herself upright, and Lore's scientist friend had to rush back over to help her.

"She's . . . alright?" Raelas asked, eyes blinking with disbelief. "She's . . ." And then she saw the corrupted leg—the corruption, and foot, sliced away.

"I stopped the spread," Alenna said. "Isolated the corruption, I think."

"You think?" Lore repeated.

Ama brought her foot down to the ground, and instinctively tried to put her weight on a foot that wasn't there. The woman grimaced, and for a second I had a moment of sympathy for her.

"We'll get you to a healer," I said. "Maybe Tokas can help, even."

Corminar glanced at me and shook his head once. Firmly.

"Well, someone out there will be able to—"

Ama responded by raising one hand into the air. Metal surgical equipment around the room started to shake, then move toward the air in front of the mage. There, a ball of metal objects formed, shaking, then vibrating with an ever-increasing intensity. The metal began to glow before our eyes, bending and then melting entirely as Ama's magicks heated it up. She whipped up her other hand to steady her magicks, Alenna having to hold the injured woman upright, and formed the molten metal into shape.

I realized what the shape was only moments before Ama shot it toward her injured limb—it was half an artificial leg.

Ama screamed as the molten metal hit her skin, but so determined was she that she carried on, morphing the metal into a shape that bound itself to what remained of her leg. Her screaming faded as the metal cooled, and everyone else in the room was too stunned to move, or to talk. Even Alenna, who was surely more familiar with this kind of stuff. The mage breathed deeply through the last of the pain, before pushing herself to her feet—one old, one new.

"Good," she said, nodding.

Maybe Ama was a lot tougher than I'd given her credit for.

"She did to *herself?*" Arzak asked.

We were back in the basement of the inn we were staying at, flagons of ale in our hands. Around my table sat Arzak, Raelas, and Corminar, while Lore and Val sat at the bar. Carle was at Ama's bedside upstairs while she got some scientist-prescribed rest. The two at the bar were talking in such hushed voices that I got the impression they were talking about me, but maybe that was just innate paranoia or having too large an ego.

"Yep."

"Maybe need her on *our* team," Arzak said. "Can get rid of this one." She pointed to Corminar; he was the butt of the joke, this time.

"Are we still one team, then?" Corminar asked, as ever going straight for the most awkward and difficult-to-answer question.

Arzak staggered over her reply. "I . . . Is . . ." She almost grimaced at the elf. "Maybe not answer for that, yet." I couldn't help but notice she glanced at Val while she said this.

"Then when?" Corminar asked, apparently not willing to let the matter drop, despite how awkward it made the vibe at this table.

"Don't know," Arzak replied, and then—perhaps in desperation to change the subject—asked, "How?"

I furrowed my brow. "How what?"

"How this Lenny save her?"

"Alenna," Corminar corrected her.

"She . . ." I started to answer, but then realized I didn't quite know. We'd seen the end result, the woman being down half a leg where the corruption had taken hold, but we knew from prior experience that this wasn't always enough. "I guess Ama was lucky?"

"Hmm." The orc nodded approvingly. "She good. We have her on team, too?"

"Just how big a team are you after?"

"Millions of us." Arzak smiled, as though envisioning it. "How is *Needlework* going?"

As the night grew dark, I caught up with Arzak and drank probably a tad too much beer. It should have been enjoyable, being able to spend time with an old friend—even if Val seemed to be painstakingly avoiding me—but there was something else casting a cloud over the affair. A thought.

Just what had Alenna done behind that curtain?

CHAPTER FORTY

The Metal Mage

I'd drunk just enough yesterday evening that I had a disturbed night's sleep. When I first awoke, it was the dead of night, not even a hint of light in the sky outside the cramped-room's window. The room was so dark that I couldn't even see Lore on the other cot, and strangely there was none of his usual snoring. I tried to ignore a full bladder and get back to sleep, but it was uncomfortable enough that I eventually realized it was a futile effort. I rose, stumbled down the hallway to the shared bathroom, trying my best not to creak the floorboards and wake anyone else up.

I couldn't resist a sigh of relief as I emptied my bladder, though I immediately regretted making noise. From the sounds of movement down the hallway, toward the rooms where the others were sleeping, I'd probably already disturbed some of them. I was quiet as I went back to my room, Lore's snoring still absent—maybe he was sleeping lightly, too—and after another half an hour or so, I drifted back to sleep.

The second time I awoke, I saw the faint silhouette of a woman standing over me.

Groggily, I snapped my hand to the dagger I kept under my pillow, and whipped it toward them. But the woman's own hand snapped down to block me.

"It's me," the figure said.

"Val?"

There was a pause. "Raelas."

"Oh," I whispered, putting the dagger down and wiping the sleep from my eyes. "Sorry."

Raelas remained quiet, then took a seat on the end of my bed. "Lore here?" she finally asked.

I squinted through the darkness at his bed, and where he should have been. I hadn't considered this as a possibility. "Not sure. Maybe not. Why? And . . . why are you here?"

"I . . . thought I heard something."

It was my turn to pause. "OK? What kind of thing?"

"Something . . . I don't know, wrong?"

"So you came to me for reassurance?" I retorted. "It's probably just some stranger in another room. People have weird snores." I glanced over at Lore, or where he should have been. "Trust me."

"Reassurance? Sure, if you're offering. It *is* just me in my room if you want to—"

"No," I answered quickly, but maybe not as quickly as I should have done.

At least there wasn't any time for Raelas to read into that moment of hesitation, because suddenly there was a noise coming from down the hallway. A noise that was animalistic, almost. A noise that was human, but not. A noise that I could only describe as . . . wrong.

"That noise," Raelas said.

We rose from the bed and stuck our heads out the door, looking down the hallway toward the source of the noise. Toward, I realized, Carle and Ama's room. Down the hallway, between us and the noise, two more doors opened. Corminar stuck his head out of one, and Val and Arzak the other. Both of the women seemed immediately more interested in Raelas standing next to me than they were in the strange noises coming from Ama's room. This was going to be *a thing*, but there was no time to deal with it now.

"Ama . . ." Raelas breathed.

I took a step out the door, toward Ama and Carle's room, when suddenly their door creaked open. It took me a moment for my eyes to adjust enough to the low light to see who it was, but then again, the large frame should have been enough of an indication.

"Carle?" Raelas asked. "What's . . ."

The warrior took a step forward without speaking, then gently closed the door behind him, turning a key in the lock. His voice was calm and measured when he finally did speak, but it was artificially so. "It's Ama," he said.

I felt Raelas tense at my side. "What's happened? Do we need Alenna?"

"I think . . ." Carle started, then drew in a deep breath. "I think it's too late for that."

A chill ran down my spine.

"What do you mean, too late? What do you—" Raelas started, but abruptly cut off when someone—some*thing*—pounded the door behind Carle.

"She's turned, Rae. The scientist failed."

"What do you mean?" the tiefling replied, shaking her head. "I saw her last night. She was fine. She was on the mend."

Carle took another step back when Ama pounded on the door once more, and only now did I realize he'd brought his sword out the room with him. "Alenna used magicks to heal her," the warrior said. "I saw those magicks fade. A blue glow. A ward, if I'm not mistaken. And when those magicks faded, then . . ."

Ama pounded on the door once more, harder this time, shaking the wood hard enough that I thought the hinges were about to give way.

Raelas gulped, and croaked, "You're saying we have to kill her."

"No. I'm saying she's already dead."

The door shook once more. And again. And again. Each time, the door seemed like it was going to come crashing down. It held, but I could see that it was splintering even in this low light. Other doors started opening at this racket, the noise waking people from their slumber. They poked their heads out of the doors, looking angrily on.

"Just what is the—" one of them started.

"Get out," I said. When they hesitated, I raised my voice, bellowing, "Get out!"

Carle and Ama's door shook once more, and this time, it slammed open.

We saw Ama's silhouette standing in the doorway, and even in the shadows I could see that something was very, very wrong. I could see the beginnings of ooze dripping from her fingertips. I could see her jaw hanging open. When she took her first step out the room, I could see that the movement was clumsy, as though she was learning to walk all over again.

Corminar reacted first.

He raised his bow, firing an arrow into the creature that was once Ama. It caused her to stagger backward, but of course it wasn't enough—we needed fire to defeat corruption like this. It bought us only a few seconds.

"Val," I said, whipping my head to her. "Get everyone out."

She seemed surprised. "Me?"

"Yes, you." Maybe it was a selfish order. Maybe I wanted her out of harm's way. This cramped hallway was no place to fight a monster like this; chances were someone was going to get hurt. But maybe we didn't need to fight here. I called after Val, "Get them far away, alright? I'm going to take this fight outside."

The witch nodded, then began ushering the onlookers out of the inn, shouting at them when necessary.

Arzak, ever fearless, charged the figure we'd once called Ama. I hoped I didn't have to remind her that she couldn't let Ama touch her—it was the usual malae rule. As Arzak approached, Carle jumped to one side, pressing himself against the wall and giving the orc ample space to get past. Too much space, really, so I wasn't sure what that meant about what he thought about her.

The orc brought her two swords arcing down in front of her, and the enemy made no effort to block them. The blades wedged themselves in a shoulder each, and Ama looked down at one of them before flicking her hand. At this flick, Arzak's two swords shot backward down the hallway, almost catching Corminar as he raised his bow.

"We're taking this out of here," I told Raelas, but she'd frozen, paling at my side. I turned and grabbed her by the shoulders, looking into her eyes. "Your friend is gone. I'm sorry. I'm so, so sorry, but there isn't time for grieving now. You understand?"

Raelas blinked up at me. "She . . . took blades to the shoulders."

"She did, yes. Now, move."

"She's not that strong," the tiefling murmured. It was as though she preferred to linger on this impossibility than face the truth—that Ama was dead.

"She is now," I said, turning away. Raelas was too stunned; I was going to need to do this myself.

Ama staggered out of her room, enraged by Arzak's attack. The orc stumbled backward, then reached toward me. "Swords!" she shouted. "Get swords to me!"

She meant for me to portal them over to her, but I wasn't going to do that. Ama had touched those blades, which meant that the corruption could still be lingering on them; we'd need to engulf them in fire before the orc used them again.

So instead Arzak turned and ran, and the monster charged after her, notably ignoring Carle, who was still pressed up against the wall.

I pressed one hand forward and opened a portal just in front of Ama, dumping her into the sky thirty yards above the inn. At the same time, I opened a portal behind me, which I stepped through to come out onto the empty street. The faintest glow of twilight's arrival silhouetted the falling monster, and I opened another portal beneath Ama to launch her back into the air once more, giving my friends enough time to step out the portal at my side.

But this particular corruption knew something of portals. Perhaps it retained some of Ama's memories, and remembered my magicks from before. Whatever the reason, it meant that Ama flicked her wrist and tore a metal drainpipe from the tavern, launching it toward herself and knocking her out of the way of the portal. She landed hard on the cobbled streets, but rose to her feet almost instantly, the landing having done little damage.

This corruption really was strong. Stronger than the man in the courtyard, even.

I steeled myself for a tougher fight than before as my friends stepped out the portal.

In the same moment, Ama flicked her wrist once more. She raised the metal drainpipe from the ground, and she brought it within arm's reach. At her touch, she imbued it with the corruption of the malae.

Then she launched it.

CHAPTER FORTY-ONE

The Gentleman Warrior

The creature with Ama's face launched the metal coated in corruption.

Of the two of us worldbenders, only I opened a portal to avoid the oncoming strike, with Raelas too rattled by the recent loss of her friend. Corminar and I fell through the portal, landing nimbly on our feet, while Arzak moved quickly enough to swipe Raelas out of the way. Carle and Val, meanwhile, prepared to strike.

"Fire!" I shouted, but the witch was already yanking something from a new apothecary bag.

Corminar's eyes lit up when he saw what she had—a small, faintly glowing glass vial. What with his *Alchemy* skill, it was only natural he'd know what it was. He responded not with words but with action, shooting an arrow to Val's feet.

The witch pulled the stopper from her vial, then yanked the arrow from the ground. As she dipped its head in the liquid, it immediately caught fire. "We knew there were malae around," she explained. "So we came prepared."

There wasn't time for me to wonder if that was a cutting remark about our *lack* of preparedness, so I tried not to.

With the twist of her wrist, the creature that was once Ama brought the metal drainpipe careening back through the air toward us. "Heads!" I shouted, ducking to the ground just in time to avoid the corruption touching me—and my hair, too, this time.

But it was only a matter of time until someone *did* get touched by the corruption, considering that Ama had such fine control over it. We'd need to strike before then, and we were going to need more than one flaming arrow.

"Raelas!" I shouted, and when she didn't reply, Arzak grabbed her by the shoulders and turned her my way. "How do these metal magicks work? Moving something that heavy has got to be draining her mana pretty quickly, right?" This question was more based on hope than any particular evidence.

"She . . ." Raelas started, voice quiet at first. "She should be out already? She uses small fragments, normally, cos that's a lot less of a drain. I . . . don't know how she's still going."

I suspected that I did know how. Alenna had told us that these corrupted people were stronger, and maybe this was why—they had higher power reserves than the person they'd once been. *Maybe even infinite,* I thought, before silencing that despairing part of my brain. That wasn't helpful right now.

As the metal mage brought the corrupted metal back toward us once more, I opened a portal to block it. The drainpipe was far too wide to fit through—at least lengthways—but I wasn't trying to magick it anywhere else. I was trying to keep it in place. It was a use for these magicks that I'd never needed, or even thought of, before.

The drainpipe smashed against the sides of the portal, reverberating backward. I thanked my lucky stars that the corruption was considered an enchantment, otherwise my *Portal Slice* ability might have cut the drainpipe into three. And then we'd have *three* corrupted projectiles to avoid.

Corminar and Val made good use of the few seconds I'd bought them, having lit a few more arrowheads aflame, but also a few chunks of wood that Arzak had ripped from a nearby market stall. Still, if they were going to do any good, then we needed to get closer.

With a snarl that was almost typical of Ama, the creature wearing her face gestured the corrupted metal around the portal. She sent the drainpipe soaring toward the three of us with the fire, recognizing them as the greatest threat.

Val, Arzak, and Corminar were too busy with their task to react in time, but fortunately I was solely focused on our enemy. I whipped my hands forward to open another portal in front of my friends, doing so just in time to prevent the metal from hitting them. It hit the edges of the portal and bounced backward again. This time, the metal had enough momentum that it bounced down into the cobbled street, scratching a line in the rock that oozed with the same black corruption.

I hoped the monster hadn't spotted that.

The corrupted tiefling flicked her hands once more, and with them, began scrawling corruption into the road, creating a perimeter around us.

"Back!" Val shouted to the onlookers, gesturing them away with sweeps of her hands. "Back! Run for your bloody *lives*, idiots!"

I couldn't have put it better myself.

Ama had crafted a perimeter of corruption that arched in a semicircle around the lot of us, the monster herself standing in the center of the open end. The beast snarled, like it had us surrounded, but we could step over the perimeter unscathed if we were careful enough, and had portals otherwise. Still, it contained the action and made movement just a little more difficult—which is exactly what Ama needed in this moment.

"Styk!" Val shouted, and I whipped my gaze back to her, Arzak, and Corminar to see that they were ready to strike.

I opened a portal in front of Val and Arzak, allowing them to appear behind the enemy armed with fire, while Corminar shot flaming arrows from where he stood. I knew from our previous encounter with corrupted tieflings that this wouldn't be enough to kill it, but it would maybe weaken it. And it would buy us more time.

Ama shrieked as Arzak's wielded flaming plank hit against her gray flesh, the oozing corruption recoiling at the touch. Immediately, the metal mage turned her attention to Arzak and Val, bringing the corrupted pipe soaring back toward them.

I moved again to open a portal to block the attack, but the corrupted tiefling had learned. Ama flicked her wrist around, and as it rotated, so, too, did the metal. It whipped around to be perpendicular to the portal, then dipped under it, still moving quickly toward the two women.

"Val!" I shouted, at the same moment that I opened a portal beneath them. Arzak and Val fell through, but like what happened before, the corruption just about caught a strand of long hair. I charged to Val's side, pushed her to the ground, and then sliced the corruption free.

The witch blinked up at me. "You cut my hair?"

"I saved your—"

"You *cut* my *hair?*"

"Not now," Arzak grunted, then burned the corrupted strands of hair with her makeshift weapon.

Meanwhile, Carle charged. He grabbed two arrows from Corminar's quiver, lit them on the arrow already nocked in the elf's bow, and then ran at Ama. He howled as he sprinted, gripping the arrows close to their heads.

"Careful!" I shouted. "Don't let her touch you!"

But the warrior seemed to pay no heed. He ran in as carelessly as he'd attack a level 1 rockrat, stabbing her with his flaming arrowheads and roaring all the while. There was a pain in his roar, as though something rooted deep within him was screaming for him to not attack the woman he'd known for so many years. Not that she *was* that woman anymore.

Carle stabbed and he stabbed, and I had to tear him away with a portal underfoot. The warrior fell through, hopefully before the corruption could touch him, and stumbled to his feet at my side. To his credit, Ama looked solidly weakened, but he'd done so at such a risk to himself that—

The warrior charged again.

"Carle, what are you *doing*?" I shouted.

"What must be done!" came the reply.

At this point, Raelas snapped back to reality. In hindsight, I think it was her watching another of her friends charging toward almost certain death that did it. Some deep-rooted part of her knew she couldn't handle losing both of them in one day.

"Not you, too!" I cried as Raelas slipped through a portal, coming out at her friend's side.

The tiefling crouched to the ground, placing her palms against it, and moments later the stone around Ama morphed into frost—an evolution of Raelas's *Frost Husk* ability, presumably. The creature turned and snarled toward her once-friend, but as it—she? it? I wasn't sure anymore—tried to lift a foot to close on Raelas, it found that it was stuck to the ground. At least for a moment.

"Arzak!" I shouted to my orc friend, lifting an open hand in the air. The orc threw me a flaming piece of wood, assuming that I knew what I was doing. I didn't, but I was working on it.

Carle attacked again with his flaming arrowheads, able to dodge the monster's mad swipes only because its feet were now frozen to the floor. Shrieking from the pain, the creature turned to snarl at Raelas, recognizing her as the source of the trap, and it now swiped at her instead.

And the frost began to crack.

Raelas's eyes widened with fear moments before the creature lunged, her own feet frozen to the spot through more figurative means. But Carle saw it coming, too.

The gentleman warrior launched himself at the corrupted woman, tackling her to the ground next to a nearby building without regard for his own safety.

Arzak, Val, and I gasped.

Carle was on top of his corrupted friend, pressed against her. There was no way he could have avoided the corruption. He'd sacrificed himself.

Before any of us could react, the figure once called Ama roared and pushed herself back to her feet with her corruption-enhanced strength. She shrieked, pushing both hands forward and then yanking them backward. As Carle stood once more, the corrupted metal drainpipe shot toward him.

He had just enough time to grab the monster and wrench her to one side. Into the path of the soaring metal fragment.

The sharp end of the broken pipe pierced the creature's flesh, going straight through before wedging itself in the wall behind her. Carle, miraculously, saved himself from being hit . . . but that didn't mean he was saved. Anything but.

The gentleman warrior gestured for me to throw the flaming plank, and I did so. As the creature with Ama's face shrieked from the subsequent pain—a shriek that grew quieter with every second that passed—I looked at Carle's hands. I looked at the black ooze dripping from them. And his arms. And his chest.

There was no cutting that corruption away.

Level ? Corruption defeated!

Worldbending: +2,300XP
Worldbending increased to level 60!
Base Points Gained: +2 INT, +2 Free Points (INT/WIS/CHA)
Ability Selection Unlocked
Select an ability from the list below:
. . .

"You . . . you let yourself get corrupted?" Raelas asked her remaining friend, half shouting, half crying. "You—"

But Carle shook his head. "I was already corrupted. Before I opened that door, before any of you knew Alenna had failed to heal Ama. She corrupted me over an hour ago. All this? I've just been . . . treading water."

As the rest of us looked on in dumbfounded silence, the gentleman warrior threw the flaming torch to Corminar.

"Do what must be done," he said.

CHAPTER FORTY-TWO

Postmortem

Corminar went to retrieve Alenna.

Faced with the two bodies in their corrupted, burnt states, we knew it wouldn't do any good. There was nothing that even the most talented healer could do to save them now, and yet it seemed the right thing to do. At the very least, the scientist might be able to explain what went wrong.

There was a school of thought—one which Raelas shared—that Alenna was to blame. That if she hadn't assured us that Ama was fine, then we wouldn't have brought her here. Carle would never have been touched by the corruption. Raelas would have lost one friend, not two.

The owner of the inn plied us with food and drink and anything else we needed, recognizing both the grief and the fact that we'd saved her inn from certain destruction—ignoring the fact that we'd also brought the destruction to her. It was a nice gesture, and one I think the pale Raelas would have been more grateful for if she wasn't in a daze.

Even Val had been sympathetic to the tiefling, in a departure from her normal glaring. She was at this very moment making her a tea in the inn's kitchen, something I'd never seen her do for anyone.

I was sitting at Raelas's side, a comforting hand on her upper back as she stared numbly at the bowl of stew sitting in front of her, untouched. And that wasn't to comment on the quality of the stew; if Lore wasn't off somewhere, he'd have been salivating at the aroma. My incomplete ability selection notification weighed on my mind, but there would be time for that later; some things were more important.

At that moment, Corminar entered the inn, Alenna at his side.

"They're out there," Raelas whispered.

Alenna nodded. "I'll see to them. I just wanted to say . . . I'm sorry, Raelas. I really thought she was cured."

I noticed that the wording was *I thought she was cured*, and not *I thought I'd cured her.*

Raelas said nothing, but turned back to the bowl of stew and shifted a shaky hand toward the spoon. I watched her take a deep breath before sipping lightly at the broth, and out of the corner of my eye, I saw Arzak slink upstairs.

As we sat in silence, and nobody would be any the wiser, I thought there might be time to review the ability selection after all, so I brought it up. There were only two choices this time.

Ability Selection Unlocked
Select an ability from the list below:

Option 1: Weaken Metal II (Worldbending)—Your magicks find flaws within metalwork and exacerbate these flaws, leading to objects becoming immediately weaker. Some enchanted objects may still withstand this spell.

This was an upgrade to an ability I'd passed on previously. There were definitely a few good use cases for it—breaking into places and shattering weapons, to name a few—but it didn't feel like enough. If I picked this, then I'd be missing out on the other ability choice, and in this case, the latter seemed to be more useful.

Option 2: Portal Relay II (Worldbending)—Up to ten small-scale portals can now be positioned stationary to an entity, and used to communicate sound. In addition, your standard portals may be used to communicate sound.

I'd been given the level 1 option of this ability back when we'd defeated Niamh, and I'd immediately come to regret passing it over. This ability came with use cases including spying on people—something I was a big fan of—but also allowing us to coordinate our attacks better as a group, as we could all be in direct communication with one another. It would almost be selfish *not* to pick this one. And I liked to think I'd grown out of selfishness.

Ability Upgraded: Portal Relay II

Portal Relay II (Worldbending): Up to ten small-scale portals can now be positioned stationary to an entity, and used to communicate sound. In addition, your standard portals may be used to communicate sound.

As Alenna and Corminar entered the inn once more, I turned to the scientist. "Do you know what you . . ." I started. "Do you know what went wrong?"

Alenna shook her head. "The ward, it . . ." She glanced at Raelas, and I took the unspoken point; maybe the tiefling didn't need to hear this.

I stood up and approached Alenna and Corminar at the edge of the room.

"I used a ward to stop the corruption from spreading," Alenna said. "You remember that book you retrieved for me? It was about using the body's power to sustain wards. That was supposed to be the cure, and I thought from my tests that it would work."

"You didn't check?" I asked.

A flash of irritation crossed Alenna's eyes. "I *did* check. The ward was stable. The corruption shouldn't have spread. But something—I don't know what—it overwhelmed the ward. It's almost like the corruption grew more powerful by itself."

"Can that happen?" Corminar asked.

"No. Not without—"

Alenna trailed off, her eyes on something across the room. I followed her gaze to see Arzak standing at the foot of the stairs, her nostrils flaring with an anger I'd never before seen in her.

"Upstairs. Now," the orc said.

Raelas whipped her head up from her bowl.

"What—" Val started, poking her head in from the kitchen.

"Now," Arzak said again. "Stuff you need see."

The grieving tiefling rose from her seat, eyes on Arzak. "What stuff?" she asked. There was panic in her tone.

The orc didn't acknowledge her in the slightest. "How many time I need say? Come now."

Val, Corminar, Alenna, and I strode over to the stairs, and Raelas whipped her hand out to grab my arm as I passed. "It's not what you think," she said.

I looked to Arzak, who held my gaze, a scowl on her face.

"What isn't?" I asked the tiefling.

But Raelas had no answer.

I yanked my arm free of her grasp and joined the others on the staircase, Arzak then leading us upstairs and along the corridor.

"I went up to Ama room, see if more information for Alenna. See if more information to understand corruption." Arzak paused. "I think I find it." She came to a halt in front of Carle and Ama's room, and she placed her hand on the door. She sighed, and then pushed. The hinges groaned as the door opened.

I saw nothing at first, only a dusty room much the same as my own. Except, this one had more stuff being stored in it—a good dozen small crates stacked in one corner of the room, away from the beds.

One of them moved. Just a little. But enough.

"Don't tell me . . ." Val said, getting there before I did.

"Malae," Arzak said.

A chill ran down my spine. "Why? What in the gods' names could they want with . . ." I started, but then an answer occurred to me.

"Ah," Alenna said. "That . . . that'd do it. That's why my ward didn't hold up—the corruption *did* grow stronger. It fed on the malae in this very room. My ward . . . didn't stand a chance."

But I wasn't interested in this anger; I now felt ire to rival Arzak's. I turned around, pushed through the small crowd at the threshold of the room, and charged down the corridor.

Raelas recoiled when she saw the fury burning on my face. "It's not what you—" she said, stumbling backward into a table, knocking glassware to the floor.

"Why?" I roared. "Why do you have them?"

"It was . . . it was . . ." Raelas stuttered, gulping.

"*Why?*" I shouted once more, striding toward her.

"It was payment!" the tiefling blurted out.

I came to an abrupt stop, perplexed by this response.

"We knew you were never gonna pay up," Raelas said. "And I think you knew we knew."

"I thought you wanted to do what was right."

"You heard our story," the tiefling replied, now shouting, too. "You know what we came from. What we had to do to survive. There's safety in coin. There's no safety in doing the right thing. But we came anyway, because we know how valuable those creatures are. *This* was our payment."

Fury blossomed through me. To think I'd thought Raelas might have been a good one. No. No, she was no hero; she was just like the rest of them. Without a word, I grabbed Raelas by the wrist and pulled her toward the staircase.

"Styk, no, I—"

"Yes, Raelas. You're dealing with them now. I don't care what else you're going through, this is too far. You saved *malae*. Malae! You know what these creatures can do, and you gambled lives on them for the sake of coin. I can stand you gambling your own lives on them, but what about everyone else? What about the others staying in the inn? What about me? Or did you not think about that?"

Raelas followed quietly, giving up any resistance. The others stayed put at the doorway as I pushed Raelas inside.

"Portal them out, and burn them," I said. "Now."

"Styk, I didn't mean to . . ." Raelas said, staggering back to her feet and coming back toward me with begging eyes. "I do care. I *did* think about—"

When she tried to touch me, I instinctively pushed her away. I didn't want her touching me. I couldn't *stand* the idea anymore.

But I didn't mean to push her toward the crates.

As Raelas fell backward into them, the stack toppled, a handful of boxes falling to the floor. We all went immediately silent, waiting with bated breath to see if any of the monsters were free.

And then we heard a familiar noise.

Shlop. An oozing black limb popped out from behind one of the boxes, climbing on top. It waited there for a moment, looking at the five of us.

Then it pounced toward Raelas.

For all her crimes, the tiefling didn't deserve this. She didn't deserve being touched by a mala. And I'd been the one to push her. I was the one who'd done it to her.

It was that line of thought, perhaps, that led to me yanking my dagger out and leaping between Raelas and the mala. My blade blocked it in midair, and I was about to breathe a sigh of relief when I felt something strangely cool touch my wrist.

When I looked down, I realized what I'd done. The mala had touched me. And the corruption began to spread.

CHAPTER FORTY-THREE

Touched by Darkness

I staggered backward, eyes bulging as I looked at the growing dark gray patch on my right arm. The corruption.

I turned around slowly, and five pairs of eyes landed on the mala's touch. Nobody spoke for a moment, stunned, their faces paling.

Half screaming, half sobbing, Val roared, "No!" She leaped forward, reaching toward me, but Arzak reacted quickly. The orc snatched Val by the neck of her dress and yanked her backward—yanked her away from me before she could touch me. Before the corruption could spread to her, too.

"I . . ." I said, still in a daze, eyes drifting to Corminar.

"Alenna," the elf said, his face betraying no emotion, still keeping his cool. "The ward. Now."

Lore's scientist friend stepped forward, and began conjuring the blue magicks of sorcery. But I'd seen what had happened before, to Ama. I knew how Alenna's magicks worked. They trapped the corruption in the already infected part of the body, using a ward that was sustained by the power of my own body. It would surely weaken me. And there was no guarantee that it would work.

"No," I said.

"No?" Alenna repeated, confused.

"*No?*" Val shouted, collapsing to the ground at Arzak's feet with tears streaming from her eyes. "What the hells do you mean, *no*? You're gonna *die*, Styk. You're gonna die! And we never even . . . I never even . . . I never got to say I was sorry." She reached toward me once more, but Arzak still held her back, face glum.

Raelas slumped against the wall at the other side of the bedroom, her eyes upon me. She let her head fall to her knees. I couldn't help but feel a rage build within when I looked at her. It was her fault that I was in this mess. Her fault, and Carle's, and Ama's, but the latter two were gone now. Raelas was the only one left, and so it was to her that I directed my ire.

But I pulled my eyes away, trying to concentrate. Trying to *think*. There had to be another way. Another way that didn't leave me a shell of a man, a ward the only thing stopping the corruption from reaching my mind, in fear for the rest of my life that it might fail, that it might take me. Or worse, that it might spread to those I loved.

I looked around. At Corminar, at Arzak, and at Val. Especially at Val, the witch who even now struggled against Arzak's hands, trying to come for me, even though it would risk the corruption spreading to herself.

There had to be another way. There had to be.

I caught myself. Here I was, thinking I could be smarter than Alenna. Smarter than someone who'd spent years researching these creatures. I didn't have anything she didn't, so who was I to—

Except . . . I did, didn't I?

I had the blood of the Architects running through me, and with this blood, access to an ancient power—the Sisyphus Artifact. It still had a charge from our defeat of Niamh. It was a charge I'd been saving for when we approached Yusef, but there was no point saving it when it meant I wouldn't be alive to face him.

Although, even then . . . how could I be sure that it would work on something like this?

There was nothing for it. I snatched the octahedron from the chain around my neck and I pushed my mana into it.

The world went black.

I looked around.

I was in the void once more. The limbo state that I'd only seen a single time before, back when I'd died facing down Jacob, the pyroknight. My instinct even now is to describe it as "dark," but it wasn't that. My surroundings were simply . . . empty. A space between life and death. A space in the aether.

Sisyphus Artifact Activated
Charges Remaining: (0 /8)
Preservation Charged Used: Respawning at Leve—————————

—————————Conflict detected.
Resolving . . .

> *Resolving . . .*

> *Conflict sustained.*

Not good.

I waited for more messages, but nothing came.

I tried to turn around in this void, and though there was no ground on which to plant my feet, I got the sense that it was working. In the distance, I thought I saw a glimmer of light, but when I narrowed my eyes, I could see nothing.

> *Warning: Emergency conflict resolution in progress. Nature of conflict: entity tainted by reality fabrics. Impossible to identify perimeter between entity and void. World structures compromised.*

Well, that wasn't encouraging. I couldn't understand much of what *any* of it meant, but I got the gist of it: I was well and truly screwed. Something about the mala's touch had interfered with the *Sisyphus Artifact*, that much was clear. But what were the implications of that? Did it mean that the malae were in touch with something fundamental to our existence? And surely that could only mean the corruption. But . . . what? And why? And just how did that help me right about now?

I tried to turn around once more, resisting against this cage of void, desperate to find an escape from this impossible place. Again, I thought I saw a glimmer of light out of the corner of one eye. When I looked toward it, it was gone.

> *Possible Conflict Resolution Option 1: Identify versions of entity in other worlds. Use copies to identify entity perimeter. Resolving . . .*

> *Resolving . . .*

> *Error————————Entity copies not found. User exists in [0] world structures.*

And that wasn't too encouraging, either, to be honest. What did it mean, no other world structures? Was this referring to the other worlds that the Players had mentioned? The ones they no longer had any presence in? Maybe they could exist across the multiverse, but I sure as bloody hells couldn't.

Again I saw light in the corner of my eye, though this time when I looked to it, it didn't fade. There were shapes in the light. There was movement. I focused my eyes as best I could, and I urged myself toward it. As I grew closer, I realized I was glimpsing back into the world. Maybe this was my way out. If I could just squeeze through, then . . .

But as I grew nearer still, a chill ran down my spine. In this tear in the aether, I saw a world that wasn't my own. I knew it wasn't mine so innately, like something within me was repulsed by it. The architecture was strange, with each structure a hundred stories tall, towering over one another, formed of rippling magicks. I saw humans and tieflings in this place, true, but I also saw reptilian humanoids, and beings covered with feather-like structures and wings of metal blades. I saw four moons in the sky above, and a sun that burned blue.

I pulled myself away, bearing to look upon it no longer.

Warning: If conflict is not resolved in the next [299] seconds, then user will be lost.

OK. That was five minutes, by my count. I didn't have long. And if the system wasn't going to resolve this for me, then I'd need to get out by myself, which meant finding a tear back to my world.

I urged myself through the void toward another glimmer of light, as though swimming through darkness. But the world I saw next was one of jungles, set inside a huge orb that rose into the sky above.

I moved on to the next—a land of humans with strange metal horses and crackling lightning magicks and glowing glass vials.

And the next, a land with wealthy realms and pink skies and palaces, where every denizen carried metal tubes in belt sheaths.

More and more glimmers of light appeared around me. Not dozens, but hundreds. I'd grossly underestimated how many worlds the Players had access to. And I was running out of time.

Warning: If conflict is not resolved in the next [59] seconds, then user will be lost.

Desperate, I willed myself to find my home world. I urged myself toward it, and I found myself soaring through the aether, dozens of worlds drifting by me, strange chills passing over my skin as I drew close. And then I saw it.

A small bedroom, filled with crates. A tiefling with her head in her hands. An elf and a human shouting at one another. A witch crying, being held back by a tall orc woman. I shot toward this world, soaring through the aether, and reached my hands into the light like it was a portal back home.

But this wasn't a portal.

And my hand didn't enter it.

I saw a body, unconscious on the floor of the inn. My own body. The corruption still spreading.

I couldn't get back.

I was trapped.

I was—

Possible Conflict Resolution Option 2: Issue entity signal to identify entity perimeter. Resolving . . .

Resolving . . .

A pain shot through me like nothing I'd ever felt before.

My limbs snapped straight, both here in this aether and out there, through the glimmer of light, back in the real world. Screams erupted from my mouths, uncontrolled, and tears of pain streamed down my cheeks.

Warning: Artifact integrity possibly compromised. Please confirm.

Conflict resolved.

I gasped as I awoke, and as my eyes snapped open, I was pleased to see not the aether, but the real world before me. I sat bolt upright, then lifted my arm to check for signs of corruption. There was no gray tint, no black ooze. I'd survived. The artifact had triumphed over the corruption.

The artifact. The void messages had said the artifact was compromised. Was it destroyed? Was it over? Could I no longer rely on it to keep me alive? And how could I be a hero without it?

As Val gasped with relief, Arzak released her. The witch ran toward me just as I felt desperately on my chest for the familiar octahedron.

It was gone.

My heart skipped a beat before I spotted it on the floor not too far from me, presumably having been dropped during the healing process. As Val ran to embrace me, I pushed her aside to scramble across the floor for the artifact, grasping it. I turned it around in my hands, looking for any signs that it was broken. But I still had that same old active effect. It was still fine. I'd lucked out.

I realized then that Val was standing over me, that I'd cast her aside for the artifact. I looked up at the witch, meeting eyes filled with despair, with terror, with anger, and cheeks lined with running makeup.

I gulped. "Val, I . . ."

The witch turned and hurried from the room.

Yusef

The barbarian arrived at Yusef's door.

"You came," Yusef said, trying not to betray the surprise in his voice; it wouldn't do for the others to know he'd had doubts. He was their prophet after all, and supposed to know for certain all that was to come. Would they follow him if he didn't?

His most loyal followers in their pale orange robes considered the man in the doorway carefully, and though nobody moved hands toward their weapons, he knew they were ready to strike. It didn't take the gift of *Divination* to know that.

"Yeah, I got your messages," the barbarian said, eyes sweeping around the room and landing for a second on the orc.

"Lore," Lillya said with a nod.

The man nodded back to her.

"And what of the others?" Yusef asked.

The barbarian swallowed. "They'll know I've left by the morning. I left a note."

"You told them you would be traveling with me?"

"I did, yeah."

"And will they follow?"

The barbarian held Yusef's gaze. It was refreshing; so few would do so these days. Not since his following had swelled in number. "You're the prophet; you tell me." The man's eyes drifted over the others in this small room, uncertain. If he had something to say, he wouldn't say it in front of the others.

"Out," Yusef said.

Of those in orange, only the orc hesitated.

"I said out, Lillya," the Player said again.

But still the orc paused, her eyes darting to the visitor. "You safe? You foresee this?"

"Would I tell you to leave if I hadn't?"

Lillya raised her eyebrows, then turned away, slamming the door shut behind her. Yusef would need to investigate the orc's recent change in manner, but he had greater priorities. He always had greater priorities.

Only when the others were long since departed from the room did the barbarian enter properly. He kept well away from Yusef, skirting around the other side of the room, then perched himself against a side table. His enormous sword clattered as metal touched wood.

"Your messengers said coming was the only way my friends would be safe. That's the only reason I came. That true?"

"I assume that your own visions showed you much the same," Yusef replied. This bit was a risk; he knew it was. But he had his magicks ready to go. He could *make* Lore see what he wanted him to see, if he had to. And nobody would see the glow of those magicks because of the obscurem he gripped in his robe's pocket.

The barbarian shook his head. "I . . . I don't know."

No matter. It was an easy fix. Yusef didn't even need to stand as he raised his hand toward the stranger, using his magicks to show the barbarian what he needed to see—visions of his friends' attack on Yusef. Visions of his friends being killed by the cult.

And then, the opposite. Visions of the man standing at Yusef's side. Of his elven friend reclaiming his homeland. Of the worldbender and the witch putting aside troubles past. Of a cultist stilling the tiefling's blade before she could kill the orc.

The barbarian stood still for a moment, the red glow of magicks fading from his eyes. "Those were clear enough, I suppose, but I can't always make sense of them. The visions. I came for my friends, but . . . maybe you could also show me—"

"How to make sense of the visions? How to control them? How to use them to seize power, to change minds and reign dominion over man?" Yusef finished for him. Again, he didn't need powers of *Divination* to see that one coming. Who wouldn't want those things?"

"No," the man said. "I was hoping you could show me how to get rid of them."

Yusef found himself caught off guard. He turned away from the man, focusing down on the papers on the desk in front of him—missives from faraway sects, reports from spies, and requests from the Council. "You want to be . . . *rid* of these powers?"

"I don't want to see my friends die over and over. I *can't* keep seeing that. I've . . . lost enough people already."

"You'd be throwing away a divine gift."

The barbarian shook his head. "I dunno about all that. I've never been one for magicks, really. Give me a sword and I'm happy, but magicks? This is all . . . this is all beyond me. Will you . . . help me?"

"There are worlds out there without magicks, you know," Yusef said. "Or, at least, worlds that aren't aware of the magicks that hold their realities together. They've created some wondrous inventions in its absence—carriages powered by steam, not horse; medicines that use the innate attributes of plants; navigational devices fixed to the poles of their worlds. Truly incredible things, and things I have seen firsthand."

"Sounds like a nice place. Why aren't you there? Why are you *here*?" It seemed the barbarian made no effort to disguise the disdain he had for Yusef. This was a man forced into a corner, doing what the prophet wanted only because he felt he had to. It wouldn't do to push him too far.

Yusef smiled. He could now say the truth. The truth that he kept from others in his flock. And why could he say it? Because nobody would believe a slayer of the Architects. "Because the magicks that bound me there faded when I died. It is true of all the worlds I visited. Reckless lifestyles, full of glutton and extravagance and a lack of concern with upsetting the locals . . . all those ended the same way. With my death. Now, only a handful of worlds remain available to me. Hence . . ." The member of the Council sighed; perhaps sharing this particular piece of information would be going too far. "Well, you'll see."

The barbarian didn't need to know about Yusef's plans. About the *Council's* plans. Not yet, at any rate. Perhaps once Yusef had sufficiently converted the man with his visions, then he might be able to trust him. But until that time, he would keep the matter of the malae to himself.

"So you can't help me?" Lore said.

"I'm already helping you. I'm keeping your friends alive. Is that not enough? Because I can ask my followers to keep you away from me, and then we'll see what happens. You never know, the fates might smile kindly upon them. Maybe only *some* of them will die."

The man's hand drifted ever so slightly toward that huge sword of his. But then he caught himself—as far as he knew, striking Yusef down would be enough to seal his friends' fates. The stranger possessed the gift of prophecy, but not so much that he would know the future for certain. Still, it was enough that Yusef could use it to plug the gaps in his own gathered intelligence.

"In fact," Yusef continued, "I think it is *you* who ought to help *me*."

"How?" the barbarian said. "How can I—"

"Your *Divination*," the Player interrupted. "Your visions. What have you seen? You say you need to be there, under the towers, when Tana completes the great plan.

"Why don't we start with that?"

CHAPTER FORTY-FOUR

Follow Them

"Out!" the innkeeper bellowed. "Out!"

I raised my hands to protest my innocence. "But we saved your inn!"

The man snarled. "You were the ones who put it in danger in the first place!"

He wasn't wrong, and that's probably why my efforts to keep the rooms ended up being fruitless. It didn't matter, not really, as there were hundreds of other inns in the city of Coldharbor. We'd just have to move to another.

Val and Arzak were downstairs, the former drinking, while Corminar, Raelas, Alenna, and I were in the hallway, trying to work out how to get rid of so many malae. We could either put them somewhere and start a big bonfire—though space was a premium in this dense city, and we didn't want to commit some accidental arson—or we could get the guards to deal with them. But then there would be questions. Questions we didn't have good answers for.

Either way, I opened a portal to the road outside and the four of us began carefully transporting the crates out of the inn, freeing the innkeeper of this dangerous merchandise. We were very careful to make sure the crates were fully sealed before touching any of them. I'd been lucky last time, but now I didn't have a charge in the Sisyphus Artifact. If one touched me, I was a goner. Honestly, even if I *did* have a charge, there was no knowing if the artifact would save me. It struggled with the corruption of the malae, or, as the artifact called it, the "fabrics of reality."

Raelas was silent the entire time, communicating only with the odd nod. Corminar had met my eye, raising an eyebrow at her. The truth was, nobody knew quite what to do with her. For all her sins, she'd just lost the only family she had in the world. Nobody could bring themselves to be so cruel to her as to tell her to go.

As we were finishing up, Arzak left the inn grumbling about something—Val noticeably not with her—and stood watching us carrying the heavy crates.

"Perhaps you would be so kind as to—" Corminar started.

Arzak interrupted him by stepping into the street and accosting a merchant carrying a near-empty hand cart. "We buy this," she said, pointing to the cart. "How much?"

The short tiefling man looked up at the huge orc, blinking, and squeaked a reply. A moment later, Arzak was placing an empty hand cart down by the pile of crates. "There. I help."

Corminar smiled up at her, and he managed to express that it was intended sarcastically. He'd really been around us for too long.

"Where Lore?" Arzak asked.

Alenna looked up from loading the last crate at that. "Yeah, I've been meaning to ask. He's been gone all night?"

The elf looked to me to answer, as I'd been the one sharing a room with the missing barbarian. "Guess so. I didn't see him leave."

"It's not like him to go without sleep," Alenna said, and I was taken aback by this very correct assessment of the gentle giant. But Alenna really was an old friend of his; maybe she knew him even better than us.

"I'll check he didn't stumble back to bed in all the chaos," I said. "You good with . . ." I gestured to the cart full of monsters.

"The weight might be a—" Corminar said, but once again Arzak interrupted him not with her words, but with her actions. She lifted the end of the cart with ease.

"Big fire in desert, yes?"

Corminar nodded. "Yes."

As the elf and the orc made their way toward the outskirts of the city, Alenna took a seat on the ground at the side of the road, and Raelas stood around awkwardly.

I turned back into the portal, and as I stepped through it, I saw the tiefling follow me through. I'd need to do something about that at some point, but right now I was glad to have another priority. I opened the door to the room Lore and I had been using, expecting to hear the familiar booming snores, but instead I only heard the creaking of the door hinge.

Nobody was in the bed, but now, in the low light of dawn, I could see that it wasn't empty. Placed gently atop the pillow was a clumsily folded scrap of parchment, and I could see upon it the large, erratic handwriting of my good friend.

The hairs on the back of my neck stood on end. Whatever this was, it surely wouldn't be good.

Feeling the presence of Raelas behind me, in the doorway, I reached forward to lift the letter from the bed and paused for a moment before opening it. As my eyes skimmed the awkward handwriting, only one thought came to mind.

"Oh, what the—"

"What do you mean 'he's gone'?"

I'd waited for Arzak and Corminar to return before revealing what I knew; the whole team needed to hear this at the same time. And, as far as I could tell, Arzak and Val were currently part of the "team" once more. We'd need them for what was to come. We were now sitting around the table downstairs in the inn, ignoring the innkeeper who was tapping his toe but had realized that, frankly, there was nothing he could do to kick us out.

"Like I said: Yusef is leaving Coldharbor. And Lore is going with him."

"Maybe Arzak and I have been gone too long. You remember we're supposed to *kill* Players, not *befriend them*?"

Alenna raised both eyebrows at that, but said nothing. Clearly Lore hadn't filled her in on *everything*.

"Does that mean you're back?" I asked. The question came out before I really realized I was asking it.

Val had no answer, but her cheeks flushed and suddenly the floor was very interesting to her.

"Why he go?" Arzak asked.

This was about the only piece of information I was dreading sharing even *more* than the fact that Lore was gone. And I was dreading it because I couldn't help but think Corminar and I had a role in it.

"He's been . . . struggling with the visions," I said. "I think more than Corminar and I realized."

"Typical men," Val grumbled under her breath. Alenna raised her eyebrows in agreement.

"What was that?"

"Nothing."

I chose to ignore it. Now wasn't the time. "He's . . . he's been seeing our deaths. Or, foreseeing, I suppose. I don't know quite what that means, but I'm starting to think here that he's been working to keep us alive all this time. And now, he says there's only one way to save Alenna's life."

The scientist visibly jumped at the mention of her name. "Save . . . *my* life? What does it . . . Does it say what happens to me?"

I shook my head. "All it says is that, after Plyas, he can't face losing any more friends. He'll do whatever it takes to keep you alive, and in this case, that means leaving with Yusef. Learning from him, maybe. I don't know, it's not clear."

"He doesn't say?" Val asked.

"No, I think he does, I just can't read his handwriting." I placed the letter down on the table, and we all pored over it.

"Fair enough," Val eventually said when we all gave up.

"Allow me to ask the question, then," Corminar said. "What do we do with this information?"

"I mean, we go after him, right?" I asked.

Arzak nodded. "Yes. Go after."

"Excellent," replied the elf. "My thoughts precisely."

Alenna slowed raised a hand. "What about . . . ?"

I could only assume the rest of the question was ". . . my prophesied death?" It was a good question, really. "Stay out of trouble," I told her. "No patients. No fights. Nothing. We'll come back with him, and we'll keep you alive. We'll find a way."

Alenna didn't say anything, but I thought she could tell that she wasn't going to change our minds on this.

I stood from the table. "Alright. Grab your stuff. We're going."

We now stood outside a familiar building in the western districts of Coldharbor, and Arzak wasn't happy.

Since we'd left the inn, I'd noticed a change in the air. The thousands of cultists in this city had spurred into action, pale orange robes fluttering as they strode around Coldharbor. It was strange that they were still here; if Lore's letter was to be believed, then Yusef had already left the city. I could only imagine their supposed "prophet" had given them a mission here. It worried me, then, when one of the cultists pushed a neatly drawn pamphlet into my hand—one offering huge sums of coin for fighters willing to join their cause. I pushed it out of my mind for now—something that I seemed to be doing a lot lately—as we had other priorities.

"No. Not this," Arzak said for the second time. "Not Tokas."

"It's Lore," Val said, echoing what I'd been about to say. "We need all the help we can get."

"You don't have to be friends with her. You don't have to forgive her for what she did. None of us have. But she wants to make amends. She'll fight for Lore."

Arzak grimaced. "I not be so sure," she said. "Because Yusef show her killing me."

CHAPTER FORTY-FIVE

To the Edge of the Desert

The prophet fled across the desert, and we followed.

Not that we necessarily knew that Yusef was fleeing us; for all we knew, he might have thought us no threat at all, not even a threat worth dealing with. Maybe it was like the situation with the Councilman flipped on its head, us now at the pitiable end of it rather than the enemy. Maybe he didn't think about us at all.

The camp outside the city was all but gone. Only a handful of tents remained, few and far between, supporting those followers who remained in Coldharbor. That was still hundreds of cultists, but in the grand scheme of things, that was nothing at all. In place of the tents, I could see long lines in the sand, indents of the wheels of heavily laden carriages. We had no such means of transport, so I could only hope that the sheer number in Yusef's party of travelers would slow them down. Otherwise, we would just have to wait until they reached their destination. And I wasn't sure I wanted to face the Player down in an arena of his choosing.

The sun beat heavily on our heads as we followed the merchants' road west. We'd thought to bring ample supplies with us—my *Portal World* was full of water flasks and food enough for the seven of us—but still the heat could be the end of us.

"Any idea where he's heading?" I called out to the disparate, quiet crowd.

"If he's continuing to tour the cities, Zelas might be his next destination," Lambkin said. "There is quite the population there; many to recruit."

"And if he's not recruiting?" I asked.

"Elassos," Tokas said. "An old tiefling fortification, up in the mountains."

"Sounds like the perfect place to—"

"Spring a trap," the tiefling finished. Good. We were on the same page.

I glanced over at the rest of our party to check that they'd heard. Arzak and Val, at the rear of the group and furthest away, wore glum expressions. They'd heard, too, then. "There's eight of us, and only one of him," I reminded them. "We've got this. Even if he does have the gift of foresight."

"No," Val said. "Not one of him." She gestured to the myriad wheel marks on the road. "Hundreds of them."

On the evening of the first day, we stopped to camp outside a small hamlet—one small enough not to have somewhere for travelers to stay. The air had grown cool in the hours after the sun had passed below the horizon, though the sand still seemed to hold some warmth.

As always, I volunteered for the first watch. I acted as though this was some selfless gesture—the others could rest—but really, I mostly wanted an uninterrupted night of sleep.

While the others slept, I kept my eyes not just on the horizon, but on those in the nearby hamlet. Curious locals stared at us from beside the village well. At least, I hoped it was only curiosity. Could they have been spies for the enemy? We knew that those in the Council had access to ample funds with which to bribe and buy loyalties, but Yusef had a power beyond even that—he could win peoples' hearts, not just their coin purses.

As I watched, the locals finally retired to their homes, their interest having waned. I returned to watching the horizon, and the dark blue sky faded to the blackest black.

Val woke me by shaking my shoulder. It was aggressive enough that I thought something was wrong, and I whipped my hand to my blade, but it was just that she didn't care about being gentle. It was progress, at least; Val was communicating with me more. I just didn't know that I *wanted* her to, after she had abandoned me.

Raelas sat, propped up against a nearby rock, eating cold beans. She glared up at Val, who acted like she didn't notice.

"We found this in night," Arzak said, throwing a pale orange robe to the ground in the center of the camp.

"Where?" Lambkin asked.

"I scouted the village," Corminar said.

"You went spying, you mean," I clarified, but moved the conversation on. "So Yusef has spies even here. I thought he might. But they didn't attack us."

"Mm," Arzak grunted. "Not yet."

We departed before the day broke, before the northern deserts lost their chill. Without the heat, we moved faster, and I could only assume we were catching up to our prey, though of course I had no evidence.

Days passed like this.

As we traveled, we stumbled across more greenery—first the odd plant here and there, but before long, oases became more commonplace. Arzak—and Val, perhaps out of solidarity—kept well away from Tokas and Lambkin. Raelas barely spoke a word. Lore's absence was a presence even greater than his usual, broad self. Only Corminar seemed to have kept any semblance of normality, though of course his benchmark of "normal" had changed since he'd watched his homeland fall.

We reached the first town of meaningful size a few days later, and all seven of us were nervous about approaching. We knew that Yusef had left spies behind, but for what purpose? He knew that we would follow him—or if not him, then Lore—but what would he do about it? Did he just want to monitor us, or was it more than that? Was he planning a trap?

"There's something wrong here," Tokas said, staring on at the town. She'd only been saying what we were all thinking, but the disdain on Arzak's face was palpable. I think I'd probably dislike someone who had been prophesied to kill me, too, though. So that was fair enough; they could stay away from each other so long as we got Lore back. That was all that mattered at this stage.

"Yes," Val said flatly, fury communicated on behalf of Arzak. "Spies. We got it."

Tokas glanced down at the floor. Even I—not someone typically good with analyzing emotions—could sense the turmoil going on within her. For all her crimes, both past and future, I couldn't help but feel a little sorry for her.

At least she had Lambkin to speak on her behalf. "What is it, Tokas?" he asked, voice gentle. "What do you see?" I noticed him put a comforting arm on her shoulder; maybe he'd gotten a tad too close to the woman he was supposed to have been monitoring.

"It doesn't . . . *feel* right," the tiefling answered.

This was hardly the meaningful answer any of us were after.

"What doesn't?" Lambkin prodded.

"There are magicks at play here, but I . . ." Tokas gestured to the sight before us. There stood small stone buildings, colored the same as the sands around us. Those inhabitants of the town looked just like all those we'd seen before; they went about their business with nothing to hint at aggressive intentions. Children played in the streets, tapping a small wooden hoop toward one of two goals. It was mundane—and that, I think, was what Tokas was trying to get at.

I opened myself to the idea of magicks before us, closing my eyes and breathing in the air as though trying to taste mana on the wind. But I tasted, saw, and felt nothing. "Val? Raelas?" I asked the other magick-users among us.

The latter shook her head. The former said nothing.

"Just you, Tokas," I told her.

"I'm not lying," she said as though anticipating doubts from some of us. I didn't doubt her, but judging by their scowling expressions, others did. "Do we have a map?"

"A map?"

"Yeah, I—" Tokas froze midsentence, drawing in a sharp breath.

"What is it?" Lambkin asked. "What's wrong?"

The tiefling paled. "Trap."

At that moment, a flash of orange appeared above me. I snapped my head up just in time to see a man appear as if from out of nowhere. His pale orange robe billowed behind him as he fell two feet to the crest of the sand dune and brought his quarterstaff down toward me. As I drew my blade, the weapon knocked against the top of my head, causing me to stagger backward and fall down the side of the dune.

Around me, I glimpsed more ambushers appearing from nowhere, launching straight into an attack on our whole party. By my initial cursory glance, they numbered not too many more than us; Yusef hadn't accounted for Val, Arzak, Lambkin, and Tokas joining our party. His spies on the road hadn't reported our number, or at least word of our number hadn't reached him before he set this trap.

The nearest assailant brought his quarterstaff down on me once more, and I responded by opening a portal beneath me and tumbling through it. I closed it just in time to see the closing portal slice through the end of the man's quarterstaff, diminishing his ability to attack but also telling me that the weapon wasn't enchanted.

As the end of the staff fell to the sand at my feet, I raised my blade and looked to the woman who was standing at my side. Not Raelas, not Val, but Tokas.

"Told you something was wrong," she said.

CHAPTER FORTY-SIX

Hurt

"Oh good," I said, "another fight."

The man with the quarterstaff charged, swiping his broken weapon wildly.

I ducked to one side, avoiding the arcing weapon, then charged in to *Stab* with my blade. My dagger hit flesh, and I pushed the attack by activating my *Closed Reach* ability.

Level 15 Recruit of the Ascendancy Cult defeated!

Worldbending: +1,050XP **Knifework**: +1,300XP

Someone shouted something off to my right, but I couldn't quite make it out over the sounds of battle.

And then someone *else* clubbed me over the head.

Raelas appeared at my side, stepping out of a portal. She turned her right arm to ice and used it to block the attack of the enemy I hadn't seen. "Duck, I said," she repeated.

"Could've said it a bit lou . . ." I started, but then my latest ability selection returned to me. With the flick of my wrist, I activated my *Portal Relay* ability, creating with it seven small portals, no larger than an apple, one for each of us. I had the ability to create up to ten of these, but I just couldn't see any point of creating more than we could use. I burst my hands forward, fingers splayed, and six of the seven small portals soared off toward my traveling companions. They slowed as they approached, then began gently circling their heads.

"What in hell," Arzak mumbled as she met the enemy blade with blades of her own.

"New ability," I shouted through my own portal, though I didn't really need to shout. "Use it to communicate."

"Styk, turn around," Corminar said.

"Yeah, communicate just like that!"

"No," the elf repeated. "Turn around. Raelas is about to die."

"Oh right." I whipped myself back to the tiefling who'd saved me just in time to see the enemy pushing down against her icy arms. I leaped into action, activating my *Knifestorm* ability while just out of range of my ally—but not the cultist. Knife wounds peppered the man's side, not quite enough to eliminate him, but enough that Raelas could push back.

The tiefling rose steadily to her feet, then headbutted the enemy. As the cultist staggered backward in surprise, I charged in for the finishing blow.

Level 19 Ascendancy Warrior defeated!

Worldbending: +950XP
Knifework: +1,650XP
Knifework increased to level 43!
Base Points Gained: +1 DEX, +1 STR, +2 Free Points (VIT/DEX/STR)

I whipped around just as I heard a cry from Arzak. One of the ambushers had struck her from behind while she'd been facing another. As a result, her right arm now sported a huge gash. My orc friend dropped her right-hand sword, leaving her only with the one I'd given her all those weeks ago—the one I'd "borrowed" from a knight of the realm.

I opened a portal to step to her side. I fell out of the portal above one of the enemies, knocking them off their feet. At the same moment, Arzak turned to meet the glowing blade of the other attacker. It was nice to know that even after all this time apart, we were still in sync when it mattered.

Arzak's blade clattered against the enemy's, and a second later the glowing blue aura of the other sword began shifting into Arzak's.

"No, no, no . . ." the enemy began to mutter as the glowing grew brighter and brighter before . . . It exploded. The magicks sent a shock wave out that knocked the enemy from her feet, but passed over me and Arzak like a gentle breeze.

"I'd almost forgotten it did that," I said, then pressed the attack on the man now stumbling back to his feet. I stabbed forward with my blade, but the man was quick to block it with his leather bracer. I tried again, to much the same result. "Oh, to hells with this."

I lowered my free hand to the ground, fingers splayed, and opened a portal beneath the man's feet, its partner high in the sky above. He fell through and began tumbling to the ground, and I turned my back, thinking the fall damage would do the trick. But when his feet hit the sand once more, it was like he'd barely fallen at all. He landed in a crouch, almost on one knee, and then rose slowly back to his feet, rage in his eyes.

"Huh. Quite a cool landing."

The man charged, blade arching through the air, and I stepped back through a new portal to avoid it.

"Let's try something else," I said, allowing myself a quick smirk. I raised my hands to— Something hit me in the shoulder. Hard. "Ouch?" I turned around just in time to see an enemy ranger about to fire a *second* arrow at me—because that's what I'd been hit by—and I slipped back through the same pair of portals to avoid it.

"On it," Tokas said over the portal relays.

A moment later, Val added between strained breaths, "Maybe spend more time fighting and less time being smug?"

OK. No more smirks.

As the same enemy charged me once more, I opened a portal in front of him and once again dumped him in the air high above. But this time, before he could reach the ground once more—and look really cool in his landing—I opened another portal that tossed him into the air above me. At the same time, I arched my dagger overhead, slicing through the man's back, rendering his light armor too damaged to be functional.

Another arrow careered overhead, missing me by a foot or more as Tokas worked her *Illusion* magicks on the enemy, making them see things that weren't there. As someone who'd been on the receiving end of that before, it filled me with more dread than I might have expected.

"Behind," Val said through the relays.

I didn't react, because I had no idea who she was talking to, and then someone stumbled into me.

"I said 'behind'!" Val shouted, this time not requiring the relay.

"Maybe tell us who you're talking to next time?" I retorted, wondering whether this was the normal good-natured bickering or actual arguments rooted in the complex feelings we had about one another. There wasn't time to find out, because another enemy launched a fireball at us.

I spun around, stepping in front of Val, and activated my *Ash Husk* ability. As Val was now forced to deal with the now armorless swordsman, I prepared myself to face down a sorcerer. There were so many fire magicks specialists out there, and I'd recently had an idea for how to deal with them.

I grabbed the fireball from midair, just before it hit me. Even with my ashen hands, this *hurt*. A lot. I screamed as I tried to work through the pain, then opened a portal at my feet. I fell through it, appearing in the air above the sorcerer, and I tumbled fireball-first.

The fire engulfed the sorcerer, and so used were they to dealing the fire damage that they clearly hadn't prepared for *receiving* it.

Level 21 Apprentice of the Boundless Flame defeated!

Worldbending: +2,250XP
Worldbending increased to level 61!
Base Points Gained: +2 INT, +2 Free Points (INT/WIS/CHA)

Though we were turning the tide on our ambushers—they were now numbering fewer than us—there was no time to waste. I turned back to Val and the swordsman, and saw that the enemy was overpowering her. Even her green-glowing magicks that summoned scorpions from the desert was not enough to slow him down. The scorpion's poison was fast-acting in these parts, but not so fast that it'd kill the man before he killed Val.

I stepped through a portal, back to the man's side, and activated *Knifestorm* once more. But the man was quick enough to block it, and even though his armor was rendered useless, he still had his blade. When my ability had run its course, he swiped with that sword and I was lucky to avoid it, staggering backward across the loose sands of a dune.

I had half a second to think before he pressed the attack, and think quickly I did. I knew he could survive a fall, and *he* knew that, too. So far, that had meant he saw no problem with tumbling from the sky, and therefore he'd made little attempt to avoid my portals. But I still had a trick up my sleeve.

I opened another portal in front of him as he charged, just in time to avoid the tip of his blade meeting my heart. The man fell through it, and . . . disappeared.

Level 27 Vice-Champion of Fallenstone escaped!

Worldbending: +2,400XP

I breathed a sigh of relief.

". . . Where'd he go?" Val asked.

The enemy was probably standing in Coldharbor's central plaza at that very moment, wondering the same question. Maybe my *Saved Portal* ability was more useful than I'd given it credit for. "Coldharbor."

A wry smile crossed her face. "Nice."

"Thanks."

She turned away after that, remembering herself and all that had passed between us.

The rest of our ambushers fell soon after that, Corminar and Lambkin picking off the last of them as they fled. "It was my arrow that felled them," the elf told us—a point that needed clarification because both had hit the enemy at the same time.

"OK?" Val said with a shrug.

I wrenched the arrow from my shoulder and winced with the pain. The witch, sighing as though it was some great chore, placed her hands over the wound and started her *Healing*. I nodded to the yellow-white glow. "You've gotten better," I said.

Val nodded. "Thanks." As she was about to turn away, I raised my hand, revealing my heavily burned palms. The witch sighed once more.

A little ways away, I saw Tokas notice Arzak's gaping wound, and the tiefling hurried to be helpful. She placed her hands over the orc's arm and began healing, generating that same yellow-white glow as Val.

"Thank—" Arzak started, then her eyes bulged when she saw that it was Tokas, not Val, who was healing her. She recoiled fast, stepping backward up the side of a dune, a gaping wound apparently far more preferable than having the tiefling so close. Than having the tiefling who was prophesied *to kill her* so close.

"I won't—" Tokas began, but the orc cut her off.

"Stay away from me. Away from me," Arzak said.

The tiefling nodded, choking back her distress. Lambkin stepped forward and placed a comforting hand on her shoulder once more.

I met the eyes of the ex-captain, and understood what he was silently telling me. We needed to fix this before something bad happened.

I just didn't know how.

CHAPTER FORTY-SEVEN

The Potential for Evil

We set off from camp the next morning just as the sky turned from midnight black to simply very, very dark blue. The ambient light of the sun was just enough for us to navigate with, and the sooner we got going, the more we could justify resting while the midday sun passed over.

I found myself trudging down the road next to Arzak, who was never the loudest among us, but had been particularly quiet since her brief argument with Tokas. I couldn't honestly say I knew what she was going through, and part of me regretted bringing Tokas along with us. But then I remembered Lore, somewhere out there, across the lands, being manipulated by our terrible enemy. We really did need all the help we could get.

Still, I could try to comfort Arzak some. "How's it going?" I asked.

"I head to fight Player who can see future, and I do so with woman who betrayed me and prophesied to kill me," came the simple answer.

"Fair enough." I gulped. "Anything I can do to help?"

"No," Arzak snapped, then after a moment she sighed. "Sorry. I have lot of stress on top of me."

"You mean you're under—" I started, then shook my head. Now wasn't the time. "It's OK. I get it. But you understand why I had to bring them along?" I nodded my head toward Lambkin and Tokas, who were at the rear of our pack by quite some way.

"I understand. Is Lore." I noted that she was echoing my earlier wording.

"Is Lore, yeah."

"Got protect him."

I nodded, and we proceeded on in silence for a few minutes.

Arzak spoke next. "You leader now, huh?"

The question took me aback. "What? No. I—"

"You say 'Why *I* had to bring them.' Not why 'we' had to bring them. *I*." Before I could protest any more, Arzak shook her head and smiled. "Is OK. I think we all know by now that you leader. Or would be. You progress fast, thank to artifact. You be stronger than all of us soon, if not already. And got brain that even Val jealous of."

I didn't answer. What could I say to this? I knew I was progressing quickly, and I was lying if I said I hadn't noticed that I was the one giving the orders these days. I looked forward, toward Val, my eyes skimming over Raelas, who was looking my way.

I still couldn't figure out how I felt about Val. Part of me wanted to run to her, to embrace her, to be with her every second. But another part roared with a furious anger about what she'd done. About how she'd left. About how she blamed me for something I could do nothing about.

And yet, she'd run to me, hadn't she? In the moments that the corruption took hold, she'd run to me. That had been her instinct. Not to flee, but to risk herself.

Arzak watched me stare. "She need time," she said, and then, "Maybe you do, too."

"She knows I can't help who my parents are, right?"

"In head? Yes. In heart . . . more complicated." Arzak kicked aside an old leather satchel that someone had discarded on the road. "We all suffer from Players. They do terrible things to us. Those wounds not close. Not completely. Is hard. But she come around, in time."

"Will she?" I found myself asking. "I don't know what I'd do if she didn't."

Arzak's eyes widened, and she came to a halt for a moment. "Maybe you tell her this. Maybe she not know. Maybe she think she love man who not truly love back."

"Does she?"

The orc shrugged. "Not my business."

"But you just said—"

"Not my business," Arzak repeated.

I shook my head. Arzak had removed her metaphorical "gossip" hat and put on her "good friend" hat once more. There was nothing that could be done about that. So I instead jumped at the opportunity to ask something that I'd been wondering about for some while. "You said everyone here suffered at the hands of Players. I know what happened to Val, to Corminar, to Lore . . . but what about you? You've never spoken about it."

Arzak remained quiet while we passed two merchants on the road, traveling the other way. We offered them polite smiles and nods, and they returned the sentiment. I could tell we were drawing close to another settlement because we passed an ever-growing number of travelers setting off with the dawn.

"Is not story I like tell."

"I figured," I replied. "You don't have to if you don't want to."

The orc shook her head. "No. Is OK. I tell. Story start in Northern Reaches. Far north. Off human maps. Very cold up there. Miss it now, in this place."

"Yeah, I bet."

"If I tell story, no interruption."

"Got it. Sorry." I snapped my trap shut.

"In far north, is frozen tundra. Hard to live in tundra. Cold, yes, but also there are beasts up there. Emerge from snowstorms. Eat crops. Eat orcs. Eat buildings, sometimes. We not always cope. Our clan, we reached south, to call in outside help. A Player answered the call, a fearsome warrior."

"Ah, and they—" I began.

"What I say about interruptions?"

"Sorry," I said again.

"You and Val perfect for each other. Two big mouths, not know when to close." Arzak shook her head. "This Player not like the others. This one, kind. This one show me ways of swords. Bought me gifts. Gave me a . . . how you say, a role model? Saved my home four times over. Took payment, yes, but was never much, and she never ask for more. I join her on journeys, on quests, left clan behind—elder gave permission. I loved her."

I resisted the urge to speak, but only just about; my mouth moved a little.

"Two years later, I watch her die. She die at hands of another Player. The second Player I ever meet. I learn that I lucky to have met her and none others. I learn that those from Ascended World not care about us. Most of them not care about us. Most of them not love us. Most of them not like El."

Silence passed over us for a moment as Arzak retreated into herself, and her memories.

"Not all Players are evil," I said, ostensibly summarizing the story, but of course thinking about a specific Player.

"Not all," Arzak agreed, though she saw right through me. "But your mother, she in Council. I . . ." The orc didn't need to finish that sentence; we all knew that the Council were involved in deadly schemes, and if my mother was a part of it, then . . . Well, I couldn't quite bring myself to think about it.

The orc glanced back at Tokas—the first time she'd laid eyes on her, as far as I could remember. "And then I meet Tokas. She save me. Not from physical danger, but from emotional. I was not in good place, and she . . . she pull me out. I love her, too, but in different way. As sister. And then . . ."

Arzak gestured generally, but it was enough for me to know exactly what she was talking about. The betrayal. Accompanying Jacob during the devastation of Plainside, if to save her children. But the tiefling was here now, trying to make up for it, even leaving her children in care back in Coldharbor to do so. I could see that Tokas was trying to make amends, but . . . did Arzak? *Could* Arzak?

"Do you think you can forgive her?" I asked.

"Forgive? How I forgive someone who betray like that? How I forgive someone who going to kill me?"

"We don't know that. The future is unwritten. I've watched Lore change it time and time again over the past few weeks, though I didn't realize at the time that that was what he was doing. You don't know what will happen."

"I know it *can* happen," Arzak said.

It was hard to argue with that, but I was about to give it a go anyway, when suddenly I heard loud voices up ahead. Turning to face the front of our pack, I saw Val standing over Raelas.

"Why are you still *here*, anyway?" the witch demanded of the tiefling.

"I . . ." Raelas started, but Val didn't give her a chance to speak.

"Cos if you're anything like your friends, then you're gonna betray us as soon as you see some opportunity to get money. We don't need that on—"

"Val," Corminar said, his voice calm. "Enough."

"What? We're not all thinking it? We should have handed her in to the guards, rather than having another liability with us."

I made a very conscious effort not to look over at Tokas.

"I have nowhere else to go!" The words seemed to burst forth from Raelas's mouth, as though she'd been fighting to keep them back. "I have no one. No one. Can't you understand that? Can't you have a little bit of sympathy?"

"After what you—" Val started, but a firm look from Corminar cut her off again.

Val wasn't wrong, though. Raelas had been collecting malae, arguably the most dangerous species alive. And she'd done it thinking only about coin. But then, if Tokas deserved a second chance, didn't Raelas, too?

"I want to be good," Raelas said. "I want to be a hero. Like you."

Val's eyes flicked to me.

"We have to give her a chance to redeem herself, Val," I said.

"Do we?" the witch replied, and then turned away.

I couldn't help but feel like I'd made another poor decision. I could only hope that Yusef and Lore weren't much further, because our group was falling apart at the seams.

I nodded to another merchant who was passing us on the road. I was again smiling, but this time trying to communicate that I was sorry for this scene he'd paid witness to.

Then I saw his face. One I recognized. One that recognized me.

Ted began to run.

CHAPTER FORTY-EIGHT

The Destitute

"No!" Ted roared, clutching his head and bolting away from us, down the road. "No! No! No! Not you! Not *you*! Leave me alone! *Leave me alone*!" From the muffled sound of his words, he was shouting through tears.

"You?" Val called out from up ahead. "What are you doing here?"

"Should not be in Auricia?" Arzak asked. The last time we'd seen him, he'd found new riches and had opened a popular new sweet shop in the capital. One which traded in enchantments under the table.

Ted didn't reply, instead continuing to flee, so I opened a portal beneath his feet and dropped him back in front of us. He hit the ground harder than I'd intended, but at least the sand was soft around here. The man scurried backward on hands and feet, looking up at me as I loomed over him.

"What you doing here, Ted?" I repeated Val's question.

"Leave me alone!" the man cried again, stumbling to his feet, his bag falling from his shoulder. He turned to run, and collided heavily with Arzak's broad chest. He bounced off it, landing back on his arse once more.

"You spy on us?" the orc asked. It was a fair enough question, considering we knew Yusef had people monitoring us. And what with how much this man hated us, it was a reasonable leap to assume he was one of them.

"Spy?" Ted spluttered. "What do you mean spy? And on *you*? I want to be as far away as possible at all times from you people!"

"Then why not in fancy shop?"

"Oh, I dunno, maybe because last time you were there, you bloody *flooded* it?"

"Huh," I said. "I forgot about that. My bad."

"Your bad?" Ted repeated. "Your *bad*? Do you know how much I had to pay the landlord for all the repairs? And that's not to mention all the stock I lost, and the customers never really came back in the same way after someone mildly *electrocuted* half of them." The man stared daggers at Val—the woman who I suspected he'd once had a bit of a crush on. That had changed, then.

"My bad," Val said, echoing me.

"Stop saying that!" Ted turned and tried to run once more, but I opened a portal in front of him. He didn't fall through it, but it was enough to stop him in his tracks. He turned back, his eyes on the satchel bag that he'd dropped in the confusion. "You ruined me. My benefactors demanded their money back—money I no longer had. I had to flee. Had to leave the human realms behind, had to come out here and start from scratch. Had to start looking for salvation."

"Salvation?" Corminar asked. He'd had the same thought as me.

"Don't tell me you're running off to join the cult."

"Cult? No," Ted replied. "I'm looking to join the Church of Ascendancy. I'm—"

"That's the cult!"

"—after a new start, in a new world. There's a man who'll grant us that if we serve him. A Player. I'm going to—"

"He's not granting anyone anything!" I cried. "He's lying to you! Seriously, why do none of you see that? Honestly, is all it takes some charismatic, strong—"

"Handsome," Val added.

I turned to her. "Seriously?"

"Mm," Arzak added. "Nice legs."

I rolled my eyes. "Some charismatic, strong, *handsome* guy and you're all falling over yourselves to believe every word he says. That's how despots get their power, you know."

Ted glared back at me.

"I read history books," I explained.

"I doubt that," the once–sweet shop owner retorted.

"That I like history books?"

"That you can read."

I replied by tossing him through a portal, just for the hells of it.

"Don't join the cult, Ted," Val said. "You're better than that. Well, you're not, but don't join it anyway."

Lambkin picked the man's satchel bag up off the ground, shaking the sand from it. This was a man who was honorable even in the face of an enemy; it was sometimes infuriating.

"We're going to kill him," I told Ted. "Your Player hero. So no point in you going. Why don't you trot back on to the Tundras and—"

The ex-captain handed the man his bag, and Ted's hand shot straight into it. I realized the mistake a moment too late.

"Lambkin, no!"

But it was too late. Ted's eyes lit up as he withdrew a round purple sweet from the bag. He popped it in his mouth, and—

The man disappeared.

"Ah," Lambkin said. "My apologies. Portal magicks, was that?"

It was a good point. For all we'd seen of Ted's enchantments before, none of them seemed close to my particular brand of *Worldbending* magicks. I looked down, seeing footsteps in the sand, and realized the truth. "Not portals," I said. "Invisibility."

We chased the footprints across the dunes, but soon they faded; Ted had an enchantment even for that.

"Hm," Arzak grumbled, eyes on Lambkin. Her ire for Tokas had now started bleeding onto the ex-captain, too.

"Wouldn't worry," I said, clapping Arzak on the shoulder. "We'll run into him again." I sighed. "We always do."

Even I was prophesying now.

Our journey northwest continued.

Nobody had gotten into an argument for a while, which I was considering a success. If we could just keep that up until we faced down Yusef, then that was fine. We could all fall apart once the job was done, and once Lore was saved.

We passed through small hamlets on the road, all of them near desolate. Corminar had thought to ask about it at one point, and the answer given was that all the young, working people had left with the cult, leaving only the old behind. They were looking for a greater life than these small desert towns could provide, and the allure of ascendancy was strong. It was no wonder that Yusef had so much success recruiting in these parts; these were places forgotten by the region's leaders, left without support, left to face the harsh realities of life.

So when we arrived at a town that was lively and bustling—at least compared to those that came before—we were a little surprised. Tokas again hesitated at the perimeter of the town and all of us slowed to a halt at her side.

"Perhaps Yusef did not travel this way," Corminar suggested, seeing what I'd seen about the town ahead of us.

"What, he veered off the merchant road?" I asked. "Like Tokas said, there's nothing in these parts until Zelas, and that's down this way."

"Maybe there was something worth going off the road for?" Val said.

Arzak shook her head, and the reasoning that followed reflected my own. "Only thing he interested in is strength. Strength in recruits. Recruits in city. Ergo, he pass through here."

"Ergo?" Val repeated, eyebrow raised.

"Did I not use right?"

"If he came through this way, then his recruitment efforts didn't go so well," Lambkin said. "Why might that be?"

I shrugged, then took a step forward. "Let's go find out."

"No," Tokas said. All this time, her eyes had been on the village, scowling as if trying to penetrate the minds of those who lived there. As if trying to hear their intentions.

"Something wrong?"

"It's as before," Tokas said. "Like when we were ambushed. I felt something. Magicks. Could be another trap."

We turned to look at the village ahead of us. The people were smiling, which I suppose was odd in itself, but it didn't exactly scream "trap." We could have simply skirted around the village to be safe, but if these people had somehow resisted Yusef's charms, then maybe it would be useful to know how.

"Alright," I said, "we'll scout it out first."

"Who put you in charge?" Val asked.

"Arzak."

Val looked to the orc.

Arzak shrugged. "Little bit, yes."

"Why would you do that? His head is big enough as it—"

"Look, I'm going in because I can portal straight back out again if anything goes wrong. That's all."

"And I'm coming," Tokas said. "If this is what I think it is, then you'll need me to sense the magicks."

"I'm a magicks user, too, you know," I replied.

"Not like this you're not."

I furrowed my brow, but didn't press the matter further; I didn't think Tokas would volunteer to walk into a potential trap unless she really thought she could help. "Fine," I said, and stepped toward the town. "But don't cause trouble."

Tokas didn't reply.

CHAPTER FORTY-NINE

Uneasy

Tokas and I walked, not portaled, into town. I didn't want to draw any attention to us in case the tiefling was right, that there was danger here. So we waited for a pair of merchants to pass us on the road, then fell in step behind them, acting as though we were with them.

"Why did you ask me to come?" Tokas whispered, glancing back at the others—and at Arzak specifically, I suspected.

"Extra hands," I replied, hoping that this would be a good enough answer.

It wasn't. "You don't want me here, not really. If you have to ask me not to cause trouble, then you don't trust me." Tokas quickly scrambled to add, "Not that I blame you."

"Let's just concentrate on the task at hand, yeah?"

But Tokas wasn't put off. "Arzak doesn't like it. Me being here. I should go."

"Once we get Lore, you can do whatever the hells you want. Until then, we need you here. We owe him that. *You*, in particular, owe him that."

The tiefling went quiet. I should have known; any talk about what she'd done to betray us was usually quick to shut her up. She just couldn't face it. I admittedly wasn't sure I could, either. At least we were both talented in emotional compartmentalization, unlike our orcish friend.

We drew closer to the town, the sights and smells—what little there were of each—tickling our senses. Sand-lashed walls in the eyes, grilled vegetables in the nose.

"You feel anything?" I asked.

"Remorse."

"Magicks, I mean. Do you feel a trap?"

"No more than before. Which is to say . . . I still think we are in danger."

I kept my eyes peeled as we entered the town proper. None of the locals seemed to be paying us any mind, not looking at us with anything more than a fleeting glance. Or were they taking care not to look at us?

I shook my head. Tokas was making me paranoid. To prove my paranoia was unfounded, I pulled out a handful of loose change and approached one of two market stalls, geared toward those on the long road from Zelas to Coldharbor.

"What'll it be, young sir?" a man probably double my age asked, looking down at me with what I can only describe as kind, purple eyes. "Water's cool; fresh from the well," he said, gesturing to the selection of waterskins on the stall in front of him. "Or I have some rations for the road, cooked this morning."

"You got something to cover my head?" I asked. "A cloth, or . . ." Something cheap enough that it wouldn't be the end of the world in terms of my wealth.

"Ah yes, got a little red to your head, ain't ya? A little red for a human, at least!" He tossed his head back and laughed as though the joke was hilarious.

I smiled politely.

"I got just the thing," the merchant continued, then pulled some cloth from beneath the table. It was sea green, the exact same shade as Val's magicks.

"I'll take it," I said, then handed over the coins, adding, "Thanks kindly."

"You're welcome, young sir."

I retreated from the stall to where Tokas was waiting for me in the shade of a building, tying the new scrap of fabric around my head. Tokas looked at it, but didn't say anything. With her, that meant she had nothing nice to say about it.

"You learn anything?" the tiefling asked.

"Only that I'm a 'young sir' around here."

Tokas said nothing.

"And you?"

"The same uneasy sensation of magicks at play. But I cannot sense the source, as though it is far away, or as though the magicks have been tied off, allowed to fester."

"Could be something as simple as a bound water spring?" I suggested. "I heard about them in Coldharbor."

Again, the tiefling said nothing, shaking her head.

"Come on," I said, holding out my arm for her to hold. "Act natural. We'll look around more."

"As a couple?"

"As a fake couple, yes. Lone travelers arouse more suspicion than couples."

Tokas hesitated. "Aren't you worried that I've just lured you out here to hurt you?"

I lowered my arm. "Well I am now you've said *that*." I shook my head. "No,

I know you won't do that. Not anymore." Tokas almost seemed pleased to hear this, but I kept my arm lowered nonetheless. "Maybe we're a couple who've just had an argument instead," I suggested.

Tokas nodded. Together, we roamed around the town, nodding and smiling politely to the locals, and I was called "young sir" a handful more times. The inhabitants of one of the houses we passed had opened up two of their rooms for travelers, and were even opening up their front room to sell food and drinks. Though they didn't seem to have quite gotten this concept down, I insisted Tokas and I stopped in for one. Where better to hear gossip than an inn? Or, at least, the closest thing this small town had for one?

The proprietor hesitated when we sat down at a table outside and ordered drinks, but that didn't stop him calling me "young sir," either.

"They are very polite in this town," Tokas noted, and I couldn't help but hear the judgmental tone that lay under those words.

When the beer came, I took a greedy sip, only to find the liquid warm and tasteless. I placed the beer back down on the table. "Not . . . amazing," I said.

Tokas hadn't touched hers, and so couldn't agree. Instead, she peered around the town, eyes narrowing.

"Everything alright, young sir?" the proprietor asked, and I worried for a second that I'd spoken too loudly. Then they continued, "Got a little red to your head, ain't ya? A little red for a human, at least!"

It hadn't been funny the first time around, but I smiled at the tiefling local and assured him all was fine.

Tokas looked at me with a furrowed brow. "What is it?"

"That's what the other guy said to me."

Her brow furrowed further. "Exactly?"

"Yeah, same thing."

"No, I mean: exactly? Word for word the same?"

I shrugged. "Yeah. I think so."

"You think so, or you know so?"

"I know so. Why's it important?"

Tokas glanced once more at the proprietor, then at the town at large. She looked back to me. "I need your blade."

I whipped my hand to the dagger in its sheath at my side, holding it in place.

"I need you to trust me," Tokas continued.

"I don't. You know that."

Tokas swallowed. "This isn't Plainside. This isn't . . . that. Please, Styk. I'm trying to do better." The words sounded awkward coming from her mouth, but that was Tokas. Staring back into those eyes, against my better judgement, I believed her. With a reluctant sigh—and one hand pointing toward the ground at my feet, ready to open a portal—I handed over the knife, pommel first.

"Thank you," the tiefling said with glistening eyes that suggested she really meant it. Then she stood from her seat and stabbed the local in the chest.

"Tokas, no!" I shouted, my stomach dropping, a wave of guilt washing over me. I'd done this. I'd given her the weapon. I'd—

But there'd been no blood.

In fact, the proprietor of this establishment didn't seem to have noticed the attack at all. He only looked back at me and asked, "Everything alright, young sir?"

Then, the illusion broke.

Ripples of red magicks appeared around us as a huge illusion shattered. The walls faded away. The people, too. The edge of the illusion spread further and further from the proprietor's chest—or, at least, where the man's chest had been, because there was no man any longer. The seat underneath me disappeared, and I fell, spread-eagled. I landed not on the ornate tiles I'd seen before, but on soft, dry sand. Even the beer was gone, but that wasn't, I supposed, any great loss.

The red, glowing ripples traveled further, until they encompassed the whole town. It wasn't just the one man. It wasn't just the one building. The whole *town* wasn't real. The whole town was an illusion. In the distance, more of the "locals" faded away from existence. In the distance, I saw the dark speckles of our allies charging toward us.

A paling Tokas staggered backward as the illusion shimmered and faded around her. "Who . . ." she started. "Who could have such power?"

I felt a chill run down my spine—a strange sensation in such a warm climate. Then I noticed something worse still. Some of the figures around us didn't fade. Some of the people *were* real, hiding within the illusion. But their faces changed. And their clothes took on pale orange hues.

One of them—one with a familiar face—stepped forward, hammer raised.

"Am sorry, spawn," Lillya said.

CHAPTER FIFTY

Fates Entwined

Lillya brought the hammer down toward my head, and then . . . stopped.

Our eyes met. I saw in hers not the wrath of battle, but regret. Guilt, even, perhaps.

"No," she breathed, loud enough that only I—and perhaps Tokas, who wasn't so far away—could hear.

"Boss?" one of the other cultists asked, eyes darting, unsure. The man looked from Lillya to me, to our friends charging forth from the distance, and then even to a riding merchant approaching fast behind them.

"This not right," Lillya said.

"But Yusef ordered us to—"

"I *know*," the orc growled. She caught herself, and her voice softened. "I know. Stand down."

Some of those in pale orange robes lowered their weapons, while others paid no attention to the orc's orders. Among the latter group was another familiar face.

"*These* are the people we're supposed to kill?" Ted said, now dressed in the uniform of the cult. He'd moved fast to join them, presumably having come across this group on the road.

"Kill them and you'll be in Yusef's favor," the other man said, as though reiterating an earlier deal. This man, too, hadn't lowered his weapons—a spiked mace.

"Ted . . ." I growled, my nostrils flaring.

"S'pose it'd put an end to them ruining my life."

"You know spawn?" Lillya asked Ted, eyebrows raising.

I groaned; the last thing I needed was for other people to be impressed by Ted. I was about to say something on the matter when Ted popped a sweet into his mouth and disappeared from sight once more. Others in the group did the same; he'd been sharing his enchantments.

"I say *stand down*!" Lillya shouted, repeating her earlier order. "This man spawn of Architects!"

Nobody else spoke. Nobody else moved a muscle. If the cultists believed Lillya about my bloodline, it didn't matter to them. They were loyal to Yusef, and he'd given them a job to do. All I could hope to do was convince enough of them not to attack, or at least to buy time until the others arrived. Even with Raelas's—fairly limited—portal magicks, there was only so fast they could move. I could hear Corminar shouting something from the distance, and for a moment I considered opening some portals of my own, but this might have been all it took to trigger the attack once more.

"She's telling the truth," I said, and caught sight of Tokas's eyes bulging; she'd never been privy to this information. "My mum, she was—"

"Yusef's orders are sacred," the loudmouthed man cut in. "We obey them at all costs."

"Even if target is Player?" Lillya retorted.

"If it's true, then you knew this when you received the orders. Nothing's changed."

The orc looked to me with sad eyes, as though to say that something had. Perhaps that something was that she'd realized she couldn't go through with it. I heard Corminar's shouting grow louder as they approached, now echoed by Val and Arzak. As I glanced at them, many of them glanced back at the horseman merchant who was fast approaching.

I counted the number of cultists—could we hope to triumph, if it did come to a fight? When I reached two dozen, I stopped counting; by then, the answer was clear. Even with the others charging in to help, we wouldn't win this one. Or, at least, we wouldn't all survive the encounter.

Still, that didn't stop me from putting my hand on the pommel of my dagger. Tokas's fingers moved, preparing to cast a spell. Neither of these movements went unnoticed, and the enemies adjusted their grips on their weapons.

"I said *stand down*!" Lillya insisted, sweat forming on her brow, and not just from the high desert sun. If this orc had changed her mind about her orders, it was because of my ancestry and nothing else. If it could convince her, maybe it could convince others. I reached my hand down the neck of my tunic and began to pull forth the object that was dangling over my chest. The Sisyphus Artifact. If Lillya could explain what it was, and who could use it, then maybe we had a chance to turn the tides in our favor.

"There is one thing that might—" I started, but then I caught sight of many of the cultists looking over my shoulder. Looking down the road at my charging allies. They must surely have known that these people were coming to my rescue, yet the expressions on their faces weren't ones of fear or preparedness. They were of . . . confusion.

And then the gentle breeze carried Corminar's cries over to me.

"Player!" he shouted. "Player!"

Tokas whipped her head to Lillya, her face paling. "He's here? You brought him with you?"

But Lillya shared that same expression of confusion as the others in her contingent. This was news to her as well. I turned around, placing my back against Tokas's, recognizing that protecting each other's backs was the best chance we had of survival if Yusef really *was* here. I really would've preferred *anyone else* in our party protecting me, though.

As I turned, I caught sight of the riding merchant once more. I caught sight of glistening, ornate armor. I realized that no sensible man would wear armor in such heat—not unless it was enchanted. And if there was a frost enchantment built into the armor, then this metal was far beyond what any merchant could afford. *That* was the Player.

"The rider!" I shouted to Tokas, and the tiefling turned around. Suddenly, the two dozen or more cultists weren't the priority; the charging Yusef was far more dangerous.

And atop his horse, he was catching up to the rest of the team fast.

"To hells with it," I muttered, then reached out an arm to open a portal in front of my friends, bringing them to my side. Many of the cultists moved as if to attack, but hesitated just enough that Tokas and Lillya's outstretched hands gave them pause. This was a fragile truce if I ever saw one.

"Could've done that sooner," Val said as she stumbled out into me, and this made my heart skip a beat. Was she back to mouthing off smarmy insults? Was she back to the Val I knew? I opened my mouth to retort, but found that nothing came forth; there was still part of me that didn't *want* all to return to normal. Not that this was the time for it.

I closed the portal as the team fanned out in the usual formation ahead of the charging Player. Those who could take a few hits stood at the front—which, without Lore and Carle around, was just Arzak. Then came me, Raelas, Tokas, and Val, or those who could inflict damage quickly at medium range. And at the back stood the greatest and second-greatest archers in the Tundras, though I was no longer interested in which of Corminar and Lambkin was which.

"Ready yourself for illusions," I shouted to the team.

"Illusions?" Corminar replied.

"Yeah, this whole town was a—"

"That's not Yusef," Raelas said, her voice still quiet.

"Well who *is* it, then?" I asked, my strained voice betraying the panic I felt.

"That's the Councilman."

I hesitated, lowering my dagger. "Wait, what? Really? And we're *worried* about that?"

The loudmouthed cultist coughed pointedly behind us. "You remember we're still here, right? Lillya, are we attacking or not?" He caught himself. "No, don't answer that; we're attacking."

"Stand down!" the orc cultist repeated, and though this still held back the tide of attacks, I could see that we were moving closer to a shattered peace with every time she had to give this instruction.

There was no time for any more words between Lillya and the rest of her team, because the Player was upon us. The man wrestled his horse clumsily to a stop, almost plowing straight through us in the process, and then looked around at everyone standing here.

"All of you?" he asked.

"All of us what?" I replied.

"Hello again," Corminar said reluctantly. "I wish I could say it was a pleasure."

"You're all together? I have to kill all of you?"

"Nobody *has* to kill anyone," I retorted. "Though honestly I can think of *one* person who—"

Lillya's right-hand man stepped forward. "We aren't here with them. We're here to kill them on the orders of Divine Player Yusef."

The Councilman raised his eyebrows. "Oh really? And how is my old friend?"

Lillya choked a bit on this. "You friend with Yusef?"

"You're a Player?" the male cultist asked. "They weren't lying?"

"I come from the upper world, or whatever Yusef calls it, yes."

"The Ascended World," Lillya and I said at once.

"Sure, that. I come from there." The Player looked around at us again, his eyes glistening, and then he started laughing.

"I don't get what's so funny," I said after a moment.

"Villain not need reason for evil laugh," Arzak said with a shrug. "They just do."

"Don't you see?" the Councilman said after a moment more of particularly irritating chuckling. "This is perfect. This is as intended. It is an opportunity for me to prove myself in front of those loyal to Yusef."

"And I suppose you're going to do that by . . ."

"Killing you."

"Killing us," I repeated. "Right. So, the one thing that you struggle with?"

The Player put his armored hands on his armored hips, threw his head back, and laughed once more. More loudly. More annoyingly. *Guffawed* might have been the better word for it, really. "I am that man no more. I have experienced the sweet taste of fresh blood. I have—"

"You been drinking blood?" Arzak asked. "You not supposed to do that. You vampire?"

The Councilman slumped his shoulders. "I was talking metaphorically."

"Right, so . . ." I started. "Let me get this straight. After we left you tied up in that basement, free to go on the condition that you don't hurt anyone, you went and immediately killed someone? And that gave you the taste for it? And then you sought vengeance on us for . . . having mercy?"

"I am rather beginning to regret allowing this man to live," Corminar grumbled. "He is not even particularly pretty."

I nodded my agreement. Agreement with the first part of that sentence, at least, though it didn't stop Raelas and Val from looking at me funnily. "Won't make that mistake twice, though, will we?" I adjusted my hand on my dagger, and the enemy's eyes bulged. He might have killed some people, but it seemed he still wasn't used to his opponents putting up a fight.

"Cultists?" the Councilman asked.

"You're probably gonna wanna call them something like 'fellow devouts' or something," Val suggested. "They don't like being reminded they're in a cult."

"We're not," that loudmouthed man in orange insisted.

Val smiled at him, making no effort to hide that she was being patronizing.

"Well, then," the male cultist said. "By my count, that's two votes versus one."

"Wait, what?" I asked. "Votes?"

"To kill you." Then he charged.

With this move, the cultist shattered the fragile peace, and all hells broke loose.

CHAPTER FIFTY-ONE

Blood on the Road

"Tokas!" I shouted, alerting her to the swinging mace about to hit her in the back of the head. I dropped her through a portal to save her anyway, but it was worth her knowing what was coming.

I'd lost track of the others in the confusion. Fights these days were so often these huge affairs, with dozens of people involved and therefore it being impossible to track what was going on. I missed the days where it was just the five of us against one enemy. Even when we were facing down the pyroknight—and almost dying in the process—I at least knew what was going on.

Tokas scrambled back to her feet at my side, and turned to face the two cultists who were charging at us. While I used *Closed Reach* to close the distance on one of them, surprising the enemy with this ability, Tokas pressed her hands forward and the bright red glow of *Illusion* magicks shot forth.

Level 22 Bladesmith defeated!

Knifework: +1,950XP
Knifework increased to level 44!
Base Points Gained: +1 DEX, +1 STR, +2 Free Points (VIT/DEX/STR)

I spared half a second to look down at the cultist bleeding out on the sand. I almost felt sorry for him. What had his crime been? He'd attacked us, sure, but he'd done so because he'd been a true believer. He thought Yusef a god, one who should be obeyed above all else. To him, *not* attacking us would have been wrong. The cultist's only crime was that he'd fallen for Yusef's lies. And when there were so many others in orange robes also telling you that Yusef was to be worshipped, you might well come to believe it.

I wouldn't have done that, obviously. But that's another matter.

"Styk," Tokas said, then kicked the other cultist in my direction, the enemy distracted by visions of her creation.

I ducked under the man's flailing blade, then hit him with my own. My dagger met the flesh of his thigh, and I twisted. A stray arrow—from Corminar, Lambkin, or enemy, I did not know—hit the man in the shoulder. I barged the man to the ground, and the impact buried that arrow deeper into his shoulder.

Level 16 Coal Merchant defeated!

Knifework: +1,450XP

I grimaced at this notification. These weren't fighters, not really. These were just people who'd had little to lose and a lot to gain from joining Yusef's cause. No wonder the Player's lies were so appealing. Yusef had power over people even from afar.

Turning on the spot, I sought out the Player who *was* here, and saw the Councilman pressing an attack on Corminar and Arzak, the orc doing her best to block the Player's summoned ghostly axe. Arzak raised her blades in a cross to defend against the enemy's axe, but in the next attack, it had changed form to a spear. The orc ducked to one side and knocked the spearhead out of harm's way, but it was a close one. Behind her, Corminar loosed arrows furiously, trying to bury one of them between the cracks in the man's armor. They were holding their own for now, but it was only a matter of time before the Councilman found a weapon shape that bested Arzak.

"Tokas, on me!" I shouted, opening a portal at my side. I didn't wait around to see if she was stepping through it; we didn't have the luxury of that much time. We were outnumbered enough that we had to focus our attacks if we were going to turn the tide, and who better to eliminate first than the Player—the man who had inspired the cultists to disobey Lillya's instructions?

A blast of red magicks coming from over my shoulder confirmed that Tokas had indeed joined me. The red bolt arced through the air, soaring toward the Player, until another blast of magicks engulfed it—this one purple. The engulfing spell changed the direction of Tokas's spell and turned it back toward her. The tiefling dived to the soft sand just in time for her own magicks to pass overhead.

As I charged at the Councilman, I cast a glance over to the right to see one of the cultists surrounded by three purple orbs, spinning around her. This was a type of *Worldbending* magicks very different to my own. I thought about shouting to one of the others to deal with this cultist, but Val, Lambkin, and Raelas were all preoccupied with not dying. Even Lillya, who was at this very moment trying to stop her own colleagues'—if that was the word—attacks, couldn't do enough to give my friends any breathing room.

"I'll take the spell-warper!" Tokas shouted, then started off toward the cultist who'd turned her own attack against her.

I jumped into the air, opened a portal in front of me, and launched myself at the Councilman. At the same moment, Arzak parried one of the man's attacks and risked throwing herself at him, shoulder first. She'd clearly seen me coming. As the Player was distracted by this sudden change in the rhythm of the fight, I brought my blade down toward his back—and activated *Closed Reach* once more.

Using the *Worldbending* ability, I could easily cut through any armor. Including this one.

The Councilman's back arched, and he roared, with both pain and surprise. His spellbound weapon changed form into a long, glowing chain, and whipped back toward me. I opened a portal beneath my feet and was halfway through it when the Player's attack soared over my head.

As Arzak pressed the attack on the Councilman, making the best of the opening I'd given her, another of the cultists charged, mace raised. It was the man who'd given us so much grief before. If I had some sympathy for the cultists before, I forgot it when I saw this irritating man running in for an attack. I allowed the man to get close, swinging his long mace toward me, and then I opened a portal between us. The heavy weapon entered the portal and reappeared on the other side—right behind my attacker.

The man cried out as I hit him with his own attack—a tactic inspired by the spell-warper. Wasting not a moment, I jumped at the man, activating my *Knifestorm* ability. The man's robe was no match for the many slashes of my blade, and I couldn't help but think Yusef maybe should have improved his cult's uniform a little.

Level 17 Chair of Town Council defeated!

Worldbending: +1,100XP
Knifework: +1,750XP

I had little time to take a breath, because before I knew it, two more of them were on me. I skimmed the site of battle to pick out a little help. I saw Val, a little ways away, facing down three of the cultists—and struggling. I dropped her through a portal without warning her, but she was used to this by now and she landed on her feet.

"Thank—" she started, then realized that I'd saved her from one fight and put her in the middle of another. Val flicked a hand forward and whipped up a dust storm, the sand darting at the faces of the two oncoming attackers.

I knew this wouldn't stop them for long, so I rushed at the nearest one. I ducked under their wild swings of their blades and this time opted for activating *Execution*, because I knew they wouldn't be able to see me until they'd blinked the sand from their eyes. The attack downed them in one.

Level 8 Schoolteacher defeated!

Knifework: +1,350XP
Knifework increased to level 45!
Base Points Gained: +1 DEX, +1 STR, +2 Free Points (VIT/DEX/STR)
Ability Selection Unlocked
Select an ability from the list below:
. . .

Stealth: +750XP

I grimaced a bit at the sight of this class; I could live with killing a chair of a town council—I'd had encounters with them in the past—but killing a schoolteacher felt like a bit much.

"Styk!" I heard Arzak shout behind me.

I whipped my head around at the shout, expecting her and Corminar to be in trouble. But instead, I saw the Councilman hurriedly backing up from the fight. "Is he . . . ?"

"Running!" Arzak shouted.

I left Val to deal with the other cultist and portaled back over to the Councilman, meaning to land another *Closed Reach* attack. But then I saw the Councilman reaching toward his waist, pulling out an enchanted-looking stone. My memory flashed back to Lev, the pyroknight's assistant, who'd been equipped with portal stones in case of any emergency. *I wonder where he got to, in the end?*

"Arzak!" I cried. "Portal stone!"

Corminar raised his bow as if to shoot the object from the enemy's hand. But it was too late. Even as the elf raised his bow, the Player was bringing the stone down toward the ground.

It crashed into the sand, activated, and . . .

There was no flash of light.

Instead, the stone erupted in a cloud of black smoke, thick enough to make me cough. I stumbled forward, wary of attack, trying to wave the smoke out of the way. I crashed into Arzak's side, then we turned and hurried straight in one direction. When we finally came out the other side of the smoke, we saw . . .

"Seriously?" I asked.

"He not serious," Arzak echoed.

We saw the Councilman running away. He shouted for his horse, who was trotting off ahead of him.

I was about to exclaim some more, but I heard shouting to my right. "Help! Styk, h—"

Back in the center of the battleground, I saw Raelas overwhelmed, desperately in need of a portal. I opened one beneath her, dropping her to my side. Then, seeing Lambkin was in much the same boat, I did the same for him, too.

Val appeared at my side looking not so happy. "Another damsel in distress, saved."

Lambkin furrowed his brow for a moment, then flicked his eyes to Raelas and realized what Val meant.

There wasn't time for any further bickering, because the remaining twenty or so cultists were running toward us.

"What do you reckon?" I asked the group at large. "Run?"

"If it is good enough for Players . . ." Corminar said.

"Run," Arzak agreed, eyeing up Tokas as she retreated to our side.

I opened a portal next to us, and one in the distance near the Councilman. If we were going to flee, we might as well take down the Player while we were at it. I was about to hop through the portal, when I caught sight of a flash of purple magicks out of the corner of my eye. The spell-warper—not dealt with, as Tokas had promised—shot one of her orbs toward my portal. It encompassed the portal, slamming it shut. Or . . . nearly shut.

I knew what would happen next, but I opened my other pair of portals anyway. Another of the spell-warper's three orbs shot toward it, closing that one nearly shut, too.

Raelas moved to try, but I shook my head.

"Don't bother," I said, then turned my back on the charging enemies. "We're going to have to run the old-fashioned way."

I sprinted across the sands, my friends at my side, and the cultists followed.

CHAPTER FIFTY-TWO

Ichor

"They catching up!" Arzak shouted.

A breeze had picked up while we were fleeing the cult, whipping up the loose top layer of sand and forcing us to shield our eyes. Only Raelas and Tokas didn't seem to bother, though whether this was due to a difference in tiefling biology, or because they thought they deserved to suffer a little to make up for past sins, I did not know.

Behind us, the cultists really were gaining on us. We'd been traveling for days by foot, under the heat of the desert sun, so we weren't exactly rested. The cultists, however, had access to horses and carriages; perhaps Yusef had chosen those most rested for the job of springing this trap on us.

"I know!" Val shouted back to Arzak, then added to me, "Sure there's no way to get those portals working?" She summoned a gust of wind to cut a path in the light sandstorm.

"Not while the spell-warper is still alive!" I cried. Looking back once more at the group of pursuers, I searched for the woman in question. She was easily identifiable from the three purple, glowing orbs hovering around her, and I soon spotted her toward the rear of the group. Protected by her fellow cultists. These cultists didn't seem to just be protecting the spell-warper from us, but from Lillya, too; they'd sensed that her loyalties were split somewhat, that she couldn't be trusted.

I saw another familiar face near the spell-warper, shouting something into her ear. A face that I increasingly wanted to punch with every encounter we had.

"Of course, *Ted's* still alive," I grumbled. I'd lost track of him in the confusion of the fight, but clearly he'd been standing back and letting his new friends do the heavy lifting. Classic Ted. It occurred to me then that this was how the spell-warper had been so on it with us; Ted had been warning her about what abilities we had. In particular, he already knew about the portals, and so cutting off our means of escape was easy.

I was conscious that I had a *Knifework* ability selection available to me, and though it seemed a long shot, there was a small chance that it could help. Keeping one eye on the shifting sands ahead of me, I opened up the notifications.

Ability Selection Unlocked
Select an ability from the list below:

Option 1: Dual Wield (Knifework)—*Passive*. You can now use a dagger in each hand with equal ability. Ability level is copied from dominant hand to nondominant hand.

I'd had this option available just five levels ago, on my previous ability selection screen, and so it was probably no surprise that it wasn't yet upgraded. At the time, I'd chosen to upgrade my *Execution* ability, which made sense considering the *Stealth* element to my build, but even at the time I'd been hard-pressed not to select this new passive.

Option 2: Parlor Tricks II (Knifework)—Impress others with a wide variety of knife-related parlor tricks, including five-finger fillet and blind throws. Has a very high chance of success, scaling further with [CHA].

Loose sand gave way beneath me, and I stumbled toward the ground. Val slowed just enough to help me back to my feet.

"Thanks."

"No problem," the witch said, sparing another glance at our pursuers.

I could quickly rule out the *Parlor Tricks* ability, even at this higher rank. I needed something for combat right about now, and I think even just generally, the time for parlor tricks was behind me; I had much bigger fish to fry these days than impressing women in taverns. There was only one more option.

Option 3: Throw III (Knifework)—Throw blades at great speed toward your enemy. Deal considerable damage to armorless areas, with additional damage scaling with [DEX] and [STR].

I couldn't help but feel that my list of abilities was starting to get a little out of control. I'd intended to keep my build tall, rather than wide, this time around, and yet here I was with three *new* options in front of me, and no option to upgrade an existing ability.

Still, though, they were good options. *Dual Wield* was a solid option always, and I'd been missing *Throw* from my previous life. Sure, I could still throw knives even without an appropriate ability, but they missed far more often than they hit. With this, I could have a realistic expectation of throwing knives to actually do damage . . . and not just to disarm myself.

Considering that right now we were fleeing for our lives, I had to choose the ability that stood the most chance of getting us out of this mess. *Dual Wield* might have been good if I'd had a second knife on hand, but as it was . . .

Ability Upgraded: Throw III

Throw III (Knifework): Throw blades at great speed toward your enemy. Deal considerable damage to armorless areas, with additional damage scaling with [DEX] and [STR].

I felt the innate knowledge and capability flow through me, and a big part of me wanted to try this out immediately. But still, I only had the one blade at the moment, and I'd have to portal it back to me. Not something that was easy to do while running away.

"What're you grinning about?" Val asked me. "I don't see what's so—" She stopped herself. "Oh. New ability? Something to get us out of this?"

"Throwing knives," I said.

"So . . . no, then." I would have been annoyed, but she smiled, gently, as she said it.

"They catching up more!" Arzak reiterated, her voice straining. "Now time for plan." She glanced at me.

"Not sure I have one."

"You not have one, then we die."

I nodded. "I'll think." I really had become the "man with a plan."

What could we do? We couldn't portal away, that much was clear. And if we kept running, it was only a matter of time before the charging cultists caught up. By then, we'd also be weaker, and less able to withstand a fight. It felt like we were trapped, like we—

I roared with pain and sank to the ground. An arrow had pierced my shoulder, entering at the back and its head sticking halfway out at the front. Again, Val stopped to pull me up to my feet, this time her eyes wide with concern . . . and fixed on the arrowhead.

"I—" I started.

"Keep running!" she shouted, practically pulling me with her.

I did my best, but as the blood poured from the fresh wound, I felt my legs growing weaker, my vision beginning to darken around the edges. "Val, I . . ."

The witch glanced at me, and from that look, she understood the rest of the sentence. "Keep running!" she cried, though she kept her own eyes fixed on the arrow. "I'm going to have to pull it through. Ready?"

Before I could answer, she yanked.

The pain erupted something fierce, and I stumbled to the ground once more. Val quickly yanked me back up to my feet for a third time before beginning to work her *Healing* magicks. "Poisoned . . ." she mumbled.

"You can't fix it?"

"I can. It'll just take longer."

"I don't think we *have* longer." I didn't need to risk a glance back over my shoulder to know that this was true. Another couple of arrows had soared past us since the first, but they were getting closer with every moment. Val said nothing, continuing to heal my wound as best she could as we ran.

Behind, I heard Lillya shouting to her fellow cultists, her voice strained and desperate. "Stop!" she roared. "Stop arrow! He spawn of *Player!*"

I think we all knew by that point that this line of negotiation had lost its power. Her fellow cultists didn't believe her. Not one but *two* Players had ordered the deaths of me and the other Slayers, and why would they want one of their own dead? To those in the Cult of Ascendancy, who thought in such black-and-white terms, it didn't make sense. Nothing would convince them of it now.

And at that moment, Arzak's much-requested plan came to me. I didn't know that it would work, but I had to try it. *So these cultists didn't believe that I had the blood of the gods flowing through me? Fine. Why don't I prove it?*

I halted midstride, Val's eyes bulging, the rest of the Slayers continuing to run. I grabbed the octahedron that was hanging around my neck, thrust it into the air, and turned to face down our pursuers.

"Do you know what this is?" I roared.

This was the riskiest part of the plan; if I didn't pique their curiosities, then they'd probably just kill me right then and there. As it was, though, the two dozen cultists stumbled to a halt . . . but didn't lower their weapons.

"Styk, I . . ." Val started, but I hushed her with a glance. Up ahead, my friends had just started realizing they'd left Val and I behind. To their credit, they stopped pretty quickly.

"Artifact of ancients," Lillya said, more to her fellow cultists than to me. "Sisyphus Artifact." She sought out a woman in the crowd. "Hualya, you remember? Months ago, Yusef mention it? Say it belong with Council? Say it meant for Players?"

One of the cultists stepped forth from the crowd. "I . . . remember. Yes. Sure."

Lillya turned back to me, pointing desperately toward the device I held in the air. I tried not to let the pain in my shoulder show, gritting my teeth through it. "That *is* Sisyphus Artifact! He use it to come back to life."

"Twice," I mumbled.

"Two and a half," Val corrected me, thinking of the corruption.

"You not see?" Lillya said. "He *is* spawn of Player."

At that, some of the cultists lowered their weapons.

CHAPTER FIFTY-THREE

Heretical Testimony

"Put down your weapons," I said, keeping the Sisyphus Artifact held above my head for all to see. Some of the cultists did, some of them didn't. "*Put down your weapons,*" I said again, this time taking on the air of command.

Only a handful, now, still held theirs, but I'd done enough that the attack was over; even if those few remaining skeptics tried anything, there were more than enough cultists presumably now on my side.

The loudmouthed cultist who'd started the attack was one of those still holding his weapon, adjusting his grip on his mace as he stared me down. "What about Yusef? He gave us a direct order. It's him we follow, not—"

"You want Player blood on hands?" Lillya demanded of him.

The man seemed lost for words.

"Hmm?" the orc pressed him. From the man's darting, wide eyes, I could see that this simple question had taken the wind from his sails.

"He has a point," Hualya said. When the orc turned on her, she hastily put up her hands. "I'm not saying we attack again, I'm not. But what do we do now? Do we return to Yusef and explain that we failed? Or, worse, that we disobeyed?"

It was Lillya's turn, now, to not have an answer. I saw the woman lick her lips before finally replying, "We will think about this." From the expressions worn by her fellow cultists, this wasn't a good enough answer for some, but it was the only answer they had.

I cast a look back over my shoulder at the rest of our party, who were stopped some way ahead of us, but making no effort to join Val's and my side. Sensible, really; they didn't know what was going on, and there could be another attack at any moment, for all they knew. I'd have to let them know what I'd done, but before that . . .

I turned to Val, expecting a grimace on her face, or some visceral reaction to the reminder that I was the son of a Player. But instead, when I turned, she simply returned to healing the wound on my shoulder once more. "You OK?" I asked her.

"I'm OK."

"With what I . . . with what I did, I mean."

Val nodded, sparing a second to look up at me. "I know."

"You're OK?" I repeated.

"I'm getting there."

Lillya approached before we could move this very stilted conversation along any further. "They not happy," she said.

"Yeah, I got that," I replied. "You think they're gonna attack again? I mean, we did kill half their friends." I was probably good to get that point out there.

The orc shrugged. "Not really friends. Yusef not like us get close. If we close then maybe we not report heresy."

"Seems like a lovely guy," Val said.

To this, Lillya had no response.

"We're going to need to ask you some questions," I said. "About Yusef." I left out the part about "so we can kill him"; I didn't think that would go down so well, even with someone who was clearly having doubts.

Lillya nodded, then glanced back at the others in orange robes. "OK. Not here."

I agreed, as we didn't want anyone else overhearing. Worst-case scenario, they attacked us again for it, and even the best case was that they'd report it back to Yusef. I opened a portal next to us, and we stepped through it, appearing next to the rest of the Slayers.

"Care to explain how you ended their attack?" Corminar asked. "I assume it was not simply your supposed smooth-talking?"

Arzak glanced down to the artifact, still in my hand, and she understood immediately. "He prove he son of Player." Her eyes flicked to Val, who shrugged.

"He did," the witch replied.

I turned to Lillya, wanting to move the conversation on. Corminar and even Raelas knew enough of all this that Val's reaction would prompt further questions. Admittedly, Tokas and Lambkin were in the dark, the latter of which had eyes bulging at this new piece of information. "Lillya, you know you're in a tricky position here, right?"

The orc in orange nodded. "We go back to Yusef, he kill us. We fail him. But will not kill you, either."

"So I have to ask," I continued, "what do you value more, your loyalty to him, or your life? Cos if it's the former, then by all means, go back to him, get killed. I won't stop you. But if you quite enjoy living, then maybe you can adjust your faith ever so slightly and worship Players in general, rather than him specifically?"

Val opened her mouth, and I knew exactly what she was about to say—that Players shouldn't be worshipped, that they were evil, and so on. But I shook my head at her; she was right, but with people as far gone as Lillya, it was best to take this one step at a time.

"I need . . ." Lillya shook her head, then pulled up a shirt sleeve to reveal a gaping wound.

There was an opportunity to win some goodwill here. "Val, would you . . ." I said, gesturing to the orc's arm. The witch nodded and set about working.

In the meantime, I saw Corminar approach a figure in orange who had wandered closer to the camp. Ted, watching on, seemingly hesitant. As Corminar grew close to the enchanter, the elf stood up straight, making an effort to stand over the young man. I couldn't hear quite what was said next, but I could see Corminar growling it, and I could see Ted's head shrinking down between his shoulders. A moment later, the elf pointed back to the rest of the cultists, some ways away, and wandered back over to us.

I watched Ted slink away as my elven friend approached. "You let him live?" I asked.

Corminar nodded. "I told him that I spared his life, but in doing so, I invoked the power of the Dawnwood. I place upon him a blood debt, his essence bound to mine until he saves my life as I did his."

I raised my eyebrows. It wasn't a voluntary reaction. "And . . . that's a thing? A blood debt?"

Corminar smiled, and for a moment I glimpsed the old Corminar—the one from before he'd watched his home fall to the enemy. The one . . . not completely *un*broken, but at least far less broken than he'd been since then. "It is not," the elf replied. "But he does not know this."

"I don't know," I said. "We might live to regret that."

"He is my charge now," the elf replied. "If he causes issues, I will deal with him, but I believe there might be something within him worth saving."

"I have absolutely no idea what you're talking about."

Corminar smiled. "Perhaps one day, I will be able to demonstrate. Until then, though . . ." He gestured to Lillya, freshly healed, being helped back to her feet by Val.

"It's time to talk," I told her. I made an effort to keep my voice calm, and gentle. We were all friends here.

What came out of Lillya's mouth next, I did *not* expect. "I have doubt about Yusef anyway."

I glanced to the others, who also remained quiet, this silence apparently intended to urge Lillya on. But the orc needed more prompting. "You . . . have doubts? You don't think he's a Player?"

Lillya shook her head furiously. "No, not this. I know he Player. My doubts about his prophecies."

My mind flashed to Lore. Clearly Yusef's prophecies were convincing enough to my friend, and he currently was the sort of guy who would know, considering he was dealing with some of his own. "They're not coming true?"

"No, I . . ." Lillya gulped.

"You can tell us," Arzak said, catching the other orc's eyes. "We might help."

Still, the orc in orange looked hesitant, but she was smart enough to know that there was no other way. She couldn't return to Yusef, and Yusef wasn't the kind of guy to let betrayal go unpunished. Her only hope of survival was for us to kill the head of the cult before he killed her. "I think his gift of prophecy flawed," Lillya finally said.

"They're not coming true?"

"No, they come true, but . . . how say this? I *think* reason he know all he know is because of spies. He have thousands of spies. All report information to him. Each of them not contribute so much that they suspect him, but contribute enough together that he knows all. Enough information make his *Divination* look powerful."

Ah.

Arzak and Lambkin nodded, and Corminar and Val were considering this thoughtfully. But across the group, I met Tokas's eyes. From the look on the tiefling's face, I knew we'd reached the same conclusion. We'd been the only ones in the town, before the trap had been sprung. Only we had *experienced* the truth, rather than simply knowing the key pieces of information.

"OK," Arzak said, "so he supplement *Divination* with spies. Not all-powerful, then. We stand chance."

"No," Tokas and I said at once. The tiefling immediately hesitated, yielding the floor to me.

But I shook my head. "No, Tokas. You tell them. You understand this more than me."

The tiefling gulped, but then drew in a deep breath to speak. "Don't you see? He's fooling everyone. He's fooling his followers, his enemies . . . maybe even the Council themselves. He's a . . ."

Tokas shook her head to herself.

"I need to go back a bit, to explain this properly. Do you remember, a few days ago, I asked to see a map?" Before anyone could answer, she continued, "It's because I had this suspicion even then. It's because I felt *Illusion* magicks in the air. I almost wondered if that village wasn't real, or if it wasn't as big as it looked."

Val shrugged. "OK? We know there's been some illusions at play; we just saw a whole town disappear in front of our eyes."

"But that's my point," Tokas continued, "it might not just be one town. How many traps did he lay for us? Did he really think Lillya would be successful, or did he have a backup plan? And a backup plan for that backup plan?"

"We don't know that he operates like that."

Tokas held up a finger to beg Val's patience. "Oh, but we do. That level of *Illusion* magicks, that is extreme. To create illusions of entire towns? You would need dozens of skilled illusionists. Or . . ."

"One very powerful person who has been training in *Illusion* their entire life," I finished.

Tokas nodded.

"You're saying . . ."

"I'm saying Lillya was right to have doubts about his prophesies," I said. "But not just because he's supplementing them. Because *he's never foreseen anything in his life.*"

The orc in orange almost choked at this.

"All these prophecies? Everything he's seen coming—our presence here, our attacks—it's because his spies told him it was coming. He's had people watching us this entire time. Dozens of them. A whole church desperate to tell him even the slightest piece of information that might help him, that he might reward them for. He's not a prophet at all. He's a false prophet."

Tokas nodded. "He's a con man."

Alia, Great Elder of Zelas

He was late.

Nobody made the Zelas Assembly of Elders wait, at least not in normal times. But these were far from normal times, and this was a man used to having others wait for him.

As the leader of the Council of Elders, Alia could not allow the others to see her disdain, or her anger. She clasped her hands around her back to resist the urge to clench them, ignoring the pain that erupted in her swollen knuckles. She strolled over to the window, taking care to appear relaxed. Alia could feel the eyes of the other elders upon her back, each of them sitting at the ornate, carved granite table; Alia had been the only one standing.

She trained her own eyes on the city of Zelas, beyond the window of the Elder Tower. They were based on the highest floor of one of the tallest towers in the city, afforded a view of almost every other rooftop or grand parade that spiraled out from the center of town. Zelas was conical in shape, the tallest towers in the center of the city, decreasing in size to mere humble shacks at the very perimeter. Without city walls, Zelas relied instead on the centricity of all their most valuable structures to hold out against any enemies. Not that there had been any since the tiefling sprawl so many decades ago.

Alia heard him coming long before the door opened, the man making no effort to disguise the sounds of his shoes hitting the elaborate painted tiles. When the servants finally opened the door of the chamber, Alia saw no sweat on the man's brow, no sign that he had made any particular effort to be here on time.

"I'm glad you waited," Yusef said.

Alia noted that this was not an apology. In fact, it only seemed to really imply that he was worth waiting for. Over the past few years, she'd been starting to wonder if this wasn't typical of Players, no matter what the legends said. "We waited," Alia echoed. "But our time is short. Perhaps we might jump straight to matters of importance?"

Yusef bowed his head in agreement. "That's my preference, too. We all have places to be, and I don't think this needs to take any longer than it has to."

There was that arrogance again. Alia drew herself tall, taking in a deep breath. "Since arriving in Zelas three days ago, you have caused quite a commotion. Key industries find themselves without employees. Mothers have lost sons and daughters to you. Our economy is on the brink of—"

"Yes, yes," Yusef said, waving Alia down.

This time, Alia failed to stop the irritation from appearing on her face. Many of the other elders noticed, but none seemed to mind; this was a slight too great, even for a Player. "Yes, yes?" the Great Elder repeated. "Yusef, this is of rather too much importance to dismiss us with a mere 'yes, yes.'"

Yusef blinked, raising his eyebrows in irritation, then approached the granite table, placing his hands upon it. "I am being pursued. I do not have time for this. In fact, I took this meeting out of good manners, but . . . no, let's get right to it."

A vision erupted in Alia's mind. Despite the images before her, the Great Elder still had enough presence of mind to note the gasps of her colleagues; they, too, had been gifted a prophecy. She saw herself and her colleagues dressed in the pale orange so fashionable of late, standing in the desert amidst a crowd of thousands. Perhaps tens of thousands, or more. She saw Yusef himself, floating above them, glowing with the magicks of *Divination*. She saw the Player raise his hands, and in a moment, they were transported.

These thousands in orange were no longer in the harsh desert environment in which they'd spent their lives. They found themselves instead in a paradise, lush with plants and flowing fresh water. No longer was the air dry, harsh on the throat. No longer was the heat something to combat each and every day. What's more, their bodies, too, had changed. Alia's skin, so leathery in the past two decades, was soft and smooth. She reached a hand out in front of her, eyes bulging, and she clenched her fist. Her knuckles no longer caused her pain. Nothing did, in fact. This was . . .

"Your reward!" Yusef shouted, his voice echoing around this new landscape. "The realm of the Architects. Your new eternal paradise."

And then, in an instant, the vision was over.

Alia, for one, needed no more convincing.

"So, will you serve?" Yusef asked. "Is this meeting over?"

The Great Elder couldn't quite believe herself when she was the first to move, running to the prophet's side and throwing herself at his feet. It had been so long since she bowed to another, and yet, with what great gift this man would eventually bestow on her . . . how could she not?

"Good," Yusef said, smiling faintly, as though this was a sight he'd seen so many times before.

"Whatever it takes, I will—" Alia started.

"Find the spawn of the Architects," Yusef cut in. "Use all your resources in the city and find he who goes by the name 'Styk.'"

"Kill him?" Alia asked.

"If you can, but that will follow anyway if you can steal the artifact he carries. The one he uses to seduce others away from our cause. Do that, and you will be rewarded as you see—"

The door to the chamber burst open once more. This time, the man standing in the doorway *was* coated in a layer of sweat that Alia—the poor, naive, old Alia—had once expected of Yusef. To Alia's surprise, she saw Yusef groan, slumping his shoulders at the sight of their latest guest.

"You? Again?" Yusef asked, though from his tone it was rhetorical.

"The Councilman does not admit defeat so easily," the other man replied.

"For the last time, Simm, you're not in the Council. We don't want you. You're lucky we even let you live, considering the mess you made in Tradum."

At this, the other man's eyes widened. "Let me live?" he repeated. "But I'm one of you! I want all the same things you do! I've even killed for the cause now." He said this last bit with a slightly strained voice. "I want in. Just tell me what to do, and I'll do it. Whatever it takes to prove myself to you, to the Council . . . I'll do it. I *can* do it."

Yusef stared the man down for a minute, perhaps two, considering him. Finally, he sighed. "There is . . . *one* way that you might prove yourself." Yusef turned to Alia and the others gathered around the table. "Elders, if you might give us the room?"

Alia leaped to follow his command, standing at the door to usher her fellow elders away. As she bowed to the Players and closed the door gently behind her—sincerely attempting not to eavesdrop—she gleaned only one word. Coldharbor.

CHAPTER FIFTY-FOUR

The Touch of the Crowd

We arrived in Zelas after dusk the following day, just in time to watch the lanterns light up around the peculiarly shaped city. The lights seemed to bloom first around the towers in the center of the city, before spreading slowly to its outskirts over an hour or so. Raelas, who knew these parts well, suggested that it was because those in the tower were rich enough to have servants to light these lanterns for them, whereas elsewhere in the city the residents lit them only when they had time.

We, however, remained beyond the perimeter of the city, using the lingering warmth of the desert sun to remain at a distance, and plan our next move. Since the revelation on the road, two days ago, we knew now just how extensive Yusef's network of spies was. It was a fair assumption that someone would spot us as soon as we entered the city, especially considering how many orange robes we'd seen on the merchants' road in the past few hours. Maybe they'd spotted us already. Maybe he *already* knew we were here.

Still, though, we needed a moment to figure out what was next. Prophet or con man, a central issue remained: Yusef was surrounded by hundreds—if not thousands—of loyal followers. We simply couldn't compete with that, even with Raelas, Tokas, and Lambkin added to our number.

"We figure out where he is, and then we take it from there," I said. "No point in planning anything until we have all the information we need. Raelas and Corminar will go in as one team, Arzak and I as the other. If we run into trouble, we open a portal and we flee. There's—"

"What, split up?" Val asked. "Have you learned *nothing* over the past couple of years?"

"I've learned to sew," I countered. I don't really know why I said that.

"Point is," the witch continued, "if we split up, we're weaker. We're easier for Yusef and his cronies to pick off. We're much better off staying together. We can still run, we can still open portals and get out of there, but we stay together, and we watch each other's backs." She looked at me as though expecting an argument.

"As the lady says," I replied.

"I'm not a lady."

"Yeah, I know." With that, I turned and led our crew of seven toward the towering desert city of Zelas.

As we reached the outermost buildings—where on other cities there might be a towering wall, manned with guards—I felt the easy buzz of the people hit me like a wave. This was a place where activity did not die down with nightfall, and from the looks of it, it was all only really getting started. The people here must have hidden from the heat during the day, with most of their trade—as evidenced by market stalls—and socialization—as evidenced by entertainers roaming the streets—happening at night. It was a place in which I felt immediately at home, like I could settle down here one day. But I was a long ways away from settling down anywhere, what with the Council's plan still barreling toward success. It was better to focus on the task at hand, and that was finding Yusef.

We'd still had our robes in our satchels, so we'd put them on before entering the city, hoping it would keep enemy eyes off us. What I'd *not* expected was that it would help us blend in quite so much; Yusef could only have been here a week, tops, and yet a huge chunk of the city seemed to have been converted to his cause. More people than not wore pale orange, and they greeted their fellow cultists with nods and broad smiles. Our best chance of finding Yusef? Ask.

I continued pushing through the ever-growing crowd.

The only problem was figuring out who was new to the cult, and who wasn't. If we accidentally asked someone with experience, like some of the contingent who Yusef hadn't left behind in Coldharbor, then they might recognize us as enemies. They might attack. And if they attacked, then there would be hundreds of cultists upon us within seconds. I knew by then that Yusef didn't have the gift of prophecy, but he'd maybe been right about one thing: if we attacked him, then his horde of followers wouldn't let us live to see the sun rise. We'd need to be careful.

Just then, I felt someone brush past me, and something tingled in the back of my mind. There was something about that brush that hadn't felt natural, something almost imperceptibly different to the feel of all those others who'd squeezed by.

My heart jumped when I realized what it was. Something I'd done plenty of in a past life.

I whipped my hand to my chest, finding my tunic sliced, and far more importantly, a complete lack of artifact dangling from my neck. "Stop!" I shouted, reaching forward where I *thought* the pickpocket had run, but the crowd was bustling, eddying this way and that. There was no way of knowing for sure who had stolen the Sisyphus Artifact.

I came to an abrupt halt, the city beginning to spin around me. I'd had that artifact with me for so long. I'd come to depend upon it. I'd taken it for granted. And now it was . . . gone? Just like that?

"Styk?" Val, who had been closest to me, asked. "What's wrong?"

"The artifact," I replied, my voice shaking. "Someone's taken it."

Val moved around me to look into my eyes, studying me. "You know who?"

I shook my head.

"They know we're here. We should get off the street." Val nodded to Arzak to gather the others, then led me by the arm down the nearest alley.

As she dragged me along, I felt the city still spinning around me. It almost came as a surprise to find that we'd stopped. I looked around, seeing Arzak and the others some way down the alley from the rest of us; Val wanted to speak to me alone.

"Val, I need it back. I can't be without it."

"It's gone, Styk. In a city like this? It's gone. You won't see it again. We need you to get your head around that sooner rather than later, if we're gonna survive."

I shook my head. "I could die."

"You didn't have any charges on it; you could've died anyway."

"Then I'll get one. I'll get the artifact back, and then I'll get a charge. We'll kill Yusef. I'll get a charge, and then I'll be safe."

Val stared into my eyes, and I got lost in her own—deep, brown, gorgeous—for a moment. Part of me wanted to kiss her then, but I knew the instinct was built on a lie; with part of me so recently snatched away from me, I wanted something else familiar to take its place.

"You know why I left?" Val finally asked.

"Because my mum's a Player," I replied. There was no point talking around this. If we were going to have this conversation now, of all times, then we might as well have it properly.

"No. Because I thought you might be turning into one of them. Not just a Player, but a *Player*. The ones we hear about. I'm under no illusion that there are more Players out there than we stumble across, but some of them are living nice, peaceful lives. Maybe they're even helping people. I'm not worried about you becoming like them, I'm worried about you becoming like Yusef. Like Jacob. Like Niamh. To tell you the truth, before I left, I thought I'd have to kill you before you killed me."

I took a step back. "That's . . . quite the admission?"

"I'd never do it, obviously," Val replied. "*Obviously*. It's you. But that was how my messed-up brain reacted to the news. I panicked. I'm not saying I'm perfect—we all know I'm so far from it—but you're not exactly perfect, either, Styk."

"You're still worried," I said, picking up on her earlier wording.

"Yes."

"After all I've done? Why?"

"It's precisely *because* of what you've done," Val hissed, sparing a glance back down the alleyway, not just at our friends, but at any other onlookers. "All this talk of being heroes, of power, of fame."

"It's not about power and fame; it's about doing the right thing."

"Yet you seem to want to do the right thing very loudly, not quietly. You want the fame. You want people to look up to you."

I furrowed my brow. "Don't *you*? Isn't that part of being alive?"

Val shook her head. "Not like that. Look, Styk, I love you. You know that. I'm pretty sure you love me, too. But I can't be with someone going down this path. I won't."

I took the opportunity to kiss her then—everything else be damned. Val returned it for a second, and then broke off, eyes widening.

"What?" I asked her. "You're surprised I've forgiven you for leaving? I suppose I was surprised, too, when I realized a few days back. But I knew what I was getting into with you. I knew it was going to be a bumpy ride."

"I didn't think you were the kind of man to let things like that go."

"Why not?"

Val shrugged. "I don't know, it's the opposite of what we're told to do, isn't it? Someone does something to hurt you, and you're expected to get them back. Hit them harder."

"There's strength in forgiveness, too, Val," I told her. "Probably more strength in that than battling it out, even. So, I choose to forgive. We don't have to be on these manic paths of vengeance all the time. I've forgiven you for leaving; surely you can be big enough to forgive me for something that I can't even help?"

"What did I *just say*, Styk?" Val hissed back at me. She glanced over at Arzak, who was now looking anywhere but at us, and blushing. "It's not your ancestry; I'd never hold that against you. It's what you're becoming."

"I'll prove it," I replied. "But how? How do you want me to prove that I'm not going to change? That I'm not going to become like that?"

The witch considered me for a moment, her eyes meeting mine, our faces still close together. "Let it go, Styk. The artifact. Let it go."

"No."

"No? You'd choose that over me?"

I shook my head again. "It's not like that. I wouldn't choose anything over you, if we had a choice. But what we're involved with—the Council, their schemes, their murders—it's bigger than us. We need every weapon we can possibly get, and part of that is the Sisyphus Artifact. We'd be crazy to let that go."

Val said nothing, but held my gaze.

"I know you know that's true," I added.

Finally, the witch sighed, and nodded. "Fine," she said, and turned away, returning to our friends down the alleyway.

"Where are you going?" I called after her.

"To go find your bloody artifact," she said.

Against my better judgement, I smiled. We weren't back to where we were—there was a lot of work to do, on both our sides—but we'd communicated. I'd take that.

CHAPTER FIFTY-FIVE

Whispers

Val shook the borrowed face away, her skin rippling back into the visage that we all knew.

"Was nobody going to mention she had changeling powers?" Lambkin asked—a question we all ignored.

We were still hidden down one of the winding alleys of Zelas, though a different one to where Val and I had had our talk. More and more we'd noticed lingering eyes upon us, owned by members of the cult, and so we'd decided to keep to the shadows. Only Val, who could change her face at will, was *perhaps* safe from spies, and so we'd sent her out to scout.

"Well?" I asked. "Any news?"

"They're looking for us," Val said. "All of them. A lot of the cultists don't have more than vague physical descriptions to go on, but they're still looking. It's a wonder we've even lasted this long."

"Though, I imagine it is only a matter of time before the hordes descend upon us," Corminar said, echoing what we were all thinking.

"Then we move fast, steal back the artifact, and—"

"There's more," Val said, and at this her face grew glum. Glummer than was typical of late, at least. We were all silent, none of us asking the obvious question, none of us quite wanting to know what Val was hesitant to say. But, of course, she had to say it. "There are prophecies spreading through the ranks."

"Well, we know those are all lies, now, don't we?" I said.

But Val's expression didn't change. "From what I've heard, they're not just coming from Yusef. They're coming from Lore, too. The Player is squeezing him for his curse, using it to reinforce his own supposed *Divination* skills. And I'm thinking, if Lore is involved . . ."

"Then maybe they're true," I finished for her.

Val nodded.

Down the end of the alleyway, the hubbub of the crowd grew louder. We all looked around the street, lit with flickering lanterns, anticipating trouble. But none came; the cultists weren't upon us just yet.

"What were they? These prophecies?" Lambkin asked.

Val shrugged. "Most of them aren't relevant to us. Most of them just seemed to be positioned to prove that Yusef *could* tell the future—tomorrow's weather, the Zelas lottery numbers, that kind of thing."

"Then he's worried we've figured it out. And he's worried we're telling his followers."

"Perhaps this why he steal artifact, too," Arzak suggested. "Want make sure they not listen to you."

"Maybe," I agreed, then turned back to Val. "You said . . . *most of them*? What about the ones that *are* relevant?"

The witch's eyes darted to Arzak, then back to me. "Just one, really. Sounds like it came from Lore himself. It says . . ." She gulped. "It says someone is going to die. One of us. And from the sounds of it, it's going to be . . ." Val again looked to Arzak, this time holding her gaze on her.

"Hm," the orc said.

"Yeah."

Arzak stood for a moment, digesting this information, and then looked to Tokas. "This change nothing," she said. "But Tokas stay away from me."

"That prophecy was a lie," Val reminded our orcish friend. "Yusef was just playing on your fears. We don't know that Tokas—"

"And I not want find out," Arzak interrupted. "Maybe Yusef kill me, yes. Maybe cultist do. Or maybe it is woman who betray us before."

Tokas took a small step backward, positioning herself behind Lambkin. This was all coming to a head, and I'd promised myself I'd do something about it before it snowballed out of control. But here we were again with more important things to worry about—namely, getting my artifact back.

"The artifact," I reminded Val, cutting off the glaring competition between Lambkin and Arzak. "Did you learn where it is?"

The witch nodded. "Yeah, I did. But you're not gonna like it."

"You're right, I don't like it," I said.

The lot of us stood in the center of the city, on the rooftop of a tall, stone, residential complex, away from the eyes of Yusef's spies. And we looked up at where the Sisyphus Artifact was stored—in a tower. A particularly tall tower.

Probably the third tallest tower in the city, though it was hard to tell from this severe, neck-twinging, angle.

It was built from brick that matched the color of the surrounding desert, stacked high and held together with the gentle blue glow of sorcery—how else could they build so high? Windows and the odd balcony marked every story, but even with this aid, I couldn't get an accurate count of how many there were. Maybe thirty. On these balconies, and around the base of the tower, we saw guards standing at attention, allowing access to the tower only to those dressed in familiar pale orange robes. The cult had already taken the building.

"I don't suppose there is any chance they are storing the artifact on the ground floor?" Corminar asked.

"It's in the Chamber of Elders," Val replied.

"And where is that?"

"Top floor."

Corminar nodded. "Lovely."

Val gritted her teeth, though this wasn't a reaction to Corminar's sarcasm; I think we were all on the same page on that front. "The way I see it, there are two ways into the Tower of Elders. We could fight our way past the guards and up every single floor—there's thirty-two, I counted—and hope that we survive to take on the elders who are protecting the artifact."

"I vote other way," Arzak said.

"The other option is we use Styk and Raelas's portals to climb the outside."

"I vote first way," Arzak corrected herself.

"How accurate can you be at this distance?" Corminar asked me. "Could you open a portal that places us at the top balcony?"

"Not from this range. I'd need to be closer. We'll have to do it bit by bit."

"I was afraid you would say that."

"OK," Val said. "We'll wait until after dark, and—"

I shook my head. "No. It could be too late by then; they could have moved it. We go now."

"But they'll see us."

"And we'll be thirty-two stories above the ground. By the time anyone reaches us, we'll have the artifact and be portaling our way back down again. We don't have to kill anyone in there, we just have to steal the artifact." It was just like the good old days.

I opened a portal in front of us, its partner on top of a building adjacent to the base of the tower, and I gestured toward it. "After you," I said to Arzak, who was closest.

"I not happy about this," she said, but she stepped through nonetheless.

After the rest of the team pressed through, I followed. And then the climbing began.

* * *

"Is high!" Arzak said, having to raise her voice over the wind. It was funny; from down below, it had seemed like a perfectly still day, but now that we were ten stories up . . . not so much.

Most of our number were crowded on a balcony below, holding the door closed against an oblivious local who thought the lock was stuck. Arzak, Corminar, and I, however, were clinging to the bottom of a window ledge and about to make our next move.

"By my calculations, we'll need to be at least three times this high," the elf said.

"This not reassuring!"

I raised my arm, pointing it up at the next target balcony—about seven more stories up—opening a muted portal in front of it. On my first attempt, I opened it too far away, but on my second, it was close enough that we would make the leap. With a little momentum, at least. But I'd thought of that, and I'd opened the other half of the pair of portals below us.

". . . Why portal down there?" Arzak asked.

"You need to let go," I told her.

The orc's eyes widened. "No force on Alterra make me let go."

Corminar sighed, then looked at me with an expressed silent question. *You sure about this?*

I nodded, and the elf released his grip on the exterior of the tower, falling through the portal and appearing in the air above us. He grabbed the edge of the next balcony nimbly.

"See?" I told Arzak.

"Hm," she replied, then after a large sigh, she finally released. Arzak tumbled toward the portal, caught the side of it against her broad shoulders, and then tumbled past it.

"Arzak!" I cried, but another portal appeared below her, dropping her back to where she'd been a moment before. This time, she hit the mark, and with the added momentum she came out flying into the stone side of the tower. I looked down to Raelas. "Thank you," I said.

"No problem," the tiefling replied. It was nice to see her coming out of her shell a little bit more, after what she'd been through. I still couldn't agree with what she'd done—mala trading was a dangerous game—but with the benefit of distance, I was starting to see how she'd been driven to it. Had I forgiven her? No, not yet, but maybe it would come. I was forgiving people all over the place these days. If *that* wasn't heroic, then I didn't know what was.

I leaped through the portal next, appearing on the balcony above, then ushered Corminar and Arzak to the ledges of a nearby window to make space for the rest of them.

"Why you volunteer *me* for this bit?" the orc asked.

"You're strong, Corminar's nimble, and I have portals," I replied. "It had to be us three."

"Corminar and Styk not afraid of heights," Arzak mumbled. "Arzak is!"

"Do you always talk in the third person when you're scared?"

"Sometimes."

Still, she got out of the way just in time for Val to come barreling through. Lambkin came through after her, and the witch caught and stabilized him. If I thought she wouldn't do the same for Tokas and Raelas—what with what had passed between them—I was wrong.

"All good?" I asked her, clinging onto a protruding piece of stone for dear life.

"Yep," Val replied. "You?"

"I'm all good."

"I preferred Raelas's flirting," Corminar piped up. "This is dreadful." This comment didn't help at all.

We proceeded in much the same way, up until the penultimate balcony where the wind had grown stronger and, more importantly, Arzak's complaining had become too great to bear. We traded her out for Raelas, who also had portals at her disposal. As the balcony wasn't quite big enough for Arzak, Val, Lambkin, and Tokas to stand there at the same time, Arzak resorted to holding Lambkin in the air to my space.

"I have never felt so degraded," the ex-captain said—something that nobody paid any attention to.

Finally, we were up on the top balcony, outside the Chamber of Elders. At least, provided that Val's information was correct. I couldn't tell if anyone had spotted us, as the distance to the ground and the loud, billowing winds made it impossible to tell, but it was worth us moving quickly. The last thing we wanted was a hundred cultists coming to the elders' aid.

As the last of our number hopped up onto the balcony, I slowly pried the door open. Inside, the chamber consisted of a large stone table surrounded by wide, high-backed chairs, each of them facing the door. I don't know if I'd been expecting the Sisyphus Artifact to be hidden away, necessarily, but what I hadn't been expecting was for it to be displayed on a pedestal in the middle of the table.

I stepped into the room, and then realized I'd missed something.

Sitting on each of the large chairs was an old tiefling, their legs crossed, their slim bodies obscured by the backs of the seats. One of them poked their head around to look at me.

I raised a hand in a pretty ambitious wave of greeting. ". . . Hi?" I said.

CHAPTER FIFTY-SIX

In the Heavens

"Hello," one of the elders replied—a woman who couldn't have been younger than eighty. I hadn't realized until now that the title of "Elder" was a literal one. Where were all the young elders at?

"Are we hello-ing intruders now, Alia?" another said.

"I was caught by surprise," the woman said, considering Styk and the others who were just now stepping in through the balcony doors. "But now that I have a moment, do we think that this is . . . ?"

"We do," replied the other. "The seducer."

Corminar, Raelas, and Val all smirked at this. Well, actually, Corminar full-on burst out laughing. "Seducer?" he repeated.

"I don't think they mean it like that," I retorted over my shoulder, but this didn't seem to do much to stop members of the team grinning at the idea.

The elder known as Alia rose slowly from her seat, her arms shaking a little with the effort. "We will have to report your trespass, you know," she said.

"Well, yeah? We figured," I replied. "Either way, though, we're gonna be taking back what you stole."

"Is it thievery when you steal from a thief?" Alia retorted.

I looked back at the rest of my team. "I mean, yes? I'm gonna go with 'yes, it is.'"

Alia ignored me. "This artifact, and those like it, was meant for the Architects. It is meant for those who bless us with their presence, having made the journey from the Ascended Realm. It's not for the likes of *you*."

Those like it? I didn't like the sound of that.

"You say that like they're here of their own free will," Val said. "Like they're so kind to be living around us. But they're—"

I shook my head at her; it wasn't that I disagreed with what she was saying, only that I knew it'd be fruitless. These people were clearly already loyal followers. I would have known that even if they weren't wearing pale orange. "I just wanna say—in case you hadn't realized—that if it comes to a fight, we're probably going to win."

The Council of Elders said nothing.

I took a step toward the table. "So, we're gonna be taking this now. And I assume you're gonna let us?"

"No," Alia said.

"OK, well it's just that you seemed to have trouble even standing up, let alone doing a whole fight."

"No," the elder repeated.

I gestured a thumb back toward the balcony, and the outside. "I could just drop you through a portal, fling you into the air out there. Just so you know."

"You're not having the artifact."

"Did you hear what I just said about throwing you into the air?"

"Hm," Arzak said pointedly behind me. I looked around to see her raising her hand. "If this is opposition, why we all need to come?"

"Well, I didn't know—"

Alia took a step toward me. It would have been menacing if she didn't seem to be having trouble with every step. "You will not have the artifact. It is our privilege to serve Yusef, and it is our duty to protect it with our lives."

"If Yusef wanted you to protect it so bad, why didn't he leave you with guards?" Val asked.

"He did," Alia replied.

We all went tense, as though they were about to spring a trap on us. But no trap came.

". . . Where are they?" Tokas asked.

"Downstairs."

"We didn't think you would come in through the window," another elder volunteered.

"You know, these Players used to feel a lot more menacing than they do these days," Val said. "The pyroknight almost killed all of us. Twice. Niamh is, well, Niamh. But this Yusef? I don't know, it feels like he's a lot more fragile than we thought, since we learned he was a fraud."

One of the elders roared with fury at this assertion, and charged at Val, dagger raised in the air. It was just a shame that this "charge" took approximately twenty seconds.

"So, are we fighting them, or . . . ?" Val asked as the elder charged at her.

"They're attacking us," I replied. "I *suppose* we'd be in our right to defend ourselves."

"It doesn't feel very heroic," Lambkin said, hitting the nail on the head in terms of my doubts.

The elder swung his dagger at Val, and the witch stepped casually out of the way. "Hey, he was the one suggesting throwing them out of windows. And he thinks he *is* a hero."

"Whatever we do, may I suggest that we do it soon?" Corminar asked. "We know there are guards below, but we do not know how soon they will arrive. Best we, as you humans say, skedaddle."

"Nobody says that," Val replied.

The elder swung a dagger slowly toward her once more, and I stepped through a portal to push him out of the way. He cried out with pain as he fell to the floor.

Level 31 Elder of Zelas defeated!

Worldbending: +10XP

We all looked down at the fallen man as the rest of the elders rose from their seats.

"Did you just . . . ?" Val started, pointing to the man who was motionless on the floor.

". . . Yeah."

"How you feeling about that?"

"Not great." I turned back to the "charging" elders. Admittedly, some of them were faster than others, though I still could have played a full game of stones before having to dodge any attacks.

"So, we're killing them?" Tokas asked.

Arzak glared at her.

"I don't want to," the tiefling clarified, "I just thought . . ."

"OK," I said, stepping aside as a weak fireball flew past me. How were even their *spells* this slow? "New plan: no more killing."

"But you just—" Val started.

"I really didn't think that was gonna be contentious. No more killing. I'll grab the artifact, and we'll get out of here. Any questions?"

Everyone raised their hands. Val blasted a fireball away with a casual summoned gust, and it caught a wall hanging. "Oops," she said. "So, no killing. Is arson fine?"

I put my head in my hands. "OK, Arzak, what's your question?"

"Do still have to leave on *outside* the building?"

"Yes. Corminar?"

"When they say *seducer*, do they mean—"

"Val?" I asked, cutting him off.

"If the artifact is here, then Yusef's been here. He trusts these people."

I caught an elder's wrist in midswing, holding their sword in place, before turning back to Val. "I don't hear a question."

"Question is, maybe we should look around quickly?"

I nodded. "Raelas, you take Arzak, Lambkin, and Tokas, and start getting down. The rest of us will have a quick look around and catch up."

Raelas matched my nod, and the four of them began their escape while the rest of us fanned out in the room. I hopped up onto the table, narrowly avoiding the swing of Alia's knife. And when I say "narrowly," I mean "it wasn't at all close."

Alia scoffed at me.

"Problem?" I asked as I crossed the table to pick up the Sisyphus Artifact. I considered placing it in my *Pocket World* storage for safekeeping, but there was something comforting about feeling it dangling against my chest. So I still opened the pocket world, but instead pulled out a piece of thin rope from my *Needlework* supplies. I pushed the rope through the loop on the top of the artifact and hung it back around my neck. When I felt its touch, I let out a breath I didn't know I'd been holding.

"The *problem* is that you should treat your elders with respect!"

"That's ambiguous."

"What?"

"I mean," I said, "is it that we should treat all older people with respect, or just this council? Because I've got an answer for each of them, neither one that you'll like."

Alia spluttered.

"Good answer," I said before turning to the rest of the gang. "You got anything?"

"Over here," Corminar said, gesturing to a stack of papers on the council's table. He leafed through it. "Follower-movement charts. There are still hundreds in Coldharbor, but Yusef seems to have realized that's a mistake; every follower west of Coldharbor is heading here, or is here already."

"He means to use them against us?" Val asked.

"Either that or something else. Perhaps we should attack him now."

"You think we'd still have the element of surprise?" I asked. "Cos I don't. I think there are more than enough cultists here already."

The elder nearest to Corminar pulled a document from the table, and from his manner, it seemed that it was a document he'd chosen specifically. I approached and plucked it from his hand.

"Got something?" Val asked.

I nodded. "He's staying in the Tower of Hope, wherever that is. And . . . Lore's there with him." At that moment, I heard a sound coming from behind the door. Footsteps, on the staircase, maybe. But was that the noise of charging guards or servants going about their business? It didn't matter, I supposed; it was time to get out of here.

I hurried over to the window, my friends running at my side, the elders behind us, moaning something about this being completely disrespectful. And I opened the first portal.

CHAPTER FIFTY-SEVEN

Loyalty

We took turns keeping watch.

The seven of us were camped well out of town, close to a nearby watering hole, but not so close that anyone would have good reason to come near. Val and Lambkin took the first watch as the last of the sun's light left the sky, and I dreamed.

I dreamed of a family. Not just Val and I—even after finding the strength to forgive her leaving, I still wasn't there yet; I wasn't dwelling on that. I dreamed of a family that included Arzak, and Corminar, and Lore. I'd never had a family before, beyond my father, and even that had been a . . . strained relationship. And my mother, the Player, I'd never met. So it was a family of choice, not of blood, of which I dreamed. Of course, one of this family of five was missing.

When Val shook me awake for the second watch, I found myself coated in sweat.

"Lore?" she asked.

"What?"

"You were talking about Lore," she said. "In your sleep."

I shook my head. "It's nothing," I replied, but it was anything but. I was only just becoming conscious of it, but while I'd slept, I'd realized what I had to do next. Over the past year and a bit, Lore and I had become close. Close enough, I thought, that I might still be able to reach him. And now I knew where he was staying.

"Alright," Val replied, then looked over at Lambkin, who was waking Tokas at the other side of the camp. "You're on. Your turn."

I nodded, and the witch began to back away, apparently about to return to the shoddy tent she was sharing with Arzak. But Val's eyes lingered on my own. I gestured to the makeshift bed. "You want to sleep here?"

"Are we there yet?" Val asked.

I shook my head. "I don't know."

"I'm sorry, Styk," she said. "I don't think I said that before, did I? I'm sorry."

I nodded, which was perhaps not the reaction she was looking for. "At least stay here until my watch is over," I said, tapping the mass of fabric I'd pulled from my pocket world. "The bed's warm. And Arzak snores."

Val raised her eyebrows in agreement. "Yeah, OK," she said. "We'll talk some more in the morning?"

"Oh, you bet we will," I replied. There was still a lot more to say, on both sides, before we could continue rebuilding this relationship.

Only when I confirmed Lambkin and Val had drifted off—it took neither of them particularly long—I approached Tokas. "You reckon you can keep watch by yourself?"

"Would Arzak like that?" the tiefling replied.

"What she doesn't know won't hurt her."

Tokas nodded. "Sure. I can do it alone. But . . . where are you going?"

"To see a man about his destiny," I replied.

"I don't know what that means."

Of course she didn't; Tokas was nothing if not literal. "I'm going to try to talk some sense into Lore."

"Alone? Is that a good idea? I could come with, if you—"

I shook my head. "No, it's best I do this alone. Less chance of raising the alarms. Will you tell the others?"

"No," Tokas replied. "I can be trusted."

That, of course, remained to be seen.

I climbed the Tower of Hope in much the same way as we'd climbed the Tower of Elders only a few hours ago. Only now, I was obscured by the thick darkness of the Armadan night, and my *Tamed Portal* passive ability meant there was little chance of others spotting my portals. Without the others—particularly Arzak—this process was easy, calming even.

As I hung from the edge of the balcony—I'd soon become comfortable with heights after mastering my portal abilities—I looked down upon the sprawling conical city of Zelas. Few lanterns remained lit at this late hour, and those few remaining were on the main thoroughfares. I watched small dots stagger home after quests that had stretched on longer than expected, or more likely, after *drinking sessions* that had stretched on longer than expected. I paused to close my eyes, just for a second, and breathe in the air.

I was calm. I was ready to work.

Keeping the calm in my heart, I continued the climb, counting the stories until I finally arrived where Lore should have been staying, only a few stories down from the top of the tower. I was painfully aware that Yusef would be sleeping nearby, and if I hadn't thought he'd be far more guarded, I might have tried a cheeky assassination attempt. As cheeky as an assassination attempt could be, at least.

I poked my head in through the nearby window to make sure that I was in the right place, and was answered not by the sight of Lore, but by his familiar snores.

"Oi," I said in as loud a voice as I dared, "sleepyhead. Wake up."

I waited for signs of Lore doing so, and was sorely disappointed. Fortunately, I'd prepared for this. I opened a portal to my pocket world at my side, reached in for my water flagon, and then upended it over Lore's head.

He snapped bolt upright.

"Woah, woah," I said. "It's me, big guy."

Lore's eyes widened. "Styk?" he whispered. "You shouldn't be here. There are guards all around this place. Especially after what you did to the elders."

"Oh, you heard about that already?"

"Yusef's furious; he—" Lore caught himself. "You scaled the tower again? Then he's seen you. You better go, before—"

OK, so that center of calm was gone already. If I needed to act fast, then I wasn't going to waste a moment. "Come with me, Lore," I said. "You shouldn't have left us. Come with me now, and I'll get you out of here. We're camped just outside town. We—"

"No."

"No?"

Lore shook his head. Even in the low light, I could see the sadness in those eyes. "If I leave, Alenna dies. It's foretold."

"Yusef's a fraud, Lore," I said, getting straight to the point. "He doesn't have the *Divination* skill at all, as far as we can tell. He does illusions. Illusions!"

"I know," came the barbarian's sad reply.

"Cool, so let's—" I caught myself; his reply wasn't what I'd expected. There was no "Oh really, Styk? Well in that case let's get the hells out of here."

"You *know*?" I repeated.

"I figured it out a few days ago," Lore said. "He only knows what his spies tell him. And what I tell him. I haven't challenged him on it or anything, but—"

"Then why in all of Tartarus are you staying here?" I demanded. "I can get you out. I have a *Saved Portal* back to Coldharbor, if you want distance. I can get you away from him in an instant. So why stay?"

"Because *I've* seen it," came the reply. That was a lot harder to argue with.

All the Slayers had been acting weird lately, but Lore was the only one of us with a good excuse; he was doing what he had to to keep us all alive. He was the one battling with the strings of fate. "If I leave Yusef, Alenna dies. I've tried everything I can to get out of it, but . . . there's nothing."

Both our heads snapped to the door when we heard movement outside. But it was the casual cough of an uninformed guard, not one charging to kill me. They weren't here yet.

"We're going to kill him, Lore," I said. "We have to."

"Good. I want him dead. I don't wanna be here, Styk. I just . . . have to be."

"Then help."

The barbarian shook his head. "I can't go with you. I really can't."

I couldn't believe I was about to say this. "I can't believe I'm saying this, but don't come with me, then. You can tell help from here."

"How? He's desperate. I think he knows you lot have seen through him. This man isn't like Jacob or Niamh; he's not actually strong. His power is in lying and making connections. And he's realized that you lot aren't falling for any of his traps. Now he knows that even the Towers of Zelas aren't safe. He'll lash out, Styk. You're not safe. You're not—"

I grabbed Lore by his shoulders. The man was rambling and needed to snap back to reality. Just what had he seen in those visions? Just how many of our deaths had he been forced to sit through? I could think of nothing else that would make him like this.

"Use that," I told him. "Use his desperation against him. We need him away from Zelas, away from his followers. *They* are his strength, as you say. If you can convince him that he's in real trouble, if you can convince him to flee, then we might stand a chance. Get him away from his followers, and we'll deal with him. Can you do that?"

Lore nodded; this, he could do.

CHAPTER FIFTY-EIGHT

To Elassos

"And where in hells have been?" Arzak demanded when I'd returned to camp in the dead of night. Tokas's and my watch had ended while I'd been gone, and the tiefling had clearly had no choice but to wake the next watchers, Arzak and Corminar.

"I went to see Lore," I replied.

"Alone?" demanded Val, sitting up from the mess of blankets in my tent.

"Oh, you're awake, too."

"You could have been hurt," Arzak said. The foot-tapping hadn't stopped, or even slowed, as far as I could see. "We say we not split up. Why you go?"

"Cos he's our friend. And we owed him a way out, if he wanted one, especially after . . ." I trailed off, but my meaning—I hoped—was obvious; after Corminar and I had overlooked how much he'd been struggling with the burden of prophecy.

"He not here."

"No. He's staying. He says if he leaves, Alenna dies. I don't blame him for choosing his friend's life over killing Yusef."

Val opened her mouth as if about to say "I do," but nothing came out.

"So pointless, then," Arzak said. "You risk life for nothing."

I shook my head. "Oh, I didn't say that." I turned to Val. "It's good you're up; I need you. We're going to need to steal some horses."

As the first light of dawn crawled its way across the desert outside Zelas, we watched two horses kicking up dust into the air. These were two of the fastest steeds that money—or, in this case, power—could buy. After the discussion I'd had with Lore last night, I had no doubt that he was riding one of them, and Yusef the other. He'd succeeded. He'd separated Yusef from the cult.

But we now had rides of our own.

As our target fled, we hopped up onto steeds of our own. We'd stolen eight— one apiece, plus one for carrying items that I couldn't fit in my pocket world. This would keep us quick, if not quick enough to catch up with Yusef on a horse like *that*. But sooner or later, he would grow tired of running, and then the battle would begin.

There would be no fragile truce this time. Yusef could no longer threaten us with visions of the future that we now knew were false. This time, when we caught him, it would end one of only two ways—we'd kill him, or he'd kill us. Just how much of a chance did he stand without his cult behind him, and with only *Illusion* magicks at his disposal?

Lore being forced to his side had really been a blessing in disguise. Yusef, perhaps considering himself some master manipulator, had thought he was strengthening himself and weakening us by bringing Lore to his side. But Lore, accidentally charismatic as he was, had gotten under the man's skin. He'd been able to do as I'd suggested. He'd played on the man's paranoia, on his fear, enough that Yusef would seek to flee fast enough that the cult couldn't follow.

Not that they weren't trying; even as Zelas disappeared behind us, we saw the familiar shade of pale orange as his worshippers gave chase. We would have to finish this fight before the cultists could catch up, but with their relatively slow pace, the longer that Yusef fled, the longer we'd have to do so. We settled in for the long haul.

Nobody spoke until the hot rays of the midday sun were upon us. We'd slowed our horses' pace so as not to wear them out, and stopped momentarily at a water hole to refill our flasks. From the tracks in the sand, Yusef and Lore had stopped here, too, and not so long ago that the desert winds had hidden those imprints.

I hurried us all back onto our horses the moment we'd stocked up on water, as we couldn't linger. Not if we wanted to catch him.

We rode once more, the road fading fast beneath our horses' hooves. This was a part of the world not well served by merchants or travelers; there was little need for established paths. If the road grew soft, it would slow us, but it would slow Yusef, too.

"You all know where he's going, right?" Tokas shouted. In the din of the galloping horses, it was no easy thing for us all to respond, so she added, "He's heading to Elassos."

I brought my horse over to her side, finding it difficult; my experience with horseback riding was very limited, considering that I wasn't filthy rich. But eventually I got there, almost as if my horse knew what I was getting at and was being considerate, even though I was pushing him hard. "Tell me," I shouted over the noise. "Why Elassos? What's there? I thought it was abandoned?"

"It is," Tokas cried back. "Except for bandits, perhaps. He won't find help there."

"Then what will he find? Why go there at all?"

"It was built back during the invasion," Tokas said. "And being a sea people, the tieflings had never really encountered fortresses like we'd seen here. But the tiefling way is to turn an enemy's strength against them, and so they established their foothold in this region by building a fortress to put all to shame, except perhaps Great Hearth. It'll have defenses; it'll have enchantments."

I nodded. "So he's setting traps for us again? He has no other tricks up his sleeve?"

"I believe we were weak enough only a year ago that these traps would have finished us," Corminar pitched in. "That we've survived so many speaks to how far we've come. Perhaps Yusef has never before needed another 'trick up his sleeve.'"

There was that. If Jacob, the pyroknight, had been smart enough—or less blinded by rage—then any traps he'd left for us could well have been the end for us. We were stronger now. *I* was stronger now. I touched the artifact dangling from my neck. Maybe we didn't have to feel fear when we rode to meet our enemy. Maybe this was what the future of the Slayers looked like—still working toward the same purpose, but no longer terrified for our lives when we did it. I, for one, could go for that.

The sun was lower in the sky, casting great shadows from the mountain range, when Elassos finally appeared over the horizon. As Tokas had promised, it really was a sight to behold. It stood atop one of the lower hills in the outer mountain range, yet with its great height, it still seemed to tower above us. The structure itself had small balconies that ran around its square floor plan on every level, punctuated occasionally by great platforms that protruded from one side or another. These platforms, supported not just by metal beams but surely magicks, too, bore handfuls of small buildings, and I got the impression that these had once been training grounds for the tiefling troops stationed there.

As we grew closer still, I saw more signs of life. There were footprints on the road—not Yusef's or Lore's, who were surely still on horseback—and there were signs of campsites. Slowly, strange shapes at the bottom of the fortress came into focus, and I saw that they were tents. Tokas hadn't been wrong; bandits really did use this fortress as a refuge. We'd just have to hope they didn't get in our way.

Faces appeared from these tents as the fortress loomed in our vision, faces attached to bodies holding curved swords and spears and preparing magicks in case of attack. But we made no effort to move for our weapons—we had bigger fish to fry—and slowly these bandits became more relaxed.

Arzak asked one of them the obvious question with her eyes, and the bandit replied in kind—looking upward to the heights of the fortress. They'd gone up there.

And where they went, we followed. We rode up the ramps leading to Elassos's main entryway—an archway larger than most taverns, with its two huge wooden doors rotting away and fire-scarred. Inside, Elassos was large enough that we didn't need to dismount. We could ride the horses up the gentle ramps that took us upward into this eerily empty, ornate fortress. Their speed was slowed, of course, but this only gave us time to inspect the glowing lines that seemed to stretch from ground floor to spire. Whatever these magicks were, I did not know, and their ever-changing color gave no indication as to which specialty they related to. All we knew was that the tieflings had once thought them important in protecting this fortress, and I prayed that Yusef didn't know more than this, either.

The horses were moving very slowly when we reached the higher floors, and Arzak—whose horse was, predictably, the most tired of all—made the decision to dismount. We all did the same, Raelas and Lambkin tying the reins to an arched pole on the wall that I could only assume had been made for this very purpose.

And then, still not a word shared, we proceeded to the topmost story.

Two men stood on the platform protruding eastward from Elassos, the sun now low enough in the sky that the spire cast them in shadow. The edges of this wooden platform were raised, but only perhaps a foot from the floor—the tieflings weren't massively concerned with safety, it seemed. Beyond that, the only object of note on this platform was, for lack of a better word, an altar—and was where all the glowing lines came together. It worried me that Yusef had chosen there, of all places, to let us catch up.

"Do you never *stop*?" the Player asked, saliva splattering the floor in front of him as he spoke with such disdain.

I held his gaze as I spoke to him. "We won't stop chasing you. We need you to realize that. So why don't we end this now, one way or another?"

Yusef's eyes darted to Lore. He was no fool. He knew that his grasp on Lore was dependent on keeping his friends alive. He'd set traps on the road, but none of them had been successful. If they had been, he'd have needed to kill Lore, and would've lost the gentle giant's grasp of *Divination*. That would have been no problem with the hordes of his cult around him, but now, if he lost Lore, he was alone.

But he would have known that. He was smart enough to anticipate that, even if he was as paranoid as Lore had said. And yet he'd come here anyway. My eyes darted to the glowing altar once more.

"One way, perhaps," Yusef replied, holding our gaze.

We stared back.

"The . . . way where you die?" Val suggested.

Yusef shook his head to himself, but said nothing, instead turning to the altar.

"What?" I goaded him. "That's it? No great speech? No threats? Just . . . that?"

"Yes," Yusef replied, and he placed his hands on the altar. "Just that." The glowing lines that stemmed out from the altar turned red in a blink, Yusef's *Illusion* magicks flowing from the altar so fast you might have missed it.

And then the tower, my friends, even Yusef himself disappeared from my sight. This was an illusion to surpass even those he'd left for us on the road, in some way using the innate powers of this fortress. There was the answer to the question. Why had he come here, even without his cult to defend him?

The answer was simple: because here was a trap that we couldn't hope to survive.

CHAPTER FIFTY-NINE

The Eyes of Our Ancestors

I stumbled forward in the artificial darkness, my dagger raised.

Yusef was in front of me. Or, at least, he *should* have been in front of me. But as I arrived where he should have been, I found nothing but the glowing red altar. He'd fled within the darkness, and I was going to have to move quickly to find him again.

I heard a muffled scream off to my right—somewhere deep in the fog-not-fog. Raelas. I charged toward her, moving as fast as I could without risking running into the point of Yusef's own knife. I crossed the glowing red lines that stemmed from the altar, and then my vision misted for a moment. I ignored it, pushing forward, until—

The platform disappeared beneath my foot.

I fell forward, opening a portal in front of me to stop me from plummeting to my doom, and opened its partner somewhere back above where the platform was. I hit the wooden platform again, hard, and I hoped that Raelas's scream from a moment ago hadn't been her doing the same—the platform, and its *edge*, was still here, whether we could see it or not.

"Are you alright, my child?" a voice came through the darkness. A familiar voice, one that pulled forth emotions of joy . . . and despair. I whipped my head around once more and approached the voice, this time taking care with every step.

A figure loomed in the darkness.

". . . Val?" I asked, though I knew deep down it wasn't. In hindsight, I realized I already knew who it was at this point, but I was deep in denial at the time.

"Come to me," the same voice replied. Definitely not Val.

I took another step forward, expecting the altar to appear in front of me once more, but it didn't. I'd lost my sense of direction in the thick fog. Instead, a familiar face appeared—one that made my heart skip a beat, but not lower my weapon.

"Mum?" I asked.

"My child." Her familiar face beamed back at me, having not aged a day since the portrait my father had treasured, or since I'd seen her image in Empress Amira's files. She held her arms out at her sides, as though encouraging me to embrace her.

"No, you . . . you're not here," I said. "You left. And you're not coming back."

"Yes," the image of my mother agreed, gazing upon me with eyes I recognized. Eyes I'd seen so many times in the mirror. "I left. I was the first of many to leave you, wasn't I? Then your father, snatched by his enemies. Then Gwin, infected by the corruption. Then Val, who left on her own accord. Yet you are so quick to forgive them."

"You're saying I should forgive you, too," I replied, then caught myself. I was arguing with an illusion. I had to remember that, or Yusef would . . . what? End me here? Trap me here forever? I didn't quite know his plan just yet.

"I'm asking a question, is all. I'm asking whether you forgave them so that you might find the courage to forgive me."

"I'm not scared, I—"

"Not scared of me, no," the woman said. "Scared of absence. If you forgive me, then you let me go. And if you let me go, then I may never return. That's it, isn't it?"

I realized then that I'd taken a few unconscious steps closer to the woman with outstretched arms. How had she done that? Or had she even done anything at all? I forced myself to stop.

"Cleo, no," I said.

"Cleo, now, is it?" the woman replied. "What happened to Mum?" Still, she kept her arms wide open.

I forced myself to step backward, away from her. "You're not real."

"No? Then how do I know so much about you?"

I held my blade higher, ready to defend myself. "Because that's how he works. Yusef. His illusions are personal. Your greatest fears made to seem real. He did it to Arzak, with Tokas prophesied to kill her, and he did it with Lore by threatening the lives of his friends. That's what this is. That's what *you* are. A trick."

The woman's smile faded. "Very well." With that, she charged, her dagger arching through the air. Instinctively I defended myself with my own blade, but then realized . . . this was an illusion. My mother, here, couldn't possibly hurt me, because she was just in my—

My dagger smashed against hers, and we rebounded.

In that moment, I saw that Cleo didn't have the same eyes as me. She had Yusef's eyes, now.

I charged, pressing the attack, activating *Knifestorm* to increase the damage dealt. But my mother—or the image of my mother—disappeared into the darkness, and my attack hit only air.

I heard another muffled cry from somewhere else nearby. *Nearby on the platform; I must remember we're on a platform.* This one I recognized—Val's. I hurried to her side as carefully as I could, wishing I didn't have the *Tamed Portals* passive as their glow might have helped cut through this darkness.

And I stumbled over a child. Well, I *would* have stumbled over a child if I hadn't instead walked straight through them like they weren't even there. This was an illusion, and it was one that Yusef wasn't inhabiting. I wouldn't have given them a second look, but then the child whimpered.

I stopped, then, and I looked down at her. It was only then that I realized this was a vision of Val. The child held up a small mouse that lay limp in her cupped, upturned hands. "I didn't mean to," she said. "I didn't mean to hurt it." The sincere distress in her voice almost broke my heart.

"It's OK," I started to say, recognizing in that moment that I was talking to an illusion, "you didn't mean to—"

"Oh, Equivalence," a voice said, emerging from the darkness. A short woman arrived at the young girl's side and cradled her. "It's OK. It's OK." The woman looked around, and in that moment I caught a glimpse of her face. Niamh's face. The Player we'd killed in the Sea of Roots. So she had not always been an enemy to Val. From the looks of it, she'd once been a friend.

I stepped backward carefully, away from the vision. I didn't know what game Yusef was playing with this, but I didn't want to stick around to find out. I kept the vision of the child and the Player in my sight as I edged away, expecting a trap, expecting—

I stumbled into something solid, and I whipped around, blade out, nearly catching Val in the stomach. "Val?"

Her eyes were fixed on the vision of her younger self.

"Is this . . . real?" I asked.

The witch hesitated before nodding.

"You never told me . . ." I trailed off, not quite sure how to phrase this question. "You didn't tell me you knew her like this."

Before Val—the adult Val—could give any reply, the vision changed. The child version of herself was older now, perhaps ten or eleven. She poked her head through a door, into some kind of village hall. There, Niamh sat at the head of an ornate dining table laden with food. But the real Val's eyes weren't on her—they were on a timid-looking couple seated at Niamh's right.

"Mum," she said. "Dad."

More parents. Yusef really needed more imagination. Though, I wasn't sure we could withstand any more imaginative traumas. "They knew her? They knew Niamh?"

"They became friends. Niamh wasn't always . . . what you saw. For a while—for many years—she was a friend to our town. She fought back the terrok infestation, dealt with the rockrats, even took down a neereagle. She encouraged my changeling abilities, supported me with them. She popped in on birthdays, brought me gifts."

A growl echoed around the fog, followed by the sound of a falling tree.

"But then we both came to understand what was happening to me. We both realized what my powers were. And she turned. She poisoned the minds of my parents, making them hate me. She destroyed my friendships. Made me an outcast. And never told me why. Why did she hate witches so much? What possible threat could I have been to her?"

Something clicked in my mind, then. I'd already come to forgive her—Yusef's vision of my mother was right about that, and probably about the reasons why, too—but now I *understood* her. I understood why she was so scared of me changing. She was scared of me turning on her like *that*. Taking everything from her that she held dear—including the Player who she'd come to love.

"Val," I said.

"Yeah?"

I nodded to the vision of Niamh. "I think it's time you got some revenge."

"She's not real."

"So what?"

Val blinked up at me for a moment, then nodded. Her attacks wouldn't hit anything, but there was maybe still a catharsis in taking down even an echo of the woman who betrayed her. The witch raised her hands, summoning her lightning magicks, and launched the attack down the table. The crackling power passed over everyone at that imaginary table without hurting them.

Everyone, but one.

A diminutive man at the closest end of the table shrieked with pain, then snapped his head toward us.

"What the . . ." Val mumbled, at the same moment that I said, "Yusef!"

As the man charged, I was tempted to open a portal underneath myself and Val to remove us from trouble. But what with this platform having an edge somewhere, I couldn't risk it; if Val fell and I couldn't see her, then she was as good as dead. Instead, I'd have to rely on my other skills for once.

I activated *Knifestorm* once more, as this ability was a more effective defense than simply trying to meet blade with blade. My dagger slashed against Yusef's curved sword, knocking him backward. But a Player—someone of Yusef's level—shouldn't have been staggered so easily. Just what was going on here?

Val pressed her own attack, relying on her lightning magicks as we were so far from nature up here. The attack made Yusef's body convulse, and I wasted no time in jumping in to stab, stab, and stab again. The man croaked as his last breath escaped his body, and then fell to the floor.

The witch arrived at my side. "That . . . was Yusef?"

I shook my head. "Can't be. He would have—"

Level 25 Swordsman of the Desert Sons defeated!

Knifework: +1,900XP

The vision faded from the dead man, revealing him for what he truly was; one of the bandits who had been camped outside the fortress. We'd thought they'd simply wanted no trouble when they'd let us by, but the truth was darker. Yusef had already enchanted them. They were part of his trap.

Whispers erupted around us, among the fog. Then screams and shouts. But were these real, or part of Yusef's trap? And just how many of our friends were still alive, within the mist? Val and I looked at one another and nodded. We had friends to save, visions to shatter, and a Player to kill.

We stepped forward, and got to work.

CHAPTER SIXTY

To Fight Our Fates

Val and I kept close to one another as we stepped through the fog, keenly aware how easy it would be to lose one another among this great illusion.

A battlefield blossomed into view.

It took me a moment to place it, considering it felt like so much time had passed since we were there. But the clear blue waters of the bay, the towering trees, the magick traps exploding against the hulls of the invading ships . . . this was just as the siege of Sunalor had been. These distressing memories could only belong to one person; the elf who had watched his homeland fall.

"Cor!" I shouted over the din of a siege in progress. "Cor, where are you?"

Val and I kept our eyes on those charging around us, both elven and Goldmarch soldiers alike, as either could turn out to be a bandit in waiting. A group of elven soldiers ran to reinforce the part of the wall we were standing on, each of them passing through us as though we weren't even there. Though, I supposed that we weren't.

And there, along the wall, I saw him. "Cor!" I shouted, waving at him. But this Corminar was busy leading troops, giving orders to a man who looked up at the trees towering overhead.

"Styk, look," Val said, tugging on my sleeve. She pointed down from the wall to the ground outside the inner city, where Corminar—*our* Corminar—battled his failure. He released arrow after arrow in frantic haste, each of them passing through the soldiers of the Golden Empire unnoticed. Did he already know that there were real, tangible threats among these illusions, or was he simply reliving an old trauma and fighting for a different outcome?

I stepped through the vision of Sunalor's inner wall, expecting to have to jump down to the other side, but the ground came up fast. There was no height difference at all in reality, and the illusion had needed to bend to reflect that. "Cor!" I shouted, charging through the enemy soldiers, having to fight my body's instinct to move around them with every step, "Cor, there are bandits in—"

I collided heavily with one of the soldiers, and it caught me by surprise enough that I bounced off them, falling backward to the ground. Before I could react, they had their curved blade swinging down toward me. The blade had just hit the flesh of my right shoulder when crackling lightning magicks soared forth from behind me. The enemy crumpled from the pain of the attack, and my elven friend, having witnessed this, pivoted to fire arrow after arrow into this soldier's back—each of them, this time, hitting.

Val's face appeared over me, and she held out a hand to pull me up. I used my left arm, not right, to grab her hand, and only when I was back on my feet did I look at my wound. It was bleeding, sure, but it could have been much worse if Val had been only half a second slower to react.

"I'll heal," the witch said. "No use in you being—"

But at that moment, I spotted the eyes of one of the charging soldiers behind her. This man wasn't looking up at the wall, like the rest of those in Goldmarch uniform; he was looking at Val. He'd seen her. As the soldier swung his blade, I yanked Val out of the way of the attack, and brought my knife up with my injured arm.

The attack was weakened by my injury, but it helped that I'd managed to bury the dagger into the man's stomach. As the man's eyes bulged, I activated *Closed Reach* to bend reality and bury the knife even further, and I twisted, just for good measure. That, alongside a couple of well-placed arrows from Corminar, was enough to down the enemy.

Level 27 Swordsman of the Desert Sons defeated!

Knifework: +2,100XP
Knifework increased to level 46!
Base Points Gained: +1 DEX, +1 STR, +2 Free Points (VIT/DEX/STR)

But there wasn't time to celebrate this minor victory, because at that moment, Corminar roared with pain. Another bandit had made themselves known in the grand illusion, this time striking at the party member who relied on distance between him and his enemy—and therefore had little in the way of health or damage resistance.

I portaled to Corminar's side, leaving it open for Val to join us, and hit the enemy with both a *Knifestorm* and a *Closed Reach* at the same time, figuring that there was nothing in the wording to say I couldn't use both at the same time. The power afforded me by the flurry of attacks plus the bended reality, allowed me to hit the enemy multiple times, and deeply, too. Normally, I would have expected any of my knife attacks not to do enough damage to down an enemy, but this time . . . it worked. My strength really had grown fast over this past year and a half.

Level 29 Swordswoman of the Desert Sons defeated!

Knifework: +2,350XP

Across the fake battlefield, lightning magicks roared out once more, and Corminar pivoted to fire an arrow at another bandit—one that Val was grappling with. As the third arrow put this enemy down, I heard a distant scream. A familiar voice. Raelas.

I met Val's gaze, and the witch nodded. Her, Corminar, and I charged across the battleground for a moment, before I remembered where we really were—on a platform suspended high in the air above the ground. I slowed the others down with a splayed hand gesture, and we proceeded hesitantly. Who knew if that scream was even real? Could that not have been part of Yusef's illusion?

Even when I saw Raelas ahead of me, my questions weren't answered for certain. Strange, warped images of Carle and Ama stood over her, terrorizing her, each of them ten, maybe twelve feet tall.

"You let us die," Ama hissed at Raelas. "That was your only job, and you failed. You're alone now. Alone for all eternity. You think your new traveling companions are your friends? No. They hate you for what you did. They'll never care for you. Not like we did. And maybe that will save their lives."

"They're not real!" I shouted, waving desperately at Raelas. I knew from experience just how convincing these illusions could be; they didn't just fool the eyes, they fooled the heart as well. "They're not—"

And then Carle pushed his sword downward, stabbing Raelas in the chest, clean through. He snapped his head toward us, snarled, and I saw his eyes. Yusef's eyes. The two giants began charging at us.

I opened a portal for Val to step through to Raelas's side—even with such a deep wound, Val's *Healing* abilities seemed to have progressed enough that she might still save the tiefling. This left Corminar and I to deal with the giant Ama and Carle.

"Cor! Ama!" I shouted, pointing at the image of the woman who'd been corrupted. The elf understood my meaning; we knew Carle's image was inhabited by someone who could do damage, but we didn't yet know if Ama was the same. I allowed myself a sigh of relief when the elf's arrow passed straight through

Ama; it meant we could focus on fighting the Player.

Yusef was probably the weakest of the Players we'd battled, at least in terms of combat ability. His power lay instead in his grip he had on others, afforded him by his *Illusion* magicks. But even the weakest of Players would be a challenge for a mere ranger and worldbender. I scoured my brain for a plan, and with so little time to think, I circled back to the familiar: portals, portals, portals.

A second later, Yusef was upon me, his sword shimmering, revealing itself as one of the curved swords of the bandits rather than the one that Carle had used. As Carle's image blinked, I opened a portal beneath myself, putting myself out of range of the Player's attacks, and when I looked back . . . Carle's eyes had changed.

I knew Yusef wouldn't have great ability with the sword, but I knew that Yusef knew that I knew, too. But the one strength he did have was his illusions. Even a fool with a sword could do real damage if his target didn't know an attack was coming. Fortunately, there was only one other figure around who Yusef could reasonably inhabit—Ama.

"Cor! Watch out!" I shouted, pointing to the giant metal mage. But I was a moment too late; Corminar dived out of the way of the tackling woman, but not before she got a hand around his ankle.

I suffered a flash of realization, then: if I'd activated my *Portal Relay* earlier, we'd have been able to keep in touch more easily, using my portals to transmit sound. I activated the ability now as I charged at Ama-Yusef, flinging two of the tiny portals that came with the ability over to Val and Corminar. The others, I kept orbiting me for now, at least until we could find the rest of the team.

I launched myself into the air with the aid of a pair of portals, and I gripped my dagger in two hands. As I soared down toward Yusef's back, I brought the knife arcing down in a *stab*. It surely wouldn't be enough to severely hurt the man—he was a *Player*, after all—but it might have been enough to get Corminar free.

As it happened, my knife tip met the ground. Yusef had left Ama's form among the billowing mist, and Corminar immediately wrenched his ankle free. That was the good news. The bad news was that we had absolutely no idea where Yusef was.

"No," I heard Val say through her mini portal relay, "you don't get off that easily. You have to live with what you've done." *The healing was going well, then.* I heard the sound of . . .

. . . an army?

The noise of the charging army grew louder and louder, and suddenly the first wave of Niamh's invasion force was upon us. Corminar and I spun around, desperately searching for who among the illusions could deal us actual damage.

"I . . ." the elf said. "I don't . . ."

We kept turning and turning, pushing our backs up against one another. As we turned, I lost track of Raelas and Val's positions in the fog; rejoining them was going to need a little bit of luck. "Keep looking," I said. "He could be any one of—"

I cried out with pain as a knife caught my side, slicing a deep gash in the flesh. I grabbed it, pressing the flesh together, trying to stop the bleeding as much as possible. I looked for the person who'd dealt the damage, but they were already lost to the crowd.

"Are you dead?" Corminar asked.

"No."

"Good." A hand came out at my side—one grasping a glowing vial. I took it from him without worrying about snatching. I could live with poor manners right about now. "It is a health potion. Dri—" This time, it was Corminar's turn to cry out.

But now I was ready. I turned the moment that the elf stopped talking, flinging my knife forward in a wild *knifestorm*. Most of my flails of my weapon met only air, but one—just one—hit. But that one cut was enough to tell reality from fantasy. I gritted my teeth through the pain of the wound in my side and pressed the attack, looking at the enemy's eyes.

Yusef's eyes.

"It's him!" I shouted, and then activated *Closed Reach* as I swung my knife forward once more. The tip of the blade met the man's flesh and he stumbled backward. Though he didn't cry out in pain, I could see a thin stream of blood running down his chest.

I'd hoped Corminar would join me in the attack, but I could see him on the ground, the damage he'd suffered being enough to down him. I threw the potion back to him, and in that split second while I was distracted, Yusef disappeared among the charging soldiers once more.

"Gods *damn* it." If we could only land one hit at a time, then for all we knew, Yusef was simply healing himself. And if we kept accruing damage at this slow but steady rate, we could all fall well before the fight was done. We needed to think of something, and fast.

I looked back at Corminar, or where he'd been, and now I saw only figments and fog. Yusef had shifted the illusion between us, keeping us separate. Keeping us weak.

I touched my side, and hissed at the pain. The damage was deeper than I'd thought; I'd been powering through before. My movements would be limited, and without the ability to use my portals in this dense fog, I was going to be slow. I just had to hope Yusef didn't take advantage of that.

I took a deep breath and pressed after him, part of me hoping that I'd stumble back across Val and Raelas, and the witch could heal me. I lashed out wildly at the soldiers, finding them all to be illusions, and was conscious all the while that by pressing on at Yusef, I was leaving Corminar unprotected. I could only hope that he'd drunk that potion and was moving nimbly through the illusion, keeping himself out of harm's way.

"She'll leave again," that voice said. My mother's voice. I looked around for her visage, but found nothing. Still, I backed away from the direction in which I'd heard it. "You know she will."

"I know no such thing," I replied. "She's sorry. I know she is."

"And that's good enough for you?"

The answer was "yes," but I wasn't going to dignify this illusion of my absent mother with a reply; there were more important things going on. I heard blade battling blade among the oppressive, dense fog, and I pushed toward it.

A beautiful human woman stood at Arzak's rear, standing back-to-back with her just as Corminar and I had done moments earlier. They fought off giant rockrats, the size of which I'd never seen before, though I could see that Arzak's swords passed through the monsters without harming them. Only the woman at her side could kill the creatures.

"Arzak!" I shouted, and the orc snapped her body around to face me. "Away from her! She's part of the illusion. She could be Yus—"

A sword point burst from her chest, and this sword very much wasn't an illusion. The rockrats disappeared in a flash, and only the woman remained. A woman, I noticed, who sported a curved blade.

"Arzak, no!" I cried out.

At the same moment, the orc blinked down at the sword protruding out of her chest. ". . . El?" she asked. Then she dropped to the floor.

I charged. I couldn't do anything to heal Arzak's severe wound, but I could at least stop this enemy from inflicting another. I burst into a *knifestorm*, this flurry of attacks being the most useful ability I had when I struggled to tell reality from illusion, and my attacks struck flesh. The woman's visage faded, revealing herself to be—of course—one of Yusef's bandit thralls. Powered by fury, I stabbed and I stabbed and I stabbed, even when the woman was falling to the floor. Even when she was *on* the floor, I stabbed, before remembering myself.

I rushed to Arzak's side, putting my hand over her chest, doing my best to stem the bleeding. But the wound was too deep. She needed healing, and she needed it now.

"Val!" I shouted. "Val! Here! Now! It's Arzak! Val!" I shouted myself hoarse, but pushed through the pain in my throat—it was hardly the worst thing going on right now.

The fog took shape around us, forming huts and forest, and it took me a moment to recognize it. Arzak's eyes bulged as she blinked around at the image of the witchfinder village, back where we'd seen the "ghosts" trapped between worlds.

And those ghosts had their eyes upon us.

"Val!" I cried out some more. "Val, *please*! We need you."

The ghosts stepped forward again. My eyes drifted to the curved blades in their faint hands.

"Val!"

I couldn't remove my hands from Arzak's chest, or she'd die. I couldn't defend myself. I could only watch as the ghosts approached, forcing me toward a dreadful decision: let Arzak die, or save myself.

The closest enemy hovered over me, savoring the moment before finally raising their curved blade.

"Val!" I shouted one last time, in vain.

Part of me wanted to remove my hands from Arzak, to save one life—my own—instead of both of us dying. But another part of me—another more sentimental part—was stronger. If this was it, then I would stare my attacker down all the while.

"Go on, then," I whispered.

The enemy swung their blade. And, with the sound of a clap, a bright red light blossomed behind them. The illusion of the ghosts shattered, revealing the bandits for what they were. All of them turned to face the woman who'd entered the fray.

Tokas.

"I'm not Val, but I can save her."

I nodded, removed my hands from the dying Arzak, and drew my blade.

CHAPTER SIXTY-ONE

The False Prophet

I roared as I arced my dagger at the closest bandit, my fury seeming to fuel the attack. A beam of glowing yellow-white light passed around me, soaring toward Arzak as Tokas yanked her back from the brink of death.

The bandit brought up their sword to block my attack, clashing against my dagger rather than flesh. I pushed into our tangled blades, holding my knife where it was, not so far from their neck. Close enough to their neck, in fact, that I activated *Closed Reach* once more. My *Worldbending* magicks bent reality further, pushing the knife another eight inches toward my enemy. Knifepoint met flesh, and the bandit recoiled from our clashed blades. I seized the advantage, opening a portal beneath them, sending them tumbling through the air at my side. I yanked my blade around, using the enemy's momentum to bury its sharp point deep in their chest.

Level 28 Swordsman of the—

No. There will be time for notifications later. I pushed them out of mind, and turned to the rest of the attackers, feeling my rage and my strength burning through me.

I kept one eye on each of the bandits with curved blades, using them as a guide for where there would be platforms underfoot, and I embraced my portals. Taking inspiration from Yusef's own strategies, I hopped around the platform, stepping in and out of portals, releasing attacks before my enemies knew what hit them and then disappearing within the fog once more. With so many of these attacks having damage boosted by my *Stealth Attack* passive and my *Execution* ability, I found these enemies dropping like flies.

I really had grown. I really had become strong. But it had required embracing my strength and putting all qualms of violence aside to see how strong I'd really become. As the last of the bandit-ghosts faded away, I breathed deeply, pushing the oxygen through me, barely feeling the wound in my side—though it had been healed slightly by my charge through Tokas's magicks.

"Styk?" Tokas asked, now crouched over the still-living Arzak.

I turned to her, becoming aware that I was grimacing, my eyes wide, but not quite caring. I'd almost watched a friend die. I was done with Yusef now. It was time to end him. I didn't know how we could, but I knew someone who might.

"Lore!" I roared through the mist, tone hard, demanding. "Lore, where are you?"

As I put Tokas and Arzak behind me, the mist encompassed me once more, the sound of the tiefling's magicks fading to a hush in a second. I heard nothing as I kept putting one foot in front of the other.

"Lore, he's killing us. You say you don't want to watch any more friends die? Well, it's happening either way!"

I staggered on through the fog.

"You say Alenna is dead if you betray Yusef?" I continued, shouting, remembering what he'd told me back in the tower. "We're all dead if you don't. Deal with that now, and Alenna later." I clutched my wound, finding my hand growing wet with thick red liquid.

I pushed on, conscious that I was leaving a trail of blood behind me. Tokas's healing had been focused on Arzak; if she'd closed my wound, then my attacks on the bandits had opened it again.

"Lore!" I shouted. "Lore!"

"He's not here," I heard Val shout through the portal relays. "He's not—" She cried out as an attack landed on her. But I couldn't help her when I didn't know where she was.

"Val?" I asked, drawing a breath.

"I'm OK. For now. Find Lore." Her reply was staggered, as though speaking for too long at one time was causing her pain.

"Lore!" I shouted again, then thought of the relays. I sent one of my remaining orbiting relays out into the fog, and I shouted some more. "Lore, do you hear me? Do you bloody well *hear me*? We're *dying*. It's slow, but we're dying. We need you. We need you *now*."

"I'm here." The voice was quiet, but steady. He wasn't hurt, just overwhelmed.

"Follow the relay," I said, then urged it back toward me. I heard his heavy feet hitting the platform. "We need to end him. Now. And we need your help doing it. What do you see, Lore? What future do you see where we escape this alive?"

"Alenna dies," came the response. I heard him both through the portal and through the fog. He was growing closer. "If I help you, she dies."

"We'll save her."

"Will we?"

I saw the big man emerge through the fog. "Look at me," I told him.

Lore met my eyes. He met my eyes with his own—soft, brown, gentle eyes. It was really him.

"We'll save her, Lore," I promised. "But right now, we need you to save *us*."

He held my gaze, and I saw terror in those round eyes. The gift of prophecy was no gift at all; it was a curse. So many times had he foreseen deaths—some illusions crafted by Yusef, others true visions, and the line between the two having grown so blurred. There was something bloodcurdlingly awful in that.

"We'll save her," I said, softly, one last time.

Lore nodded, then turned, his eyes glowing yellow.

"Lore?"

"This way." He moved with a confidence that the dense fog shouldn't have allowed, with the edge of the wide platform potentially springing itself on us with every step. But then there were those glowing eyes he had, yellow with the hue of *Divination*. Since we'd last spent time with him, Lore had learned to better control Niamh's curse—that he could use it for this purpose showed that it wasn't all bad.

I pressed after him, taking care to keep close, unwilling to put one foot wrong, even though I always had portals to get myself back on the platform, should the worse happen. But the worse did not happen, and soon we saw a familiar sight ahead.

The strange altar stood before us, those glowing red lines illuminating the fog, and casting a crimson color over Lore's face. Through Val's relay, I heard a cry. "Whatever you're doing, better do it quickly!" she said.

I met Lore's eyes. We didn't need to communicate any further; we both knew what had to happen next. Lore charged toward the altar, throwing himself into the air with his Bane Sword swinging in an arc above him. I opened a portal in front of him, in midstep, launching him further into the air above the altar. As he fell, he brought his sword arcing down toward the amplifier of Yusef's power.

Alone, it might not be enough. But I had one last trick up my sleeve.

As Lore fell through one pair of portals, I stepped through another, bringing myself into the air at Lore's side. I reached out in the air, twisting my body around as we fell, and I put my hands around the pommel of Lore's greatsword—with its enormous size, there was room enough to spare.

It had taken me far too long to realize the great thing about my *Closed Reach* ability. It read, only: *Bend reality to narrow the gap between blade and target by up to eight inches.*

At no point did it specify that it had to be *my* blade.

Bane Sword clashed against stone, and the moment I felt the two connect, I activated my *Closed Reach* ability. The greatsword split the stone, creating a gash eight inches deep, causing the red, glowing lines to brighten and fade and brighten and fade, more erratically with every second that passed.

Then, the altar exploded.

All around us, the fog faded in a blink, revealing my allies and the great injuries they'd suffered battling both past and present.

A great, final, wave of red magicks erupted from the etched stone, throwing me and Lore backward and through the air. Lore fell in a heap on the platform, while I arced through the air, relying on my portals to keep me from falling to my doom. I leapt through the portal and landed at Val's side.

The witch was clasping her stomach, hurriedly healing a wound that had bled profusely over her exposed skin and torn clothes. I stepped over to support her, and looked around. Only one of the bandits was still standing, but that was a matter quickly seen to by Corminar, who was probably the least wounded of us, excluding Lore. Presumably he'd gone through his deep supply of potions to still be looking so well. Raelas was on the ground, bleeding but breathing and being seen to by Lambkin—notably *not* a healer, and injured himself from his own battles with the illusions—while Tokas still worked on Arzak's once-horrific wound.

And that left only one more: Yusef.

The Player stood at the stairwell, snarling as he stared the lot of us down. He'd lost his advantage; the illusion was shattered. But the team were in no place to battle a Player, even one as weak as him. With only Lore uninjured, it would be a hopeless task.

Unless we could flip the situation on its head. I cast my eyes around, looking for the answer.

"You lot just won't *stop*, will you?" Yusef spat. The man had once carried himself with a grand presence—one appropriate to his image as, for lack of a better word, a god. But now, the person before us, snarling and tired and spitting as he was, he revealed himself as just another man. A mortal, at least in this world.

Corminar raised his bow.

"Do you *know* what you endanger?" the Player shouted at the elf. "Do you know?"

"We will end the Council's scheme before—" Corminar started.

"Yes, yes, the *scheme*. But do you even know what that scheme is? Do you understand why it's important?"

Lore took a step closer to Yusef, his sword still in his hand. This was enough to get the Player's attention. "And *you*!" he shouted at his temporary traveling companion. "Do you know what you've done? Alenna will surely die, now. That's more blood on your hands."

I could open a *Saved Portal*, get Lore back to Coldharbor in a moment, but the barbarian's eyes were on Yusef.

"Maybe we can still save her," the Player said. "Come. Join me. Defend me against these others, and I will help you with her."

I heard this as a desperate bargain, but from the wide-eyed expression on Lore's face, he heard it as anything but. The barbarian, slowly, reluctantly, sheathed his sword, and ambled over to Yusef's side.

"Lore, no," I breathed. "Really? He—"

"I told you, Styk. I ain't gonna watch another one of you die."

Yusef smiled at this. With Lore still untouched, he was the strongest of us. With the barbarian at his side, we definitely wouldn't be able to defeat him.

But then Lore looked to me, and for a moment, I thought I saw something twinkling within his eyes. He half turned to Yusef. "What was that you were about to say?" the barbarian prodded him.

Suppressing a grin, I understood. With the flick of a hand behind my back, I cast my magicks.

"About the scheme?" Lore pressed the Player, stepping in front of him to keep the enemy's attention on himself. "Maybe they should know. Maybe they'd stop chasing us then."

Yusef, straightening his back and regaining a posture more typical of the man—and more in keeping with his image—smiled. "The scheme? Sure, I'll tell you. It's simple. Our Ascended World is dead. Let's not mince words, especially as everyone here knows that. When it died, we were all forced into the games— or, worlds we created as a game, at least. Worlds formed of powerful magicks that only accelerated the destruction of our home."

"A game?" I repeated. "Our existence, our world is a *game* to you? We're alive! Living, breathing creatures in a living, breathing world! If you cut me, don't I bleed?"

Yusef shrugged. "Well, yes, but it's not real blood. Not in the way that mine is. Your blood was created by magicks; ours, with the birth of the universe, evolving over millennia. You are . . . a lower life-form."

Well, that's a pretty cut-and-dry way of looking at it.

"And these worlds . . ." the Player continued, "they turned out to be only a temporary measure. There are only so many, and over the decades . . . we have died in so many. For some members on the Council, this is the only world left to them. For others, me included, we are alive in only a handful. These worlds aren't enough. They could never be enough."

"So what's the solution?" Lore asked, pushing the Player for information. We were nearly there. So close now. We just needed a little more detail to seal the deal.

The Player smiled; he took great delight in this scheme, it seemed. "Create a new world. Use the magicks of all those other worlds we created to make a new world, one in which we are immortal, and can live out eternity in peace. Not all can come with us, only those surviving members of my kind and a few select locals. That's what you miss out on, you see. If you stopped hunting my Council, maybe we could reach a deal. Maybe *you* could join us in heaven, rather than being left here, in a dying world."

Nobody said anything, letting these words linger in the air for just a moment. This was it. We just needed one final push.

"So, we could buy our way into this new world?" Lore asked. "But you'll take all your followers with you, right?"

Yusef cast his head back and laughed. "Take them with me? No. They'll stay in the crumbling, magick-stripped hellhole we leave behind."

It was Lore's turn to laugh. He stepped away from the Player's side, ambling back toward me and Val, and he smiled at Yusef. Though I was exhausted, I couldn't help but join in; there was something infectious about it. And then Corminar, and Val, and even Lambkin began to laugh, all because they knew one thing.

They knew the job was done.

Because, of course, it wasn't just my relay portals that transmitted sound. *All* my portals did, now. Everyone in hearing range had heard Yusef's admission, his truth about the Ascended World and the fate of his people—but so, too, had all those on the other side of the *Saved Portal* I'd opened two minutes earlier, behind Yusef. So, too, had all those devout cultists the Player had left behind on Coldharbor's main plaza.

Thousands of them. All staring at the portal that had appeared before them. All silent, because they dared not interrupt the man they worshipped. All hearing Yusef's plain and simple truth: that he'd lied to them. That he'd told them a great and terrible lie.

A moment too late, Yusef turned. He saw the portal. He saw *through* the portal, and he realized what he'd done. I took great delight in his smirk fading, in his eyes widening.

From Coldharbor's dusty streets, the cultist horde charged.

CHAPTER SIXTY-TWO

Illusion's End

The cultists charged.

I staggered backward as the masses swarmed Yusef, emboldened by their rage just as I had been. So many years they'd followed him, worshipped him, all with the promise of a divine reward. But now they knew it had been time wasted, that there was no world to ascend to. And, as was often the case with mobs, they'd fed on each other's anger.

I wouldn't get my artifact charge. Not for this Player. But there were many others out there to take down—a whole Council to kill—and I'd realized my true strength. We would take the fight to them, and we would concede no quarter. We would hunt them down, and we would kill them all. Yeah, there would be plenty of time for artifact charges later.

I never saw Yusef die, and I barely even heard him scream, as the crowd attacking him had grown so large. Val and I had needed to take a few steps back to make space for the rabid hundreds, each of them wanting a piece of the man who'd deceived them. I caught sight of Val eyeing me, her brow furrowed, curious that I was allowing Yusef to be defeated by others. Through all this, the only reason I knew that the Player was defeated was the notifications that began piling up.

5 x Swordsmen of the Desert Sons defeated!
Level 44 Veilcaster defeated!

Worldbending: +16,150XP

Worldbending increased to level 62!
Worldbending increased to level 63!
Worldbending increased to level 64!
Worldbending increased to level 65!
Base Points Gained: +8 INT, +8 Free Points (INT/WIS/CHA)

Ability Selection Unlocked
Select an ability from the list below:
. . .

Knifework: +7,250XP
Knifework increased to level 47!
Knifework increased to level 48!
Base Points Gained: +2 DEX, +2 STR, +4 Free Points (VIT/DEX/STR)

Level up!
You increased to Level 21!

It was an almost disappointingly low amount of experience considering all we'd been through, but then again . . . my involvement had been far from the finishing blow, as far as the System was concerned. Maybe I was lucky to even get this much. And there was a new ability selection to pick from! Yet . . . still, all this felt somehow incomplete.

"You OK?" Val asked, and it took me a moment to realize she wasn't talking to me.

Lore nodded, but shifted from foot to foot, looking at the crowd still charging through the portal, not yet fully aware that their vengeance was already complete. "Yeah, I . . ."

"Alenna," I said.

The big man nodded, meeting my eyes.

I returned the nod in kind, and allowed my *Saved Portal* to close, stemming the flow of once-cultists from Coldharbor. "Be ready," I said, and then opened the *Saved Portal* once more, in front of him. Lore was through in the blink of an eye, rushing off to see Alenna, to make absolutely sure that Yusef's illusion of her death had been just that—an illusion.

"Don't suppose you could . . ." I started, pointing down to the deep wound on my side. While Val got to work healing me, I looked over at Tokas and Arzak, the former helping the latter back to her feet.

"How's it feel?" the tiefling asked. "Are you better? Are you going to be OK?"

Arzak looked back at Tokas, then reached a hand forward and squeezed the tiefling gently on the shoulder. "Thank you, Tokas," the orc said, and I was surprised to see that her glistening eyes seemed to display sincerity. Not that Arzak was ever much of one to disguise her true feelings. "You not ever going to kill me, were you? Just silly illusion. Silly illusion, is all. Sorry for doubting."

"Alright, enough!" Lambkin shouted at the crowd, waving his hands to encourage the cultists back through the portal. "It's done! Better get home before you all get stranded here." This last thought alone was enough to begin to reverse the flow back into Coldharbor. But I was more interested in what Arzak and Tokas had to say than the sea of orange heading back home. From Lambkin's glances in the same direction, I suspected he was, too—but was trying to hide it.

"It's OK," Tokas said. "I still . . . I did what I did. I have to deal with the consequences. Tim's helped me realize that."

Arzak and I reacted to this in the same way—with a quizzical expression. "Tim?" the orc asked.

Tokas nodded toward Lambkin.

"Hm. He should stick with Lambkin."

I opened my mouth to agree, but was distracted by Val patting my wound. "All done." She cast a glance over to Raelas, who was on the ground, struggling back to her feet, clearly sporting a broken leg. "I suppose I better . . ." Val shook her head in exasperation, then hurried over to the tiefling's side.

As I turned back toward Arzak and Tokas, not at all trying to hide that I was watching them, the orc looked over at me. Arzak shot me a quick, almost apologetic glance, then turned back to Tokas and let out a deep, long breath. "You should join us. Come back to team. Not all forgiven, but . . ."

Yet already Tokas was shaking her head; if she'd wanted that once, then she did no longer. "I'm . . . I'm grateful. But I think that's behind me now. I have children to raise. And I don't think . . . I don't think I'm cut out for this life anymore. Tim and I, we'll stamp out the last of the mala trade, then we'll go home."

The man in question—Tim—appeared at my side, also looking over at the tiefling and the orc. Well, the tiefling, really; his eyes were fixed on her.

"You're going with her?" I asked him.

Lambkin nodded. "Yeah, I . . ." He allowed himself a laugh, and I couldn't blame him; the battle was won, and we deserved a little joy. "I guess maybe Sae wasn't my soulmate after all. We find love in the strangest of places, don't we?"

"Yeah, you can say that again." Almost against my better judgement, my eyes slid over to Val. The witch stood over Raelas, working her *Healing* magicks on the tiefling, and from the looks of it, actually treating the woman with kindness. I felt a smile cross my face, and then Val—perhaps sensing my eyes upon her—looked back at me. She returned the smile in kind.

"You think you two will work it out?" Lambkin asked.

"Yeah," I replied. "Yeah, I think I do."

Lambkin stuck out a hand and clasped me around the shoulder—an act of friendship. How far we'd come since our first encounter, with him trying his best to kill me. As Lambkin moved away once more to encourage the cultists back through the portal, I drew in a deep breath.

The battle was done. We'd survived it. That was another Player death under my belt, and a cause for celebration—even if there were so many other members of the Council still to contend with. For all we knew, their scheme could still go ahead even without Yusef. In fact, it almost certainly *would* still go ahead; this didn't seem like the type of plan that they would just give up on. And while our world was still threatened, we had work to do.

Still, we could take this moment for ourselves, just this once.

While Val finished up with Raelas, I took a look through the ability selection I'd just unlocked. There were just two choices on this particular level.

Ability Selection Unlocked
Select an ability from the list below:

Option 1: Enhanced Portals II (Worldbending)—*Upgrade to Enhanced Portals.* Create a portal to another location within current range of sight or within a thirty-yard radius. Support up to three pairs of portals at once. Uses mana to open portals only.

Three pairs of portals sounded handy in principle, but the limitation then was on my ability to coordinate six portals at once, rather than any ability limitations. I struggled enough with two pairs of portals, so I was hardly jumping at the bit to accept this ability choice.

And that was before I even saw the other option.

Conflict encountered. System adaptation complete. Unique ability choice unlocked. Unique ability choice strongly recommended.
Option 2: Titan Husk (Worldbending)—*Replaces Ash Husk.* Warp your flesh to totally withstand all physical damage effects from everything including fire, frost, lightning, poison, and corruption.

So my encounters with the malae had done some good. The artifact, in resolving my conflict with the so-called reality fabrics, had triggered something spoken about as though it were only a myth—a unique ability choice. These unique abilities were created through unique circumstances—circumstances that the Architects of the System had never truly accounted for. And in this case, my encounters with the malae had forced the System to provide me an ability that withstood corruption.

Even without the corruption resistance, this would have been a fantastic ability. We might've well been done dealing with Yusef's malae, but even without this corruption resistance coming in handy, this was still an ability worth having.

I was just about to lock in my choice when something magical happened, something so perfect for the situation that it seemed created by divine intervention.

Corminar found a bottle of wine.

CHAPTER SIXTY-THREE

Reasons to Be

I say Corminar *found* a bottle of wine.

What I really mean is that certain parts of the recently fractured Cult of Ascendancy gave wine an almost religious significance. Wine was the drink of the gods, that which should be gifted to them, that which should be kept on hand in case the prophet should return to them. The recently healed Corminar had spotted it in the hands of a cultist—held as if about to be used as a weapon against their now-dead leader—and had chosen to relieve them of it.

The ranger stuck an arrowhead in the cork and then wrenched it out. I could only assume he'd made sure not to use a poison-coated arrow.

With the flick of his hand, Corminar gestured the seven of us over to the edge of the platform, where he sat with his legs hanging over the edge, hundreds of feet above the ground.

"Is safe?" Arzak asked.

Corminar took a big swig of wine, then gestured to me and Raelas. "There is no longer the mist of *Illusion*, and we have two worldbenders among our number. I am sure they will catch us should we fall."

Val shrugged, then joined the elf at his side, hanging her legs over the edge, too. Corminar handed her the bottle, and she swigged from it just as greedily as the elf had. They shared their love for alcohol.

Wait, so do I. I hurried over to join them, and Val handed me the bottle. It was good wine. Dry, just as I liked it, but smooth. I didn't have the vocabulary to describe it more than that—did it have notes of berries, perhaps?—so I instead handed it off to Raelas as she joined us. Soon, it was only Arzak who remained standing away from the edge, her fear of heights still controlling her, but we could forgive her a little fear just this once.

Lambkin, at the end of our line, offered the bottle to Arzak, who creeped over to the edge timidly, stretching her arm out as far as possible so she wouldn't need to get near us.

As I stared forward at the long shadows stretching east, I closed my eyes. Nobody said a word for a few minutes, each of us enjoying the respite, the view, maybe even one another's company, though I suspect they were enjoying the wine first and foremost.

"You didn't kill him," Val said at last. "Yusef; you let the cultists take him down."

I shrugged. "Didn't see there was any other way. We were all weak from his illusions. We needed them."

Maybe it was the wine talking, or the world-shatteringly impressive view in front of us, but what Val said next surprised me. It wasn't just the words, but the way she said them, too. "I'm sorry, Styk. I'm really, really, well and truly sorry. You shouldn't forgive me, that's—"

"But I have."

"Yeah, you have, haven't you? Cos you're better than me."

"Val, don't. Don't think I'm better than you—I've messed up so many times in the past. Got people killed. Hurt people I care about, sometimes even intentionally. You messed up, sure. I'm not pretending you didn't. But we've *all* been through some stuff, and we all carry it with us. And what I saw back there . . ." I gestured back to the platform where I saw her younger self's encounters with Niamh.

"Still," Val said, reaching over to hold my hand. "You forgave me, and I'm gonna do everything I can to make sure you don't regret it." She, very hesitantly, put her head down to rest on my shoulder, only letting it settle when I didn't recoil. And then, when I didn't, she squeezed my hand, too.

We sat like that for a while, even Arzak eventually beating out her fear of heights to join us. The landscape before us turned from yellow, to blue, to black, as the sun set behind the mountains. And up here, at the top of the tower, the wind grew bitter.

Lambkin was the first to pull himself back from the edge and stand. "I suppose we better be going. Check in on the kids—the minder will be relieved to see us, I reckon."

Tokas, using Lambkin's hand to pull herself back to her feet, shot the man a dirty look. But then she smiled; she knew he didn't mean it. We watched them leave through the portal I'd left open.

Next, it was Raelas's turn to stand, perhaps sensing that she was now the odd one out.

"So," Val said, turning to look up at the woman, "you coming with us?"

The tiefling immediately became very rigid, apparently stunned by this extended olive branch.

"We could use all the help we can get," Val pressed.

But, just like Tokas, Raelas shook her head. "I appreciate the offer and all, but you already have a worldbender. And one far stronger than me, at that. I'll help you, sure, but I'm not gonna join you. I think, after all this . . . I think I've got to find my own place in the world. Not as a team, but as me. As Raelas. Besides, you've exposed the Players with what you did here, haven't you? You're gonna need someone to go around spreading the word."

Raelas stepped toward the *Saved Portal* back to Coldharbor, then paused at the threshold. She looked over her shoulder and blew me a kiss, this act making it Val's turn to go rigid. "Be good, handsome."

And with that, she was gone.

I felt Val's wrath before I saw it.

"I hate that woman," the witch said.

"But you just offered for her to—" I started, then shook my head. This wasn't a conversation I needed to have; now was a time for celebration, not . . . whatever this was.

And this left just the Slayers. The Slayers without Lore, at least.

"We reckon Lore's OK?" Val asked as though she'd read my mind.

I saw a cloud of dust lift from the dark sands below, a group of riders charging for Elassos. Cultists from Zelas perhaps, not yet aware that it was too late to save their prophet. "He's been through a lot," I answered. "With not much help from any of us, I gotta say. We really need to learn to communicate better."

"Hm," Arzak agreed.

"He'll be OK, though, given time. Maybe we can figure out a way of getting Niamh's curse removed? I think he'd like that."

"Would we not rather he learns to control it?" Corminar asked.

"I think that's up to him."

Corminar nodded his agreement, but kept his eyes lingering on Val and me, the witch's head still resting against my shoulder. "I must ask, have you two worked out this ridiculous argument now? We are stronger as a full team, and so I hope that you have."

"It's not—" Val started to say, but then she caught herself. Maybe she'd been about to claim that the argument wasn't ridiculous, but then realized that she didn't believe that. "We're working on it," she eventually said, and then glanced up at me.

I nodded back my reply, and in silence we stared across the desert once more. With a sigh, I brought myself back to my feet, taking care not to topple over the edge—something that was slightly more likely to happen with the equivalent of a glass of wine in me. "Come on, let's get off this platform," I said, waving the team toward the portal back to Coldharbor.

"More wine when we get there?" Val asked.

"Of course," replied the elf. "Provided that I am able to select the—"

But he didn't get to finish that sentence, because at that moment, the cultists we'd seen riding over from Zelas appeared on the platform. My initial instinct was to fight, and then to simply step through the portal and leave them behind. But then I noticed that it was Lillya—perhaps the friendliest of all the cultists—standing at the head of the pack.

The orc stared down at the dead Yusef in the center of the platform. "Oh," she said.

"Yeah, sorry," I replied. "If you were here to help him, then I'm afraid you're like two hours too—"

"No," Lillya said, cutting me off. Only then did I recognize the glimmer of urgency in her eyes. Urgency that existed even after Yusef's demise. "Something I need tell you."

"Perhaps it can wait?" Corminar asked, eyeing the portal. "I have a thirst for northern Armadan wine, and it is a thirst not easily quenched."

"No, we—"

"We've earned a rest," Val added, gesturing to the dead Yusef. "Let us celebrate for a bit first, before we get caught up in—"

"*No*," Lillya said, forcefully now, cutting off even Val. "You not understand. It *not over*."

Val looked at the dead illusionist. "It looks pretty over."

Lillya ignored her, and raised a flimsy piece of parchment into the air, waving it at us. A letter. "Found in Tower of Hope. In Yusef's room. Your fight isn't over, there is—"

"The Council?" I asked. "If it's the Council, then we know. We're on it. But like Val said, we—"

"Yusef in contact with person in Coldharbor," Lillya said, now speaking over me. Whatever this was, apparently it really couldn't wait. "Someone he bought mala breeding program from. Someone he gave *lot* of coin to, to fund research. It is someone who want to revive old tiefling tradition. You know one? Turn enemy strength against enemy. We need destroy malae before Coldharbor is lost."

I took an unconscious step backward. I'd missed something. I'd known there were loose ends, questions we'd unearthed without any answers, but we'd been so focused on killing Yusef that I'd put them to one side. But we knew the mala breeders had been here before Yusef ever arrived. We knew there had been others involved in this dangerous industry. We'd just not realized they were right under our noses.

I asked the question that I already knew the answer to. "This person in Coldharbor, that Yusef was dealing with, do you know their name?"

"Alenna," Lillya replied.

Lore's visions of Alenna's death *hadn't* been an illusion. He really had foreseen it. We'd stumbled into the chain of events that may well have caused her to die, but in a much more real sense; it had been her own actions that would lead to her death. Her dances with demons, her drive to dissect the malae, to understand them, maybe even to use their power. Without Lore at her side, there would be nobody to protect her against her own mistakes. Nobody to protect her against the corruption.

"I understand now," I said.

Ability Unlocked: Titan Husk

Titan Husk (Worldbending): Warp your flesh to totally withstand all physical damage effects from everything including fire, frost, lightning, poison, and corruption.

As I ran for the portal, I locked in my ability choice. I was going to need it.

Alenna

Alenna knew the moment was upon her the second she heard the door slam open.

The man who stood in her doorway was no hulking warrior, possessed no long limbs or bulging muscles, but then again, Alenna didn't need him to. All she needed was a willing host. Someone who wanted to grow stronger.

"Did he send you?" Alenna asked. The man nodded, so she gestured him over to her operating table.

This wasn't the first man whom her benefactor had sent her way—far from it—but it was the first since she'd found the answer. There, in that book that Lore's friends had retrieved for her, had been the spell that she could use to stop the corruption spreading—a ward sustained by the life-force of its host, a ward that prevented the corruption from reaching the brainstem.

It had taken a few attempts to perfect the spell, of course. Alenna regretted that nasty business with the metal mage, and even more so all the damage that had followed. Ama would have been lost without Alenna's intervention, but that large gentleman warrior should never have been hurt. That life weighed on Alenna, but she kept herself going with the knowledge that if she was successful, no lives would be lost to the malae ever again.

As the man settled on the stone platform, Alenna tapped the enchanted gems, and they blossomed into life, casting a vivid light all across the patient.

"What do I call you?" she asked.

"Simm," came the reply, "though people call me the Councilman." This last bit seemed like it was added as a second thought.

"Simm it is," Alenna replied, which seemed to cause the man to grumble. "Do you know why you are here?"

"Yusef said you could make me stronger. Unstoppable, in fact. He used the words 'perfect soldier.'"

"And just what would you give up to become this perfect soldier, Simm?"

"Everything."

Alenna nodded. "Correct answer. Let's begin." She turned away toward the metal cabinets at the rear of her room, and began undoing the first lock. With this first lock, protections fell away—wards against sound, against light, against anything she could think of. There was no overdoing it when it came to caging the malae. Inside, crammed into a box too small for it, was one of these creatures. Alenna was comfortable enough with these boxes for now to know that she could hold it without danger to herself, though she still kept both eyes on it for any sign of escape.

"The malae have always been a problem in the Beached Armada," Alenna said as she placed the mala box down and set out her tools. "The first one ever reported was found here, you know that? It was a few years after the invasion—that long ago. The invasion force, they'd had no real trouble with the people living here, but battling the malae? That nearly destroyed them."

She took a step back, making sure she had everything in place—the patient, the mala, her tools, and the borrowed spell book.

"And as a result, we lost our ways. We forgot our central tenet—fight fire with fire, use our enemy's strengths against them. That applies for monsters just as much as it does for people, I reckon. And the greater the strength, the greater the power we can extract. That's how I'll make you the perfect soldier, Simm. I'll imbue you with the power of corruption. Are you ready?"

"Oh yes," her patient replied.

"Good."

Alenna got to work. It was the ward that she'd focus on first; this was the most important step, and there could be no flaw in her work. If the ward had even the slightest gap, the corruption would find it in time. Her patient would end up as one of those walking monsters, barely conscious yet just conscious enough to know that the corruption now controlled them. And Lore's friends weren't around right now to handle one, so she would need to be extra careful.

The ward glowed as she established it, before fading away as she tied off the magicks and allowed the man's soul to feed it. She kept her hands on the man's neck, just where she'd placed the ward, testing it, pushing at it, seeking any sign of weakness. But Alenna was right; she'd perfected it.

"OK, Simm," she said. "You're about to feel a slight pinch." Before her patient could react, Alenna lifted the box, pressed it against the man's chest, and slid open one side, exposing flesh to corruption. She slid the side of the box back into place a moment later. There was no point overdoing it; even the slightest touch would fester, though it would take longer to do so. This gave Alenna time to escape if anything *did* go wrong.

The man cried out with pain as the mala touched his flesh, and the ward briefly glowed to life once more, reacting to this corruption. This ward would stop the corruption spreading to the man's brain, but in theory it would also prevent the patient from spreading corruption with his touch. If such a powerful being could spread corruption as easily as that, then Coldharbor was doomed, so this really was the most important aspect of the procedure.

Alenna opened her mouth, beginning to talk to distract the man from the pain. He was turning into a living weapon, but he was a person, too. She would spare him the torture as much as she could. "I know it hurts, but it's for a good cause. Think of all you'll do when you're the strongest being to walk Alterra. You'll be able to destroy all the malae without risk to yourself, their corruption unable to hurt you. You'll save us all. You'll be worshipped. Doesn't that sound good?"

The scientist lit her torch and pressed the flames against the wound on the man's chest, causing him to cry out louder.

"It hurts to become a god," she said. "But it's worth it." It had to be.

After Alenna finished up the procedure, she stepped back from the patient as far as she could manage, her back up against the wall. She would give this Simm as much space as she could, but she needed to know whether or not this procedure had been successful. If it had, she would give him his orders. If it hadn't . . . well, that didn't bear thinking about right now.

The man stopped screaming. His breathing grew quieter, then silent, and then Alenna could no longer see his chest rising and falling.

". . . Simm?" she asked.

The man didn't reply, though his eyes were open.

"Simm, are you—"

At that moment, the corrupted man swung his legs down from the platform, and he stared at her in silence with cold, black eyes.

"Oh good," Alenna said, relieved. "You're alive. That's good. Could you just reassure me that it's still *you* in there?"

"It is still me," the man replied. His cold eyes didn't change.

Alenna resisted the urge to swallow. "OK, great. The hard part is done. The next part? You find the malae. You kill them. You save us all, and—"

Simm charged forward from the stone table in a flash, his limbs empowered by the corruption surging through them. Alenna barely had time to blink before the man's hand was around her neck.

She tried to cry out, but the man squeezed tight. All she could do was gasp for air.

"That sounded like an order," the patient said. "I'm *done* taking orders from the likes of you. You think I care about being worshipped? You think I care about this world anymore, now that I know what the Council intends? No. I care about only one thing now: revenge."

Alenna gasped for air, struggling against the firm hand wrapped around her neck. "Please," she wheezed. "Let me—"

The perfect soldier squeezed.

CHAPTER SIXTY-FOUR

Corruption Returns

As I stepped back through the portal, I expected to emerge into chaos.

But there was only the usual hustle and bustle of the city, particularly in the main plaza, and with the cult only just starting to scatter. If there had been any of the screaming and panicking that I'd been expecting, then I of course would have heard it from the platform—what with my portals communicating sound these days.

This was good. This meant that whatever Alenna was really up to, she hadn't finished it yet. Part of my mind couldn't help but worry that Lore had hurried straight for her—what if he stumbled across something he shouldn't? Just what would she do to protect her secret, and would she do it to a man she thought of as a brother?

The last of our team, Corminar, stepped through the portal, and I looked back through it at the orc. "You coming?" I asked. "Last chance."

"Can get me back to Rose Home?" Lillya asked.

"This is as close as you're gonna get."

The orc in the orange robe shrugged, then stepped through with a handful of other cultists from Zelas. I allowed the portal to shut behind her; whatever was coming next, I suspected I'd need two pairs of portals to—

Someone screamed.

It was distant, barely noticeable above the din of the cultists crowding the square, but it was the sort of noise I'd been listening for. Sounds of panic. Alarm bells—this noise metaphorical, existing only in my head—started ringing. "Where?" I asked Corminar, the only other person in our group to have noticed the scream, and the only one of us with superior elven hearing.

"Southwest," he replied. "Perhaps two hundred yards."

I nodded, oriented myself based on where I'd once seen the sun set over Coldharbor's western sprawl, and began to push through the crowd in the direction the elf had said.

I heard scoffs and tuts erupted behind me as I pushed through without any regard for people being in the way, and without worrying about stepping on people's feet. The scream could have been nothing. I *hoped* it would turn out to be nothing, that I would irk all those people without solid cause. But, as these stories so often go, the person who'd screamed had done so with good reason.

A woman stood, unmoving, in the center of a main road that led directly out of town from Coldharbor's main plaza. Others on this busy street gave her a wide berth, staring and cowering and fleeing. In a time long since passed, I might have done the same, considering this woman's skin had turned gray, and a black ooze was just now beginning to seep from her pores. The people of Coldharbor were well versed in corruption by now; they knew it when they saw it.

"Corminar!" I shouted, but the elf was already moving. He grabbed a glowing glass vial from his alchemist's satchel, and he tossed it to me. I snatched it from the air in the same moment that I *portal sliced* into a nearby cart, sending its bags of produce tumbling onto the ground. I snatched a plank of wood from the debris, then poured the contents of Corminar's potion over it.

The wood burst into flames.

"I should—" Arzak started, reaching out to take the flames from me.

"No," I said. There wasn't time to explain my latest ability selection, but now that I could use *Titan Husk*, I was the person safest to approach the corrupted woman. Still, the team could do with fire of their own to defend themselves. I touched the end of my makeshift torch to the scattered wooden debris of the shouting merchant's cart, setting it alight, and turned back to the enemy.

When I met her eyes, I saw no life behind them.

I drew in a deep breath. We could do this. We'd done this before. I just didn't think we'd ever have to do it *again*.

I raised the torch in one hand, and my dagger in the other, and I activated my new ability for the first time. As with *Ash Husk*, my skin rippled and changed— but it settled on no solid form, instead continuing to warp and shimmer. As I crossed the dusty road toward the enemy, it looked for a moment like she wouldn't react, that the corruption had not yet taken hold enough for her to do more than stagger around town. But then, at the last moment, an oozing arm whipped up to block my attacks.

I bounced off the arm, hitting the dirt hard.

"Styk!" Val cried, fear sharp in her voice. I'd not explained, of course. She didn't know that I could resist the corruption now, with this new ability. Maybe that was an oversight, an unkindness to let her think I was about to die. *Oops.*

I thrust a hand up in the air, flashing the witch a shimmering thumbs-up sign, before opening a portal on the ground and falling back through it. I landed in front of the enemy once more.

"I forgot how strong this made you," I said.

The corrupted woman didn't reply.

As I charged in again to attack, I became peripherally aware of more shouts and screams erupting around me, but I was too focused on this fight to give them a second thought. I feigned with my dagger, causing the enemy to swing their arm up to block once more, and then I stepped through a portal. Appearing behind them, I brought my flames down upon their back. The monster's flesh sizzled.

It wasn't enough to kill the beast. Far from it. Fire was the corruptions' weakness, but it still took a good deal of it to get anywhere. Last time we'd fought one of these, I'd dumped masses of flaming *Needlework* supplies on it. Since then, however, I'd not had a chance to stock back up. I did have one advantage over last time, though; I could touch it.

I leaped onto the monster, feeling the oozing corruption against my rippling flesh. As before, it was cold to the touch, almost so cold that it felt like a burn. I ignored the sensation and wrapped my limbs around the creature, holding on tight while pressing the flames against it. To distract the monster, I also opened a portal beneath it, sending the pair of us high into the sky above Coldharbor.

We tumbled toward the ground, spinning. The monster hissed with the pain of the torch now pressed against its chest. Despite being weakened by the flames, it was still strong enough to wrench me away, and a moment later, we tumbled separately. I caught sight of crowds fleeing down streets below, and saw not one but two pillars of smoke. Then it hit me—where there was smoke, there was fire.

And I could control where we landed.

One of the pillars of smoke was just one road away, on a narrow street that ran mostly parallel to the main road we'd been on. I put my arms out at my side, trying to stop myself spinning, and then focused on opening a portal both above the fire and below the falling monster.

My aim was true, the corrupted woman falling through the portal and landing on the source of the smoke, but now I had two new problems: I didn't know if the monster was dead, and I was now fifty yards away from a very sudden stop.

I dealt with the "me being about to die" problem first, opening a portal beneath me and another near the pillar of smoke—but this one facing upward. As I'd practiced a couple of times before, I waited until I was at the peak of my soaring back into the air, then opened a portal directly beneath me. I fell through it, landing back on the streets of Coldharbor.

The source of the pillar of smoke was a burning building—a bakery, in fact. Both customer and patron had long since fled the establishment, which lent itself to me returning to a tried-and-true technique: dropping a building on the monster.

I whipped my hands forward, using them to aim properly, and I *portal sliced* and *portal sliced* at the burning beams of the ceiling, until the two-story building collapsed in on itself—and the monster burning within.

Level ? Corruption defeated!

Worldbending: +6,700XP
Worldbending increased to level 66!
Base Points Gained: +2 INT, +2 Free Points (INT/WIS/CHA)

Knifework: +1,300XP

I staggered backward from the falling, burning building, coughing the billowing dust back out of my lungs. To my left, I saw Val, Arzak, and Corminar running down the alleyway from the adjoining street.

"How did you . . ." Val asked, staring at my rippling skin.

"New ability. I'm corruption-proof. Will explain later." In situations like these, there wasn't time for full sentences. Panicked ex-cultists, still in pale orange robes, ran down the street with wide, frantic eyes. And the shouting grew louder behind me.

I turned around slowly, already knowing what I was about to find. That's when I realized *why* everyone had fled the bakery. It wasn't just the flames, it was what had *caused* the flames: another of the corrupted locals.

"Just how many of these things *are* there?"

If there was more than one, then chances were there were more than two. Chaos was taking hold in Coldharbor, and quickly the city was spiraling out of control—these monsters being at the heart of it. We needed to take these down while they were few in number, else this would get out of control. This rapidly spreading corruption had the potential to destroy not just the city, but Alterra itself.

"How could Yusef want this?" I asked, more out of exasperation and panic than because I was actually looking for an answer.

But Val gave me one anyway. "He couldn't. Something's gone wrong."

I nodded, then charged into battle once more. As I struck a monster with fire, I felt something weighing heavily in my gut—a sense that we couldn't kill the corruption quickly enough.

A sense that we were doomed.

CHAPTER SIXTY-FIVE

Birthright

Level ? Corruption defeated!

This was the fourth monster of its kind that we'd killed, and even the result-ing *Worldbending* and *Knifework* skill level increases weren't enough to offset my growing nausea. Corminar had very narrowly escaped being corrupted himself at one point, and if we kept going like this, this possibility would end up an inevi-tability. With Coldharbor falling around us, we needed to switch up our strategy, or else we were only giving this city a few more hours of life.

"Styk . . ." Arzak grumbled, presumably getting at just the same thing.

"We gotta find the cause," I replied while scanning the streets for more signs of trouble. In the midst of the spreading chaos, it was hard to tell what was a threat and what was simply people fleeing in terror.

"Any thoughts on . . ." Val started, then she found the answer herself. "Alenna."

I nodded, opening a portal in front of us that stretched as far in the distance as I could reasonably aim. "Come on. Let's go pay a visit to the good scientist."

We stepped through the portal into a crowd of people running north, though whether they were fleeing a corruption or simply carried along by the waves of panic was yet to be determined. I had to push through these throngs of people just to make enough space for Val, Corminar, and Arzak to come through the portal behind me, then stood on tiptoes to aim another portal down the street.

"Styk! Val!" I heard someone shouting through the crowd. Lambkin, Tokas following at his heel.

"Thank the gods we found you. We were just coming back to the portal—the city's gone mad."

"Yes, we see this," Arzak replied, her eyes scanning the surroundings for trouble while Lambkin and I spoke.

"You know what's happened?"

The ex-captain shook his head. "Only that the corruption is spreading fast. We ran into one of those monsters back there. Even the soldiers here took some convincing to fight it rather than running, though I can hardly blame them."

"You took it down?"

"With some trouble, but yes."

"We had to put down a few soldiers touched by the corruption," Tokas explained, as ever saying the hard part without hesitation.

"We could do with more of those soldiers," I replied.

Lambkin pressed his lips together. "You'll be lucky; they're fewer and further between with every second that passes."

"Err . . ." Val said.

"Come on," I told Tokas and Lambkin. "We're heading to Alenna's surgery. If we can find the cause of all this, then maybe we can still turn the tide."

The pair of them nodded, and I turned to open a portal once more. Every second counted. With each—

"Styk?" Val said, interrupting my line of thought.

"Yeah?" I asked as we stepped through the portal to get us closer to Alenna's place of work.

"You want an army? Well . . ." She gestured around us, and it took me a second to understand what she was pointing at. The sea of pale orange robes. The Cult of Ascendancy, still in Coldharbor in their thousands. And with their reason to be so recently taken away from them. "The city needs a hero, Styk. And you're right—it's you. It has to be you."

These words, coming out of that mouth, almost made me stagger backward. Wasn't this at the heart of how Val worried I was changing? Wasn't it my desire to be a hero that had created that wedge between us? "You get it now?" I asked.

Val nodded. "I get it."

I held her gaze just for a moment before remembering the urgency of the situation, and I got to work. I activated *Portal Relays*, and sent all but one of them soaring off into the city, scattered through the streets as much as I could without losing track of them.

More screaming erupted from down the street, and Tokas, Arzak, Corminar, and Lambkin hurried off to deal with its cause—inevitably another local touched by the corruption.

I looked through the portal relay at the views from the nine other relays shimmering in and out of sight, and I . . . hesitated. The pressure got to me, at least for a moment.

I felt a hand on my arm. "You got this," Val said.

I nodded. I did, indeed, have this. I looked into the relay, at the hundreds of cultists in orange, and I prepared myself. I wouldn't be able to get the word to all of them, not even with my relays, but I could spread the word to enough. If I was successful, word would travel, even among the chaos.

I took a deep breath, and I prepared myself to speak. *Don't say cultists, don't say cultists*, I told myself.

"Attention, cultists!" I bellowed through the relays.

Oops.

"My name is Styk. Some of you may know me, while some of you might have only heard whispers. I am the man whom Yusef—the deceiver—wanted dead. A member of the team who exposed him for what he is. But, above all, I am a man with the Architects' blood in my veins. If you've heard such rumors, know this: they are true.

"But I'll make no promises about an Ascended World. You heard it straight from Yusef's mouth; the Ascended World is dead. There is no divine destination for you. There is only this world, just this world that you see around you. A flawed world, full of flawed people"—I glanced at Val—"but one that's beautiful nonetheless. And this world needs saving.

"I call on you—each and every one of you—not to run, not to flee this threat that spreads through Coldharbor, but to stand and fight. Save not just this city, but this *world*. *Be* the heroes that you've always wanted to find in the Players. Stand and fight." I took in one last deep breath as I bellowed my final instruction. *"Burn the corruption wherever it takes hold!"*

There was a moment of near silence, at least as much as there could be in this falling city, but then . . . someone roared. It wasn't the roar of anger, of frustration, but a battle cry. A battle cry that spread through the ranks of the orange sea, that stopped them in their tracks, that had them pick up weapons and stand their ground. My words had had their desired effect. We had ourselves an army.

Seizing upon the opportunity of the emboldened cult, I charged into the already raging battle of Slayers versus corruption.

And dozens of cultists charged with me.

We amassed hundreds of cultists as we fought our way across the city of Coldharbor. With so many on our side, so many following my bellowed commands, we could defeat the corrupted quickly. It almost felt like we were turning the tide, eliminating the enemy fast enough that we might still triumph. But we could only speak for the streets we fought down—elsewhere in the city, the corruption was likely still winning. We could hurry to Alenna's surgery all we wanted, but even if we found and eliminated the cause, if enough of the corruption was left to spread elsewhere, our fight would be lost.

We needed to split our attention.

"Corminar!" I shouted, summoning the elf to my side. He appeared near instantly. "Take some of the cultists west. Destroy any corruption that's festering there. Understand?"

But Corminar had paled. "It shouldn't be me," he replied.

"What? Why? Now's not the time for you to suddenly get humble."

"You want me to lead. I am no leader. Sunalor proved that."

I clipped him around the ear.

Corminar scowled. "What on Alterra are you—"

"Sunalor wasn't your fault, alright? Nobody could've saved that city; the locals were too outnumbered. Anyone could have led Sunalor to its defeat."

"Anyone, perhaps. But it was me. I cannot—"

I ignored him, then repositioned two of my portal relays to echo my voice over part of the amassed cultist force. "Forty of you, with him!" I shouted, pointing to Corminar's head.

"Styk, as I have said, I cannot—"

"Learn from your mistakes." With that, I turned, leaving him with a crowd of those in orange robes. He could either flounder, or he could do his job. I knew him well enough to be sure he'd do the latter. I didn't look back.

We charged across the city, our horde pouring through portals and into the next, even before the last had closed. We battled the corruptions as much as we could, doing our best to end them quickly—because for every minute that passed, another seemed to crop up in its place. As we neared Alenna's surgery, I glanced down a main road to my right, and saw that chaos had taken hold.

"Tokas!" I shouted. I would have asked for Arzak, but without Lore, I needed her brawn. I was going to have to trust the woman who'd betrayed us. "Take more of them," I told her.

The tiefling nodded.

"Head east. Do as I told Corminar; eliminate all—"

"No," Lambkin interrupted. "I'll take them. Tokas, get the children to safety."

I considered him for a moment. He'd been a captain, once. He knew how to lead, at least a small unit. He was no worse a choice than Tokas. I nodded.

"Soldiers!" I shouted once more through the portal relays. "Another forty of you—with this man here!"

Lambkin raised his blade in the air in salute, to signal that he was the man I was referring to. Tokas, meanwhile, turned away, heading back toward where her children were hiding, hopefully still safe. It had to have been duty—or, no, guilt—that had kept her with us for so long. She began to run, then dithered for a moment, turning back to Lambkin just as he looked back at her. She took another few seconds away from her kids to run back and kiss the man, planting as passionate a kiss on his lips as ever I'd seen. I'd never expected *this* to happen when I'd agreed that Lambkin could watch over her.

But there was no time for these kinds of thoughts. I turned and led our remaining contingent of fifty or so on, spreading the remaining eight relays between myself, Arzak, Val, and the cultists.

Even someone who didn't know our destination could have realized we were getting close. The devastation in this part of the city was greater than any we'd seen; buildings crumbled by unseen forces, fires blazing in the ruins, but above all else, it was . . . quiet. All those but the few trying to fight the corruptions had long since fled this part of Coldharbor. I tried to ignore the uncomfortable feeling in my gut, and I pressed on; if anyone would know the truth of what happened here—and how to stop it—it was Alenna.

Her surgery remained standing, for the most part. If she had any control over the creatures, it wouldn't have been damaged at all, so the fact that it was still largely intact was surely down to luck. I wasted no time in kicking the door open and bellowing her name.

"*Alenna!*" I roared.

But I saw no Alenna. I saw only the broad frame of my friend, kneeling in the center of the floor, crying and clutching . . . *Ah. There was Alenna.* Guilt blossomed forth in my stomach; I'd assured Lore that the visions of Alenna's death had been planted by Yusef, a means to control him. They might well have been a means to control him, but my mistake was thinking that meant they *couldn't* be real. Lore's betrayal of the Player—as I'd encouraged—had led to this moment.

Lore looked up at me, meeting my eyes. But there was no accusation in those eyes, no blame, at least not directed at me. "I should have known," he croaked. "I should have known."

Shouting erupted outside the premises, followed by the inevitable scuffle of a fight.

"Mourn later. Survive now," Arzak said, before disappearing through the doorway once more to join the cultists in battle.

Val approached Lore, putting a gentle hand on his shoulder. "She's right. I'm sorry, but she's right. We have a city to save."

"A world," I added. "Who did this, Lore? What happened here?"

But as it turned out, the barbarian didn't need to answer. A man stepped forth from the shadows, covered in dust, debris, blood, and . . . the ooze of corruption. A man we should have killed when we had the chance.

"I did," the Councilman said. "I happened."

And then I understood. All that was happening outside? All the chaos, all the death? It was nothing more than bait. The Councilman didn't care what happened to this city, or to the people in it. He just wanted us here.

Because in those otherwise cold, dead eyes, I still saw the hunger for vengeance.

CHAPTER SIXTY-SIX

Coldharbor Screams

"So this is it, then?" I asked the Councilman. "Your big moment? You make some big speech about how we embarrassed you, pushed you into becoming this monster? That now you're out to seek vengeance?"

"Well, I—" the Player started, but I cut him off.

"I think it's clear to all of us what's happened here. Alenna made you like this, right?" I gestured to his body, oozing and gray. "You heard that it could make you stronger? Maybe even strong enough to stop us making a fool out of you?"

"I—"

"Cos let me tell you, mate; we're *still* gonna make a fool out of you. And this time, we're not gonna let you go."

I reactivated my *Titan Husk* ability, my skin beginning to ripple and warp, and I charged. In the moments before I hit him, the Councilman only laughed. What did he think was about to happen except that he'd corrupt me, that he'd add me to his horde? He thought his vengeance was going to be simple.

I was about to prove that it was not.

My blade pointing straight forward, I used the momentum of my tackle to add strength to the *stab*. The enemy didn't even bother blocking me. My knife-point went straight into his flesh, almost like a knife through butter, but much more gross. And my momentum had me crashing into the man's abdomen.

He'd counted on this, I think. Why avoid a single attack when you were strong enough to withstand it, *and* it would spell an end to your attacker? Not just an end, even, but extra strength for your own personal army, as created by his spread corruption. But, of course, I did not get corrupted so easily, not anymore.

I twisted the knife in the man's flesh, then put all my weight onto it to cut downward. The man didn't so much as flinch, and the pallid gray flesh seemed to close up behind my cut, the ooze working its magicks. I recoiled from the monster, taking my knife with me, and the enemy's eyes widened.

"You're . . . you're not . . ."

I heard Lore stumbling to his feet behind me, Val still presumably at his side. The Councilman's eyes darted to each of them. It was all very well him getting close to me, but he couldn't touch *them*. If he did, they'd be lost forever. So it was worth keeping his gaze on me.

"I told you," I replied. "I'm here to make a fool out of you."

The enemy's eyes snapped back to me.

This time, it was his turn to charge.

I opened a portal behind me and stepped through it, leaving it open for the Councilman to follow. In the close proximity of Alenna's surgery, Lore and Val were in danger, but in the street outside there was a little more room to play with. I appeared out of the portal just as Arzak and the cultists were finishing off the latest monster, but they still needed just a few more seconds.

"See?" I told the Councilman as he appeared charging through the portal, and I opened another pair to dart out of his way. "Whatever you do to yourself, we'll be stronger. We'll still resist you. And you're not getting away this time."

The Councilman charged at me once more, roaring with fury, and I stepped through another portal. Out of the corner of my eye, I saw Arzak's sword blazing with the power of absorbed fire magicks. Finally, she put the final, killing blow in the other enemy. I'd bought them enough time.

I appeared out of another portal behind the charging enemy, this time slashing once more. I knew it could do no good without fire to back it up—my attempt at an attack earlier proved that once and for all—but it was enough to anger him. It kept his focus on me—the one man he could not corrupt.

As the Councilman turned, I slipped through a portal and out of his reach, ready to—

An oozing chain snapped through the portal just as I let it close, wrapping itself around the wrist of my knife arm. A second later, it crushed it.

I fell to the ground, seeing black and overwhelmed by pain. My knife had long since fallen. Where, I could not see. All I could think about was the pain shooting up my right arm, and that my fingers would not move. "Styk!" I heard someone shout, but in my daze, I couldn't tell who.

A figure loomed over me. I blinked up at it, trying to bring them into focus, but my eyes wouldn't behave—whether that was from the tears or the overwhelming pain, I didn't know. No. I knew who it was. I knew who it must have been.

"Cultists," I mumbled, meaning to give an order, but found my voice escaping me.

Flaming dots peppered the man looming over me, glowing orange orbs that try as I might, I still couldn't bring into focus. But I knew what they were. They were the same flaming arrows that I'd seen the cultists fire at a half dozen corruptions by now. Sometimes, they'd been enough to bring the enemy to their knees. For a creation like the Councilman, however—a creation that Alenna had worked on directly—I knew it wouldn't be enough to fell him.

As it turned out, it wasn't even enough to distract him from me.

The blurry figure moved, and a moment later I felt a fresh pain erupt in my jaw. My head hit the dusty ground, hard. With the sky spinning above me, I put out a hand to try to steady myself, to try to push myself back to my feet. But the moment I did so, another force bludgeoned me, sending me back to the ground.

I spat the blood from my mouth, pressed my hand against the dirt, and opened a portal. I didn't care where I opened the other side; as long as it was away from here, it didn't matter. But as I tumbled through, the oozing metal chain reached for me once more, this time snatching me by the neck. I dangled in the air as this metal snake wrapped itself tighter around my neck. It could have snapped it in an instant—even in my current state, I knew this—but I was saved by the Councilman wanting to savor the kill.

I forced my vision back into focus just in time to see the battlefield thirty yards below me. The Councilman held his snakelike weapon through the open portal, and two dozen cultists fired their flaming arrows at him once more.

But then, there was Val.

A huge web of roots burst from the dusty ground, spreading in the blink of an eye. A moment later, it was as though the root structure of an ancient tree had grown around the Councilman, trapping him, but also—

The cultists fired their flaming arrows once more, and Arzak brought her flaming sword down upon the roots. They caught fire instantly. Whatever plant Val had chosen to summon, it was dry and highly flammable—just what we needed in this situation.

I heard the Councilman scream in the same moment that the snaking chain weapon released me, and I lashed out to grab at the edge of my open portal, steadying myself for a moment so I could work out what to do next. My right hand didn't cooperate, having been crushed by the chain, and so I hung there for a moment by my left hand alone. The edge of the portal felt strange against my flesh, an almost tingling sensation to it, one that made my fingers grow numb. If I hung for much longer, then my fingers might grow so numb that I lost my grip entirely.

Looking down, I saw the monster use his immense strength to rip himself free of the burning roots. His skin hissed as it touched flame, but other than that, this damage barely seemed enough to even slow him. This corruption was stronger than any we'd seen before—any Alenna had *created* before—and so we'd need a lot more fire than that. I scoured my brain for possibilities.

Before, I'd dumped the burning contents of my pocket world on these creatures. There were two problems there: my pocket world was currently completely devoid of any *Needlework* supplies, and I wasn't sure that would be enough to kill the Councilman anyway. Our other success had come from dropping burning buildings on these corruptions, but . . . this was going to be easier said than done, with an enemy as powerful as the Player below me. Still, it was our best bet, and there wasn't enough time to give it any more thought, because the Councilman now turned on my friends.

I released the edge of the portal, allowing it to close as I plummeted, then opened another beneath me that had me fall on top of the enemy. I grabbed him around the neck with my injured right arm, then tried to bury my knife in him with my left. It was . . . not my most successful attack ever. The point of my blade barely broke flesh, but then again, that wasn't my intention. I attacked him only to get his attention back on me. And on that point . . .

. . . I was also unsuccessful.

The Councilman spun, his snakelike weapon flailing out at those who surrounded him. Arzak leaped to the ground just in time for the weapon to skim overhead, but others weren't so lucky. The weapon clipped three of those in orange robes, hitting them hard enough to knock them from their feet and have them sailing through the air. Two of them hit a stone wall, hard, while the other tumbled along the street, picking up scrapes and broken bones as she went.

I reached for the metal chain, knowing already that I wasn't strong enough to disarm this enemy, but I could at least restrict his movements. As I grabbed the weapon near the man's hand, I hung upon it, weighing it down—and even the Councilman could use it as a flail no longer.

But he could still change its shape. The chain warped beneath me, shrinking in length and growing in width, and I released it just in time to avoid being sliced by the sharp edges of the newly formed axe. The Councilman swung it at me faster than I'd anticipated, and though I staggered backward, the axe caught me on the chest, striking a deep gash through the center. If I kept taking hits like this, I'd be useless. Unless Val could somehow find the time to heal me.

I kept stepping backward, my eyes darting around for something—anything—we could use against him, and I tried my best to ignore the pain blossoming in my torso. There was no time for pain, now. If I embraced pain, it was over. If I let myself feel the pain, there would be so much more to come.

The Councilman's attention was now well and truly split. Even my recent attacks hadn't been enough to keep him focused on me. I opened my mouth to let loose some more cutting remarks, but before anything could come out, the enemy snapped their attention to the nearest of the cultists.

The woman in orange met the enemy's gaze, and then—very understandably—turned to flee. But it was a losing battle. This creation was stronger, faster than any of us could ever hope to be. The Councilman closed the gap on the cultist fast, then leaped into the air and came down upon her. When he landed, he grabbed the woman by the head, and for a moment I thought he was about to twist. Instead, however, he let his oozing corruption bleed into her. This was how the corruption had spread through Coldharbor, how he'd drawn us back here. But it was also yet another weapon in his already great arsenal.

"We keep on like this, and it's only a matter of time until we lose!" Val shouted from across the dusty street.

"I know!" I shouted back at her, frozen, unsure what to do next.

"Any ideas?"

I scoured my mind once more, desperate, thinking through every possible permutation of not just my abilities, but Arzak's, and Val's. And I came up with . . . nothing.

But then I saw the large silhouette of Lore, standing in the doorway of Alenna's surgery, his eyes glowing more brightly than ever with the surging magicks of *Divination*.

"I have one," he said.

CHAPTER SIXTY-SEVEN

Underpowered

I didn't need Lore to say it twice. If he had a plan—whatever it might be—then that was better than anyone else could say. With the flick of my unshattered wrist, I sent one of my portal relays soaring toward him, giving him the ability to easily give commands.

Whatever his plan, I assumed it had something to do with those glowing yellow eyes. His *Divination* powers were active, and he could foresee the battle to come, at least in some sense. Of course, these magicks were always inevitably flawed, but flawed or not, they were powerful. Maybe something good would come of Niamh's curse after all.

"Arzak, charge!" the barbarian shouted.

The orc did so without hesitation. I didn't know whether this was because she shared my understanding of the situation, or if she simply trusted Lore with her life, but I supposed it didn't matter. He'd told her to charge, and charge she did.

"Left!" Lore cried.

Arzak shifted one foot to the left just as the Councilman turned, his ghostly chain flailing toward her. The weapon missed by perhaps a foot, though would have struck true if Lore hadn't seen this coming.

"Duck!"

Arzak ducked. The next flail of the enemy's chain whipped over her head. She drew closer to the enemy, and raised her still-flaming sword. It was at this moment that everyone else—me, Val, and the dozen or so cultists—realized we should press the attack while the Councilman was distracted. Many of the cultists peppered the enemy with attacks, though I suspected only the one capable of summoning fireballs was able to deal any damage. Val and I, however, knew enough about the spread of corruption that we looked instead to the person that the Councilman had put his hands upon—and turned into a monster.

The ex-cultist's skin was paling fast, their once–bright pink irises turning black. How much time did we have until the corruption took over their mind? How long did we have while they were still themselves?

And did it make sense to kill them before it took hold?

"Val," I said, and the witch met my eyes. She nodded.

I portaled us over to the corrupted woman's side in an instant, and we wasted no time in striking. Val sent waves of lightning magicks coursing through the woman's body, pausing only to let me in for a *closed reach stab*. Even in my left hand, my blade dealt significant damage to the robed woman. We were early enough; the corruption hadn't taken hold so much yet that only fire would kill her. But that meant we'd killed the woman, not the monster.

Level 8 Town Planner defeated!

Knifework: +1,500XP
Worldbending: +300XP

I pushed the notifications aside immediately, not needing the reminder of the innocence of the woman we'd just killed. From the glum expression on Val's face, she felt the same. We switched our attention back to the Councilman, on whom Arzak was landing attack after attack with her flaming blade. And with Lore to instruct her—to foresee the enemy's attacks—she avoided getting corrupted in the process.

"Now, Styk!" Lore shouted through the relay.

I moved before my mind could process it, opening a portal at my side and stepping into the space next to the enemy. I had no fire magicks at my disposal, but that didn't mean I was useless; I could still draw the enemy's wrath.

I sheathed my trusty blade, instead grabbing a discarded knife from the ground—I say "discarded" when I really mean "fallen from a dead cultist's hand"—and made first use of the ability I'd gained while chasing Yusef across the desert. It was an ability I'd made plenty of use of in my first life, despite it being a simple one. Sometimes it was those simple abilities that were most versatile. I *threw* it.

The blade was slightly rusty, and not as sharp as it could have been, but still it was enough. As I released, the knife tumbled through the air, soaring toward the enemy's shoulder. I was crouching, scrambling for the next projectile even before the thrown blade wedged itself deep in the Councilman's shoulder. As the enemy hissed, I *threw* once more, but this time I aimed to do more than just draw this monster's attention.

I knew only fire could deal damage to someone touched by corruption, but that didn't mean my *Knifework* was useless. I could still use it to turn the tide. I *threw* this second blade not toward shoulder, but toward eye. Even thrown from my left hand, activating an ability made the knife hit true. I heard a squelch as the blade point pierced eyeball.

The Councilman roared, clutching at his now-ruined eye, then charged at me.

"Time to run, Styk!" Lore said, though I didn't need the gift of *Divination* for that one. I opened a portal behind me, falling through it clumsily. As I stepped out the other side and let the portals close, I stumbled into a fallen cultist and tumbled toward the ground. Out of instinct, I put out both hands to break my fall, and immense pain shot through my right arm when I landed on my crumpled hand.

"Styk!" Val shouted, but she wasn't fool enough to rush to my aid.

As the half-blinded Councilman turned to my new position to charge at me once more, I splayed my left hand against the ground and used it to open a portal back into Alenna's surgery, and out of sight.

I just needed a moment to gather myself.

I looked around at the interior of the building, as though I might find the solution to our inevitable defeat, when the front brick wall crumbled. Debris and dust washed over me, knocking me from my feet once more, and though this time I didn't have time to put out my hands, I still landed on my injury. The roof creaked above me as part of its support had been taken away, but I had arguably bigger things to worry about—like the ghostly chain shooting toward me once more, through the hole in the wall.

I tumbled through the portal, once again back outside, and shouted, "Could have warned me!"

But across the dusty, body-littered street, I saw Lore blinking. I saw the yellow-white glow in his eyes flickering. He'd made enough use of the power that it was waning on him, in need of time to recharge. If he had a plan to finish this, we'd need it sooner rather than later.

"Lore?" I shouted, prodding him into action.

"I . . ." he started. "I think I see . . . *Duck!*"

But it was a moment too late. The Councilman whipped his ghostly chain at me, knocking me from my feet yet again, and following the attack through enough to hit four of the remaining cultists. All five of us soared through the air, though I only saw—*felt*—where I landed. I hit my head against something hard as I came to an abrupt stop, and in the initial seconds after the impact, that hit was what I focused on. But then I saw the splintered wood piercing through my left calf, and the pain followed soon after.

The Councilman wasn't one to leave it there and call it a day. He moved with the momentum of his pointed ghostly chain, whipping it around him and back at me once more. I tried to scramble back to my feet, but my left leg wasn't strong enough to support my weight. I tried instead to open a portal, to fall backward through it, but I was a fraction of a second too late. The chain soared toward me, its sharp point shooting toward my chest, and—

Roots burst up from the ground in front of me, knocking the enemy's weapon from its path of attack at the very last moment. Again, the Councilman roared in frustration—these Players couldn't deal with anything not going their way—and this block was enough to turn the enemy's attention onto Val.

And Val couldn't escape his attacks so easily.

The weapon soared back around for a third attack, once again leading with its sharp point. Val saw it coming, diving out of the way, but the Councilman had expected that. His weapon diverted at the last moment, its point burying itself in Val's side.

She howled, and my stomach lurched.

Suddenly, the pain in my leg didn't seem so bad anymore. Nothing seemed as bad anymore. I had only one thought in my head: this man needed to die. Now. I pushed myself back to my feet, my left leg shaking beneath me, my mind ignoring the pain.

The Councilman warped his chain back into an axe once more, and moved as if to stand over Val. As if to finish her off.

"Pathetic," I spat, half conscious that my saliva was red, not white.

The enemy's head snapped toward me. He shot daggers with his remaining eye, his injured one healing, but healing slowly—and entirely black with the ooze of corruption.

I tried not to look at Val, to keep my eyes squarely on the Councilman. But I saw it—the pool of blood appearing around her. She was alive, for now, but wouldn't be for much longer. And she was our only healer.

It was now or never.

I opened a portal beneath me, dropping through it and out above the enemy, pointing my blade down and activating *stab*, just as I had done against the pyroknight all those moons ago. I knew it wouldn't kill him. I knew it was just a distraction. But I'd seen Arzak charging in for the attack at the same time. Maybe my distraction would be enough. Maybe it would give Arzak the opening she needed.

The ghostly axe warped into chain once more.

It snatched me from the air, grabbing me by the ankle.

The Councilman hung me upside down in front of his smiling face.

"Revenge," he said.

CHAPTER SIXTY-EIGHT

Corruption Falls

"Revenge."

It was just one word, but it communicated so much. It was his goal, sure, it was why he'd come here—but it was more than that. It spoke to the Players' disdain for the people of this world. It said that revenge was justification enough for all this, the destruction of half of Coldharbor, the hundreds or thousands dead, and the corruption that threatened to consume all of Alterra.

And it pissed me off.

I met the gaze of the half-blind, corrupted Player for just a moment before I activated another rarely used ability. Using my *Shrill Perimeter*, I created a circle around us, about twenty-feet wide, that glowed gently with the purple magicks of *Worldbending*. And then, as soon as it was created, it activated—there was an enemy inside the perimeter to trip its banshee sound.

The noise startled the enemy—perhaps his senses, not just his strength, was bolstered by the corruption—and his weapon loosened its grasp on me just enough for me to slip to the ground. But I never hit the ground, of course, instead disappearing through another portal and out another that set me upright once more. My left leg half buckled as I landed on it, and I had to grab for a nearby wall to steady myself.

It was the semidestroyed building that had once been Alenna's surgery that I found myself next to, though I hadn't aimed there specifically. Flames, whether from Arzak's sword or one of the few flaming arrows, had blossomed into life on the wooden structural interior of the building, though it was just another in a sea of falling structures.

"Lore?" I shouted, trying not to let my voice sound strained. "Any luck with your . . ."

I met his eyes. His regular, nonglowing eyes, only a wisp of the *Divination* magicks left to rage behind them. He'd exhausted Niamh's curse for now, at least until he rested. And at this rate, we would be dead long before he could. I glanced around. There were just four of us left standing: me, Lore, Arzak, and one lucky ex-cultist. Four of us against Alenna's creation, who seemed little closer to falling than at the start of the battle.

". . . Lore?" I tried again. "We're really gonna need some prophecy, buddy."

"I . . ." he said. "I . . . I . . . got it." His eyes flashed yellow, and he opened his mouth to bellow orders through the portal relay. "Arzak, get ready to—"

The Councilman's chain whipped back on itself, catching Lore off guard and swiping him from his feet. I flung one hand forward, meaning to open a portal beneath him and remove him from danger, but the enemy was faster. The point of the snakelike weapon swung around once more, and pierced Lore clean through his right thigh. The big man screamed.

With Val bleeding out fast across the street, we had no healers, and we were long since out of Corminar's health potions. However we were going to finish this, it needed to be just me, Arzak, and—

The last cultist screamed as they fell.

It needed to be just me and Arzak.

I stepped through a portal to stand next to my orcish friend, then turned to nod at her. Arzak returned the nod in kind. We both knew our chances here were slim, but what else could we do but go down fighting? We had a job to do, and—whether Val believed it or not—we were heroes. We really had no choice in the matter.

The Councilman turned slowly, his glowing metal chain scraping across the dusty street. His right eye was nearly completely re-formed at this point, but instead of the brown irises and white sclera, there was only black. The gods alone knew whether he saw in the same way out of that eye, now.

"Ready, Arzak?" I asked.

"To die?"

"To fight," I replied, though I couldn't really deny the other part, either. Maybe this was how it was always going to end; the Slayers would stumble across an enemy too great to handle, and we'd die in the inevitable fight. Maybe that was always going to be my fate, ever since I stumbled across Val in the prison below Umlok's castle. But that didn't mean I had to like it.

"Strike through the portals, Arzak," I said.

Before waiting for her to reply, I opened a portal in front of Arzak that afforded her an attack on the enemy. She was swinging her flaming blade even before the portal had fully opened, and fire and metal struck corrupted gray flesh. As the Councilman turned to the portal, I snapped it shut, and opened another off to another side. Again, Arzak struck true and hard, and the flames hissed against corruption.

We managed that only once more before the Councilman turned to the source of these attacks. This forced me to instead open a portal beneath us to avoid his chain's attack. We fell through it, landing clumsily on the ground. Arzak remained steady on her feet, while I collapsed to the debris-covered street. I didn't try to move, though, because my leg would only give way once more, and I could do all I needed to, even from this low vantage point.

Without wasting another second, I opened a portal in front of where Arzak was already swinging her flaming sword, and flames struck the enemy's back.

"No," the Councilman roared as flames hissed against corruption, and he turned to grab Arzak's sword by the blade using his free hand.

The orc's eyes widened, instinctively pulling her weapon back through the portal, though still the Player didn't lose his grasp. I closed the portal, knowing that it would remain open until flesh left its boundary, but thinking this would still disorient the enemy enough to give Arzak an advantage.

Instead, the portal closed.

The portal closed *through* the Councilman's arm.

All were still, all were silent for a second as we took in this latest development. The only sound was the faint *thud* of severed limb against hard cobble ground, Arzak's weapon still in its grasp.

I hadn't evolved my portal abilities. There was no good reason that they would close around a living being. No good reason, except . . . what if the System didn't recognize the Councilman as being alive anymore? What if the corruption had spread too far throughout his system?

And what if this was just the advantage we needed?

With the flick of my good wrist, I opened a portal and dropped the enemy's forearm and Arzak's blade to my side. I reached out, prying the corrupted flesh from the weapon, meaning to give it back to my orcish friend before the Councilman could react. But I was too slow.

Roaring some animalistic, definitely-no-longer-human roar, the Councilman launched into an attack on the now-disarmed Arzak. The enemy's weapon, still in chain form, whipped toward the orc just as she dived out of the way, tearing a great gash across her chest and shoulder.

I hesitated just for a second before launching her weapon back to her, thinking this might be enough to remove the orc from the fight. But Arzak was made of solid muscle; it would take more than one—admittedly deep—tear to remove her from the fight. Opening a portal, I released the flaming sword back into the air at her side, and Arzak caught it with her still-good arm.

As the Councilman's attention flicked back to the armed orc, I moved to open a portal within him, meaning to slice him in two. But still, I found I could not open a portal through the man, and instead I would need to lure him through one before I could close it on him.

The opportunity came immediately, with the Councilman turning to meet Arzak's attack, swinging his chain around, and with it, his arm. I opened a portal just in front of him, but before I could close it around that wrist, the Player reacted. He yanked his arm out of the way of that closing portal, avoiding my attack. In that same moment, I caught sight of his other arm, severed at the elbow. Except . . . it wasn't. Black ooze rippled around the wound, and slowly but surely, the corruption rebuilt the missing limb out of its own form. We simply couldn't get a break.

"Arzak!" I shouted as I prepared to open a portal once more, "Strike now. Strike—"

The Councilman's chain whipped over the head of Arzak, the orc dodging it deftly. But it became apparent less than a second later that Arzak hadn't been his target.

I had.

The chain whipped around my legs as I dived out of the way. One ankle escaped, but the other was quickly entwined in the enemy's weapon. The Councilman yanked me off my feet, pulling me into the air once more, but this time using my body to block Arzak's flaming attack.

I could withstand the flames due to my *Titan Husk* ability, but that didn't mean they didn't hurt. A howl of pain escaped my lips.

The Councilman used me as a shield to push against Arzak, blocking her attempted attacks with my back, my shredded shirt falling from my torso, my ability to fight back eliminated by the pain. He pressed closer, still using me as a shield, pushing me into Arzak's sword. And in the same move, he pushed the sharp edge of Arzak's flaming sword into Arzak.

I felt Arzak collapse behind me before I realized that this was it, that my orcish friend was now out of the fight. The Councilman must have realized it at the same moment, because his chain released my leg, dropping me to the ground. As far as he was concerned, the fight was over; I could never be strong enough alone to pose him a challenge.

I caught sight of Arzak trying to stagger back to her feet, breathing deeply, her torso mangled by burn and tear alike. She grunted as she tried to rise from her knee, but . . . ultimately, it was too much.

I really *would* need to fight on alone. And yet, I could barely stand.

Grunting just as Arzak had from the exertion, I forced myself back to my feet, one leg very shaky beneath me. Perhaps the Councilman was right. What chance could I have against him at even the best of times, much less when I was wounded? Maybe it was over. But that didn't mean I would go down without a fight.

As the Councilman rounded on me, weapon still in chain form, there was time for only one last attack.

I reached down, and I grabbed Arzak's flaming sword from the ground. It wasn't a knife, but it was a blade, and my *Throw* ability really only specified *blade* after all. I stared where I was aiming—right at the Councilman's head—and I drew in a deep, deep breath. This was it. All or nothing.

I threw the flaming blade.

As soon as the weapon left my hand, I knew I had struck true. The sword tumbled point over pommel as it soared through the air, across the short distance between me and the strongest enemy we'd ever faced. I drew in another breath, this one sharp, to match the pain in my stomach, and I waited for point to meet skull.

But that moment never came. The Councilman morphed his weapon back into axe form, and that axe came up to knock the blade away at the last possible moment. Arzak's blade rebounded into the ground at the man's feet, hard enough that it buried itself point-first.

My leg gave way beneath me.

"It's over," the Councilman said, echoing the thought I'd had at that very same moment. "It's over."

I said nothing, but dropped my head back onto the dusty, bloodstained street.

"You really shouldn't have humiliated me so," the enemy continued.

I thrust a hand in the air and shooed the Councilman away. "I'm really not in the mood."

"To die?"

"For this classic villain monologue thing. We get it. You won. Now are you going to end it, or what? Cos I really don't need to hear the inevitable justifications for all your murder."

"It is not murder," the Councilman said. "I see that now. I am a higher order of being. This is more like . . . pest—"

"Yeah, yeah. I've heard it all before. Pest control, right? Love it. Good justification. Really nice." If I was going to die, I might as well annoy my murderer. This was the way all men in my family died.

"I will allow you, at least, to die on your feet."

I groaned. "Do I have to?"

"Do you . . ." the Councilman stumbled over his words. "Yes. Stand up. Now."

"Why?"

"I want to see the light go out behind your eyes."

I sighed again. "You've changed, man."

The Councilman kicked me.

"Alright," I said, starting to pick myself off the ground, but taking my time about it. "Alright." A moment later, I stood face-to-face with the man who would kill me.

But he didn't attack. Not yet, anyway. Instead, he asked me to . . . "Beg."

"You're not finding this very satisfying, are you?"

"*Beg*. Beg for your pitiful life."

"No."

"*Beg*!" the Councilman shouted one last time.

"Or what, you'll—"

An explosion of red magicks washed over us. I staggered backward, but not from force—there wasn't any—but from surprise. And as I staggered, I saw shapes form around me. *My* shape. Hundreds of me circled the battleground.

And in the distance, standing down the desolate, devastated street, I saw a familiar shape. It was just as before. Just as with the pyroknight. It was Tokas, of all people, who returned to save the day. She was injured, her right sleeve torn from her dress and one hand clasping a bleeding wound. She'd had to fight to get here, but fight she had. Though she was on the cusp of defeat, still she joined the battle. Still she gave everything she had.

I didn't waste the opening Tokas had given me, and I made sure to move among the crowd of my fake selves. As I moved, so, too, did they, in this way and that, completely obscuring the location of the real me.

This infuriated the Councilman, who roared with anger and began attacking the illusions with his ghostly axe. Tokas had bought me time for another attack, but I'd need to make absolutely sure this one would work.

I thought about all I'd learned while I'd watched my friends fall. We knew already that fire was the only way to put a stop to the corruption. Even slicing off flesh could only slow the monster down for so long—his once-missing arm was now almost re-formed. But I also now knew that the System no longer recognized the Councilman as human. I could use that to *slice* him, but I could also . . .

That's it. The only thing that still might work.

"Tokas!" I roared, and my illusion selves echoed. "Make them charge him!"

My illusions turned on their spots, whipping their heads toward the enemy, and a moment later a hundred fake selves were running at him. The Councilman shifted his axe to chain form and attacked wildly, chain flailing between the illusions. And while the enemy was distracted, I opened a portal.

This portal, unlike the others, had no partner. With this attempt, I sought not to throw the Councilman elsewhere, but instead capitalize on the fact that the System no longer recognized him as human. This time, I stuffed him into a pocket world.

Just before he fell, the Councilman whipped his chain out once more. The chain passed through the illusions of me, but—perhaps accidentally—caught the already injured Tokas. The attack threw her hard against the wall of a nearby building, resulting in a gut-wrenching *crunch*. She collapsed to the ground, and the illusions vanished instantly, but I had no time to check on her; for all I knew, the pocket world wouldn't hold the Councilman long.

As soon as the enemy was inside, I closed the pocket world's entrance, and portaled myself over to Val's side. She was looking bad, really bad, but I couldn't help her. The priority had to be killing the Councilman.

I grabbed Val by the shoulders, and wrenched her around. "There!" I shouted, pointing to Alenna's burning surgery. "Roots, there. As flammable as you can manage."

I couldn't make out her slurred response, but Val's hands glowed green with *Witchcraft* magicks, and roots did indeed encompass the surgery before Val passed out.

When the fire of Alenna's surgery was a raging inferno, I opened the portal to my pocket world once more. The Councilman tumbled out into the building, corruption hissing against the flames, and I let my leg collapse beneath me once more.

I watched with bated breath as monster fought fire and roots, and sighed with relief only when I received a familiar notification.

Level ? Corrupted defeated!

Worldbending: +31,050XP

Worldbending increased to level 68!
Worldbending increased to level 69!
Worldbending increased to level 70!
Worldbending increased to level 71!
Worldbending increased to level 72!
Base Points Gained: +10 INT, +10 Free Points (INT/WIS/CHA)

Ability Selection Unlocked
Select an ability from the list below:
. . .

Knifework: +15,600XP

Knifework increased to level 50!
Knifework increased to level 51!
Knifework increased to level 52!
Base Points Gained: +3 DEX, +3 STR, +6 Free Points (VIT/DEX/STR)

Ability Selection Unlocked
Select an ability from the list below:
. . .

Level up!
You increased to Level 22!

Descendant of the Architects defeated!

Sisyphus Artifact: Charge replenished!

Sisyphus Artifact: Leveled up!

Artifact Upgrade Unlocked
Select [2] upgrades from the list below:

---

1. Increase Charges VI [9 > 10]

---

2. Extend Active Period II [1,000 > 1,500]

---

3. Increase Effect I [+1,400 percent > +1,900 percent]

---

4. Add Experience Preservation Charge IV [+1]

I turned back to the battleground, and my friends bleeding out around me. I could make my upgrade selections later; I knew what I would pick. For now, I needed to make sure everyone was OK.

I dropped to Val's side, trying to gently shake her awake.

"You really saved me there, Tokas," I shouted over to the tiefling. "Arzak is right. I think you should really consider joining us again."

There came no reply from Tokas. Val finally stirred, but she wasn't with it enough to do any healing. I'd need to look elsewhere.

"Tokas, I need a hand over here," I called out to her. "If we get Val back on her feet, we can make sure we can save as many as possible."

Still, Tokas didn't reply.

It was at this point that I looked over at her. She was still where she'd fallen, unmoving.

". . . Tokas?"

CHAPTER SIXTY-NINE

Til Death

It rained on the day we buried Tokas.

Arzak thought it was the gods at work, so rarely did it rain in Coldharbor. But that was the way things went sometimes. Sometimes the weather really did reflect your mood.

It was far from the only funeral held in Coldharbor that day. So many had lost loved ones to the misdeeds of the Councilman. So many mourned. There had been broader devastation, too; people had lost their businesses, their homes. Huge stretches of Coldharbor had been leveled. The road to rebuilding would be long and arduous. If we'd realized the truth sooner, perhaps all this could have been avoided. Perhaps lives could have been saved. Perhaps Tokas would still be with us.

And yet, despite all this, the citizens of Coldharbor had still made great efforts to thank us. The people of Coldharbor had paid for Tokas's funeral, had given us rooms in the untouched palace, and put great wealth in the hands of Lambkin, to be given to Tokas's children when they came of age. The people we met, despite so many having lost their own friends, gave us their most sincere condolences.

There were so many funerals held in Coldharbor that day, yet only the funerals of Tokas and the cultists we'd fought alongside had attendance numbering in the thousands.

Arzak gave the eulogy. I'd heard it dozens of times before, as I'd helped the nervous orc practice it overnight, and so instead my attention drifted. Tokas, for all her crimes, hadn't deserved this. I couldn't shake the feeling that I was responsible for her death. That we all were. If we hadn't been so involved in petty squabbles—Val and I particularly guilty of this—maybe we would have been paying more attention to the world around us. Maybe we would have realized what the Councilman was capable of. Maybe we would have realized the truth of Alenna's experiments.

As if Val was thinking the same thing, I felt her hand slip into mine and give it a gentle squeeze. I squeezed back.

The mood was low, understandably, in the aftermath of the funeral. Arzak had left with Lambkin and the children, leaving the rest of us in the temple, now the only ones there.

Lore had the lowest mood among us. He sat on the wooden bench with his head in his hands, unmoving. We'd all been to two funerals in as many days, though the turnout for his old friend's had been . . . not quite so extensive.

I took a seat at his side. "I don't think I said it before, but I'm sorry about Alenna. I know she was about the closest thing you had to family."

Lore didn't move, but I knew he'd heard me. It was just all too much.

"And about what she did . . ."

At this, the big man moved to look at me. "She did what she thought she had to," he said. "Alenna was always a fan of the old tiefling stories. Always believed there was a truth in turning your enemies' strengths against them. I guess she was just . . . putting her money where her mouth was."

"Yeah." I said no more, letting Lore continue on his own. After all, this wasn't really a conversation. It was a chance for Lore to let out some of those feelings he'd been bottling up.

"She'd go to any lengths to save her people. I get that. I would, too. But it . . . it doesn't help the pain."

I put a hand on the man's shoulder. This time, when he put his head in his hands, he sobbed.

On the way back to the palace rooms that had been generously gifted to us for as long as we were in Coldharbor, Lore came to an abrupt halt.

Even those in the streets around us stopped to stare. People here knew us. Not just me, the descendant of a Player, but the rest of the team, too. We were the heroes who had saved Coldharbor, if also the heroes who had watched Sunalor fall. The reverence that the people here had once had for the Players had seemed to drift onto us instead. People wanted to help us. People smiled when we spoke to them. People hopped to serve, even if we would ask them not to.

It only occurred to me now that this meant that Tokas had been successful. Her goal here had been to reveal the truth of the Player, to show the people that these outworlders weren't what everyone thought they were. That Coldharbor now recognized *us* as the real heroes instead of the Players meant that the tide was turning. In time, maybe we could count on others, too, to bring the fight to the Council. Hopefully Raelas was out there, right this minute, spreading the word.

"What is it, Lore?" Val asked, her voice soft.

"There's one more thing I have to do," the barbarian said. "Will you guys wait for me, in Coldharbor? Just for a few days?"

"Sure, but what is it? What are you doing?"

"There are still malae out in the desert. In the canyon. We need to destroy them."

I nodded. "OK, sure. We'll come with you, and—"

"No," Lore said, and for a moment I thought I glimpsed the yellow magicks of *Divination* behind his eyes once more. "No, you two . . . stay here. Trust me."

I nodded, and watched Lore turn away. He spoke to the people of Coldharbor, many of them freshly out of pale orange robes, and asked for volunteers to go with him, on a mission to eradicate the mala menace. The locals, still in awe of us, stumbled over themselves to volunteer, and it wasn't long until Lore had near enough an army, most armed with torches.

Out of the corner of my eye, I glimpsed Val staring at me. "What?"

"You sure you don't want to go? Don't you want to be the hero?"

I watched as Corminar joined Lore to lead the locals out of town. "I want to be a hero, sure. But I've never wanted to be *that* kind of hero. I just want to be good. To help people. That's all. Maybe get a little rich in the process for all my hard work, sure, but I don't need the fame. That's for other people. Besides . . ." I nodded to Lore. "I think he needs to do this."

My and Val's room in the palace had a balcony with a view over all of Coldharbor, in all its devastation and its beauty. I stood on the balcony, my eyes defocusing, and breathed in the crisp, fresh air coming off Coldwater Bay.

I was level 22 now, and far stronger than any other level 22 out there. I'd benefited from the restart, from the experience boost afforded me by the Sisyphus Artifact. *I* was the one who'd ended the Councilman—though not without the team's help. I was the strongest of us, now.

The XP that had resulted from the fight only bolstered that. I'd added an experience preservation charge to the artifact, meaning I could afford to die yet again without losing anything. And I'd increased the effect of the experience point gain up to a massive 1,900 percent. I now grew at twenty times the rate of anyone else. More and more, I was becoming unstoppable.

And that was to say nothing of my two latest abilities. Both had been upgrades, but important upgrades they were.

Stab IV (Knifework): Put your weight behind your wielded blade and force the tip through all but the toughest hides and armor. Damage scales on [STR]. Damage increased by an additional [+100 percent].

I now dealt double damage with my blade, and could pierce almost all armors. That was what had drawn me to this upgrade rather than any new ability; rendering my enemy's armor useless made me surely unstoppable. But there was the *Worldbending* ability upgrade, too.

Portal Slice III (Worldbending): *Passive.* Portals can now be spawned within nonsentient objects. Doing so slices through all objects except those specifically imbued with *Worldbending* protections.

The applications of this upgrade were near endless. I could now use my portals to slice through practically any nonliving thing. I could slice through weapons, armor, brick walls . . . you name it, I could slice through it.

No other level 22 person in Alterra could hope to be this powerful. More and more, the rest of the Slayers were no match for me. I suspected that if it came to fighting any of them—not that I would—I would win handily. Only the Players, the Council themselves, could hope to pose any resistance.

I found something stirring within me, then, as I stood on that balcony. A . . . temptation, perhaps, for lack of a better word. I'd told Val I had no interest in being the sort of hero who needed fame. But . . . why not? Who deserved it more than me? And who in this world had done more to deserve it?

My gut twisted when I caught myself on this path of reasoning. This was exactly what Val had been afraid of, back when she'd left. She'd feared me going down this route, becoming the Player that my mother was. But the worst part was that she was right. I *did* have the potential for it within me. I would have to wrestle those demons.

"You alright out here?" Val asked.

I turned back to see her standing in the balcony's doorway, wearing a necklace and a thin green silk dress that left little to the imagination. I realized my jaw was hanging loose after maybe only fifteen seconds. "Where'd you get *that*?" I asked.

Val turned on the spot, giving me a good view. "You like it? I asked one of the palace staff."

"It suits you."

"I know." Something crossed Val's face then, a flash of darkness. Had she known what I'd been thinking? What I'd been wrestling with? "Styk?"

". . . Yeah?" I asked, trying to ignore the pit in my stomach.

"Forgive me."

I breathed a sigh of relief. She wasn't onto me. Not yet. "You've gotta stop asking that. I told you, I already have."

"I know. It's just . . . I still feel I have to make it up to you."

"Hence the dress?" I asked.

"Among other things."

I traced her figure with my eyes once more, my vision settling on the necklace. It was small, silver, and had the shape of a knife in a cage. "You have the palace staff bring that, too?"

Val fingered the pendant gently. "No, I've . . . had this a while. Since Lore's farm. It's supposed to symbolize where we met. In a prison. With a butter knife."

"That was before . . ." I wasn't sure I'd ever seen Val blush before that moment, but blush she did. "You've known that long?"

The witch nodded, and I kissed her. In that moment, I felt all the pain we'd caused each other, all the anguish, all the uncertainty slip away. We were back together now, and I didn't want us to ever part again.

"You still want to make it up to me?" I asked. "I want two things."

"Tell me."

"I want us to talk to someone about our relationship. To stop squabbling. To sort out any issues between us."

"Done. And the other?"

"I want us to stop wasting time. I want you to marry me."

Arzak was squealing with joy. I don't think I'd ever heard her *squeal* before.

Val had just told her the news, and the two of them were unabashedly stealing glances at me from the palace steps. I shook my head, trying to ignore them, focusing instead on the contingent marching back to the palace.

Lore and Corminar stood at its head, but at this distance—and in the dim light of the setting sun—I couldn't see their faces. Surely they sensed from Arzak now jumping up and down with joy that something had happened. But if they'd picked up on it, their body language didn't show it.

Some ways away, Lore turned to his contingent, said a few words, and his party of Coldharbor residents began to disperse. Their job was done. The two Slayers approached, and then I saw that I had been right; their faces were glum. My stomach lurched.

"News?" Corminar asked, eyebrow raised, nodding to Val and Arzak.

≠Lore looked at me, eyes glowing yellow more brightly than ever. "The malae," he said. "They were gone."

"We found only tracks," Corminar said. "Hundreds of carriages. Heading south. Heading for the Goldmarch."

"The Council," I said.

Simultaneously, Corminar and Lore nodded.

EPILOGUE

Cleo

The Council called Cleo their greatest assassin, as though this was a generous compliment. In truth, however, Cleo wasn't just *their* greatest assassin, she was perhaps the greatest assassin in all of Alterra.

Such a line of work was a dangerous game. Just one mistake, just *one*, likely spelled the end of any assassin. They would be captured. They would be put to death. But Cleo had never made a mistake, and she had worked jobs numbering in the hundreds.

As head of the Council, Tana preferred to operate within the guidelines of the law whenever possible. The less attention they could draw to their world-ending misdeeds, the better. But it wasn't always possible to operate without drawing blood, especially now that Yusef's Cult of Ascendency had disbanded. Now that they had no church to manipulate—and now that there were whispers in the streets about the Players not being quite what they appeared—Cleo's work would only get more important from here on out.

Alterra's greatest assassin had tracked her targets across half a world, always one step behind them. She had come close to catching them in the Tundras, but a stolen ship had caused her to lose her tail. And then, later, she'd heard rumors of half of them being in one place, and half of them being in another. But this could not be true; a team of elite Player-slayers would surely know that they were stronger together.

It was the death of a non-Council Player that had finally drawn Cleo's attention back to the team in question. She'd ridden from Westbara, her horse's hooves pounding against the dry sand as she'd rode north.

And when she'd reached Coldharbor, she'd discovered a city less hospitable to Players than ever before. Cleo kept her hood up, her identity secret. Surely few would recognize her even without her shielding her face, but the assassin was not one to take any chances. That was how she'd survived for so long.

Cleo asked around the city, a greased palm here, a knife-to-the-throat there, seeking out the location of the five adventurers she'd been sent to kill. The answer was one that she'd not expected: that these five were considered heroes, that the city had given them chambers in the palace itself for as long as they required. And "as long as they needed" seemed to include a wedding between two members of the team. This was not good news; the palace would be heavily guarded, and her targets less accessible.

Still, she had killed in palaces before. Guards hadn't stopped her.

Cleo rode to the palace, her best dagger and strongest poisons at her side, her Cloak of Illusions wrapped around her shoulders, but with no magicks yet flowing through it. The wedding was not hard to find, being that so many of Coldharbor's business leaders and government had turned out for it. And with so many faces that were surely unfamiliar to the targets, Cleo could easily slip in.

The assassin saw the bride first, a beautiful woman with long black hair, harboring the secret of her *Witchcraft* abilities. Cleo would kill her last—it was the strongest of them, the Bladespinner and the Warrior, with whom she was most concerned. But then the assassin caught sight of the groom. The Bladespinner. One of the men she was obliged to kill.

Her son.

Cleo's stomach lurched.

He'd grown up so much since she'd last seen him. He'd been a kid back then, back when she'd last passed through that small farming village. His father was gone already, his grave unkempt, and her son was already on his path to becoming a fully-fledged criminal. Like mother, like son, she supposed.

Cleo had never intended to call in on him. She knew she had a son, of course, but she had practically forgotten during all those years on her mission in the Badlands. It was only as she'd passed through that town once more that she remembered, and her curiosity had gotten the better of her.

The assassin had expected to feel nothing for the boy she'd left on his father's doorstep, but upon seeing those eyes—the same eyes that she saw every time she looked in the mirror—she found something stir within her. Not love, not quite. But certainly *something*. A fondness, perhaps. Maybe even a connection.

When Cleo had turned and left the village immediately, she'd told herself that it was to avoid the boy recognizing her. But in truth—and she knew this deep down—it was because she feared what would happen to *her* if she stayed too long.

She'd never expected to see him again, and yet here he was. The man she'd been paid to kill. Not "Styk," really, but Riley. That was the name she'd given him. That was the name she'd written in the note for his father. Yet he'd opted for a different one—what did that say?

It was cruel, to kill a man on his wedding day, but cruelty had never been an issue before. As little—not so little, anymore—Riley took his bride to the floor, Cleo stepped through the crowd.

And then Cleo felt something she'd never felt before. Not on a job, at least. She prided herself on operating free of emotion, of killing without guilt. But here, presented with the truth of her targets' identities, that pattern was broken.

Her hand trembled as she reached for the dagger that hung at her side. The knife felt heavier than ever before.

After scouting her for the Council, Tana had asked Cleo only one question: just how far would she go to secure them their new world?

It was time to find out.

Cleo stepped forward through the joyous crowd just as her son turned away. She prepared to draw her blade, ready to strike at the others in the chaos that followed, ready to end the lives of her five—

"Hello," the bride said, her eyes upon Cleo. "I don't think we've met."

"I . . ." Cleo started, and she felt her hand release her dagger. "I . . ."

Deep brown eyes stared curiously back at her.

"I just wanted to wish you happiness," Cleo said. Before the bride could reply, she turned and hurried from the palace grounds.

What had she become?

About the Author

O. S. Marrow is a progression fantasy author with a particular interest in the philosophical and metaphysical. His passion for writing started at a very young age, as he scribbled down fan fiction inspired by his favorite books (none of which should ever see the light of day). Marrow currently lives in London, United Kingdom, and is often seen staring out of his study window, searching for the perfect next word.

RESPAWN YOUR CURIOSITY

follow us on our socials

 podiumentertainment.com

 @podiumentertainment

 /podiumentertainment

 @podium_ent

 @podiumentertainment

www.ingramcontent.com/pod-product-compliance
Lightning Source LLC
Chambersburg PA
CBHW030515120726
47904CB00005B/1474